Dear Reader,

Those of you who read my books know that these days I write contemporary romantic thrillers as Jayne Ann Krentz, historical romantic suspense as Amanda Quick and futuristics as Jayne Castle. At the start of my career, however, I wrote classic, battle-of-the-sexes-style romance using both my Krentz name and the pen name Stephanie James. This volume contains one or more stories from that time.

I want to take this opportunity to thank all of you— new readers as well as those who have been with me from the start. I appreciate your interest in my books.

Sincerely,

Jayne Ann Krentz

JAYNE ANN KRENTZ

WRITING AS STEPHANIE JAMES

THE MAN IN THE MASK

HQN™

ISBN-13: 978-0-373-77264-3
ISBN-10:   0-373-77264-5

THE MAN IN THE MASK

Also available from

JAYNE ANN KRENTZ

CONTENTS

FABULOUS BEAST

For Suzanne, Barb and Elaine.
Friends in this business are not a luxury, but a
necessity. We are all committed to the same goal:
keeping each other sane.

CHAPTER ONE

"IF YOU'RE THE U.S. CAVALRY, YOU'RE a little late." The badly battered man with the silver eyes and the ebony cane managed a rather grisly parody of a smile before sliding slowly down the brick wall of the alley. He sank to his knees on the dirty cobblestones, bracing his shoulder against the bricks behind him. "But better late than never, I suppose."

The silver gaze was abruptly hidden by dark lashes as the man closed his eyes in pain. Although the extent of his injuries was obvious, he never relaxed the savage grip he had on the handle of the ebony cane.

Tabitha Graham, who had rounded the corner of the old alley only seconds before, stood staring in horrified shock at the sight of the beaten and bloody man. Her eyes widened in astounded recognition, and then she dropped the huge armload of packages she had been carrying.

"Oh, my God!" she breathed, heedless of the small fortune in souvenirs and trinkets she was abandoning in chaos at the entrance to the alley. She rushed forward, crouching at once beside the dark-haired man. "What happened?" Desperately she tried to remember her first aid.

There was a fair amount of blood on the man's khaki

shirt and slacks as well as on his face, but he didn't seem to be bleeding profusely from any one deep wound. Tabitha held her breath, struggling to control her own shock and anxiety so that she could deal with the physical shock and pain the man must have been experiencing. No severe bleeding. And he was breathing, albeit painfully.

Taking a resolute grip on herself, Tabitha mentally ran through the list of vital signs to be checked first. It had been so long since she'd taken that first-aid class! Her hands moved on his kneeling figure, brushing gently over the broad shoulders and down to his waist, seeking the extent of the damage. When she lightly touched his rib cage, he gasped.

"Would you believe I walked into a brick wall?" he managed in an attempt at macabre humor. He didn't open his eyes. It seemed to be taking all his strength just to remain on his knees, leaning against the side of the alley.

"I might believe several people pushed you into that brick wall," Tabitha muttered as she finished the superficial inspection. "Here, lie down. You're not losing a great deal of blood and except for possibly a cracked rib, I don't think anything's broken. Are you feeling faint?"

"Hell, no. Women faint. Men pass out." He slumped a little farther down against the wall.

"Well, do you feel as if you're going to pass out?" Tabitha demanded, reaching out to steady him.

"Yes."

"Please. Lie down." She tried to ease him onto his side. "I think we should get your feet elevated. Don't want you going into shock. As soon as you're more comfortable I'll go for help."

"No!" The silver eyes flew open and she read the sudden command in them. "The ship sails in about half an hour, doesn't it?"

"Yes, but I don't think…"

"Listen. I'd rather be treated by the doctor on board the ship than risk getting stranded on this backwater island. Lord knows what kind of medical care is available here," he said urgently.

Tabitha chewed on her lip. "I'm not sure you should be moved."

"I'm damn well not going to spend the night in this alley!" He closed his eyes again and groaned as he changed position slightly. "Please. You're from the ship, too, aren't you?"

"Yes."

"I thought I'd seen you on board," he muttered. "Look, if you'll just help me get back to the wharf, I'd really appreciate it."

Tabitha frowned, realizing how important the matter was to him. He really didn't want to find himself stranded on the small Caribbean island where the cruise ship had docked for the afternoon. She couldn't blame him, she decided. If their positions had been reversed, she knew she'd rather trust herself to the medical care available on board the huge passenger ship than to the unknown facilities available locally.

"All right," she said reassuringly. "I'll find a way to get you back. Just stay still while I go flag down one of those crazy taxis."

He didn't answer; he didn't appear capable of answering. With a last anxious look at his hunched figure, Tabitha leaped to her feet and raced back toward the mouth of the alley. She nearly tripped over the sack containing the woven basket and the carved wooden dragon that had been among her last purchases.

Out on the narrow street she hailed the first small car which came into view. There was no need to worry about whether or not it was a taxi. One of the first things she had discovered when she'd gotten off the ship earlier in the day was that when a cruise ship was in town, every available car somehow metamorphosed into a taxi. The driver of this one screeched to a halt in front of her and grinned broadly.

"Taxi, lady?"

"Yes, but I need some help. There's another passenger. He's in the alley and he's been hurt. Will you give me a hand getting him into the car? We'll pay double the fare, naturally," she added quickly.

"Sure, lady." The man grinned even more cheerfully and jumped out of the somewhat banged-up automobile. "St. Regis very friendly island. Glad to help."

Without waiting, Tabitha turned and hurried back into the alley. The dark-haired man had sunk a little lower onto the cobblestones and his eyes were closed again. She could see the cold moisture on his brow and her sense of urgency increased. It was hot here on the island, but this man looked as if he were having chills. She noticed that his large hand was still clamped fiercely around the handle of the cane.

The cab driver whistled as he saw his other passenger. "Very bad. You need doctor, yes?"

"He wants the one on board the ship," Tabitha said

hastily as the man with the cane tried to shake his head. It was obvious that the pain made the small movement sheer torture. "Here, give me a hand," she added and went forward to gently but firmly begin the difficult process of getting the battered man to his feet.

The car driver shrugged and obligingly stepped forward to help. Tabitha winced as she saw the whitening brackets on either side of the victim's hard mouth. The lines whitened even further as she and the taxi driver got him to his feet. But her fellow passenger said nothing as the three of them began the walk to the waiting car. Tabitha knew it was because it took his full willpower simply to make the journey.

Together she and the driver got the dark-haired man into the cab, and Tabitha slid into the back seat beside him. Her arm went around the man's shoulders in an instinctive effort to both comfort and steady him. She felt him stifle another groan of pain and then realized he was leaning heavily against her. His bruised face was turned into her shoulder and the brown lashes drooped against the high line of his cheek.

"Good medicine," the cab driver announced, reaching under his seat and withdrawing a small bottle of rum. He handed it back to Tabitha. "Give him some of this, lady. It help."

Doubtfully Tabitha took the bottle. "Do you really think he should have any alcohol?"

The silver eyes of the victim opened briefly, focusing on the rum bottle. "Definitely," he muttered huskily. He tried to raise a hand toward the bottle, but Tabitha moved it firmly out of reach and uncapped it. Then she painstakingly wiped the neck.

"All right, but just a small sip," she cautioned, holding the bottle to his lips. It was an unsteady process because of the manner in which the driver was whizzing the small car through the one main street of town toward the wharf. The vendors lining the street didn't even glance up from their wares as the car whipped past. They were accustomed to the local style of driving. The cruise ship would be leaving in less than half an hour and no one wanted to miss a last-minute sale. The street was rapidly emptying of tourists.

The dark-haired man swallowed the sip of rum Tabitha allowed and tried for another. Tabitha pulled the bottle back from his mouth. "I really don't think you should have any more," she explained anxiously.

He raised his silver eyes to meet her uncertain sherry brown gaze. "Please?" he whispered. "I hurt, lady. I hurt so much."

Knowing she could offer nothing else in the way of immediate relief, Tabitha relented. Her victim swallowed greedily from the bottle and then, without any warning, he collapsed completely. One moment he was drinking rum, the next he was sprawled across her lap, his dark head resting on her thigh.

"Oh, my God," Tabitha whispered. "Hurry, driver. *Hurry!*" She stared down at the man in her lap. The blood from the small cuts on his face was staining her white cotton pants. Her fingers fluttered soothingly along his wrist, seeking a pulse. The beat seemed reasonably strong, she discovered in relief. Her eyes wandered over his inert body once more.

She had seen the man more than once during the three days the cruise ship had been at sea, but always

from a distance. She had no idea who he was. The ebony
cane which he still grasped even in his semiconscious
state had always been in evidence when she had seen
him on deck or in the dining room. It was a necessity,
not an affectation, because the man walked with a
decided limp.

He was heavy, lying across her legs, Tabitha thought
fleetingly. Solid and hard and heavy but without an
ounce of fat. Rather like a large, sleekly muscled
animal. The dark, coffee brown hair was thick and cut
conservatively in an apparent effort to tame a slight
wave. The dark pelt was tousled now, a result of the
violent activity the man had recently undergone, but the
casual disarray of it did not make him look any younger.
From a distance Tabitha had idly decided that he was
probably almost forty and she saw nothing in him now
to change that opinion.

In fact, Tabitha realized, up close the lines etched
into his face indicated that he might even have passed
his fortieth birthday. There was a fixed, implacable look
about the aggressive nose and forceful jaw. The broadly
carved features were neither sensitive nor aquiline. She
could not read either intrinsic compassion or cruelty in
the profile; simply a hard, unyielding strength. What
had happened to his left leg to leave him with such a
marked limp? she wondered. Perhaps an automobile
accident.

What on earth had occurred in that miserable little
alley? Had he been attacked by a group of young toughs
who had been lying in wait for an unsuspecting tourist?
With his limp and the evidence of the cane, this particular man might have seemed an especially easy target.

Curiously Tabitha reached into his pocket and found a worn leather wallet. Flipping it open, she discovered a Texas driver's license issued to one Devlin Colter. Whoever had assaulted him hadn't gotten the wallet, fortunately.

Devlin Colter. At least now he had a name. As the taxi came to a sliding halt in front of the docks, Tabitha hastily slid the wallet back into the pocket of Colter's khaki slacks. He stirred as she did so, reacting apparently to the cessation of motion rather than to the fact that she had been going through his pockets. Tabitha suddenly felt a little guilty.

"We're at the ship," she murmured soothingly. Her fingers gently stroked his arm. "I'll ask them to bring out a stretcher."

"Please don't," he muttered thickly. "This is going to be embarrassing enough as it is. Just help me out of the cab, will you?"

"Of course, but I really think…"

Devlin Colter didn't appear to be paying much attention to what she thought. His whole concentration was on getting to a sitting position. She heard him swear feelingly as he managed the feat. Then the cab driver was jumping out to assist his double-fare passengers.

Two of the cruise ship's crew lounging near the gangway saw Tabitha and her fellow passenger and hurried forward to assist.

"Have the doc paged, Emerson," one of the men said briskly as he took the weight of Devlin Colter. "And notify the captain. Looks like one of our passengers met up with an accident on shore." His eyes narrowed as he turned to glance at Tabitha. "Car accident?"

"No, at least I don't think so. I found him like this in an alley near the main market area. I think he's been beaten up by some punks."

"Yeah, that's what it looks like. We've never had any trouble on St. Regis before," the crewman said unhappily as he and another man guided the stumbling Colter toward the gangway. "Here, you take his cane. It's in the way."

"No," Colter growled through clenched teeth as he fought for consciousness. "I'll keep it."

Tabitha's heart twisted as she witnessed his desperate need to hang on to the ebony stick. In a moment of crisis some people cling irrationally to seemingly insignificant objects. The cane had probably come to be an extension of himself over the years, and Colter undoubtedly felt awkward and unsteady without it.

"I'll take good care of it," she promised gently, taking hold of the cane. "And right now it really is in the way." For an instant she didn't think he was going to surrender it. As he stood braced by the two members of the ship's crew, Devlin Colter opened his silver eyes wide enough to regard Tabitha through two narrow slits. He seemed to realize he was in no shape to fight this small battle.

"Take it," he muttered. "But stay with me. Give me your word that you'll stay with me for a while."

Tabitha was oddly touched at the stark pleading in his low, rough voice. She answered without thinking. "I'll stay with you as long as you want me."

The silver eyes pinned her for a timeless, assessing moment. And then, apparently satisfied at what he had seen, Colter gritted, "Yes, you will, won't you?" As if the decision to trust her with his cane sapped the remainder of what little energy he had left, Colter slipped into a faint.

No, Tabitha reminded herself as she followed the two crewmen who were carrying him, Colter hadn't fainted, he'd passed out. She clung very tightly to the ebony cane.

Two hours later she was still obediently clutching the cane as she sat beside the white-sheeted bed in the small but well-equipped sick bay. Devlin Colter had wandered in and out of consciousness while the ship's doctor tended to his wounds, but each time he had stirred restlessly and opened his silvery eyes, he'd caught sight of Tabitha nearby and the image had appeared to reassure him. Now he was sleeping, a reasonably normal sort of sleep thanks to a sedative. His body bore several strips of tape and bandages and there were dark bruises under his eyes. The ribs, fortunately, had only been battered, not broken, although the doctor said they would cause considerable discomfort for several days. Still, all things considered, Devlin Colter was in fair shape for a man who had undergone a severe beating in a back alley.

What was it about the sight of her which had calmed him during his restless moments? Tabitha wondered fleetingly as she sat holding the cane. He had seemed lucid when he was awake so she didn't think he was hallucinating. He didn't seem to be mistaking her for someone else.

Not that she was the kind of person who generally got mistaken for someone else, Tabitha reminded herself dryly. If anything, people were more inclined to overlook her altogether. Quiet people often got overlooked. Sometimes that suited them perfectly. Sometimes it was frustrating.

A quiet woman who was hauntingly beautiful probably wouldn't have known what it was like to spend most of her life as an observer of others. She would probably have been considered tragic and vulnerable and in need of a man's protection. Some male would have long since swept her off her feet.

But Tabitha Graham had not reached the age of twenty-nine years without learning that she was not the hauntingly beautiful, tragically quiet type. Instead she felt rather average when it came to looks. Her toast-colored hair was cropped in a blunt cut which swung gently along the line of her jaw, neither short and sassy nor long and sultry in style.

The light brown hair framed a set of features that were softly molded, almost wholesome. Wholesome was a word Tabitha didn't care for at all, even if it did suit her gentle mouth and slightly tilted nose.

It was the sherry-colored eyes which somewhat miti-gated the wholesome effect. They were faintly slanted at the outer corners, and there was a flare of intelligence and humor in them which could not be completely dimmed.

As far as the rest of her was concerned, Tabitha had to admit that the term wholesome probably was as accurate as any. Unfortunately. There was a soft round-ness to her breasts and hips which no amount of dieting ever seemed to diminish. All dieting managed to achieve, Tabitha had long since realized, was a stale-mate in the battle against outright plumpness. The endless food available on board a luxury cruise liner was not contributing to the war effort. Or if it was, it was definitely on the wrong side. But that was all right, she had assured herself three days ago. This was supposed to be a vacation and she was entitled to enjoy it.

With that thought in mind, she had purchased loose-fitting cottons for the Caribbean cruise, clothing that would not remind her of how much she was enjoying the food. Her white, drawstring pants which were now stained with blood and dirt were accompanied by a square-necked, handkerchief-hem, white top. The only jewelry Tabitha had on was a silver pendant designed in the shape of a griffin. The small sculpture with its lion's body and eagle's head was a fierce little creature drawn from the pages of a medieval bestiary. As she absently fingered the beast, Tabitha abruptly remembered the tiny, dragon carving she had left lying at the entrance to the old alley.

It wasn't the only souvenir she had left on the cobblestones in her haste to rescue Devlin Colter, but it was the one she would miss the most. It had been an especially charming beast with a handsome head and delicately detailed claws. Ah, well, Colter was an even more interesting beast, she thought humorously. A small, private smile curved her mouth just as his silver eyes flickered open.

"Don't worry, I've still got it," she assured him, holding up the cane.

His gaze went briefly from her face to the cane and back again. "Thanks," he said seriously. "Thanks for everything. I owe you."

Tabitha shook her head, smiling. "Don't be ridiculous. Anyone would have done the same. I just happened to be the first tourist passing that alley after you got clobbered in it. Which reminds me. The captain would like to talk to you when you're feeling up to a chat. I guess he's got a few questions about what happened. The steamship company doesn't like having its passengers beaten up while visiting places like St. Regis. Whoever it was didn't get your wallet, by the way."

Devlin continued to stare at her for another moment. The weakness and sedative-induced drowsiness in him was obvious. "I suppose I should be grateful for small favors," he managed dryly. "Who are you, anyway?"

"Tabitha Graham. From Washington."

"D.C.?"

She grimaced. "State of. Every traveling citizen of the state of Washington has to explain that for some reason! People always assume the D.C."

He nodded once and then winced as the motion apparently sent a wave of discomfort through his head. "You look more like the state of than D.C." The silver eyes closed for a moment as he took a couple of careful breaths.

"How can you tell?" Tabitha asked curiously.

He didn't open his eyes. "I used to live there. D.C. types are a little harder, a little more…" His voice trailed off as he searched for a word.

"Sophisticated?" Tabitha supplied dryly.

"I guess. You look sort of soft." His eyes were still closed.

"Wholesome? Healthy? Sweet?" she added helpfully.

"Yeah. Maybe." He was clearly tiring; losing interest in the analysis. That didn't surprise Tabitha. She was accustomed to men losing interest. Just as she thought he was drifting back into sleep, however, the silver gray eyes slitted open once more. "What do you do up in the state of Washington, Tabitha Graham?"

"I run a small bookshop in a little town on Puget Sound. It's a wholesome, healthy, sweet sort of occupation," she confided cheerfully. "What about you?"

There was a small pause. She didn't know whether he was simply assimilating her words or whether he had actually fallen asleep. Then Colter said quietly, "I have an equally wholesome, sweet and, until now, healthy occupation. I run a travel agency."

"Uh oh. Let me guess. You're going to take St. Regis off your list of recommended tourist stops as soon as you get home, right?"

"The temptation is strong."

"What happened in that horrible little alley, Devlin?" she inquired softly.

"Call me Dev." He paused again, gathering his strength. "I'm afraid it was exactly what it looks like. I got clobbered by a couple of young toughs who were anxious to supplement their annual income."

"Well, they didn't get your money!" Tabitha exclaimed in satisfaction.

"That is, of course, a great comfort," he muttered. "Frankly, I'd rather they had asked politely for the traveler's checks I was carrying instead of trying to take them off me the hard way. You'd better tell the captain I'm awake."

Tabitha got to her feet and stepped closer to the bed, frowning down at him intently. "Are you sure you're ready to talk to him?"

"I'm sure." He slanted a glance up at her serious expression. "Hang on to my cane for me, will you? I don't seem to be in any condition to hang on to it myself."

She smiled reassuringly. "I'll keep track of it for you. Do you want anything else before I leave?"

"A small bottle of whiskey would be much appreciated."

"Oh no, I don't think so. Not on top of all those pain-killers you've got in you," Tabitha said quickly.

"The pain-killers leave something to be desired. Please?" He tried a tentative, ingratiating smile that amused Tabitha.

"No. I'm sure the doctor would never approve. Now you get some rest while I go tell the nurse you're awake. She can notify the captain." Tabitha smiled again and touched his arm as it lay under the sheet. Then she turned quickly and started for the door.

"Tabby!" he called after her, sounding suddenly concerned.

"Tabby?" she echoed, swinging around in surprise as she reached the door. Her brows came together in a straight line.

"Sorry," Dev apologized at once. "Something about you reminds me of a tabby cat." He lifted one hand in a vague gesture of explanation.

"Uh huh. Sweet and wholesome. What did you want, Dev?"

"I just wanted to remind you of the cane."

She shook her head. "Believe me, I won't let it out of my sight." Grasping it firmly, she continued out the door. He really was fixated on the ebony cane, she thought with a touch of compassion. The poor man must feel terribly uncertain and unsteady without it. His limp made him vulnerable, she realized as she went about the business of notifying the nurse that the patient was awake. Tabitha didn't know many vulnerable men. It was intriguing to meet one.

She was still considering that notion an hour later in her cabin as she dressed for dinner. The easy-fitting, yellow pullover dress she had chosen was both comfortable and reasonably attractive. There was nothing startlingly chic about it, but on the other hand it wouldn't embarrass her, either. A perfect Tabitha sort of outfit, she decided as she brushed her hair into the familiar soft curve. It wouldn't draw attention.

She hesitated for a moment after setting down the brush and then decided to exchange the silver griffin pendant for a wide brass bracelet which had a small unicorn engraved on it. Then, satisfied, she picked up her purse and prepared to leave the tiny stateroom. She had her hand on the doorknob when the phone on the night table rang shrilly. Tabitha blinked in surprise. She didn't know anyone else on board ship well enough to expect a call. Someone had probably dialed the wrong room. She lifted the receiver a little impatiently.

"Tabby?"

She arched an eyebrow in astonishment, identifying that low, rough voice at once. "It's okay, Dev," she half-chuckled. "I've still got your cane. It's safe and sound."

"Oh. Well, thanks, but that's not exactly what I was calling about. I was wondering if you might consider bringing me a little soup or something."

"Soup! Didn't the nurse order dinner for you?"

"I'm not in sick bay any longer. I'm back in my cabin. I couldn't stand any more of the antiseptic look."

"Are you sure you shouldn't have spent the night there?" Tabitha demanded. "After all, you've got a lot of recovering to do."

"I can do it just as well here in my cabin. If I can get a little food, that is," he added meaningfully. "What about it? Do you think you could wangle a little something from the kitchens?"

"I can try," she agreed slowly, wondering why he simply didn't call a steward. Maybe he just didn't feel up to explaining why he wanted to be served in his cabin tonight. He did sound awfully weak. "Okay, I'll see what I can do. What's your cabin number?"

He told her and then hung up the phone, sounding more exhausted than ever. Tabitha replaced her own receiver thoughtfully. The poor man was apparently traveling alone, just as she was. And just like herself, he didn't seem to have made any friends on board, at least none he felt he could call upon in a situation like this. Tabitha felt herself warming toward Devlin Colter. He appeared to be a quiet, self-contained person who was not accustomed to imposing on people. A person who did not fit easily into the cheerful social life on board the cruise ship.

A person rather like herself.

It took some explanations and a short discussion with a member of the purser's staff, but Tabitha eventually arranged for dinner to be served to Devlin and herself in his cabin. She felt a small sense of triumph as she knocked on his door half an hour later with a steward in tow.

His voice was groggy as he instructed her to enter,

and she realized at once that he wasn't looking any better. Lying in bed, naked from the waist up except for assorted bandages, Dev appeared more bruised and battered than she had last seen him. Tabitha halted on the threshold of the room, eyeing him dubiously. His precious cane was in her hand.

"Are you sure you shouldn't be in sick bay?" she asked.

"I'm sure," he growled, his eyes running over her almost curiously as she walked into the room. "The bruises are just starting to color up a little, that's all. They'll look even worse tomorrow." He watched her set down his cane.

"You sound like an expert on the subject," she noted dryly as she motioned for the steward to carry in the tray full of food she had selected.

Dev's gaze went from her to the tray as the steward set it down on the small table by the bed. "Good grief, I ordered soup. You look like you've brought along a full-course dinner."

"The clam chowder is for you. The rest of the food is for me." Tabitha smiled, remembering to tip the steward as he backed out of the door.

"You're eating here with me?" Dev glanced at her interestedly. "I appreciate that. It's a little lonely down here all by myself."

"I figured it might be. Let's see what we have. Can you sit up in bed?"

"With a little help."

"Oh, of course." She stepped across the short expanse of space and carefully placed her arm around his shoulders. The feel of his warm skin elicited an unexpected sense of awareness in her. She felt the movement of the sleek, hard muscles of his shoulders as he groaned and struggled awkwardly to a sitting position. His masculine strength coupled with the feel of his bronzed skin made her abruptly nervous. As he settled into the pillows, she moved back quickly, nearly bumping into the tray full of food.

"Careful, that was my chowder that almost fell on the rug," he observed casually.

"Sorry," she mumbled and quickly turned her attention to preparing his soup. By the time she had it placed on his lap together with a chunk of sourdough bread, Tabitha was feeling in command of herself once again. It was obvious her touch hadn't had the same unsettling effect on Dev as the feel of his body had had on her! The man was in absolutely miserable shape, she reminded herself forcefully. The last thing he would be thinking about right at the moment was his own semi-nudity. And even if he had been, she thought good-naturedly, it didn't follow that her touch would necessarily spark a chord of awareness in him. Men didn't react that way to her even when they were in prime condition!

"Oh good," Dev was saying with a genuine trace of enthusiasm in his voice. "You brought along some wine."

"That's for me, too." She chuckled, busying herself with the dishes on the tray. "It's to go with my lobster pâté and my fettuccini." She uncovered the last of her own dishes, a spinach salad, and glanced up in time to catch an appalled expression on Dev's face.

"You're going to sit there, eat all that good food and drink all that excellent wine in front of me without even offering a bite or a sip?"

"You said you only wanted soup," she pointed out calmly, arranging her chair at the little table.

"I think I've changed my mind," he countered weakly, his eyes following her hands as she carefully poured out a glass of wine.

"I thought you might," Tabitha agreed with a satisfied nod. "That's why I ordered double on the fettuccini and had the steward bring along another wineglass." She produced the second glass from behind a silver tureen and smiled appealingly. "I checked with the doctor, and he said the drugs should have worn off sufficiently by now to allow you some alcohol."

He sighed in exaggerated relief. "For a minute there I was beginning to suspect there might be a cruel streak beneath that wholesome, sweet facade!"

Tabitha laughed lightly as she handed him a toast point covered with pâté. "I enjoy good food too much to deny it to someone else. Given your present condition, though, there's not much you could have done about it if I'd chosen to sit here and torment you by eating every last scrap myself."

He winced. "You've got a point there. I couldn't wrest that wine bottle away from a fly tonight. Damn, but I ache! All over, too. Even my feet seem to hurt. Look at this," he added in outright disgust as he picked up his soup spoon, "my hand is shaking. Of all the stupid, idiotic…"

"It's just reaction to the shock your body's been through," Tabitha said soothingly, and rose instantly to cross back to his side. "Here, I'll help you." She took the spoon from his unsteady grasp and began ladling up the chowder and holding it to his lips.

"When I ordered dinner, I didn't expect to have it hand-fed to me," Dev groaned. But he downed the soup with definite enthusiasm. By the time they got to the fettuccini he was feeling strong enough to handle his own fork.

Tabitha watched the process with a sense of pleased satisfaction. If she hadn't taken it upon herself to order the remainder of the meal, her patient would only have had some soup tonight. Not nearly enough for a man his size. Half-amused at the gentle, nurturing impulse she was feeling toward Devlin Colter, she magnanimously gave him the last of the beaujolais wine.

"Wow, that tasted good." He sighed, leaning back farther into the pillows as she took the empty glass from his hand. "I was a lot hungrier than I thought. And that wine is a lot more help than the doctor's pain pills!"

"You look exhausted," she informed him, arranging the empty dishes on the tray. "What you need now is some sleep."

"Yes, I know. But it's rather nice to have someone to talk to tonight. Any chance of your staying for a while?"

She turned in surprise to find him watching her with a shuttered, half-pleading expression. He really did want her to stay. Perhaps the shock of being so badly beaten by a band of thugs left even a strong man like this feeling uneasy at the thought of facing a long night of pain alone. "I'll stay for a while if you like," she murmured gently. "Would you like to play cards or something?"

"No." He shook his head a little restlessly. "Just…talk to me, okay? I'm sure I'll fall asleep fairly quickly."

She got the unspoken message. He wanted her to stay until he was asleep. Moving her chair closer to the bed, she instinctively put out a hand to touch his brow. "How's your head?"

"Hurts like hell, just like the rest of me," he admitted gruffly. He turned his face slightly toward her in a move that brought his forehead more firmly against her palm. "Your hand feels cool. Nice."

"Maybe a damp washcloth would help." Tabitha pulled her hand away, aware once more of that faint trace of unease she experienced whenever she touched him. Rising, she went into the small bath and located a washcloth. When she returned a few minutes later to place the dampened cloth on his forehead, his dark lashes were drooping, veiling the silver eyes. He was clearly exhausted.

When she draped the cloth across his brow he groaned a small sigh of relief. "Feels good," he mumbled without opening his eyes. He groped for a moment with his hand, found hers and placed her fingertips against his temple. "That's where it hurts the most."

Tabitha chewed uncertainly on her lower lip for an instant and then realized that all she really wanted to do was help relieve his pain. Carefully she began massaging his temple. He responded with another muttered sigh, and she sensed his body relaxing. The hard, set lines of his face eased a little and the dark lashes stayed closed. Such an unhandsome face, she thought wonderingly, but such beautiful eyes. Like a dragon.

The image that thought produced caused her lips to curve upward in another of her private, little smiles. It was some time before she realized Dev had fallen asleep.

For a few moments longer she continued to massage his temple, and then she carefully withdrew her hand. It was time to go back to her own cabin.

"No." It was a husky plea, thick with sleep. Her hand was caught in his and pushed back to his head. Then Dev shifted slightly, the restlessness evidence of the pain which still assaulted his body.

She couldn't leave him yet. He needed her. Tabitha took a deep breath and moved from the chair to sit beside him on the bed. It would be easier to go on massaging his head from that position.

As if he sensed that she wasn't going to abandon him to a lonely night of discomfort, Dev Colter fell more soundly asleep. Tabitha stared down at him, aware that she had a strange, protective feeling toward this man who was still very much a stranger. Perhaps because she had been the one to rescue him from that dirty alley and get him safely back to the ship; perhaps because he seemed to need her care tonight. Whatever the reason, she felt a strong desire to soothe and comfort him. He needed her. No man had ever really needed her before.

His vulnerability was new to her. She found it appealing in an unexpected fashion. It made him seem unthreatening and hinted at a sensitivity which most men seemed to lack.

Tabitha realized that she could like Devlin Colter very much, and the knowledge sent a wave of pleasurable warmth through her. She would take good care of him.

CHAPTER TWO

TABBY CAT.

She lay curled beside him on the narrow bed looking for all the world like a soft, purring tabby cat. Except that she wasn't exactly purring, Dev corrected himself, as he examined the woman beside him. She was sound asleep. What would it take to make her purr?

He kept very still on his side of the bed, watching as the Caribbean dawn began to filter through the state-room window. He realized wryly that he wasn't avoiding movement just because of a reluctance to reawaken the aches and pains of yesterday in his stiff muscles, but rather because he was strangely reluctant to awaken Miss Tabitha Graham. He knew that when those huge sherry-colored eyes opened, they were going to be filled with acute embarrassment and with that watchful, distant caution he had seen in them yesterday and once or twice during the preceding three days.

Dev decided he rather liked her the way she was now, her soft, satisfyingly curved body curled in a relaxed and trusting sprawl alongside him. It took an effort of will to resist the temptation to reach out and stroke the full line of her sweet derriere. But he realized that if he gave in to the urge she would undoubtedly awaken, and he wanted to delay that event as long as possible.

It wasn't just the rounded curve of her rear which intrigued him; Miss Tabitha Graham also had a pleasantly full bosom. The old-fashioned word made him smile unexpectedly. He straightened his mouth almost at once when the expression tugged painfully at bruised and cut flesh. But his gaze continued to linger on the outline of Tabitha's breasts beneath the cotton knit dress. It would be interesting to see how the soft mounds reacted to a man's touch.

No, he decided with an unusual restlessness, not just to a man's touch; to *his* touch. Would the nipples harden into small, dark pebbles? If he succeeded in eliciting a reaction like that would she then part her soft, rounded thighs and let him slide between them?

Hell, what was the mater with him this morning? Here he was, stiff and sore in every muscle and his mind insisted on busying itself with a fantasy which, if actually carried out, would prove to be sheer torture to his bruised frame. Not to mention the fact that it would undoubtedly scare Miss Tabitha Graham right back to her own stateroom, never to re-emerge for the duration of the voyage.

And it occurred to Dev that that was the last thing he wanted to do. He didn't want his tabby cat to disappear; she was proving to be very pleasant to have around. There was something infinitely comforting and soothing about her presence, and he was unfamiliar with comforting and soothing women.

When she had rounded the corner of that alley yesterday, he had sensed almost immediately that she wasn't going to panic or flutter about uselessly. After the initial shock of seeing his battered condition, she had dropped everything, literally, and come to his rescue. He had known as soon as he felt her gentle touch on his aching body that she could be trusted. How he knew that, he couldn't have said. Dev Colter had not made a lifelong habit of trusting people, but he had learned to trust his instincts. They had kept him alive this long.

On the way back to the ship he had let himself be comforted by the warmth and softness of her body. He could still remember the shape of her thigh beneath his cheek as he'd sprawled on her lap. When he'd awakened from the doctor's ministrations, it had been reassuring to see her sweetly anxious face light up with that gentle smile. No woman had ever looked at him quite like that before. The urge to call her with a plea for dinner later had been irresistible.

Dev's mouth hardened grimly as he realized what the direction of his thoughts was doing to his body. Perhaps it was normal for a man to have a few fantasies when he woke up to find a woman, any woman, lying beside him! And when that woman was the same creature who had rescued him and comforted him, perhaps it was even more normal to do a little fantasizing.

But regardless of the normalness of the situation, Dev had enough perception to know that throwing himself on top of Miss Tabitha Graham, even if he had been physically capable of the action this morning, would only result in unmitigated disaster. She'd flee and that was the last thing he wanted.

Dev Colter was discovering that he was hungry for

more of the gentle, soothing comfort he had received yesterday. In fact, he wanted a hell of a lot more of it. It was not a commodity which had been particularly abundant in his life. At forty he was suddenly aware that he was rather greedy for what he had missed. He had enough self-control not to jeopardize his present good luck by giving in to the urgings of his body. When Tabitha stirred slightly, he instantly closed his eyes. He'd trust his instincts in dealing with her.

SHE AWOKE WITH A FEELING OF disorientation. For a moment Tabitha delayed opening her eyes, trying to assimilate the elements of strangeness which were impinging on her. The steady, throbbing feel of the ship's engines was familiar enough, but nothing else seemed quite right. For one thing there was a solid, warm body next to hers on the bed. Tabitha's eyes flew open in alarm as reality came back with a thud.

For an agonizing instant she lay perfectly still, hardly daring to seek out Dev Colter's face. What must he be thinking? How could she have fallen asleep like that last night? There was a distant recollection of easing herself down beside him so that she could rest a little while she massaged his temple and then nothing until now. How excruciatingly embarrassing for both of them!

But when she found the nerve to raise her eyes to his face, she heaved a sigh of relief. He was still asleep. Her incipient embarrassment faded to be replaced by concern. Poor man. He must be exhausted. Thank heaven he had been able to get some rest.

Carefully Tabitha eased herself out of the narrow bed, aware of a distinct feeling of purely feminine pleasure. What rest Dev had obtained was attributable, in part, to her. Hurriedly she collected her sandals, which had apparently fallen off during the night, and slipped out of the stateroom.

A hasty glance up and down the corridor determined that no one was witnessing her early morning departure from a man's room. Not that anyone on board would particularly care, she assured herself wryly as she made her way back to her own deck. Everyone on board was there to enjoy himself or herself to the fullest and certainly wouldn't begrudge others doing the same!

But Tabitha was not accustomed to making any kind of spectacle of herself and the thought of someone smirking over her departure from a man's cabin was enough to bring a wave of warmth to her cheeks. She hated scenes of any kind and she was especially horrified at the thought of finding herself the center of speculative attention. She liked to think it was because she was sensitive, but the simple truth was that she lacked the self-confidence to carry off such a situation and she knew it.

With a vast sense of relief she gained the privacy of her own stateroom. A nice, hot shower would restore her usual calm, she decided at once, stripping off the yellow cotton knit dress. Catching sight of her nude body just before she stepped into the bath, she gave a self-mocking smile. What would Dev Colter have thought if he'd awakened to find her lying next to him?

Would he have found anything at all appealing in her gently rounded frame? Probably not. Tabitha sighed philosophically. She had learned long ago that while men sometimes admired full breasts and hips, she apparently lacked the sensual voluptuousness which made such a shape truly attractive. And her ex-husband had made it abundantly clear that she also lacked the fiery, ardent nature which might have compensated.

Grimacing, she went into the shower and turned on the water. As soon as she was out she would order breakfast for Dev. He had been hungry last night and presumably would be again this morning. He needed to eat for strength, she decided determinedly, and immediately began planning a strengthening sort of menu for him. It was quite pleasant to lose herself in the activity, and it restored her equilibrium.

By the time she knocked on his door half an hour later she was feeling quite in command of herself and of the situation. His answering invitation to enter seemed to come with reassuring alacrity.

"Good morning," Tabitha said cheerfully as she walked into the room, once again followed by a steward carrying a tray. "How are you feeling? I've brought breakfast."

Dev was sitting on the edge of the bed, dressed in a fresh pair of light tan pants clasped around his hard waist with a dark leather belt. Contrasting with the bandages he still wore, his nude upper torso was sleek and bronzed in the early morning light, and his dark brown hair had been brushed into place. It still bore a trace of dampness from the shower. His silvery eyes focused on her immediately.

"Great. I'm starving again. I was just wondering whether or not I had enough strength left after that shower to make it up to the dining room. It was very thoughtful of you to do this, Tabby."

Tabitha glowed at the genuine note of gratitude in his voice. Such a nice man, she thought happily. Polite, grateful for small favors, sensitive, vulnerable. For what more could a woman ask? Perhaps this sort of man wouldn't care if a woman's roundness couldn't exactly be described as voluptuous?

"Do you need any more pain pills?" she asked, airily dismissing the steward so that she could dish up the grapefruit and scrambled eggs herself. "I can ask the doctor for another packet, if you like." She uncovered a plate of toast, peering down at it to make sure the cook had remembered to butter the bread.

"I think I'll survive on aspirin today," he murmured, watching as she bustled about the tray.

Aware of his eyes following her every move, Tabitha hastened through her preparations and then motioned him to the chair on the opposite side of the small table. What a relief to know he had still been asleep when she'd awakened this morning!

"I've been trying to decide whether or not you should spend the day in bed," she told him as he cautiously sat down across from her. "It's obvious you're still not feeling very well."

"I still ache a bit here and there," he admitted. "But I think the sun might feel good on my poor, battered body. What do you think?" he asked humbly.

"You might be right," she agreed thoughtfully. "The warmth might be good for those aching muscles. We'll fill you full of aspirins after breakfast and then go find a couple of vacant deck chairs near the pool. How does that sound?"

She thought she saw a flash of something close to

relief in his eyes before he nodded and agreed. "It sounds delightful." He paused and then went on softly, "I haven't thanked you for helping me get to sleep last night, Tabby."

She blinked in sudden uncertainty. How much did he remember about last night? In the next moment she relaxed as he gave her a blandly polite look. "It was quite all right. You don't owe me any thanks. I was glad to do it. What did the captain say when you told him what had happened on St. Regis?"

Dev shrugged and then stifled a small groan, regretting the movement. "He said he'd check back with the local authorities but that probably not much would be done. This sort of thing happens occasionally everywhere in the world. I should never have wandered down that alley in the first place," he added ruefully.

"How were you to know it would be dangerous?" she countered roundly. "Heavens, I was about to do the exact same thing. A few minutes earlier and it would have been me who got attacked."

The level glance he gave her was suddenly unreadable. "How did you happen to wander into that alley when you did?" He dug into his grapefruit.

"I was following a sign on the wall outside which said there was a sculptor's studio at the other end," she explained easily. "I had already found the most interesting little wooden dragon at another shop, and I was hoping to find something else equally fascinating before I went back to the ship. You never can tell what will turn up at little, hidden shops."

"What sort of things do you collect?" he asked curiously.

"Things like this," she said, holding out her hand to display a ring done in an intricate design.

Dev frowned over her fingers. "What is it?"

"A sea serpent! Can't you see the little fins and the odd-shaped head?"

"Er, yes, now that you mention it. Uh, you collect sea serpents?" he asked very politely.

Tabitha smiled in amusement. "I like fantastic creatures. Dragons and unicorns and griffins and harpies. There's something about mythological animals that I find fascinating. I can't really explain it."

"Maybe it's because you're part tabby cat," he suggested softly.

She looked up in surprise and then chuckled. "Tabby cats are hardly fantastic creatures. Quite ordinary animals, as a matter of fact."

"Any creature is fantastic to someone who isn't familiar with it. If a man had never seen a tabby cat up close, he might be quite amazed when one wandered into his life." Dev's words were spoken in a slow, thoughtful tone.

Tabitha stared at him in astonishment. "You're absolutely right, you know,' she said very seriously, plunging into her favorite topic. "When the medieval monks wrote their bestiaries they had to describe a lot of creatures they had never seen. It was natural that the unfamiliar ones seemed quite strange to them."

"Bestiaries?" he queried.

"Books of beasts," she laughed. "They were books of natural history. Full of information on flora and fauna. They were serious attempts at biology but a lot of the information on animals from far-off lands got a little garbled in the translation process. Perfectly understandable, of course, given the limited methods of communication at the time. It's rather fun to sit down with a bestiary and figure out just what kind of creature a griffin or a unicorn really is."

"What do the bestiaries have to say about tabby cats?" Dev's mouth crooked into a small smile, and his eyes asked her to share the humor.

"Not much, as I recall," she retorted dryly. "Something about cats being useful for catching mice, I think. It's a very short entry in most bestiaries. Perhaps a case of familiarity breeding contempt." Determinedly Tabitha decided to take charge of the conversation. She didn't care for the personal tone it seemed to be assuming. "Are you on board this ship to scout out new itineraries for your clients?"

He hesitated as if reluctant to change the topic and then gave in gracefully. "That's right. One of the perks of being in the travel business."

"Have you been in the field long?"

"Quite a while," he answered vaguely.

"You must have seen a great deal of the world by now," she said enthusiastically.

"A fair amount," he agreed dryly. "Is this your first cruise?"

"How can you tell?" she asked, grinning.

"You seem to be a little reluctant to join in with the others. I've noticed you a few times during the past couple of days, and you're always by yourself."

She flushed. "I could say the same thing about you."

He looked pleased. "Had you noticed me before you encountered me in that alley yesterday then?"

Something about the boyish pleasure in his eyes made her laugh out loud. "Yes, as a matter of fact, I had."

"It's the cane," he decided, abruptly morose. "People tend to notice a man with a limp."

"If you think they noticed you when you had a limp, just wait until they get a load of you covered in bandages and bruises!" she teased gently.

He muttered something in disgust. "You've just convinced me to spend the day in the cabin instead of on deck."

"Nonsense," she scolded roundly. "I think you're quite right. The sun will feel good, and I refuse to let you sulk down here in your cabin when going topside is bound to be therapeutic. Besides, with a shirt on, the only visible marks are going to be the bruises on your cheek and under your eye. They'll give you a mysterious, dangerous look. Very appealing to the ladies. Just wait and see."

"I'm on board for business purposes," he stated aloofly, "not to appeal to the ladies.'

Sensing that she had somehow offended him, Tabitha impulsively reached across the table to touch his hand. "I'm sorry. I was only teasing you." When he nodded a bit shortly, accepting her apology, she quickly withdrew her hand. His eyes went to where her fingers had rested on his skin, and then he picked up his fork and resumed eating the scrambled eggs.

Tabitha smiled happily to herself. She really did like this man who was capable of being embarrassed at the thought of serving as a titillating source of interest to women. Such a pleasure to encounter a male whose ego wasn't overly inflated! And she could empathize with him completely. She would have reacted exactly the same way if someone had intimated she might be capable of drawing the attention of the males on board.

The day ahead stretched forth invitingly. With a strong sense of proprietary interest in the man she had rescued, Tabitha took charge of the day's activities. Dev seemed quite content to let her establish the schedule, responding to her gentle bullying with satisfying gratitude. Dutifully he obeyed her injunction to avoid overdoing it in the sun and acceded to her choice of chicken with peanut sauce for lunch. She also made sure he consumed invigorating tea at the morning break and several scones which were served at three in the afternoon.

In between these times she obtained a deck of cards and played gin rummy with her recuperating patient. And all the while the conversation flowed easily between them. Dev talked about his adventures as a travel agent, and she told him about the small pleasures of running a bookshop in a quaint Victorian fishing town.

"We have something in common," he observed at one point as she beat him for the third time at gin rummy. "Both of us know what it is to be struggling small-business people."

The thought of a similarity in their careers pleased Tabitha and her normally small, private smile widened into something approaching brilliance. Dev stared at her for a moment as if he'd lost track of his thoughts. Then he appeared to remember what he had been about to say.

"Listen," he went on earnestly, "just because I'm not up to having a swim, don't let me keep you out of the pool. It's getting quite warm out here, and I'm sure you want to cool off a little."

Tabitha's eyes widened in dismay. "Oh no, I'm fine, really, I am. I'm enjoying the warmth." Have this man see her in a bathing suit? Not a chance!

Now why should she feel so awkward at the thought? she asked herself grimly. She'd been swimming before in the cruise ship's pool, heedless of what poolside opinion might be. But she was accustomed to receiving only mild glances that quickly slid off and went on to more interesting targets. In her demure bathing suit, with its small skirt at the hips, she felt she achieved a certain anonymity amid the bevy of sleek maillots and bikinis. This afternoon, however, simply because they had spent so much time together and had gotten to know each other, Dev was bound to give her more than a brief, disinterested once-over glance if she were to change into a swimsuit. She'd certainly give him more than a quick look if he were to change!

"Go on, Tabby," he encouraged. "I'll just stretch out here on the lounger and rest a bit while you cool off. Everyone else is in the pool!"

"I don't…well, that is…" She fumbled to a halt. There really wasn't a whole lot she could use for an excuse. And she didn't want to make him think she was self-conscious about the prospect of having him see her in the suit. Besides, he was a gentleman and a friend. He wouldn't be judging her against the other women, would he? Dev Colter was too intrinsically gracious to stoop to that sort of masculine cruelty. "All right, if you're sure you don't mind being deserted for a while, I'll go downstairs and change. Be right back."

She was shy, Dev thought, hiding his amusement as he watched her hurry off toward the staircase which led to the lower decks. Was she really embarrassed at the thought of flaunting that nicely rounded body in a skimpy little swimsuit? He liked the small, growing signs of awareness he was seeing in her. The notion of having her aware of him as a man was satisfying. Still, he cautioned himself, he had to go slowly. The desire to pounce on her was increasing every hour he spent in her company but instinct told him it would be disastrous. Better to have her relaxed and open, slipping over the edge into sensual awareness before she quite realized what was happening.

Dev settled back in his lounger, wincing as he jolted a few still-healing muscles. Then his mouth tilted upward faintly at the corners as he closed his eyes and waited for the return of his tabby cat. He felt rather like a medieval hunter setting out to capture an unfamiliar creature described in a bestiary. The knowledge that he was deliberately setting lures and baiting traps took him by surprise. What was it about this woman that made him want to keep her near? Was it just that he was luxuriating in the soft comfort she offered? Probably. It was a rare treat.

Women in his life tended to fall into one of two categories. They were either lethally dangerous or else they were cute, sexy creatures who found him temporarily fascinating because of his past. He made a determined effort to avoid both varieties. Unfortunately, there didn't seem to be a whole lot of choice in between the two extremes. Or perhaps, up until recently, he hadn't realized what he was missing. How did a man know to go looking for something when he wasn't fully aware that it existed?

Tabitha emerged on deck twenty minutes later swathed in a huge, oversized towel. She smiled a little uncertainly as she came toward him, hugging the towel closely. Conscious of his role, Dev returned the smile, keeping the greeting light and totally unthreatening. He wanted the tabby purring comfortably.

"Here, I'll hold your towel for you while you go in the pool." Casually he held up his hand, making it nearly impossible for her to avoid complying. It took her a couple of seconds but then, apparently deciding she was being ridiculous, she let the towel unwind and handed it to him with a brave nonchalance that made him want to chuckle indulgently.

"I'll be right back," she assured him, turning at once toward the pool. He watched as she first sat down on the edge and then slid into the water. It was a hell of a swimsuit, he decided dryly. He hooked his arms around his knees, sitting up to watch as Tabitha dutifully began swimming laps. The suit was black with tiny little nondescript flowers scattered about. High-necked, with wide straps and a little skirt designed to help conceal the roundness of her hips, the garment stood out amid the gaily colored bikinis and maillots simply because it was so utterly different! He wondered if she realized that in seeking anonymity she had unknowingly made herself somewhat unique on the sun deck of the ship.

Even though it had been designed to conceal rather than reveal, there was only so much a swimsuit, any swimsuit, could cover however, and Dev found himself thoroughly enjoying the sight of Tabitha as she gamely went back and forth in the pool. She was so soft looking, he thought wonderingly. Soft and gentle and feminine. He remembered the touch of her hand on his forehead the night before and took a deep breath. A determined man might resort to violence to obtain that kind of softness for his very own.

And he'd sure as hell resorted to violence for less reason than that in the past!

But violence wasn't the way with a woman like this. He narrowed his eyes against the sun as Tabitha emerged, dripping, from the pool. He watched the way she shook back her warm-colored hair and then he realized he wasn't the only one whose eyes were following the progress of the staid little swimsuit. With instinctive male alertness he pinpointed the one or two other knowing masculine gazes, and he frowned in unaccustomed displeasure.

Almost simultaneously he realized something else. Tabitha was totally unaware of the other eyes on her. It wasn't a casual pretence of unawareness inspired by feminine self-confidence but a genuine lack of consciousness that she was attractive. It was as if she simply didn't believe herself the type of woman to draw a second glance from any man. Perhaps it was that very lack of sensual response on her part which made the other masculine gazes slide on past to other swimsuits.

But none of these other men had nearly gotten themselves killed in a back alley on some scroungy Caribbean island and then had this woman come to their rescue. Nor had they discovered the warmth and gentleness in her touch as Dev had the previous night. He decided he preferred to keep the information to himself.

"I've been thinking about tonight," Tabitha began hesitantly as she neared Dev's lounger and quickly picked up the towel he extended. As soon as she got it wrapped around her she felt instantly more comfortable. His gaze had remained politely on her face as she approached, and his smile was one of genuine welcome. Such a nice man. He neither leered nor ignored. Her eyes sparkled with enthusiasm as she took the seat beside him. "Are you going to feel up to having dinner in the main dining room?"

"I'm feeling better by the minute. And thanks to all the food you've been stuffing down me today, I think my energy level will be high enough to manage the exertion of dinner," he said, chuckling and leaning back against his folded arms.

"Oh good. Well, I was wondering about perhaps seeing the purser and getting your seat assignment changed. There's an empty place at my table and as long as you're not traveling with anyone else…?" She tried not to chew on her lower lip as she waited for his reaction. He had been so amenable to every other suggestion she'd made today that when this idea had come to her in the pool, she had decided to risk the potential rejection.

"I'd like that, Tabby," he murmured, closing his eyes against the glare of the sun. "I'd like that very much."

Tabitha's smile was very private this time as she leaned back to let the heat of the day finish drying her body. Her self-confidence soared. Dev wanted to have dinner with her. She was suddenly enormously glad she'd taken the initiative. Perhaps he'd been wondering how to do it, himself, but hadn't wanted to seem too demanding of her time. Dev Colter wasn't the kind of man who would want to push himself into a woman's company unless he was sure she wanted him to do so, she thought smugly.

That smug feeling was still with her as she entered the dining room on Dev's arm that evening. Dressed in a gauzy, free-floating, white dress trimmed in turquoise at the hem and throat, she felt light and delicate beside his solid strength. He was wearing a dark, linen sports jacket over tan trousers, and the ebony cane in his hand seemed to lend an air of dignified restraint to the total picture of lean, conservative masculinity. Best of all he acted as if she were the only woman in the whole room.

"You look very charming tonight, Tabby," he murmured as they took their seats. "I only wish I could ask you to go dancing later on."

She glanced up in surprise and confusion. "Oh, will you be too tired, do you think?" she asked weakly. She had been hoping the evening would extend well beyond the dinner hour. The tinge of disappointment was almost painful.

He gave her an odd glance as he picked up his menu. "Not too tired. But I'm afraid I don't dance." His silver glance slid sideways to the cane hooked on the back of his chair.

Relief flooded through her. "Good grief, is that all you're worried about?"

"Well, it does rather limit my capabilities on the dance floor," he drawled a bit coolly.

"So who wants to dance? I'm not really a very good dancer anyway. We'll sit at one of the little tables and drink gin and tonics and make brilliantly perceptive ob-

servations about all the other people on the dance floor."
She chuckled.

Dev studied her for a moment. He seemed about to ask
a question but shelved it as the others who had been
assigned to their table began to arrive. The conversation
quickly became general. The two other couples, both in
their mid-fifties, had heard of the affair on St. Regis and
were full of interested concern as they discovered themselves seated next to the victim. Somewhat to Tabitha's
surprise, Dev seemed quite willing to talk about it
although he chose to emphasize her own part in the
matter.

"Believe me, I was never so glad to see anyone in my
life as I was Miss Graham here when she came around
the corner," he announced feelingly.

"Not quite true," Tabitha heard herself retort. "You
said that if I were the U.S. cavalry, I was a bit late, as I
recall!" She turned to the others, astonishing herself
with her willingness to make a joke of the whole thing.
"It was one complaint after another, you know. First that
I was late and then that I wouldn't let him pour an entire
bottle of rum down his throat in the taxi on the way to
the boat and later, when he asked for a bowl of soup,
that I showed up with a full-course meal. There's no
pleasing some men!"

Dev contrived to look hurt. "Well, I really could have
used the rest of that bottle of rum the taxi driver
offered!"

One of the other men at the table laughed loudly.
"I don't blame you, Colter. Sounds like good
medicine to me!" He picked up his whiskey sour and
swallowed thirstily.

It wasn't until Dev had escorted Tabitha to a seat in the elegant cocktail lounge after dinner that he asked the question she had seen in his eyes just before the meal.

"Why don't you dance?" he inquired blandly as he ordered drinks.

Tabitha lifted one shoulder dismissingly. "Not enough practice, I suppose. It takes a fair amount of experience to feel confident on the floor, you know."

His mouth twisted. "To tell you the truth I wasn't much good even before my accident. Now the cane gives me the perfect excuse to stay safely seated."

"Your accident?" she began delicately, aware of an avid curiosity.

"Umm." He nodded unhelpfully and then, instead of responding to her unasked question, he went on with another of his own. "So why haven't you acquired much practice, Tabby? Don't they date in that little Victorian village where you have your bookshop?"

She smiled. "Definitely. We're not *that* antiquated. But since my marriage ended, I haven't gotten out a great deal." She bit her lip. "Actually, I didn't get out a great deal before my marriage. Or during it, to be perfectly precise."

He gave her an odd glance. "When were you married?"

"A couple of years ago. It didn't last long, I'm afraid. Only about a year."

"What happened?" Dev asked.

"I guess you could say it was cancelled due to lack of interest," she tried to retort brightly, but a flash of remembered humiliation came and went briefly in her eyes.

"Which of you lost interest in the other?"

She eyed him with the first, faint trace of wariness she had yet experienced around him. "Are you sure you want to discuss this particular subject?"

He smiled with a reassuring gentleness that immediately relaxed her. "It's probably a case of failure loving company. My ex-wife lost interest in me right after my accident."

"Oh!" Tabitha exclaimed, her heart going out to him at once at hearing the bold statement. "I didn't realize… Well, I know exactly how you feel. It's rather demoralizing, to say the least, isn't it?"

"When your mate loses interest? To say the least," he agreed dryly. Then he went on with warm assurance. "I can't see anyone losing interest in you, though, Tabby."

Her smile flickered brilliantly at the compliment and then faded into a self-mocking grimace. "Actually, the surprise was that Greg married me in the first place. I was the kind of girl who made a fortune baby-sitting in high school because I never had a date. In college I was the sort who always got her term papers done early, because I had plenty of free evenings to study. Later I made a success of my little bookshop, because I had plenty of time to devote to it. When Greg came along, I was as astonished as everyone else was when he asked me to marry him! I hadn't exactly been besieged with offers."

"What happened, Tabby?" The silver eyes pinned her intently.

She shrugged. "What I didn't understand at the time and what he didn't bother to tell me was that he had moved into town in an effort to recover from a blazing love affair which had gone wrong. I guess I seemed like a quiet, undemanding sort of female who didn't remind him in the least of his lost love. It was a classic case of marrying on the rebound and it proved a disaster. I knew almost immediately that I was never going to be able to satisfy him, and when I found out he was always comparing me with the great love of his life, I realized it was all pretty hopeless. He realized it, too. And then his dream woman came back into his life. That resolved the situation rather quickly. Greg and I were divorced almost at once."

"And he went back to his blazing love affair?"

"Yes. It was all for the best. But the experience didn't improve my ability on the dance floor," she concluded in an attempt at flippancy. Then, very bravely, she asked, "What about you, Dev? Did your wife really leave you because of your accident?" Her eyes were dark with sympathy.

He shrugged, glancing down at his drink, and then raised his gaze once more to her concerned face. "The marriage had been disintegrating long before the accident. I hadn't proved to be what she wanted in a husband. I suppose my lifestyle sounded more exciting to her than it really is. Or perhaps I sounded more exciting to her than I really am," he confided dryly. "People sometimes think that if you're well traveled, you're a jet-setter type. And I'm not, to put it mildly. I'm just a hard-working businessman. It took me quite a while to recover from my accident, and by the time I had, we had decided to go our separate ways. She found someone else before the divorce was finalized."

"We seem to have several things in common," Tabitha observed softly.

He looked at her and then he smiled. "We do, don't we?" There was another short silence and then he added in an even quieter tone, "You don't bore me in the slightest, Tabby."

"That's the nice thing about a shipboard romance, isn't it?" she said without stopping to think. "By the time boredom sets in, the boat is back in port and everyone can go his or her own way." Almost instantly she wished her tongue would dissolve in her mouth. Lord! Now he was going to think she was suggesting that he have a shipboard affair with her! And she hadn't meant that at all. Had she?

But Dev appeared not to have picked up on the awful ramifications of her words. Instead he only smiled benignly and glanced around at the dancers who were beginning to crowd the floor. "How many of these people do you suppose are only involved in shipboard romances?" he asked easily. "I'll take the first guess. I'll bet that couple over there in the far corner is having an affair."

Grateful for the diversion, she played the game with him. "How can you tell?"

"Look at the way they're all wrapped up in each other."

"Maybe they're newlyweds."

"No rings."

"Hmm. You're very observant," she said, rather surprised he had been able to pick up such a small detail from such a distance across a dark room.

"I have good eyes." He shrugged, as if it were an unimportant fact about himself he had long since taken for granted. "Good ears, too."

"Better than normal?" she asked, firmly resisting the

impulse to make a Little-Red-Riding-Hood-style comment. He had clearly intended no humor in the remarks.

"So I've been told," he confirmed idly. "Your turn."

"Okay, I'll choose that couple near the bar. I'll bet they're involved in an affair, too."

"Nah. They're married."

Tabitha frowned. "Rings?"

"Yeah, but that's not what gives them away. Look how he keeps glancing over his wife's shoulder at the blonde by the window. He's flirting like hell."

"You sound very knowledgeable," she accused.

"I'm a man. I understand my own sex," Dev growled.

"And married men always flirt?"

"That one does. Let's see, who else can we find?"

"This could make an interesting parlor game," Tabitha murmured, getting into the spirit of the thing.

Two hours slipped past and Tabitha realized she was enjoying herself with unaccustomed abandon. She even allowed herself more than her usual two drinks and was beginning to feel quite bubbly. It was probably the alcohol in part, but she knew that she was high on something besides the unaccustomed number of drinks. She was enthralled with the relationship that was blossoming between Dev Colter and herself.

"You look very happy," he observed as they ambled out on deck to drink in some of the moonlight and the sea air. Actually it was Tabitha who ambled. Dev still moved with a great deal of stiffness. Even when he was healed, he would be less than agile with that left leg of his, Tabitha thought compassionately. He would still be vulnerable. Her expression softened dreamily at the thought.

"I am," she said simply. "I've had a lovely evening." An unfamiliar self-confidence was welling up in her as she leaned against the rail and clung lightly to his arm. "I can only think of one more thing that would make it perfect." For a second her heart almost stopped as the words left her mouth. Surely this wasn't Tabitha Graham talking?

Dev looked down at her, his hard face shadowed in the moonlight. Only his silver eyes seemed light and reflective. "What's that, Tabby?"

She took a deep breath and then, with a fragile sureness which was entirely new to her, she lifted her face and raised her hands to splay against the front of his jacket.

"Would you mind very much if I kissed you good night?" she asked politely.

CHAPTER THREE

"IT'S ALL RIGHT," SHE MURMURED with a reassuring smile when he said nothing in response to her inquiry. "I'm really quite harmless. Tabby cats are, you know."

"I'm not so sure about that," Dev said quietly. "But the appearance of being harmless and gentle is probably part of your charm. I wouldn't mind at all if you kissed me good night. But I should warn you that it's been a long time since I said good night to a woman under moonlight. In fact, it feels like it's been forever."

Tabitha lifted sensitive fingers to touch the side of his hard cheek, her eyes like sherry wine as they revealed her sympathy. He seemed so very vulnerable physically and now, she sensed, he was also vulnerable emotionally. "Has it, Dev?"

He inclined his head once, a little shortly, and she had the distinct impression that he was embarrassed about his lack of sophisticated experience. Then he leaned against the railing and hooked the ebony cane over the metal beside him. "I've spent a lot of time alone since Amanda left. Too much, it seems, if you have to be the one to ask me whether or not you can kiss me. I should have swept you off your feet with a romantic assault out here on deck," he concluded wryly as he softly folded his large hand over her fingers, which still rested lightly on his chest.

Instinctively Tabitha moved a little closer, her face lifted anxiously. "Don't be ridiculous, Dev. If you had tried to stage a grand assault, I would have wondered what in the world was going on. It wouldn't have been in character for you at all!"

"No?"

She shook her head firmly. "Dev, you're special precisely because you're not like other men. You're sensitive and, I think, a little shy. Just like me. I feel comfortable with you. Don't you understand? Men always seem to be playing some sort of macho game and you don't do that. You're honest and gentle and you don't try to flirt with every beautiful woman who walks past. You and I are friends. We have things in common. All of that is so much nicer than having to worry about playing a game, don't you think? It's because I feel we're on the same wavelength that I felt comfortable asking if I could kiss you."

"And if I'd assaulted you instead?" he asked half-humorously, silver eyes gleaming.

She laughed up at him, the amusement mirrored in her warm gaze. "I would have thought you probably had too much to drink. I'm not the kind of woman men assault, but more importantly, you're not the kind of man who goes around pouncing on women."

His gaze narrowed slightly. "Are you sure that doesn't make me a little dull?"

"It makes you wonderful," she whispered happily and stood on tiptoe. Her fingers went lightly around the back of his head as she raised her lips to brush them against his mouth.

That flower-soft caress was truly all she had intended. A part of Tabitha, sensitized by the intriguing new relationship which was developing between herself and the man she had rescued, had simply wanted a touch of intimacy. Something in her had wanted to deepen the closeness just a bit. Or perhaps it was merely a desire to broaden the spectrum of the friendship being established.

Whatever the basis of the impulse, Tabitha knew she mustn't go too far with it or Dev would wonder what had gotten into her. She didn't want to frighten him off by demanding more than he was prepared to give. No, she had planned to limit the kiss to just a brief gesture of affection.

What she hadn't counted on was the unexpected warmth of his mouth against hers, nor the faint tremor in his hand, which still enclosed her fingers. She withdrew until there was an inch or so between her lips and his, but she stayed on her toes and her hand at the back of his head did not move.

"Again?" she heard herself ask huskily.

"Please." His voice was even huskier.

Very carefully she leaned against him this time, finding a distinct pleasure in the feel of his hard chest against her full breasts. When she moved her mouth lightly against his, he muttered her name and the sound of it was strangely intoxicating.

"Tabby. Sweet Tabby."

Almost imperceptibly his fingers tightened around her hand, pressing it against his jacket. Then she was aware that his other hand was settling ever so hesitantly at her waist, resting on the curve of her hip. He was just as nervous and uncertain about all this as she was,

Tabitha thought wonderingly. Perhaps it would be easier
for her if she took the initiative. A vulnerable, sensitive
man like this would be anxious not to press matters
farther than she wished them to go.

Relaxing into the role of the one who must set the
pace, she felt a little more of her weight rest against his
solid frame. He seemed so substantial, so strong, ab-
sorbing her lighter weight with ease. If she hadn't
already learned of the other side of his nature, she might
have been nervous about the strength in him. But she
did know of his sensitivity and his vulnerability, and so
she let herself enjoy the delicate moment.

It was strange being the one who sampled and tasted
and set the boundaries. There was a curious freedom in
it, unlike anything else she had ever known before.
There was no painful agony of suspense, wondering
whether or not she would attract or bore her partner.
There was no nervousness about how far to let the situation go. Instead she experienced a heady sense of excitement.

His dark hair seemed crisp and inviting to the touch
and her fingers began to move a little awkwardly in it.
She felt another tremor pass through his body and her
own anticipation increased. He wasn't bored, she
thought exultantly. Her touch was eliciting a response
in him; she could feel it!

The moment when her mouth parted invitingly
beneath his passed without her actually being aware of
it. One instant there was a barrier between their tongues
and the next she was tasting the inside of him.

She heard someone moan softly and realized belatedly that it was herself. The next shiver she sensed was

one which flowed through her body, not his. Her feeling of anticipation was elevated by several quantum leaps, sending her senses into an unfamiliar whirl.

For an endless moment she explored the intimate taste of him, unaware that her nails were sinking delicately into the back of his neck. He was taking most of her weight now as he leaned against the railing and somehow his legs had spread apart. She was standing cradled between his thighs and the heat of him passed easily through the thin gauze of her dress. He was so warm and inviting, so undemanding, yet welcoming.

She was becoming hungry, Tabitha realized distantly; even a bit greedy. The urge to learn more intimate details of his body was rapidly deepening. She mustn't scare him off, she reminded herself. She didn't want to do anything that would spoil the unfolding relationship.

His tongue played with hers as she caressed the inside of his mouth with exquisite care and it followed as she led the way back into her own mouth. Once she had him inside, she moaned softly again, inviting him to explore as he would.

For some reason his legs seemed to tighten around hers and the strong hand at her waist dropped lower on her hip, kneading gently. But mostly Tabitha was aware of the incredible thoroughness with which he used his tongue. She was becoming captivated by what she had found. The blossoming sensuality she was experiencing was totally new to her. Above all she must not push it.

"Tabby?" he rasped a little thickly as she reluctantly withdrew her mouth from his.

"It's all right, Dev," she mumbled a little unsteadily.

"I know things are moving too fast. Don't worry, I won't let them get out of hand."

"Tabby," he began carefully, as though searching for difficult words. "Tabby, I…"

"Don't," she pleaded, stopping his mouth with her fingertips. Her eyes smiled warmly up at him. "Don't say it. I know this is taking both of us by surprise. I wouldn't dream of spoiling it by rushing things. I expect it's the moonlight and the wine. Neither of us is too accustomed to romance, apparently!" Her curving lips invited him to laugh with her at the situation in which they found themselves.

Dev stared down at her for a long moment, silver eyes opaque. "I, for one, am not very familiar with it at all," he finally murmured.

"I know. That's one of the things I like so much about you," she told him honestly.

"You do?"

"Umm. I feel like I'm dealing with someone I understand. Someone who has the same reservations and concerns I do. The same fears."

"What fears?" he questioned deeply, apparently having a little difficulty in swallowing. Poor man. Was he so very nervous of her?

"About building something meaningful between two people; about wanting to be certain there's real depth in a relationship before committing yourself to it. Oh, Dev, I feel I know you so well!" Tabitha exclaimed in satisfaction. "We have so much in common. I know neither of us wants a casual fling. It's no wonder we don't fit into this crowd on board. We're both a couple of misfits, aren't we?"

"In a way." He sounded almost cautious as he intently studied her upturned face. "I have to admit that neither of us seems quite what the cruise line had in mind in the way of potential passengers when it printed up the brochures! I'm on board for obvious business reasons. What made you buy a ticket, Tabby?"

"Fantasy, I think," she told him whimsically. "I had this image of what a Caribbean cruise would be like, you see. Balmy nights and sunny days filled with exotic color and excitement. Maybe I thought I would become a different person on board, I don't know. All I do know is that after I'd been on the ship one day, I realized I was the same old me and ten days at sea wasn't going to change things."

"Would you really want to be different? Even for ten days?" Dev asked in a gently neutral tone.

"I think every woman who thinks herself rather average has fantasies occasionally about becoming a femme fatale, about living a romantic adventure. Don't men have personal fantasies about being someone different?"

The question seemed to take him back for a moment. An unreadable expression flitted across his face and then he said slowly, "They do. I'd be lying if I said they didn't. There have been times lately when I've wished I was another kind of man."

"Oh, no," Tabitha interrupted with conviction. "Don't wish that! I wouldn't want you any different."

"You like the man I am?"

"Very much." She touched her fingertips to the lines at the side of his mouth, automatically soothing the uncertainty she sensed in him. "I like the man you are very much, Dev Colter. I wouldn't change a thing."

He gave a sideways glance at the ebony walking stick slung over the rail. "Not even the cane?"

She smiled at that. "The only reason I might be willing to see that changed is because of the pain your accident must have caused you. Other than that, no, I wouldn't particularly want to see it changed, if you want the truth. It gives you a distinguished air, like the gray in your hair."

"Thanks!" he muttered wryly. "The gray is a sign of being nearly forty, Tabitha."

Tabitha lifted her fingertips from the lines at his mouth to the flecks of silver in his deep brown hair. "I love the gray in your hair. Like moonlight caught in the shadows."

"I think you've been reading too much fantasy, but I won't complain," he groaned. Both of his hands had settled on her waist now, and she still stood between his thighs. "So here we are, two people who would like to live a fantasy and en route we've found something else, hmm?"

"That's a nice way of putting it," she whispered. It seemed to Tabitha that his fingers curved with a small amount of force into the curve of her hip. Or perhaps it was simply her imagination.

"Tabby, if this is reality, I think I prefer it to a romantic adventure on the high seas," Dev said huskily.

Her breath caught in her throat as her mind spun with all the potential implications of what he was saying. "So do I, Dev. I've thoroughly enjoyed this evening. I only wish you weren't still recovering from that awful incident on St. Regis."

"I feel much better," he assured her quickly.

"You don't have to pretend with me." She chuckled. "I'm the one who saw you in that alley, remember? I know very well you must still be hurting in any number of spots! And it's undoubtedly time you were in bed. You know what the doctor said, lots of rest."

Aware of where her duty lay, Tabitha stepped back out of his arms and took his hand in hers. Deliberately she started toward the entrance to the lower decks.

"Are you going to tuck me in tonight, Tabby?" Dev asked as he obediently followed.

She tried to analyze his tone, wondering if he sounded hopeful or was simply making a small joke. Then it occurred to her that his head might be aching. Perhaps he was obliquely asking her for another massage. "Have you got a headache?"

"No, I don't," he answered automatically and then blinked as she looked back at him inquiringly. His voice trailed off abruptly as if he had said something he wished he hadn't. Then he essayed a crooked little smile. "But it was very pleasant having you stay with me last night until I fell asleep."

"No one likes to suffer alone." She smiled as they headed down the long corridor lined with stateroom doors. "I was very happy to stay with you." At least he seemed to think she had left him after he'd fallen asleep. It was nice to have that confirmed. It made everything so much more comfortable between them. She looked up as they arrived at her cabin door. "Well, good night, Dev. I hope you sleep well."

"I'll call you before breakfast in the morning," he said deliberately. Then he added quickly, "That is, if you'd like to have breakfast together?"

She took pity on his suddenly anxious expression. "I'll look forward to it." Then, feeling very confident about what her reception would be, Tabitha balanced herself again on her toes and brushed her mouth lightly against his. "See you in the morning," she said before he had a chance to react. She stepped inside her own cabin and closed the door. Her own aggressiveness was enough of a shock to herself. No point in alarming him with it, too!

Out in the corridor, Dev watched the stateroom door shut firmly in his face and his knuckles whitened around the curved handle of his cane. Damn it to hell! This was taking more out of him than he had expected. How much patience did she think a man had?

With another muttered oath he started on down the corridor to his own room. There were only five days left on the stupid cruise. Five days left to figure out how to let Miss Tabitha Graham talk herself into bed with him. Well, he shouldn't complain, he told himself as he opened the door to his cabin. Look at the progress he'd made this evening. He'd made himself seem so nice and safe that she'd actually taken the initiative out on deck. And to think he'd spent the previous hour in the cocktail lounge wondering how to go about taking her into his arms without scaring the daylights out of her!

But it had all worked out very nicely, even if she had cut him off far too quickly. Dev shut the door behind him and set down the ebony cane. Tabitha was going to find herself in his bed eventually. He just had to be patient. You couldn't stalk a tabby cat with an elephant gun. Subtlety was called for here.

It was strange, he decided as he caught sight of the grim set of his face in the mirror, he would never have thought himself the subtle type. But then, he'd never tried to attract a woman like Tabitha Graham, either. A man was never too old to learn new tricks, it seemed. Then he winced as he sat down on the edge of the bed, his fingers going to his bruised ribs.

He might not be too old to learn new tricks in some areas, but there was no doubt that he was too old to be dabbling in his former line of work. How in hell had he ever let Delaney talk him into making that pickup on St. Regis?

Painfully, wishing he had another bottle of whiskey handy, Dev undressed and got into bed. It was really much more pleasant when Tabitha was around to fuss over him. He shouldn't have automatically denied the headache. Unfortunately he had spoken without thinking, and by the time he'd realized his tactical error it was too late. If he'd just thought it out beforehand, he could have had her here right now using her wonderful fingertips on his forehead.

Muttering about his failure to think fast enough on his feet, he reached out to switch off the bedside light. Then he lay staring out at the moonlit darkness beyond the window.

There was no point kidding himself. Tabitha had no idea at all of the kind of man he was. She had given him a fantasy role. To her he was gentle and vulnerable and sensitive. Just the kind of man she wanted. If he kept his head and didn't make any serious errors during the next couple of day, she would crawl into his lap like a trusting little cat. And then he would find out exactly what it took to make her purr.

With that thought in mind, Dev closed his eyes and went to sleep. He did not stay awake long enough to ask himself just why it was so important to make Tabby purr.

THE SHIP'S ITINERARY THE FOLLOWING DAY included an afternoon stop at another of the lesser-known islands on the list detailed in the brochure. Tabitha was looking forward to it with great anticipation. She bubbled over at breakfast as she read the description given in the ship's daily newsletter.

"It says here that a lot of expatriate-artist types have established a colony on the western tip of the island and that passengers from the ship are welcome to visit," she informed Dev over fresh papaya.

"I take it you'd like to visit the colony?"

"Definitely! No telling what sort of unusual things might be going on there."

"I'll bet." He chuckled.

"I meant in the way of creativity," she told him repressively.

"So did I. Put a bunch of free-spirited artists together on an island, and there's no telling what sort of creative endeavors they'll get up to."

"You're teasing me," she accused, but the knowledge left her feeling remarkably light-hearted. It was the sign of a good relationship when each party felt free to gently tease the other, wasn't it?

"You're right. I'll look forward to seeing the colony as much as you will," he assured her blandly. "Another cup of coffee?"

"Please." Then Tabitha frowned. "Are you sure you're feeling up to the trip? How are your ribs this morning?"

"A little sore, but nothing that should stop me from accompanying you."

And they didn't, apparently. Tabitha double-checked several times during the afternoon to make certain Dev wasn't overexerting himself, but he seemed able to maintain the pace she set. Together they toured the small shop at the art colony, and Tabitha fell in love with one item after another. A wide variety of work was being done in all sorts of media from woodworking to pottery and weaving.

"Look at this lovely dragon design, Dev," she exclaimed jubilantly as she examined a woven wall hanging. "He's going to look great over my fireplace."

Dev eyed the hanging thoughtfully. "He does appear to be looking for a home. Look at those pathetically pleading eyes. Too bad about the big teeth and the fiery tongue. Who'd want to take a chance on him as a house pet?"

"Don't be ridiculous! I would! He's gorgeous." She began rolling up the hanging. "And a perfect copy of a small German bronze figure I have."

"How did dragons make their way into bestiaries? From fairy tales?"

"The monks weren't that naive," she sniffed. "They knew the difference between fairy tales and real life. No, they probably came from descriptions of large serpents like pythons. And there are some other big reptiles in the world which could have been described as dragons. When you think about it, it's not hard to imagine some real-life dragons."

"Well, if you're going to take him home, I'd very much like to buy him for you," Dev said. "To replace the little carving that got left behind on St. Regis."

"Oh, that's okay. You needn't do that," she said hurriedly, pleased at the offer.

"I'd very much like to, though, Tabby. Will you let me?"

She cocked her head to one side at the soft note of entreaty in his low voice, and then she gave him a dazzling smile of acceptance. He really wanted to do this. How could she refuse? A man like Dev Colter would feel guilty at the knowledge that he'd been the cause of her leaving her trinkets behind on St. Regis. Such a thoughtful person!

"That's very kind of you, Dev. If you're quite sure you want to do this…"

"I am."

She lifted a shoulder in helpless appreciation. "Then thanks. I'll think of you every time I look at him," she added with a grin.

"What is it about him that's going to remind you of me? The fiery breath or the nasty-looking tail?"

"I think it's the eyes," she said musingly and then blushed as she realized it was the truth. Brilliant silver pools filled with a barely masked vulnerability. That was what she saw when she looked into Dev's eyes.

That night she again floated into dinner on his arm, and it seemed to Tabitha that her conversation had never been so witty and intelligent. The evening drifted past on dragon's wings, full of magic and shimmering excitement. Dev must have felt some of the sorcery, because he seemed as wrapped up in her as she was in him. Everywhere she led, he followed, willingly changing conversational directions, duplicating her order of turbot with cucumber sauce at dinner and insisting that she choose the wine.

So enthralled was she in the warm, vibrant relation-

ship which seemed to be developing that Tabitha was
unaware of the increasingly frequent glances she was
receiving from more than one nearby male passenger.
Her animation and sparkling excitement were like
small, glittering lures that frequently caught the attention of others. But after so many years of playing the
role of observer rather than participant, Tabitha was not
equipped now to recognize that kind of subtle masculine attention.

Dev, on the other hand, discovered he'd developed
a whole new set of instincts where Tabitha Graham
was concerned. Sitting across from her in the cocktail
lounge later he saw disaster approaching long before
it walked over to the table. He did some quick evalua-
tion of the situation even as Tabby began a detailed discussion of basilisks.

"That's the creature that supposedly kills with only
a glance," she was saying chattily as Dev watched a
rugged, athletic-looking, blond man start toward the
table. "It could be a completely fabulous creature with
no basis in reality, but some people have pointed out that
it could simply have been confused with some reptiles
which can spit their venom. Those poor monks sitting
around their tables dutifully writing out bestiaries had
no way of verifying many of the reports they got about
animals in far-off places, remember. At any rate,
although any creature who looked straight at it report-
edly keeled over, the thing was apparently vulnerable
to weasels. That was the theory at the time."

Dev tried to produce a basilisk-style stare which he
directed at the blond man who was now directly behind
Tabitha. It had no effect, probably because the other

male had eyes only for Tabby. He'd taken one glance at Dev's cane earlier in the evening and had undoubtedly concluded, quite accurately, that it limited the older man's social activities. And the band was a very good one that night. Dev knew Tabitha was about to be asked to dance.

"Excuse me," the man said with a smile that came straight off a California beach. "Would you care to dance?" Tabitha looked up in surprised confusion. Before she could respond, the stranger turned to Dev and went on coolly, "I'm sure you won't mind if I borrow her for a while, will you?" Left unspoken was the rest of the sentence but Dev heard it, anyway. *After all you can't ask her out on the floor. Why shouldn't I take her away from you?*

The casual challenge had an unexpectedly savage effect on Dev. He was not normally the possessive type, and even if he had been, he knew Tabitha well enough by now to know she was hardly the kind of woman who would play two men off against each other even if she got the chance. Hell, Tabitha wouldn't know *how* to play that kind of game. But the knowledge didn't lessen his purely masculine reaction to the blond beach boy.

"I beg your pardon?" Tabitha was saying, glancing up at the stranger with a puzzled expression in her huge, sherry eyes.

"I asked if you'd like to dance. The name's Steve, by the way. Steve Waverly." The man gave her another of his sunny grins, confidence radiating from every pore. He had assessed Tabitha's companion and decided there was no threat from that quarter.

"Oh," Tabitha murmured, sounding rather flustered,

but nonetheless pleased, "that's very kind of you, but I'm really not much of a dancer, I'm afraid. Not much practice, you see. And I was right in the middle of telling Dev, here, about basilisks. And weasels."

"Weasels?" The stranger's smile slipped a bit as he attempted to follow the conversation.

"You use weasels to get rid of basilisks," Tabitha explained kindly. "They might not actually have been weasels, of course. There is some speculation that they were mistaken for mongooses which do tackle snakes. And since basilisks may have been a type of snake, it makes sense that mongooses might…"

She was interrupted by a muffled groan from the other side of the table. Instantly her head came around in frowning concern. Dev gave her his bravest smile. "Sorry, honey. My ribs are acting up again. You know the doctor said they would be sore for a few days." He gingerly put a hand inside his jacket, testing the bruised ribs. "And I'm afraid all that exercise today might not have been the best thing for my leg. It's aching a little. But don't worry, I'll just take a couple of aspirin while you have a dance with Mr. Waverly. Maybe that and another couple of drinks will deaden the pain."

Instantly Tabitha was on her feet, Steve Waverly completely forgotten as she rounded the table to take Dev's arm. "You will not sit here and gulp aspirin and alcohol! Of all the silly notions. What you need is more bed rest. I should never have dragged you off to that artist's colony this afternoon. How could I have been so thoughtless? And now I've kept you up till all hours when you ought to be sleeping. Come along, Dev. I'm taking you back to your cabin right now!"

Dev allowed himself to be assisted to his feet, his fingers closing strongly around the handle of the cane as he smiled blandly at his puzzled foe. "If you'll excuse us, Steve?"

Tabitha seemed to remember Waverly's presence. "Oh, yes, please excuse us, Mr. Waverly," she said with a charming smile. "Dev is still recovering from a terrible incident back on St. Regis, you know. He needs plenty of bed rest. See you later," she added rather absently as she took Dev's arm and started him out of the cocktail lounge.

They had almost reached the door when Dev pulled back slightly. "Just a second, honey, I forgot to leave a tip. You wait here and I'll be right back."

"I could take the money back to the table," she began earnestly.

"No, that's all right. Won't take a second." He patted her hand reassuringly and turned back into the crowded lounge. Using the cane with a polite ruthlessness, he forged a path back through the dancers until he found the table Steve Waverly occupied alone. The younger man glanced up in astonishment as Dev approached.

"Listen, weasel," Dev drawled in chillingly polite tones that immediately got Waverly's complete attention. "I think we need to clarify a small matter here. Just so there's no misunderstandings, the lady is private property. Come near her again and I will take you apart piece by piece. There are plenty of other more exotic creatures on board this ship. Stay away from my tabby cat."

Waverly's handsome face went through a variety of expressions as he rapidly reassessed the situation. Dev was pleased with the final wariness which settled into the other man's blue eyes. He nodded in satisfaction, not feeling any compunction at all in having used nearly forty years of harsh experience and the resulting masculine assurance to quell his younger rival. Dev knew damn well he could be intimidating when he chose, and tonight he found himself choosing to be exactly that: thoroughly intimidating.

"Good night, Mr. Waverly," he murmured arrogantly, turning back toward the door with masterful confidence. Through the bobbing dancers he could just barely make out Tabitha's anxious gaze as she searched impatiently for him. Dev smiled to himself, quite pleased. He remembered to inject a hint of brave suffering into his smile as Tabitha caught sight of him and came forward to take his arm once more.

"Did you leave the tip?" she asked politely, guiding him out the door.

"I left a tip," he murmured in satisfaction.

"I'm sure it will be appreciated."

"I can only hope so."

"How's the leg?" Tabitha inquired as he leaned more heavily on her arm.

"It aches, I'm afraid," Dev admitted. It wasn't altogether a sham, either, unfortunately. The damn leg was hurting a bit tonight. And so were the ribs for that matter. Forty years might buy a man enough experience and confidence to intimidate younger rivals but they also brought some less pleasant rewards such as the aches and pains generated by all that accumulated experience.

The discomfort, however, was almost worth it just to see the warm concern in Tabby's eyes as she led him back to his room. Dev felt the gentleness of her touch

on his arm and sensed the tenderness she wanted to
extend. The evening was going very well, he decided.
Very well, indeed.

"Is the leg hurting very badly?" she asked anxiously
as he opened his cabin door.

"It's felt better," he told her grimly.

She chewed on her lower lip for a second. "Look, why
don't you get into a bathrobe or something, and I'll
massage it for you," she finally offered. "Would that help?
And I can put a compress on your ribs, too, if you like."

Dev sighed in satisfaction and tried to make it sound
like a suppressed groan of pain. "That would be fantastic, Tabby. How can I thank you?" He leaned the ebony
cane against the wall and steadied himself with a hand
braced against the bathroom door. "I'll be right out as soon
as I change," he told her calmly. He was proud of the
casual tone of his voice, especially given the fact that his
blood was starting to move with a heavy beat in his veins.

She was waiting for him when he emerged from the
bathroom a few minutes later. He was dressed only in
a beach towel that he had wrapped carelessly around his
waist. He saw the way her wide eyes lingered on his
bare chest before she quickly raised them to his face.
"Sorry—" he smiled easily "—I don't have a robe."

"I see. Well, lie down on the bed and let me at that
leg. I'll get a cloth from the bath for your ribs, too," she
said industriously, looking everywhere but at his half-
naked body.

He sank heavily down onto the bed which she had
already turned back for him and watched indulgently as
she scurried around the room, collecting a warm damp
cloth and her nerves. He liked the way his near naked-

ness had thrown her into awkward confusion. She was becoming increasingly aware of him, he realized. It was just a matter of time.

Carefully arranging the sheet so that it covered as much of him as possible, Tabitha eventually settled down to the task at hand. At the first touch of her gentle fingers Dev closed his eyes and exhaled slowly. It was going to be a toss-up, he decided, between the way she aroused him and the way she relaxed him. But he knew which sensation was going to carry the day. Already his body was tightening with awareness.

"That feels so good, Tabby," he growled as she worked on his aching leg. "Much better than aspirin."

"How did you hurt your leg, Dev?" she asked in a soft voice, as if afraid of intruding on his privacy, but unable to resist the question any longer.

"I had an accident a couple of years ago. Zigged when I should have zagged," he returned as nonchalantly as possible.

"A skiing accident?"

"No, uh, car accident," he corrected automatically. The story should be automatic by now. He'd told it enough times. "Got cut with some flying glass."

"Yes, I can see the scars," she whispered, tenderly kneading the area around the knee where the evidence of the accident still persisted. He heard the gentleness in her voice and smiled to himself. It was so nice to have her fussing over him like this. Who would have thought after all these years that he'd find himself wanting to immerse himself in a woman's tenderness? Having a female for an occasional bed partner had always seemed more than sufficient in the past.

It wasn't just her attention and compassion he was enjoying, Dev realized with a flash of honesty. He was also enjoying playing the role she had assigned him. He rather liked being the kind of man she admired. Tabby found him intelligent, a stimulating conversationalist, well traveled and very much the gentleman. With her he actually felt like a cultured, gracious businessman who was on a cruise for pleasure as well as business. God! She'd be utterly appalled if she knew what sort of tip he'd actually left behind in the cocktail lounge this evening!

But Waverly deserved what he'd gotten. Tabby was Dev's own private discovery and damned if he was going to let another man come along and steal her away just when he had her halfway into bed.

Actually, she was sitting on his bed right now. He felt her adjust the warm compress on his ribs.

"Any better?" she asked after a moment.

"Much. You're a natural nurse, Tabby. Probably missed your calling by going into the book business."

He kept his eyes closed, aware that her hands were fluttering a bit awkwardly on him now. She wanted to touch him more intimately, he realized, and she didn't quite know what kind of excuse to use to do so. Maybe he should pretend to fall asleep again. Last time she had stayed all night. If he could get her to lie down beside him tonight, he'd have it made, he was sure of it. Experimentally, he tried a yawn.

"You must be exhausted, Dev. Will you be able to sleep with your leg hurting?"

"It's not hurting nearly so much now," he told her in a voice that was rapidly thickening from something besides weariness. How much more of this was he going to be able to take? When would she realize how his body was reacting to her? Damn it, she'd been a married woman. Regardless of how lousy her husband had been in bed, she must know when a man was becoming aroused! Maybe he should just grab her. Hell, he'd waited long enough, hadn't he? She was so close and he *knew* she was aware of him as a man.

But if he could just hold off a little while longer, she'd take the initiative, and he wouldn't have to risk spoiling her image of him as a shy, vulnerable gentleman. His hand clenched under the sheet. How much longer?

Dev sensed Tabitha's increased agitation. Her own sensual awareness was there in her touch now. He could hear her increased rate of breathing and even though he steadfastly kept his eyes closed he had a mental image of what the action was doing to her lovely breasts. Her rounded thigh was pressed against his as she sat beside him on the bed, and it was all he could do to resist closing his hand over the intriguing curve.

When she leaned over him to adjust the sheet, he held his breath. Perhaps now. Last night she'd found the courage to kiss him good night. If she tried that again this evening, he would simply close his arms around her and pull her down onto the bed. His mind raced with the image of what he would do next. It would be easy to roll over on top of her, trapping her beneath him with one leg while he stifled her protests with a kiss.

No, he couldn't wait any longer. When she leaned down to kiss him good night, he'd risk losing his status of gentleman and grab her. Hell, a man couldn't wait forever.

"Good night, Dev. I'll see you in the morning for breakfast." Suddenly her hands had left him.

Dev's eyes snapped open in dismay as he realized there wasn't going to be any good night kiss. She was halfway out the door before he could think of anything to say and by then it was much too late. A second later the door closed solidly behind her.

"Damn it to hell!" he gritted, his clenched hand lifting to pound impotently into the pillow. "Damn it to hell and back! What went wrong?"

It seemed to him that his leg ached worse than ever.

CHAPTER FOUR

TABITHA KNEW EXACTLY WHAT HAD gone wrong. She'd
lost her nerve at the crucial point and, since Dev was
too shy and too sensitive to take the initiative, she had
lost the opportunity. Damn!

Back in her cabin she paced the tiny floor space and
wondered what would have happened if she'd let the
massage turn into lovemaking. She was almost certain
Dev wouldn't have rejected her. It had seemed as though
his body had grown tighter, harder, under her hands
instead of more relaxed, and there could be only one
reason for that. She had managed to arouse him, she was
sure of it. Poor man. He must wonder at her intentions!

In all honesty, what were her intentions? She certainly had not set out to seduce Dev this evening. Her immediate concern had been his bruised ribs and aching
leg.

But somewhere along the line she had realized what
was happening to both of them. And she'd lost her
nerve.

The knowledge of their mutual attraction had shaken
her far more than she would have expected. After all,
she had been a married woman! Still, the lessons she'd
learned from a husband who had found her boring had

been drilled into her so well that it was difficult to escape them. It was difficult to be sure that she had at last found a man who found her interesting.

He was like her in so many ways, she thought. Perhaps, in a way, he was even more withdrawn and vulnerable. After all, in addition to his unhappy marriage, he'd also suffered that terrible car accident. She'd seen how aloof and distant he'd held himself during the first few days of the voyage, never mixing with the other passengers.

Yes, he was even more cautious than she was when it came to relationships, Tabitha decided, and that meant that it was up to her to keep the wonderful association developing.

In other words, if there was to be any hope for something meaningful between Dev Colter and herself, she was going to have to take the initiative and seduce him. He was simply too uncertain, too vulnerable to do it on his own.

Deliberately seduce a man? She, who had never been given any reason to think herself either sensual or irresistible? Whose husband had made it very clear that she was a nonentity in bed?

But Dev Colter was not her husband. He was as different from Greg as night from day. Dev would not expect an acrobat in bed. And in spite of his physical weight and strength, Tabitha just knew Dev would be a tender and infinitely gentle lover. Perhaps even a lover who could let her find out for herself if there was any hope of releasing a sensual side to her nature—a fantasy side.

"Face it, woman," she lectured herself in front of the mirror. "You're falling in love with the man. And you were the one who said she'd never get involved in a shipboard romance!"

Could she let this marvelous man just disappear from her life without making some effort to cement a more permanent bond between them?

What would have happened if she'd obeyed her impulse to touch him more and more intimately tonight? What if she had tried another kiss? Would he have responded? Dealing with a basically shy male had its advantages, but it also had a few drawbacks, she decided ruefully. It left her with the task of making the final decision.

There were only a few days left on this trip. So little time left. If she was going to do anything substantial, it would have to be soon. Resolutely, Tabitha lifted her chin and eyed her reflection. Damn it, she was falling in love, *really* falling in love for the first time in her life. Was she going to let her natural hesitation and shyness ruin her one chance?

But set out to deliberately seduce a man?

With a groan of dismay Tabitha sank down onto her bed, chin in hand, and contemplated the enormity of what she wanted to do. On top of everything else there was the awful risk that she was misinterpreting things terribly. Perhaps Dev wasn't all that interested in her. Oh, God. How awful if she put him in an embarrassing and untenable position by trying to seduce him! *Mortifying!*

The alternative was to return to Port Townsend and go sedately back to work in her bookshop without ever having learned the truth about his feelings for her. She knew she would never forgive herself for her cowardice. Dragon-seducing was dangerous work, however. She didn't feel very well equipped to tackle the job. Tabitha groaned again and flopped back on the pillows, staring at the ceiling.

There was no repressing the excitement and the sense of wonder she experienced as she fell asleep considering the immediate future. It was as if her whole life were focused on a crucial turning point, leaving it up to her to choose the final path. Never, since the day she had decided to go into business for herself, had she felt quite so poised on the brink.

It took great courage to don the flowing, colorful caftan without first putting on a bra the next morning. Anxiously Tabitha stood in front of the mirror and eyed the effect. Wasn't she a little too well rounded and a little too old to be going without a bra? On the other hand the turquoise and red garment was so loose-fitting that Dev might not even notice the absence of a bra beneath the material!

The question was, would Dev be attracted to the sensual shape of her unconfined breasts even if he did notice? Fingers drumming on the counter, Tabitha hesitated. Maybe she looked better with the bra on. No, she didn't droop or anything and nearly every other woman on board dressed quite freely. With a brisk nod of decision, she decided to leave the bra off.

Feeling enormously daring and quite liberated, she ran a brush through the soft bell of her hair and located her sandals under the bed. She'd take things a step at a time. Breakfast without a bra came first.

The knock on her door came just as she was lacing up her sandals. She took a deep breath and went to answer it with her most casual smile.

"Good morning, Tabby," Dev began calmly as she

opened the door. "I came to see if you were ready for breakfast." As if he had been standing in the room ten minutes earlier, watching her dress, his silver eyes flicked down, sweeping across the bodice of the caftan.

"I'm starving," Tabitha said, hurriedly stepping out into the corridor before she lost her nerve. Oh, lord! He'd noticed. She was absolutely sure of it. So what was his reaction! "How are you feeling this morning?" she remembered to ask.

"Quite refreshed," he drawled, taking her arm in a grip that seemed more intimate than usual. Did the back of his hand always come into contact with the side of her breast when he took her arm or was she just more conscious of the warmth this morning because there was one less barrier? "I always seem to sleep well after you've tucked me into bed," he went on lightly.

He seemed to be waiting for something. She sensed the hesitation in him and all at once understood it. He was wondering whether or not to kiss her good morning. Feeling more confident because she'd had good luck with the action before, Tabitha smiled and braced herself lightly against his shoulder with one hand. Then she brushed his mouth with the most fleeting of kisses.

"I'm glad," she murmured.

"That I sleep well after you've put me to bed? So am I." As she eased back down he lowered his head and returned the kiss. This time the contact held longer and there was a warmth to it that lingered long after Dev broke the kiss.

The greeting signaled the start of the day, and the sunny hours rolled past with a sensation of rapidly coalescing intimacy. Dev seemed more than willing to be led down the primrose path, Tabitha decided in wry humor as she stretched out beside him on a pool lounger. He might be shy but he was not disinterested!

"Do you feel up to a little swimming this afternoon?" she asked conversationally as he sat down beside her. They had both changed into swimsuits, and she found her glance wandering toward the curling mat of hair that formed a large triangle on his chest. Apparently he had removed his bandages, and more than once she had to drag her eyes away from the spot where the tip of the triangle disappeared into his trim swimsuit.

"I think so. How do the bruises look?" He glanced down at his ribs, more or less giving her free license to do the same.

"Much better," she managed with an air of briskness. God, he was hard. Hard and lean and wonderfully sleek. She wanted an excuse to touch him, any excuse. "A little black and blue still, but definitely healing," she went on, extending her fingers to the line of his battered ribs. His skin was warm from the sun. He glanced up, his silver eyes meshing with hers, and she forgot to withdraw her hand.

Without a word he covered her hand with his own, pressing it briefly against his chest, and then he released it to get to his feet. "Last one in buys the drinks tonight," he announced cheerfully. He began moving the few feet to the pool's edge without the aid of his cane, the limp very pronounced. It certainly didn't totally incapacitate him, however!

"Hey!" Tabitha exclaimed, realizing she was being left behind. "No fair. I didn't get any warning." She dove in about two seconds behind him, surfacing a moment later to find him laughing down at her. "For a supposedly wounded man with a definite limp, you move awfully fast," she accused.

"A man will do a lot when the provocation is sufficient. For a tabby cat, you seem to take fairly well to water."

"I still think we should run that race again. I deserve a head start, being the weaker sex and all!"

"I wouldn't dream of setting back all the progress made by the women's movement."

She grinned. "That's very noble of you. Try this bit of progress on for size!" Taking him by surprise, she managed to push him over backward in the water. He went under very nicely. But he managed to circle her wrists with his own, and she found herself following him below the surface.

For an instant the world was transformed in the abruptly silent, watery environment. Tabitha couldn't resist. Taking her courage in both hands, she let herself float down until her body lay along his and then, eyes tightly closed, she kissed the strong line of his throat. His hands seemed to wind themselves into her hair, holding her head in place, and she felt her legs tangle excitingly with his. It was a moment of magic and undeniable passion.

The magic ran out at the same instant as the air in Tabitha's lungs. Realizing she was about to try breathing water, she kicked reluctantly free and surged to the surface. Automatically her eyes scanned the faces of the nearest sunbathers.

"Worried that someone may have noticed?" Dev

asked softly as he came up beside her. "Don't fret about it. They'll think you're a mermaid."

Tabitha blinked water out of her eyes. "Dangerous creatures, mermaids," she managed to say lightly, striking out for the side of the pool. She hoped no one had noticed that little scene but it was hard to tell. She still wasn't accustomed to this seduction business!

"Why are they dangerous?" Dev asked, trailing beside her in the water.

"Sailors who hear their calls at sea and follow them are never heard from again," she told him in dark tones. "They lure men to disaster."

"I thought the ladies who lured sailors to their deaths were the Sirens," he protested laughingly.

She liked his laughter, Tabitha decided. She liked it very, very much. "Well, there's some confusion between Sirens and mermaids in the various bestiaries. You can't blame the scribes for getting them confused. All they were really sure of was that you had to be damn careful of the creatures. In fact, there are a lot of general cautions about women thrown into the texts. The female of the species is often rather dangerous, I'm afraid. Or at least the medieval people thought so." She smiled brilliantly.

"You know how men are about learning from history," Dev rasped softly. "They have a bad habit of forgetting the lessons of the past no matter how many times they're repeated."

Tabitha drew in her breath, a wave of excitement coursing through her. "Meaning you're going to turn a deaf ear to all those warnings about Sirens and mermaids and Harpies?"

"Meaning I don't think I have anything to fear from a tabby cat," he corrected, silver eyes gleaming in the sunlight. "I'm not really dealing with a Siren or a mermaid, am I?"

She searched his face, uncertain of his real message. "No," Tabitha had to admit. "Probably not. But you said yourself that to a man who's never seen a tabby cat, she might seem very unusual."

"She does," he told her whimsically. "Unusual and charming and very appealing."

"But not dangerous?"

"I'm not sure yet."

Tabitha treaded water, staring up at him for a moment longer. Then she made up her mind. Not dangerous, hmm? Delicately she grasped his slick shoulders, letting herself slide closer. He didn't move as she closed the distance between them. Probably thought she was going to kiss him again, Tabitha decided mischievously. He was getting to like her kisses, she knew.

Very deliberately she bent her head and sank her teeth lightly into his bare shoulder.

"Ouch!" Startled, he drew back.

Tabitha didn't let him go. She smiled blandly up at him. "I've decided I don't like being labeled as 'not dangerous.'"

He eyed her a little warily. "I see. I, uh, won't make the mistake again."

"Good." She released him to swim to the side of the pool again. "Hungry? It's almost time for tea and scones." She had him properly confused now, Tabitha decided gleefully, even somewhat intrigued. She hadn't missed the speculative light which had gleamed for a moment in his eyes. This certainly was a delicate game, this business of seducing a man. You had to be so careful not to go too far and scare the victim, yet you couldn't be too hesitant or nothing would be accomplished!

It was as they left the dining room and headed toward one of the lounges on board that Tabitha reminded herself of the two staples of sophisticated seduction: alcohol and verbal innuendoes.

Matters had been proceeding very nicely up to this point, she decided, vividly aware of the feel of Dev's hand on her back. He had been finding one excuse after another to touch her all evening, and she had been encouraging the contact. The dress she had on was a swirly, little thing, loose but also of quite thin cotton in a vibrant, coral shade. Her bra had once again been left behind in her stateroom. She was very conscious of the lack of it when the evening breeze on deck plastered the coral cotton against the length of her body.

The overall effect was a bit more than she had intended, Tabitha realized as she saw her escort's eyes drop almost lazily to the outline of her breasts. Fortunately they soon entered the darkened cocktail lounge and during the process of finding a table, Tabitha recovered her composure.

Alcohol and innuendoes. Booze and sexy conversation.

She would get Dev Colter just a bit tipsy, she decided judiciously. Enough to lower some of his natural, gentlemanly reserve. And then she would talk about sex.

"Don't forget I'm buying the drinks this evening," she said cheerfully as they sat down. "Even though I have definite qualms about the manner in which the race at the pool was conducted, I *did* lose. Never let it be said I'm not noble in defeat!" She smiled up at the approaching steward. "We'll have two gin and tonics. Doubles."

"Doubles?" the steward repeated politely.

"Doubles," she said firmly and then turned the smile on a rather watchful Dev. Now for the titillating conversation. She took a deep breath and widened her smile. "Did I ever tell you how interested the scribes who wrote the bestiaries were in the, uh, mating habits of the various animals?"

He blinked. His long, dark lashes lowered briefly and then lifted to reveal a politely interested silver gaze. "No, I don't believe you did. A subject of great interest, hmmm?"

Tabitha cleared her throat. She had started this and she was damn well not going to falter now. As soon as the drinks arrived she launched into her lecture on the sex habits of medieval animals. "They thought elephants extremely modest, you know. So chaste that an elephant couple had to chew on a bit of mandrake in order to overcome their natural shyness about sex."

"Mandrake?"

"Ummm. I guess the scribes thought it served as an aphrodisiac."

"Rather like a modern-day couple having a few drinks before testing each other's inclinations?" Dev suggested in mild interest.

She peered at him a little sharply and then relaxed. He seemed genuinely interested in the discussion. "Well, yes, as a matter of fact. I guess that is a good parallel." She groped for another piece of information. "They thought that the virility of a horse was hampered if you cut its mane," she continued brightly.

"Something to keep in mind next time I go to the barber."

Tabitha frowned for an instant, trying to decide whether or not he was joking. "The texts don't draw any lessons for human males on the matter," she told him dryly.

"I see. What other interesting facts have you gleaned from the bestiaries?" Dev sipped his drink, watching her expectantly.

"Well, vultures, it seems, don't go in for sex," she confided smilingly.

"No sex?"

"It was thought that lady vultures just gave birth whenever the notion struck them." That didn't sound very sexy. What else could she remember? "They thought vipers had a particularly violent method of propagation. After mating, the female viper bit off the male's head."

"Do you mind if I have another drink? This discussion is getting somewhat gruesome."

Tabitha straightened and signaled to the steward. "Heavens, no. I'll get it for you. I'm still paying off my loser's debt, remember? We'll have two more," she instructed the steward.

"Doubles again, ma'am?"

"Yes, please." Tabitha went back to her lecture. "Where was I?"

"The female viper was biting off the male's head, I think," Dev reminded her gently.

"Oh, yes. Well, if it's any comfort, the monks writing

the bestiaries didn't approve of such activity. They drew a few sharp lessons from it and passed them along for the, er, edification of human females."

"What sort of lessons?"

Tabitha experienced a moment of awkwardness which she overcame with another sip from her drink. Then she leaned forward and lowered her voice very meaningfully. "They strongly advised human wives not to resist the approaches of their husbands."

"In other words, not to plead a headache?" The silver gaze gleamed.

Tabitha nodded. "Here's your drink. Might as well take advantage of the fact that I'm buying, hadn't you?"

"Might as well." He downed a healthy swallow and waited for the next bit of bestiary lore.

"They thought partridges did it a bit too often. The birds were thought to be very sexually aggressive, constantly trying to mate. So much so that they often wore themselves out, poor birds."

"Fascinating."

"Lions were strongly approved of because they were thought to be loyal to their mates," Tabitha went on chattily. "There's not much information on the mating habits of dragons and unicorns, though. No one really knew too much about them, it seems."

"Perhaps it's just as well."

"You're probably right," she agreed thoughtfully. "Some things are better left to the imagination. Would you like another drink?"

"I haven't had a chance to finish this one," Dev pointed out politely.

"Oh. Well, perhaps in a few minutes."

"Thank you. You're very generous in paying off your debt." His mouth kicked upward at the corners.

She smiled brightly. "I try."

"Do you lose often?"

"Actually, no. I don't get involved in many contests," she explained with a chuckle.

"A non-participant?"

"Since kindergarten, I'm afraid. How about you? Were you the kind who went out for the team? Or did you tend to keep to yourself?"

"I've never been much of a joiner or a team player," he admitted. There was a small silence and then he held out his empty glass. "I'm ready for the next drink."

"I'll order you a surprise this time. Something a little different." They had so much in common, Tabitha thought blissfully as she selected a Tequila Sunrise for her escort. So very much. Did he see it, too?

"The entire evening is turning out to be one surprise after another," Dev drawled as the steward departed once more with an order.

"And we're only halfway through it," she retorted. But the sense of mounting excitement rippling through her was already making her head spin. Everything was going wonderfully on course. Dev showed every indication of being more than mildly interested in following her sensual lead. All she had to do was keep matters moving in the right direction and not lose her nerve in the process.

Gamely she plied Dev with drinks, watching hopefully for signs of relaxed inhibitions. She went back to anecdotes about the mating habits of animals from the bestiaries, and somehow the conversation seemed to keep its sensual orientation without much effort. There was nothing overt about the innuendoes, naturally. Dev wasn't the sort of man who would embarrass her with blatantly sexual remarks, unlike some men who had imbibed several drinks. But somehow everything seemed to be overlaid with a touch of sensuality.

Perhaps it was simply the combination of her mood and the balmy Caribbean night. By the time they left the cocktail lounge, Tabitha felt she had the situation completely in hand. Dev was, in fact, eating out of her palm. She had the heady realization that she could do just about anything she liked with him just then.

"Are you tired?" she asked, deliberately resting her head on his shoulder as they came to a halt by the rail. She let her arm wind around his waist.

"No," he murmured in her hair. "As a matter of fact, I feel much better tonight than I have since St. Regis."

"Not even a headache? How's your leg?"

"My head and my leg are fine, thank you."

"I see." There went the obvious excuses for guiding him downstairs to his cabin. She would have to try something more direct. "Aren't you feeling even a little tipsy from all those drinks I ordered for you?"

"Pleasantly high would describe the sensation." His breath gently fanned her hair as she snuggled closer.

'You don't want to lie down or anything?"

"I hadn't thought about taking a rest. Didn't feel I needed one."

"Dev," she said, lifting her head with sudden resolve, "I don't think I got around to telling you about the mating habits of tabby cats this evening."

She felt him go very still. Tabitha, herself, could

hardly move now that she'd made her most suggestive play yet.

"No," he finally said, his voice sounding rather muffled, "I don't believe you did. How would you describe them?"

"Right now, I think it's fair to say they could be described as quite...quite *wanton*." Tabitha turned in his arms and circled his waist with both hands. Then she lifted her face in the moonlight, inviting his kiss.

CHAPTER FIVE

TABITHA SAW THE SILVER FLAME of desire in Dev's eyes as he obediently lowered his head and she knew she had won. She had succeeded in seducing him. The knowledge bloomed in her like wildfire, sending small shivers down her spine and making her senses tingle. She had actually made him want her!

As his mouth closed over hers she crushed her breasts against the hard planes of his chest, hoping he would thrill to the contact as much as she did. The husky groan from deep in his throat told her he was surgingly aware of her now.

"Oh, Dev," she whispered, lifting her fingers to twine them in his hair. "Tell me you want me just a little. Please tell me. I want you so much...."

"How could I resist you, tabby cat?" he muttered hoarsely as she nibbled suggestively on his lower lip. "So soft and warm and sweetly sexy." His arms closed more strongly around her, urging her closer.

Tabitha didn't hesitate. She buried her lips against his throat and let herself melt against his hardness. She was vaguely aware that he had hooked the cane over the railing and was leaning back, balancing both of them. Once again his legs had parted and she was between them, luxuriating in the intimacy of the embrace.

"A sleeping dragon," she murmured, her voice stirring with barely suppressed excitement. "I feel as if I'm waking a sleeping dragon."

"Do you see me as a beast, then?" he growled, gently dropping tiny kisses along the line of her shoulder.

"A fabulous beast. Gentle and strong and noble. A beast of legend."

"Tabby, Tabby, your imagination overwhelms me," he groaned. Dev's hands slipped down her spine to the contour of her hip.

"It's not my imagination. You are all those things. You're also shy and vulnerable and sensitive. The perfect man," she sighed. "And I've been wanting to make love to you all day. Will you mind very much?"

"Tabby, I'm yours tonight," he rasped thickly. "Take me and do what you will with me."

It was exactly the response for which she had been praying, but still Tabitha hesitated as a thought struck her. "Do you really mean that? It's not just the alcohol talking?"

"The alcohol?" He sounded as if he were only half-aware of the question.

"I've…I've been plying you with drinks all evening long," she explained in a burst of honesty that she instantly rued.

"You wanted me drunk?"

"I wanted you…*relaxed*," Tabitha corrected firmly.

"Ah, I understand. You used alcohol to lower my inhibitions and now you're worried I'll regret it all in the morning, is that it?" She couldn't tell what he was thinking. His voice sounded very muffled again as he put his lips to her wind-tossed hair.

"Will you, Dev?" Uncertainty flared for a brief moment.

She felt him shake his head. "No, sweetheart, I won't regret a thing. I know I shall wake up in the morning with wonderful memories of tonight."

"If you're quite sure…"

"I'm sure," he affirmed. Was that a hint of impatience she heard now in his voice?

Tabitha gathered her courage once more. "Well, then, would you like to come downstairs with me, Dev?" She pulled back, her hands still on his shoulders and searched his silvery gaze. The moonlight in his eyes made them mysterious pools which she couldn't fully delve, but there was no denying the passion she saw there. Wordlessly she lowered her hand, taking one of his in a gentle grip.

Dev followed silently as she led him toward the stateroom decks. All the way down the long corridor to her room she was pulsingly aware of his heavy, dark presence. Pushing aside the qualms and uncertainties she ought to be experiencing, Tabitha reminded herself that she was following her heart tonight. There was no need for fear or nervousness. If she gave in to either, Dev would leave in an instant, she was certain. He would do nothing to frighten her.

No, she decided as she unlocked her cabin door. This was what she wanted.

"Tabby?" Her name was a question as she resolutely closed the door behind him and she came close to touch his arm reassuringly.

"It's all right, Dev. I know what I'm doing."

"Do you?" he asked obliquely, his hands settling on her shoulders as she smiled tremulously up at him.

"Yes, Dev, I do. I want you. I…I care for you very much. I've been hoping all day long that you feel the same."

"How could I not want you?" he said simply, letting his fingers trail through her hair in slow wonder. "Oh, God, Tabby!"

She opened her mouth beneath his, inviting him inside and responding intensely when he accepted the invitation. She was falling in love with this man. There could be absolutely no doubt now. No one else had ever reached her in quite the same way, and she had never felt this flickering enchantment with any other man. Dev Colter was truly a fabulous beast: a silver-eyed dragon waiting for her to awaken him fully.

Slowly, with infinite care, she slipped her hands inside his jacket and pushed it off his shoulders. The garment fell to the floor. The feel of his smoothly muscled shoulders held her attention for a long moment as she tasted his tongue in her mouth, and then she began the unsteady task of unbuttoning his white shirt and unknotting the striped tie he wore.

Undressing Dev Colter proved to be a most satisfying endeavor. This was the first time she had been totally free to explore his body, and Tabitha found herself fascinated. It wasn't only the feel of his firm contours that aroused and intrigued her, it was also the utterly masculine scent of him, tinged as it was with aftershave and soap. And then there was the crisp, curling cloud of chest hair which drew her coral-tipped nails like a magnet. Wonderingly she let her thumbs glide across his flat, male nipples.

"Tabby, you're going to drive me out of my head tonight," he grated feelingly. She was aware that his fingers were trembling slightly as they found the zipper of her dress, and the knowledge warmed her. Poor Dev. He was so uncertain and nervous, so anxious to please. Tabitha was touched even as she allowed freer rein to her own passion.

When the dress fell at last in a wave at her feet, Dev drew in his breath as her full, round breasts came into view. For a moment Tabitha felt a shaft of unease, and then she saw the glowing appreciation in his eyes as he scanned her gentle figure and she relaxed. He found her pleasing, she thought triumphantly.

Wearing only the satin triangle of her underpants, she pressed herself closely against him and snuggled languidly when his palms cupped the curves of her derriere. She felt the strength of his fingers as he clenched them excitingly into her flesh. Tabitha trembled.

"Dev, I've never felt quite like this before," she confessed, letting her lips sample the flavor of his skin. "When I'm with you I feel marvelous. Passionate and exciting and sensuous."

"That's because you are passionate and exciting and sensuous." He slid his hands up her waist until they hovered just under the weight of her breasts. Then he let his thumbs gently rasp the nipples.

"Oh!" Instantly the tiny buds responded, forming hard, tight buttons of desire. Tabitha moaned, her eyes closing as she swayed more heavily against him.

"You make me feel exactly the same way," he confided deeply, holding her close.

"You don't mind that I'm seducing you tonight?" She smiled against his shoulder, confident now of her welcome.

"I can't even think straight at the moment. How could I mind what you do to me? Take me to bed, Tabby, please!"

She nipped erotically at his shoulder as she found the buckle of his belt and unfastened it. In another moment he was dressed as she was, in only his briefs.

"You're wonderful," she breathed in blatant admiration as she stepped back to drink her fill of his hard, muscular frame. "Sleek and strong and wonderful! Oh, Dev!" Moving forward again, she arched herself fluidly into his warmth, her fingers digging deeply into the coiled muscles of his back.

Somehow they were moving, shifting backward the few steps to the bed, and then Tabitha sank down, drawing him after her. Dev followed urgently, willingly giving himself up to her gentle touch.

Inflamed now with the sensual success she was achieving, Tabitha pushed imperiously until he fell onto his back. Dev watched with a lambent flame in his eyes as she knelt beside him and began to explore the sleek hardness of his body.

"Tabby, you must be a Siren or a mermaid. Anytime you call, I'll come. I could never resist." He gasped as she lightly scored the inside of his thigh with her nails and then he sighed as she sprinkled hungry kisses down his chest to the pit of his stomach. Her growing love for him was eliciting a surprising inventiveness from her, she realized. Never had she experienced such an overwhelming urge to explore a man's body.

Lost in a world of passionate discovery, Tabitha barely heard his muttered words. She listened only for the harsh sound of his heavy breathing and the gasps of desire which told her that whatever she was doing was right. His strong thighs twisted as she caressed him, and the thrusting evidence of his desire was hard and eager when she found it with her tender fingers.

"My yes, Tabby!" Then he seemed to lose control, pulling at her until she sprawled along the length of him in a silken tangle. "Now, honey, take me, now!" he blazed fiercely. His fingers went at once to the bit of satin at her hips, jerking it down over her full buttocks. Obediently Tabitha kicked the little garment free and then she came back to him.

Impulsively she settled astride his hips. *It would be like riding a dragon,* she thought fleetingly. And then, as his hands guided her firmly down onto him, she tensed, aware that he was far, far different from her ex-husband and in more than just a mental or emotional way.

"Dev?" The breath stilled in her throat as he waited, poised beneath her. She sensed the restrained power in him and for the first time, Tabitha hesitated.

"Are you suddenly afraid of me, Tabby?" he demanded softly, not trying to force her to complete the union. "You know I won't hurt you. Come close and make sweet love to me, little cat."

Then, his hands grasping the satiny contours of her thighs, he eased her down. Tabitha gasped as he filled her slowly and completely with his hardness. The shock of the union was unexpected. Her nails dug into his arms as she braced herself against the heavy impact he had made on her body.

As if he understood that she needed a moment to adjust to him, Dev held himself still beneath her, his hand soothing and coaxing on her thighs. She heard the fiery string of sensual words that he uttered in a dark, persuasive voice, and the combination of his tone and his touch made her body relax once more.

"That's it, honey," he growled as she slowly returned to the erotically reckless state she had been in only a moment earlier. "That's my tabby cat. Come and purr for me, sweetheart. Don't be afraid of me. You see how well we fit together? I would never hurt you. Just relax and love me. Let me lose myself in you. Just relax, honey."

The hypnotic words had the desired effect and as her body accepted his completely, Tabby forgot the shock of the intrusion. Besides, inside her now all was glittering, swirling fire. The heavy strength of him, which had momentarily intimidated her, was now a source of unbelievable excitement. She gave herself up to it with an abandon she had never known before.

Like riding a dragon.

The ride was infinitely more exhilarating than she could possibly have imagined. In her wildest fantasies, Tabitha had never thought herself capable of this thrilling response. Her body soared and spun, locked with his until the distant goal beckoned so urgently she could no longer turn aside. Caught in the slipstream which carried them both, Tabitha heard herself cry out, felt her body tauten in mindless tension, and then came a shivering release that left her weak and breathless.

Even as the sound of Dev's name left her lips, she

was aware of him thrusting with even greater force than before and then he, too, was calling out. His voice was a thick, impeded shout of satisfaction that was wholly masculine and utterly timeless.

Playing the patient, sensitive gentleman definitely had its own rewards, Dev decided with languid, lazy pleasure as he came slowly out of the long aftermath of lovemaking. Countless rewards. Intensely gratifying rewards. He had gauged Tabitha Graham to perfection. She had climbed right into his lap just as if she knew where she belonged. He would bear the small marks of her claws with great satisfaction, remembering the passion which had incited her to leave the little nail marks on his shoulders.

Never had he allowed himself to be so sweetly seduced. His mouth curved with wicked delight as he lay with one arm around Tabitha and waited for her to stir. He had loved it, every minute of it, from the moment this morning when he had made the tantalizing discovery that she had deliberately failed to put on a bra, right up to the part where she had plied him with liquor and lectured him about the mating habits of animals. Fantastic. He would remember this night as long as he lived. If only there were more time left on the cruise! The thought of turning Tabby loose in a few days was very unpleasant.

He would have to do something about that. Nobody but a fool would let someone like Tabitha Graham walk out of his life. He'd never met anyone like her, and he had a fairly good idea he wasn't likely to run into anyone similar again. There had to be some way of ensuring that she would be around to seduce him again and again. And one of these days, when she was no longer shy of him, he would return the favor in full measure!

He was contemplating just how he would go about that task when Dev saw her lashes flutter. Lazily he propped himself on his elbow and stared down at her.

"You can't hide forever, Tabby. Open your eyes and look at me, sweetheart."

Her lashes lifted and wide sherry eyes regarded him with something between trepidation and hope. Dev leaned down and kissed the tip of her nose.

"I wasn't hiding," she protested carefully. "I was just sleepy."

He smiled. "Sure you're not feeling shy?"

"Maybe. A little."

"Not used to seducing men, hmm?"

"Well, no, now that you mention it," she retorted gamely. But he was right. She did feel shy and wary and rather unsettled. He looked happy and contented, though. Wonderingly she traced a path along the line of his perspiration-damp ribs. The bruises were still quite visible. "Are you all right?" she asked. "Nothing hurts?"

He grinned and Tabitha swallowed under the impact of the expression. "Nothing hurts. Nothing at all. I feel fantastic. How about you?"

"I, well, to tell you the truth, it was a…a very interesting experience," she told him, her eyes going to the level of his chest.

"A very interesting experience!" he echoed, sounding slightly taken aback. "What on earth does that mean?"

"It means I've never felt anything quite like what

just happened," she admitted candidly. "I…I told you my husband found me boring. Well, I'm afraid I found him a little, er, boring, too. You see, he didn't have much patience with me, and I guess I wasn't a very warm sort of wife or something." She coughed a bit awkwardly and pressed on. "At any rate, I've never…that is I hadn't experienced the full…I mean…" She floundered to a stop and raised her eyes pleadingly. "You know what I mean."

"Ah, Tabby," he groaned softly, "you amaze me. How could anyone as sweet and warm and loving as you are have gotten this far in life without learning the full extent of your own passion?"

"I don't think anyone has ever thought me particularly passionate before," she said very honestly. "I've never even thought of myself as passionate. I've never really been able to let myself go before. But with you I feel free somehow. Free and brave and even sexy. Oh, Dev, I think it's because we're so much alike, you and I," she continued earnestly. "Don't you feel it, too?"

"I think I understand you perfectly," he murmured.

"You didn't mind being seduced tonight?" she asked hopefully, eyes brimming with her feelings. She was in love. There could be absolutely no doubt now. Never had she felt like this.

"I loved being seduced tonight. In fact, I was going to ask you if you felt like seducing me all over again?"

"Again?" She looked up at him in astonishment. *Again?* After what they had just been through?

"I wouldn't dream of demanding too much of you," he began quickly as he saw the clear hesitation in her. His tone was humble and very anxious. "You've been more than generous tonight. I should go back to my cabin now so that you can get some sleep. After all, a woman like you would probably appreciate some privacy now. I don't mean to invade your life and force myself on you...."

"I don't mind," she interrupted quite bluntly. "I don't mind at all." Smiling invitingly, she put her arms around his neck and pulled him down to her. Dev needed no second urging.

TABITHA AWOKE THE NEXT MORNING WITH the feeling that her whole world had changed during the night. The knowledge brought with it a disorienting mixture of anticipation and uncertainty, pleasure and shyness.

For a long, private time she contented herself with simply gazing at the sprawled form of the man sleeping beside her, noting every detail with eyes that revealed her new-found love. How could she have been so incredibly lucky? Who would have thought that this cruise would bring her a man like him? He was so perfect, so absolutely perfect for her that it was almost frightening. She was old enough to know that life seldom offered such ideal relationships.

What if Dev didn't feel the same way about her?

What if he grew bored as her husband had grown bored?

What if he was only interested in a short-term affair?

No! He wasn't the kind of man who would have allowed the situation to develop as far as it had if he didn't feel as involved and committed as she did. Dev Colter was too much like herself to do that. Whatever else happened, she would always be certain that his feelings for her during the night had been genuine and deep. Determinedly she pushed back the covers and slipped out of bed, heading for the bath.

Of course she *had* been guilty of rushing things last night, she chided herself in the shower. There was no way she could deny the fact that she had set out to seduce the poor man and had succeeded.

The thought of herself as a seductress gave her a certain gleeful excitement, but it also brought with it uncertainty. What if she had pushed Dev a little too quickly? What if she'd hurried him into a physical commitment before he was quite ready? Perhaps she shouldn't have taken the initiative. Would he be resentful of her efforts this morning in the clear light of day? She was frowning over that notion when the shower curtain was pushed aside.

"Good morning," Dev said gently, silver eyes raking her worried expression. He smiled. "I had the feeling you might be in here berating yourself for being such a charming Siren last night." His eyes were warm, roving over her wet, nude body with remembered pleasure. "Having second thoughts?"

"A…a few," she admitted, vividly aware of his nakedness as well as her own. Under the force of the hot water she could feel her skin turn pink from the tips of her breasts to her earlobes. She buried her face industriously in a washcloth. "I mean, only if you are," she mumbled into the cloth. "I shouldn't have rushed you, Dev. Perhaps you weren't ready for that."

"If I seemed less than ready last night, I sincerely apologize," he drawled meaningfully.

Tabitha went redder than ever. "You know I wasn't referring to your…your…"

"Sexual prowess?" he interposed politely.

Was he teasing her? Or did he think she might have found him disappointing last night? That possibility made her lower the washcloth. She swung anxious eyes to his. "Oh, Dev. You were perfect last night," she breathed.

He stepped into the shower and circled her waist with large hands. "So were you," he told her simply. Bending his head, he kissed her forehead. "Stop worrying. You'll never get anywhere as a seductress if you get into the habit of having second thoughts the next morning!"

Her mouth curved tremulously. "Seductresses shouldn't have consciences?"

"Nope. But it's obvious you do, don't you?"

"I rushed you last night."

"I enjoyed being rushed."

"You're quite sure?"

"I'm positive," he murmured, nibbling appreciatively at her neck.

She relaxed and the smile on her lips curved a bit wider, lighting her sherry-colored eyes. "Well, if you're not going to gnash your teeth in dismay and ask how I could have been so callous as to get you drunk and then take advantage of you…"

"I'm not."

"Then I suppose I shall just have to ignore my qualms, hmm?"

"As long as you don't ignore me," he agreed. Dev caught her hand and spread her fingers across his chest.

"I'd never do that," she assured him earnestly.

"I think I'm going to hold you to that promise." He found her wet mouth with his own as Tabitha eagerly leaned into his strength.

By the time they had finished breakfast the ship had dropped anchor in the harbor of yet another of the out-of-the-way islands on its itinerary. Once again Tabitha had done her research.

"What's this one got to offer?" Dev asked, peering doubtfully toward shore as the tender boat carried them toward the dock.

"You ought to know, you're supposed to be checking it out for your clients, remember?" she chuckled.

"Somehow all these islands are beginning to seem alike."

"A fine attitude for a tourist agent!" She examined the brochure in her lap, the sea breeze ruffling her hair as she bent over the colorful paper. "It says not to miss the gardens of the secluded old hotel on the hill to the east of the town. Apparently they were designed by a famous English landscape artist sometime during the last century for a plantation owner. The plantation went under and has since become a hotel patronized only by the elite."

"And now us. There goes the neighborhood," Dev sighed. "I've heard of the place, though. Three hundred dollars a day for a room. Haven't been able to talk many clients into trying it lately."

"Well, the gardens are said to be spectacular. There's even a maze! That should be fun."

"Thinking of abandoning your lover somewhere in it and leaving him to wander helplessly forever?"

Tabitha jerked her head up in astonishment, struck by the hint of something other than teasing buried in his voice. Was he genuinely worried that she wasn't feeling as committed this morning as he was? He was so very vulnerable, she thought with love. "Never," she vowed a bit gruffly. She could hardly say more. They were already docking.

Dev nodded, apparently satisfied, and took her hand to help her off the boat. Somehow, even with the necessity of wielding the cane, he accomplished the task with a kind of formal grace that made Tabitha feel cherished. His strength more than compensated for his limp, she realized. This morning, dressed in familiar khaki slacks and a shirt with the cuffs rolled up on his forearms, he seemed very vital and overwhelmingly masculine to her. Every time she looked at him she remembered what making love to him had been like and the recollections, she feared, showed in her eyes.

The day, which had begun so brightly, began to take a curious turn for the worse shortly after she and Dev arrived by cab at the elegant former plantation home.

It was nothing she could put her finger on at first, merely a sense that Dev's mood had begun to undergo a subtle change. She noticed it first as they sat eating lunch in the dining room which looked out onto the beautiful formal gardens.

"Something wrong with the pear chutney?" she asked, watching as he toyed with the food on his plate.

He glanced up quickly and smiled. "No, of course not. Why do you ask?"

She shrugged. "You're not exactly wolfing down your food with your usual enthusiasm. Are your ribs hurting again?"

Was he being that obvious? Dev wondered as he denied the query. Or was it just that Tabby was so aware of him now that she was able to pick up on his moods very quickly? He would have to watch it or he'd ruin the whole day if he wasn't careful.

Still, there was no ignoring that uneasy sensation he'd experienced as soon as they had stepped out of the cab. Tabitha's enthusiasm had carried both of them up the grand steps and into the stately, open air lobby of the hotel before he'd had a chance to identify the prickly feeling.

But as soon as they'd sat down to lunch, Dev had realized the restless sensation wasn't going to disappear. It was intensifying. Two years was a long time to be out of the business, he thought, but some of the old instincts lingered apparently. The last time he'd experienced this disturbing feeling had been when he'd gone into that alley on St. Regis. Twice in one week didn't seem fair, not when he'd been free of the annoying habit for two years. Damn it to hell. Why had he agreed to get involved with Delaney again?

"Are you going to try the lemon syllabub?" Tabitha asked cheerfully, examining the dessert menu.

"That sounds good," he agreed promptly, not wanting to sound hesitant. She was already curious enough about his attitude. Deliberately he made himself eat the last of his curried lamb and rice, trying to appear enthusiastic. The excellent food was practically tasteless. He simply couldn't concentrate on it or enjoy it. What the hell was wrong?

There was nothing that could be wrong. Not here on this pleasant, sleepy little island in the Caribbean. Everything that had been wrong had already taken place on St. Regis. He should be clear of that by now.

But what if he wasn't? What if he'd unwittingly dragged Tabby into something connected with that mess? His fingers tightened around the wineglass before he carefully set it back down on the table. It was stupid to try to bury the prickly restlessness under a dose of alcohol. If there was trouble near, the last thing he needed was to be even a little under the influence when it hit.

The first priority was Tabby. In his thoughts that one conclusion leaped to the forefront immediately. Nothing else mattered as much as protecting her. She wasn't a target, of course, but being with him might make her one. Dev swore again, vastly annoyed with himself.

"Dev? Are you sure your ribs aren't hurting?"

He smiled a little, eyes softening as he absorbed the worried expression on her gentle face. It was rather pleasant having her worry about him. He was getting more than a little accustomed to the luxury. And maybe she was offering him the easiest excuse for cutting the day short. If she thought he was in pain, she'd rush him back to the ship, and that was beginning to look like the only way of erasing this uneasy chill down his spine.

"Well, to tell you the truth…" he began ruefully.

"I knew it!" she exclaimed, tossing down her napkin. "And you were going to play the macho role and pretend nothing was hurting, weren't you? Idiot! It's all my fault, too."

"Your fault?"

The red stain on her cheeks was delightful, he decided in amusement. "Because of last night," she mumbled, turning to search for the waiter.

"You're determined to go on some kind of guilt trip over last night, aren't you?" he teased her softly. "You woke up this morning berating yourself for seducing me, and now you're convinced you forced me to overexert myself. Stop worrying, honey. The ribs are just a little sore because I'm still recovering. That's all. Honest."

She was already madly signaling to the waiter, though, and it seemed simplest just to sit back and let her take charge of rescuing him again. She was so good at it, Dev decided in pleased satisfaction. Look at the way she ordered the waiter about. She was even abandoning her syllabub. Dev stifled a grin at what that sacrifice might signify. She eyed him critically as the waiter went off to prepare the check.

"I'm going to run to the rest room while he's getting the bill. I'll be right back, okay? Then we can head for the ship. I think you should be lying down," she added with a crisp nod.

"I'm sorry to ruin the day like this," Dev said in his most humble tones. It wasn't hard to fake the regret. He genuinely did regret spoiling her tour of the island. But that nagging unease wasn't getting any milder, and he'd learned long ago not to disregard it. Probably a false alarm this time, but with Tabby around he didn't intend to take chances.

"You're not ruining the day!" she assured him at once, getting to her feet. "Now you just sit right here. I'll be back in a minute."

He watched her go, thoroughly enjoying the way her body moved beneath the light material of the red-and-white-striped tunic she was wearing. The garment was unbelted, naturally. All her clothes seemed light and airy and unconfining. But somehow the very undefined line made her all the more provocative to his eyes. And now that he knew exactly how beautifully those breasts and that sweet rear curved, his imagination was quite capable of filling in details.

She disappeared down the long hall that led toward the rest room facilities, and Dev turned his attention back to collecting the check. The waiter was hurrying across the room with it already, inspired, no doubt, by Tabby's firm injunction. Dev tossed down a credit card and then waited impatiently while the transaction was completed. With any luck Tabby wouldn't dawdle in the rest room. At least she wasn't the kind of female who felt compelled to repaint her face at every opportunity.

He signed the credit slip and then glanced at his watch. She'd been gone almost ten minutes now. How long should he give her? She'd said she would be right back.

The gnawing unease grew. With a brusque movement Dev reached for his cane and got to his feet. The tension was getting to him, he thought. He wanted Tabby out of this place. False alarm or not, he wasn't going to stick around to find out what was wrong. He'd go knock on the rest room door and tell her to hurry. He could always plead that his ribs had taken a turn for the worse.

But it was the situation which was taking a turn for the worse. He knew it with growing certainty as he made his way down the paneled hall to the door discreetly marked "ladies." Even as he knocked, he was already afraid of not getting a response.

What the hell could be wrong?

But something *was* wrong. Terribly wrong. There was no one inside the rest room as Dev discovered when he impatiently disregarded the proprieties and pushed open the door. No one at all.

The gardens. Perhaps she'd decided to take a quick look at the gardens that had been described in the brochure. One could only see a portion of them from the dining room, and he knew she'd been intrigued by the idea of the maze somewhere in the middle.

Damn it, if she'd decided to take a quick trip outside without telling him…! He cut off the thought with a disgusted grimace. He'd hardly given her any reason to think she shouldn't go outside alone. How could he blame her if she'd dashed out for a quick peek at the maze? The perspiration was beginning to dampen his khaki shirt as he started down the hall toward the entrance to the formal gardens. He should have told her he was in great pain. He ought to have pleaded much more severe discomfort. Then she wouldn't have decided to take the little side trip to the gardens.

Outside on the wide veranda he stood gazing at the sweep of heavily landscaped grounds. Over a century of carefully assisted growth had created a near labyrinth of luscious plantings. Magnificent, tall hedges, huge shade trees and tangled thickets of exotic flowers all combined to form a dense pattern of foliage which stretched across a couple of acres. Some formal garden! The jungle appeared to have had a strong influence during the years. There was no way he could see anything clearly beyond the first few yards.

There was no sign of Tabitha. No sign of anyone, in fact. The gardens were silent.

Dev's fingers tightened on the cane as he considered his options. There weren't a whole lot of them. Maybe she'd gone in search of the maze. It was supposed to be somewhere in the middle of that conglomeration of greenery.

Before he'd made it past the first few ten-foot-high hedges, Dev knew disaster hovered near. The prickly feeling down his spine was rapidly turning into a full-scale alarm.

When he rounded the next wall of boxwood he was almost prepared for the sight that awaited him.

Tabitha was there all right. She was standing very still, her huge eyes wide and fearful as she gazed at him.

The man with the gun in his hand had his free palm clamped firmly over her mouth. He was thin, lanky and his long hair was dark and greasy looking.

"It's about time you came looking for her, Colter. Thought we might have to send a message or something. But Waverly was pretty sure you'd come looking when your girl friend didn't return to the dining room."

Steve Waverly, the irritating weasel who had tried to dance with Tabitha two nights before, sauntered out from behind a hedge. He still had that California beach-boy grin, Dev thought disgustedly.

"Game's over, Colter," he said laconically. "Let's have the film."

Only years of training kept Dev from gritting his teeth in self-disgust. How could he have been so stupid? He should have guessed that Waverly had been after more than just Tabitha. Who the hell was he and how did he know about the film?

Something about being around Tabitha had dulled his highly developed senses, Dev decided grimly.

Around her, other things seemed more important. He could only hope that his lapse wasn't going to cost both of them their lives.

CHAPTER SIX

"LET HER GO, WAVERLY. TABBY'S not involved in this."
Dev didn't really expect that bit of logic to have much
of an effect and it didn't. Steve Waverly just smiled a
little more broadly and shook his head.

"Now, you know I'm not about to do that. Not until
I have the film. Then as far as I'm concerned both of
you can go back to the ship. In the meantime Miss
Graham here is going to play the part of incentive for
you."

Tabitha's eyes flickered warily from one man to the
other. The long-haired man with the gun who was
holding her never said a word. It was clear Waverly was
the one in charge. Dev concentrated on him, trying not
to see the fear in Tabitha's questioning gaze.

"Waverly," he said very softly, "I told you the other
night that if you came near her again I'd take you apart.
And that was just if you asked her to dance. Can you
imagine what I'm going to do to you for manhandling
her like this?"

The toothy smile sagged for a fraction of a second
before it was tacked firmly back in place. Good, Dev
decided sardonically, he hadn't completely lost the
old charm. He could still put a trace of fear in a man

like Steve Waverly, even though Waverly's henchman held a gun. Too bad he simply hadn't dumped the younger man over the side of the ship when he'd first made a nuisance of himself. Would have saved a lot of trouble.

"Your lady friend isn't going to get hurt and neither are you. All we're after is that film you picked up on St. Regis. Then the two of you can go back to being happy-go-lucky cruise passengers." Waverly threw a derisive glance at Tabitha, who was watching him as if he were a snake. "That is if your tabby cat—wasn't that what you called her?—if she doesn't mind continuing to play the role of convenient cover for you. Will you mind that, Miss Graham? Now that you know what's going on, are you going to object to sleeping with him? He just used you to give himself a little protective camouflage, you know. Paired off with you, he appeared to be merely another male passenger who was having a good time on board ship. Helped him pass the time very pleasantly, I imagine. Kept him from getting bored."

Tabitha made a muffled sound behind the hard palm that was slapped across her mouth. The words were unintelligible but her eyes were blazing. It occurred to Dev that she was not only terrified; she was furious. If her temper was akin to her passion, Tabitha Graham might turn into one hell of a dangerous commodity when angered. Strangely enough, it would have been impossible before now to even imagine her truly furious. She was such a gentle little thing!

"She's not interested in your analysis of our relationship, Waverly. Let her go."

"Not a chance.'

"I haven't got the film," Dev said wearily. "It's back on board the ship. Hidden in my cabin."

"I don't believe you. You wouldn't let it out of your sight until you handed it over to your boss. We both know that!"

"Do we?" Dev inquired with deceptive mildness.

"Tell him to shut up and hand over the film, Steve," the long-haired man whispered urgently. He was clearly much more nervous than Waverly. Which didn't make for a good situation. If there was one thing worse than a man with a gun, it was a nervous man with a gun.

"Don't worry. Mr. Colter will cooperate, I'm sure. We just have to convince him we're quite serious." Waverly made a production out of lighting a cigarette as if he had all the time in the world. Given the fact that no one else seemed to be wandering down into the gardens from the hotel, that might be quite true, Dev was forced to acknowledge.

"How did you learn about the pickup on St. Regis?" he asked as if only idly curious.

"The man who tried to stop you in that alley survived." Waverly smiled, narrowing his eyes against the smoke from his cigarette. "I guess you didn't know about that interesting tidbit, did you? We found him in the trash bin at the far end of the alley where you'd stuffed him after you practically killed him. Did you think he was dead?"

"I wasn't sure," Dev said dryly. "I knew he was unconscious, though, and I didn't want to leave him lying around to litter the streets." Well, hell. It had taken almost the last of his strength to dump that guy into the trash bin in the hope that he wouldn't be discovered for some time. Looked like it had all been a wasted effort. Out of the corner of his eye Dev saw Tabitha looking at him incredulously. This whole thing must be coming as one hell of a shock to her. Later he would try to explain everything. Right now he had business to transact.

"Well, he made it, and he gave me the identification I needed on you. Our information was that whoever was assigned to the pickup would be traveling on board the cruise ship, but we couldn't be sure which passenger was our rabbit. Once Jeffers managed to tell me about the tall bastard with the cane, I was able to spot you." Waverly glanced at Tabitha, who glared back. "I'll admit I couldn't figure you out, Miss Graham. Definitely not Colter's type from what we knew of him. Then I finally realized he was just using you for cover. Sorry you had to get involved in all of this but that's the breaks, I guess." He stepped toward her. "Speaking of breaks…" Almost casually he fingered the line of her jaw. "I'd hate to have to resort to breaking various and sundry bones in your soft little body."

"Get away from her Waverly!" Dev snapped, ice layering every word. He watched, trying to keep his glance stony as Waverly turned toward him. Then the other man smiled bleakly and very slowly allowed his hand to trail down the line of Tabitha's throat to the curve of her breast. Dev knew he was on the edge of losing his control completely as he watched the other man touching Tabitha with such obscene intimacy. *"Get away from her!"*

"Sure, Colter. Just as soon as you hand over the film."

"You can have the goddamned film. Just turn her loose!' Dev growled savagely.

Waverly stepped forward a couple of feet and politely extended his hand. "Film first, I'm afraid."

Tabitha tensed, knowing she was never going to have another chance. The thin, lanky man with the greasy, long hair was concentrating almost completely on the drama the other two men were acting out. It had to be now or never.

With a muffled shout, she twisted, throwing herself sideways against the man with the gun. He really wasn't all that much heavier than herself, she realized distractedly.

He yelled as she fell against him, stumbling awkwardly beneath the unexpected assault.

"Tabby!"

She heard Dev call her name as she toppled to the ground on top of her victim but all she could think about was the gun. The thin young man was proving to be far stronger than he looked. She would never be able to outfight him. He squirmed violently beneath her, still gripping the gun, although he couldn't yet raise his arm to use it.

"You bitch!" he shouted tightly, lashing at her with his free hand. "Get off me, you damned bitch!"

Almost simultaneously Tabitha heard Dev's cane whistle through the air in a violent arc that cracked against Waverly's face. Then, just as she realized how hopeless her own attack was going to prove, Dev was in front of her, his foot coming down on the gunman's arm. The man screamed, but his hand clenched spasmodically around the handle of the pistol instead of releasing it.

With a desperate heave the thin man threw off the

scrabbling Tabitha, sending her crashing against Dev, who staggered briefly under the unexpected impact of her body. Instantly Tabitha pushed free, scrambling to her feet, but she didn't need to hear Dev's short, explicit oath to know that it was too late.

"Waverly! The gun!" The long-haired man on the grass hurled the weapon frantically at his companion even as the edge of Dev's hand came down against the side of his neck in a devastating blow that rendered him unconscious.

Dev stumbled awkwardly as he tried to regain his balance after delivering the karate chop. He cursed the cane and the stiff leg which was slowing him down. Time was running out. He would never be able to get to Waverly in time. The other man, holding his head with one hand where the cane had drawn blood, was just closing his fingers around the handle of the gun.

"Tabitha! The maze!" Dev steadied himself with the cane and jerked at Tabitha's wrist. Without pausing he yanked her after him as he plunged into the narrow entrance of the dense, boxwood maze. God! He would have given his soul in that moment for the old speed and coordination that he had once taken for granted along with the rest of his acute senses.

At least Tabby had the sense to keep her mouth shut and not demand explanations at this point, Dev thought with some satisfaction as he pulled her deeper and deeper into the maze. He relied on instinct to orient him.

Tabitha wasn't asking questions because she was too busy fighting down panic and anger. The walls of the maze loomed incredibly high, blocking out much of the sun; the dense foliage was so thick it was impossible to see from one aisle into the next. This was a real maze, she thought in stunned wonder, not just some gardener's whimsy. Whoever had constructed it originally had intended for the final product to be a real challenge. What did Dev think he was going to accomplish by dragging both of them in here?

Then again, he might have decided there wasn't much to lose. Waverly had the gun. She and Dev were unarmed.

Even as that realization dawned, Dev was halting her, pushing her flat against the prickly wall of the corridor in which they now stood. An instant later, Tabitha understood why he had stopped. The corridor was a dead end.

He turned to her, silver eyes like slivers of steel. Tabitha stared up at him in dumbfounded amazement. This wasn't the man she knew. This couldn't be the gentle, vulnerable, self-effacing man she had seduced last night! This Dev Colter was a man of forceful action and danger. She realized she was almost as afraid of him as she was of Steve Waverly and the thin man who had held the gun on her. Tabitha's mouth was abruptly dry.

"Don't move. Not an inch," he growled almost soundlessly. "And don't say a word. We're only going to get one chance. Nod your head if you understand."

Mutely Tabitha inclined her head once in a jerky little nod. Her nails pressed anxiously into her palms. He continued to stare down at her a second longer, and then he turned back toward the entrance of the dead-end corridor in which they stood.

Tabitha stayed where she was, pressed flat against

the boxwood wall, and stared after him. He moved soundlessly on the grass which carpeted the maze, but she had the feeling that he would have moved just as lightly over dried twigs or stones. Even with his obvious dependency on the cane, there was a feral quality about Dev, a quality she ought to have noticed long before this. Why hadn't she?

The answer came almost at once: Because she had wanted to see another kind of man altogether. Her imagination had created as unreal a beast as any that ever graced a medieval bestiary. Now she was faced with the very real man behind the fabulous construct created by her own desires.

She watched, aware that there was another beast prowling the maze besides Dev. Steve Waverly had followed them through the boxwood entrance, and there was no reason to think he had turned around and retreated. He would know his quarry was unarmed and he seemed to want something Dev had.

Dev halted for a moment before stepping out into the next angled aisle of the maze. Tabitha heard the faintest of soft, snicking noises as he lifted the cane for a moment, and then, to her fascinated horror, she saw the wicked, steel blade that had emerged from the tip of the cane. Her eyes were glued to the deadly sword as Dev glanced back over his shoulder. The intent mask of his features grew colder and more brutal than ever.

Slowly she raised her eyes to his face, and Dev wanted to curse aloud at the expression he saw in them. For God's sake! Did she think he could take care of Waverly by being Mr. Nice Guy? The sword cane was little enough defense against the gun as it was. She looked as if she didn't want him to have even that much of a weapon!

No, he told himself in the next breath, it wasn't that she wished him unarmed. She wished him to disappear, along with the entire situation. Hell, he was going to have his hands full trying to pacify her after this was all over. She was clearly half in shock. Abruptly he turned away, not wanting to suffer another instant of that accusing, pleading glance. First things first.

Soundlessly he slipped out into the adjoining passage. His stiff leg kept him from the smooth, gliding pace which had once been his to use at will, but at least it didn't keep him from being able to move altogether. He didn't dare rely on the cane now. It had to be kept ready for the instant it would be needed. How far into the maze had Waverly come?

Dev paused to listen, trying to revive all the old instincts and the once-highly attuned senses. Too bad he hadn't listened to those senses earlier. He might have been able to avoid this stupid mess altogether. If anything happened to Tabby, it would be all his fault. The thought made him clench the ebony cane more violently than ever. Deliberately he relaxed the grip. Tension wasn't going to do him any good. It obscured the awareness he needed at the moment.

There, behind him, back toward the entrance to the maze. He turned cautiously, willing the faint, rasping sound to repeat itself. Slowly he made his way down the narrow corridor. Would Waverly be fool enough to blunder through the maze looking for him? Or would he realize the danger of hunting when you couldn't see around the next corner? Dev glanced down at the tip of the sword in his hand. All he needed was an instant's warning. Just one lousy instant of advantage.

The rasping sound came again. Waverly was moving deeper into the maze, certain he held the only weapon. Dev felt the infuriating stiffness in his knee and gritted his teeth. He had told Delaney he had no business getting back into this life. A man pushing forty and cursed with a game leg was hardly prime material for this kind of work.

The faint, rasping sound came once more. Waverly was either not terribly worried about giving away his location, or he simply didn't know how to move silently. The younger man would be in a hurry to wind up the situation before other tourists came wandering down into the garden. Perhaps that urgency would make the damn beach boy careless. Dev deliberately slowed his breathing, striving to focus all his attention on his sense of hearing. Then the boxwood wall beside him vibrated ever so slightly.

Waverly was in the neighboring passage.

The question, Dev realized grimly, was how could he be certain which end of the passage would be open. He might turn the corner up ahead and find himself facing another wall of thick boxwood. Or he might find himself facing Waverly's gun.

The only sensible thing to do was to station himself at the intersection ahead and wait. Waiting was one thing he could do far better than Waverly could. Younger men tended to be far more impatient. Yeah, Dev told himself evenly, I'll wait this one out.

He advanced to the intersection and then pressed his back to the wall, his head turned to the side so that he could watch the opening. Eventually Waverly would find his way past this corridor entrance. The maze wasn't so complicated that it couldn't be searched by someone intent on doing exactly that. At least in this position, Dev thought, he was between Waverly and Tabitha. She was in a dead-end corridor and there weren't any other intersections between him and her except the one he had just come through.

And Waverly was still on the other side of the boxwood wall. Dev could hear the faint sound of the other man's breathing now. Then Waverly lost his patience altogether.

"Listen to me, Colter," he hissed, his voice so unexpectedly close that Dev instinctively tensed. "All I want is the film. Bring it to the front of the maze and I'll let both of you go."

Sure you will, Dev thought silently. What kind of a fool do you think I am, kid? Just keep coming this way.

"Can you hear me, Colter?"

Dev waited silently. Waverly's voice was a little farther away now. Was he going to search another corridor before he came down the one which formed the intersection Dev was guarding? Apparently so.

The waiting was always the worst part. But when your life depended on it, you learned to wait. Patiently.

The minutes clicked past. Occasionally Waverly called out persuasively, but Dev just went on waiting. Sooner or later the man had to come down this corridor.

Steve Waverly eventually made his way down the narrow passage which joined with the one in which Dev stood. The younger man was making very little effort to cover the sound of his movements now. It was obvious he was getting nervous about the unfinished business. It was that nervousness which gave Dev his opportunity.

Waverly came down the corridor at a trot, moving much too hastily and too noisily. Dev gathered himself. As he had told Tabby, there was only going to be one chance. He waited one more excruciating second, buying all the advantage he could.

Then, when he sensed that Waverly was only a couple of feet from the intersection, Dev threw himself out into the passage, the blade of the sword cane slashing unerringly around in a curve, searching for its prey.

Steve Waverly yelled in astonishment as his intended victim emerged from the corridor to the right, but before he could squeeze off a shot, cold steel had sliced a scarlet ribbon across the arm which held the weapon. The gun fell from nerveless fingers. Waverly screamed again and clutched at his bleeding arm.

"Don't move or the next thing I slash will be your throat."

Dev emphasized his words by letting the tip of the sword cane lie menacingly alongside Waverly's neck. The blond man froze, his eyes glazed with pain and fear. Cautiously, the sword never moving an inch, Dev balanced himself on his good leg and used the other to kick the gun farther out of reach. He didn't dare attempt to lean down and pick it up. The awkward movement might make his balance too precarious. Damned leg.

"All right, Waverly. Let's go. Turn around and head back toward the entrance."

"For God's sake! I'm bleeding to death!"

"You'll live. Unfortunately. Now *move!*"

"Listen, Colter. We can make a deal here. I'll split the profit off that damn film. You can have Eddie's share."

"Eddie's your good buddy lying unconscious out there on the grass?"

"That's right. Forget him. You can have his portion."

"Why do I get this nasty feeling that you can't be relied on, Waverly?" Dev prodded his victim gently with the cane, and the man moved uneasily back down the corridor.

"You can trust me."

"Sure. Even if I could, I'd still want to slit your throat for the way you used my woman. That was a mistake, Waverly. A bad one. Give me half an excuse right now, and I'll kill you for that."

"I didn't hurt her!"

"You threatened her. And you touched her. Didn't I tell you just the other night that I'd take you apart if you came near her?"

"Colter, listen to me!"

"Oh, shut up, Waverly. Just keep moving."

"Which way? I'm lost." Waverly glared furiously around as he came to a halt at the next intersection.

"To the right," Dev said automatically, his sense of direction as sound as it had ever been in the past. Some instincts, apparently, didn't fade. "Now left."

Without hesitation Dev followed the proddings of his inner senses, pushing Waverly through the entrance of the maze a couple of minutes later. "Lie down on the grass over there by your good friend Eddie." He waited as Waverly did as he was told.

"What about my arm?"

"What about it?" Dev asked carelessly. Then he raised his voice. "Tabby! Can you hear me? Come on out of the maze."

There was a moment's silence.

"Tabby!"

"I hear you, Dev." Her voice sounded very faint.

"Come on out. Everything's under control." Hell, his tone still sounded gruff, Dev realized vaguely. It was hard to leach out the violence when your body still hummed with it. "Tabby!" he tried again.

"Dev, I'm trying but it's confusing."

"What the hell…?"

"It's a maze, Dev, remember?" There was a touch of asperity in the question. Her voice sounded even more faint.

"Tabby, I can't come and get you. I've got to keep an eye on Waverly. Listen, on your way out, watch for the gun he dropped. Bring it with you."

There was no answer this time. Dev waited again, but now he didn't feel patient. He wanted to see her again, reassure himself that she was safe, and then he wanted to get rid of Waverly and friend. The sooner this mess was cleaned up, the better. Delaney could handle what was left of it. Dev knew that all he himself wanted was to return to the ship with Tabby. He was going to be busy enough explaining everything to her.

Three more minutes ticked past.

"Tabby? What's keeping you? Just walk back out the same way we went in."

"I'm not sure which way that is! And stop yelling at me!"

"I'm not yelling at you. But I haven't got all day!"

"Then just go ahead and leave without me!" she called back furiously.

At the caustic tone in her words Dev winced. She was more than a little upset, he realized. "Tabby?"

"I think I'm at the center of the maze."

"Orient yourself with the sun!" he called back, aware that he must sound rather irritated by now. "Hurry up."

This time he received no answer at all. Several more minutes went by. Dev felt his annoyance growing. Was she playing games with him? If that was the case... "About time you got here!" he muttered as she suddenly appeared at the entrance. He had never been so happy to see anyone in his life.

But his expression didn't convey his relief. Tabitha emerged to find him glaring at her, and she froze for an instant at the tableau of the three men. Dev was standing guard with the edge of the sword hovering close to a sullen-looking Waverly. The thin young man on the ground hadn't yet awakened. Tabitha swallowed and wondered if he might be dead.

"I see you found the gun. Good. Bring it here, Tabby." There was a sense of exaggerated patience in his tone which thoroughly annoyed Tabitha. This was all his fault in the first place! Wordlessly she went forward and handed over the gun. As soon as he had it in his hand, Dev sheathed the sword in the cane with a small movement of his finger on a hidden button. Then he leaned against the ebony stick with a stifled groan.

Tabitha resolutely ignored the sign of pain. Never again was he going to deceive her with his small, insidious tricks! Her chin came up and her eyes narrowed. "Now what?" she asked aloofly.

He slanted her an assessing glance. "Now we get rid of these two. I suppose you'd better go back to the hotel and get some help. Have them call the local police. I'll have to explain all this to the authorities."

Obediently Tabitha swung around, grateful for any excuse to depart the violent scene.

"Tabby?"

She glanced back warily. "What?"

"If you couldn't remember which way we had gone into the maze, how did you find your way out from the center so quickly?"

She shrugged. "I remembered something I read somewhere about how to escape from mazes."

He stared at her in surprise. "What's that?"

"You put your hand against the wall and never lift it off. That way you don't go over the same territory twice." She couldn't keep a tinge of pride out of her voice even though she was still furious and resentful.

"Tabby, that's just an old myth! If that's the technique you used then you were merely very lucky!" Dev growled.

"An old myth? But, Dev, I'm something of an expert on old myths, remember? And on the whole I've found them to be much more reliable than modern lies told by modern men like you." Without waiting for a response, Tabitha turned back toward the hotel.

Damn! Dev thought, it's going to be a long night. He glared down at Waverly. "You're to blame for all this, you stupid bastard. Why the hell did you have to get so damn greedy?"

Waverly, wisely sensing that his luck had already run out, kept his mouth shut.

The island police, spiffy in their summer-weight, khaki uniforms, arrived twenty minutes later. Tabitha did not return with them.

By the time Dev had explained the situation, put through a call to Delaney from police headquarters and managed to extricate himself from the sticky scene, he was not in a good mood. Delaney had taken the whole thing much too cavalierly as far as Dev was concerned.

"You've still got the magic touch, Dev," Delaney announced cheerily from the other end of the line. "I told you that you did."

"The old touch, my ass. I nearly got killed, Delaney. What's more I nearly got my woman killed. I was a fool to let you talk me into this. Oh, hell, why am I standing here in this nearly one-hundred-percent humidity trying to reason with you? You've got a one-track mind."

"That's how I got where I am. Plus instincts, of course. I've got good instincts, too, Dev. Just like you. We're two of a kind."

Dev closed his eyes in disgust. His leg was aching again. He wondered what the odds were of getting Tabitha to massage it for him. "Listen, Delaney, we can argue this out later. The ship sails in forty minutes, and I'm going to be on it. I'll make the delivery when I return to the States. In the meantime, try to keep creeps like Waverly out of my way, will you? This was supposed to be a trouble-free assignment designed to help me get my feet wet again as I recall."

Delaney laughed. "See you soon, Dev. Enjoy the rest of your cruise." He hung up the phone before Dev could think of a suitably cutting response. So much for Washington, D.C. types. Bastards. Now it was time to go back to the ship and deal with Washington, state of, types. Sweet, little tabby cats who had had their fur ruffled the wrong way.

He would soon stroke Tabby back into a warm and purring mood, Dev promised himself as he took his leave of the somewhat confused island police. "Don't worry, someone will be along soon to pick up Waverly and good, old Eddie there," he assured the chief. "Just keep them under lock and key until then, okay?"

"Of course, Mr. Colter, we are only too anxious to cooperate. But we would like a few explanations," the balding, middle-aged man informed him with a frown. He was a good cop and he didn't like confusing situations caused by visiting Americans. Americans were always confusing, it was true, but this instance was a bit more annoying than usual.

"The gentleman who arrives to take charge of these two will be happy to explain everything," Dev said smoothly. Damned if he was going to hang around and make excuses. The first priority was to get back to the ship and find Tabitha.

She was probably hiding in her cabin even now, nervous and anxious and full of questions. He'd rather answer her queries than those of the chief of police, Dev decided, flagging down a taxi.

Poor Tabby. She had been through a lot this afternoon. Actually, he owed her a favor. If she hadn't made that move against the guy with the gun, things might have been far more complicated than they had been. Dev smiled to himself as the cab whisked him back to the docks where the tender boats were making their last runs to the ship. She had plenty of spirit, and she'd kept her head when the chips were down. He realized he couldn't wait until he had her back in his arms.

He would explain everything, and then he would make sweet love to her until she had forgiven him for the upsetting afternoon. There wasn't a doubt in his mind that she *would* forgive him. How could someone as compassionate and gentle as Tabby Graham refuse to accept his apologies? It was only a matter of time before he once more had her in the palm of his hand. Dev relaxed a little at the thought.

But sweet, compassionate, gentle Tabitha Graham was not in her cabin. She was, in fact, nowhere on board the luxury liner. And the huge ship had sailed before Dev, grilling everyone from the lowliest steward to the captain, discovered that Tabby had returned to the liner only long enough to collect her things from the stateroom.

Then she had left once more, heading for the island airport, where she had caught the first plane back to the mainland.

Trapped on board until the ship reached its next destination, Dev spent the evening alone in his cabin with a bottle of whiskey. After every swallow he glared at the ebony cane which concealed the bit of microfilm in a hidden compartment in the handle.

It had been a damned Washington, D.C. type who had designed that cane.

Turkeys.

Dev took another swallow of whiskey and made up his mind. He was going to get as far away from Washington, D.C. as soon as possible.

CHAPTER SEVEN

A WEEK AFTER HER RETURN TO PORT TOWNSEND a rare fury still smoldered in Tabitha's heart.

Devlin Colter had used her.

Every time the thought of being used crossed her mind, Tabitha experienced another blazing surge of anger. Never had she known any emotion as fierce and violent as the rage she had felt since that fateful afternoon in the maze.

No, that wasn't strictly accurate, she was honest enough to admit a few days after her return. There had once been another kind of emotion that had flared just as wildly and had been just as rare. She had learned of the other fire the night she had seduced Dev.

Passion and anger. She had never known the meaning of either as she did in the wake of her experience with Dev Colter. Seven days after her escape from the island, Tabitha concentrated fiercely on the anger. The memory of her own passion was far more disturbing and better left alone as much as possible. She threw herself back into work at her shop, The Manticore.

Dev had toyed with her, played a game of pretend. Tabitha gritted her teeth every time the realization went through her mind. She would be unpacking a carton of books and find her fingers trembling with fury as she tried to wield the knife she was using on the cardboard.

Or she would be thumbing through her beautiful collection of bestiaries and come across a picture of a dragon. The sight of it would cause her to snap the book shut with a brutal movement.

A game of make-believe. Why had he indulged such a silly pastime? Just because he thought she made a good cover for his activities? Because he had been bored? Because she had been the one to get him out of that alley and he had felt a fleeting gratitude?

None of the possibilities was pleasant, and none of them did anything to soothe her fury.

God, what a fool she had made of herself! How he must have laughed to himself that night when she had set out to seduce him by plying him with drinks and tales of the mating habits of the animals in her medieval books! The red stained her cheeks once more as she remembered that awful night.

Ten days after her return home, Tabitha was shelving new paperback mysteries in her shop when the memory of her own passion danced, unbidden, once more through her mind. This time her hand stilled in the act of placing a book in the rack.

This time her fingers didn't shake with fury and humiliation.

For a long moment Tabitha simply stared unseeingly at the book in her hand, her face revealing the absorption of her own thoughts. Damn it, she had known passion, real passion that night. She had thought herself in love, and she had set out to seduce the man of her dreams.

Whatever else you could say about that embarrassing and infuriating evening, she had been successful. She had made love to her dragon and even if he had been secretly laughing at her, he had responded.

There could be no doubt about that! she reminded herself feelingly. And he hadn't been the only one who had responded. Her own reaction had been deeply, startlingly fulfilling; unlike anything else she had ever known.

It was true that she had been making love to a myth—a man who didn't really exist except in her own imagination—but she had done it rather well. Yes, damn it, she *had* done it rather well. Dev Colter might have been amusing himself with her, or he might have been deliberately using her, but he had been satisfied that night, she would stake The Manticore on that small fact.

Tabitha's gentle mouth twisted wryly as she shelved the last of the mysteries and headed back toward the front counter. If only he had been the man he had pretended to be: a wonderfully vulnerable, sensitive, shy man who had needed her. How perfect it all would have been.

The chiming of the bell on the door broke into her morbid reverie. With an effort of will Tabitha forced herself to remember that she had a business to run and that meant summoning up a pleasant welcome for potential customers. The young couple who entered looked like the professional, browsing type but one never knew.

"We saw the poster of the phoenix in the window and wondered if you have a copy for sale?" the man inquired politely. His girl friend, her long hair in braids, looked hopeful.

"It's a beautiful poster," she said quickly.

"I've got several in stock," Tabitha informed them, striving for a gracious tone as she delved under the counter to find the rolled up, plastic-encased posters. "Take your pick. Phoenixes are popular with artists."

The young couple pored over the various paintings and sketches of the mythological bird, most of which depicted the creature in the classic pose of rising from its own ashes.

"I think this one would look good on the living room wall," the young woman finally announced decisively. "It's got all the right colors for that room."

Idly Tabitha glanced at the poster that had been selected. "You picked one of the more accurate paintings," she approved. "A lot of analysts think the phoenix was probably a purple heron which got sacrificed to an Egyptian sun god periodically. The bird in that painting looks nice and purple."

"Our interior designer would call it mauve," the young man said, grinning good-naturedly. "Okay, we'll take this one. When we get it framed, it's going to be fabulous."

Tabitha nodded, dutifully writing up the transaction and handing over a rolled copy of the elegant poster. As the couple turned to leave the shop she began re-rolling the rest of the phoenix collection. There was quite a variety in the artwork, some of which had been commissioned by Tabitha herself specifically for sale in the shop, but all of the art showed a regal bird gloriously reborn after a fiery death. The pictures struck a responsive chord in her own mind.

She, herself, had gone up in flames that night she had

seduced Dev Colter. What were the odds that, like the phoenix, she, too could be reborn?

The tantalizing thought came and went in her head all during the long afternoon. Whenever the shop door opened, it interrupted some variation on the teasing possibility of becoming a different woman. Damn it, she *had* been a different woman that night she had lain in Dev Colter's arms. She had been vibrant and alive and passionate.

Why couldn't she be that way again? Deliberately Tabitha went to the special section of the shop where she housed the reproductions of medieval bestiaries and took down several of the magnificently illustrated volumes. Hauling them over to the counter, she opened each one to the section on the phoenix and began to read.

Phoenixes, it seemed, only went through their fiery regeneration once every five hundred years. Well, allowances would have to be made on that score, Tabitha told herself dryly. She was going to turn thirty in another couple of days; surely that milestone in a woman's life could substitute for the five-hundred-year mark of a phoenix's! She stared at all the various woodcuts and drawings of the birds, moodily trying to imagine herself as a renewed and entirely different woman. A woman like she had been that night on the ship.

But such a woman needed a man to appreciate the radical change, Tabitha told herself derisively. Where was she going to find such a male? She knew plenty of people, having lived in town for the past six years, but they all saw her as she was, a quiet, unassuming woman who hadn't been able to hold onto a husband for more than a few months. They had all felt very sorry for her when Greg had left, of course, but Tabitha doubted that any of them had been very surprised.

What she needed was a way of formally announcing her new image, Tabitha decided. She would give herself a thirtieth birthday party.

It was a cinch no one else would remember to give her one!

With the care and precision of a determined military commander, Tabitha devoted herself to the plans for her thirtieth birthday party. Just the act of organizing it was something of a catharsis. Her pent-up rage and humiliation gave her the necessary energy to see the huge undertaking through. She had never planned anything on such a scale in her life, and it took more work than she would have imagined.

"You want two cases of that Cabernet?" her friend at the wine shop asked dubiously. "Are you sure you don't mean just two bottles?" He knew as well as anyone else in the neighborhood that Tabitha Graham did not entertain on a grand scale.

"Two cases, George," Tabitha confirmed, "and a case of the Sauvignon Blanc '81, too. Now let me see your cheese selection. And I'll want a large quantity of sourdough bread, too. Can you order that for me?"

"Well, sure, but, if you don't mind my asking, why do you need so much food and wine, Tabitha?" George Royce scratched his graying head and smiled at her with curiosity.

"For my thirtieth birthday party, George. Oh, by the way, you and your wife are invited. Bring anybody else you can think of, too, please."

"Anybody else? How big a party is this going to be?"

"As big as I can make it!"

The sign went up in the bookshop window the day before the event. Done by a friend who had an art gallery down the street from Tabitha's bookshop, it depicted a beautiful version of a phoenix and announced to all and sundry that everyone was invited to Tabitha's home the following day.

"You're going to get some freeloaders with an open invitation like that," Sandra Adams warned as she walked into the shop that afternoon.

"That's all right. I've got plenty of food. A few freeloaders won't matter," Tabitha declared airily. "Are you coming, Sandy?"

"Oh, sure. Wouldn't miss it. Everyone's coming. We're all a little curious. What happened to you on that cruise, Tab? You seem different, somehow."

Tabitha smiled serenely. She had taken to wearing all her clothes without a bra this past week, and more than one person had commented on the "change" in her. And she'd caught more than one pair of male eyes straying to the loose fitting shirts she was wearing with her jeans. The open attention was still a little awkward to handle at times, but Tabitha was grimly sticking to the plan.

"I had a wonderful time. Found out what I've been missing all these years, Sandy. You wouldn't believe how people act on those cruise ships."

"I've heard stories." Sandy grinned. "To tell you the truth, Tab, I think it's terrific. I mean, the change is for the better. You seem more lively somehow. Even Ron noticed it."

"Is he coming?" Ron was Sandy's brother, who visited frequently from Seattle.

"You bet. He was planning on coming to Port Townsend this weekend anyway with a couple of friends. They'll be there. You know Ron. Offer him free beer and food and he'll turn up for anything."

Several young tourists in the shop jokingly called attention to the sign and asked if it truly was an open invitation. Tabitha assured them it was. To her delight a few said they might stop by on the evening of the party.

Tabitha used one of the books from the home entertaining section of The Manticore to help design the arrangement of food and beverages. Anxiously she went over and over the details, leaving nothing to chance. It was a bit frightening to plan a party of this magnitude. What if no one showed up?

That secret fear of all neophyte party-givers was still haunting her the evening of the party as she dressed in a dashing, black dress bought especially for the occasion from a friend who owned a boutique. The dress was a floating thing of sheer, black cotton designed with a wide, bateau neckline and full, dolman sleeves. It was bound at the waist with a wide, red leather belt that emphasized the curves above and below.

Any threat of poor attendance was dispelled almost as soon as Tabitha finished brushing her hair. The doorbell began to ring, and it didn't stop for the next hour and a half. Nearly everyone who had been invited and several others who had seen the sign in the shop window showed up to celebrate Tabitha's thirtieth birthday and to satisfy their curiosity about the change in Tabby Graham.

Circulating through her overcrowded living room, Tabitha did her best not to disappoint any of the curious. The blazing fire on the hearth made a fine focus for the event. Someone had already settled on the sheepskin rug in front of it.

"I never realized what a nice job you had done on this old cottage," Sandra Adams exclaimed, glancing around the room as Tabitha pushed a glass of wine into her hand. "I really love all those framed prints of your weird medieval animals. Somehow it all mixes very nicely with the black sofas and the polished wooden floors. And that rug under the glass coffee table is fantastic! Where did you get it?"

"It was a lucky find in Seattle." Tabitha smiled, glancing with just a trace of unease at the fringed rug she had once loved so much. It showed a fabulous dragon, complete with wings and gleaming eyes, and it reminded her far too vividly of the beaten and bloody dragon she had discovered in the alley on St. Regis. Both were creatures of myth, having no basis in reality.

"Oh, here's Ron and his friend now," Sandra observed, swinging toward the door as it opened to admit her handsome younger brother. Ron Adams was about twenty-five and blessed with over six feet of height. He worked out regularly at a Seattle health club, and it showed in the well-sculpted lines of his chest and shoulders. He wore his jet black hair in a casual, wind-blown style that nicely complemented his dark eyes and the tan he got skiing every winter.

The man who accompanied him was about the same age and sported a dashing mustache. Both took one look around at the lively throng and seemed to approve.

"Over here, Ron!" Sandra called above the din.

Tabitha glanced assessingly at the younger man as he approached. She had met Ron once or twice in the past, but she doubted if it had been a memorable occasion for Sandra's good-looking brother.

"Hi, Tab, nice to see you again. Thanks for the invitation," he drawled, his dark eyes running appraisingly over the thin black cotton dress his hostess was wearing.

Tabitha was learning to recognize that speculative gleam in a man's eyes now. She had seen it more than once this past week. The first time she'd ever seen it had been when Dev Colter arrived at her door the morning she had chosen not to wear a bra for the first time. That particular undergarment was tucked away in her lingerie drawer tonight, too. Gamely she ignored a twinge of self-consciousness and summoned up her brightest smile.

"I'm glad you could make it, Ron. And I hope your friend enjoys himself."

"Oh, he will. Any beer?"

"Lots of it. Help yourself."

"Great. I'll be right back." His gaze strayed again to the black dress.

"Hmm," Sandra murmured as her brother disappeared in the direction of the serving area. "Why do I get this funny feeling that Ron is suddenly developing an interest in older women?"

Tabitha chuckled. "Not likely," she demurred. "But from my point of view, I have to admit I've heard some good things on the subject of younger men."

"Something along the line of 'Get 'em young and train 'em right'?" Sandra giggled. "Not a bad idea. Good luck with him, Tab."

Tabitha was aware of the embarrassed flush in her cheeks, but she managed a small grin.

Ron wasn't the only male who reassessed Tabitha Graham that night. As she determinedly threw herself into the role of hostess, Tabitha was aware of several glances, and there never seemed to be a lack of masculine assistance when she needed help opening new bottles of wine or carrying trays of appetizers.

On the one hand it was all very flattering, but on the other it didn't seem quite real. Or perhaps it was the free flow of wine which gave a tinge of unreality to the evening. The stereo was never silent, and the crowd in the living room seemed to swell rather than diminish throughout the evening. Thank heaven she had bought all those plastic glasses, Tabitha thought fleetingly at one point. She would long since have run out of her own glassware.

By one o'clock in the morning Tabitha was beginning to wonder how such an evening concluded itself. As far as she could tell no one seemed anxious to go home. Ron Adams was constantly around now, consuming her beer and wine in great quantities. His friend had disappeared long since with an attractive blonde whom Tabitha didn't recognize. Sandra Adams was involved in an intimate discussion with a young fisherman she had discovered near the fireplace. Throughout the room the laughter and the alcohol mingled.

By two o'clock some of the throng finally decided to take their leave. Tabitha, who had lost count of the glasses of wine she had consumed, cheerfully waved goodbye from her front porch and then turned back to the doorway to find Ron waiting with yet another glass for her.

"Great party, Tab," he mumbled quite thickly. His dark eyes gleamed once again with male speculation. "How old did you say you were?"

"Thirty," she murmured, sipping at her wine. Everything was beginning to take on a hazy, dreamy aspect that was really rather pleasant, she thought.

"I'm twenty-five," he told her and then smiled hugely. "I hear it's the latest trend."

Tabitha blinked, momentarily losing track of the conversation. It had been harder and harder to concentrate on such things for the past two hours. "Trend?"

"You know, men having affairs with women who are older."

"Ah, yes. The latest trend." Tabitha nodded wisely.

"There's something kind of exciting about it," Ron confided.

"I'm all for excitement."

"Me, too. Life is too damn short. Best thing you can do is fill it full of excitement," Ron agreed with a profundity born of a rather high percentage of alcohol in his bloodstream.

"Absolutely." Tabitha took another swallow of wine and somehow lost her balance on the porch. Carefully she put out a hand and braced herself against the wall. Then she smiled once more. "Get 'em young and train 'em right."

"Get what young?" Ron took a step closer and had to grab at the wall himself.

"Males."

"Male what?"

"Male whatever," Tabitha explained with a vague wave of her hand. "Puppies, dragons, basilisks, you name it. Best to get 'em young and train them properly. Older ones are likely to be mean and vicious."

"No kidding?"

"Yup."

"I want you to know," Ron said very carefully, if rather unsteadily, "that I consider myself very trainable." He edged a little close, using the wall for support.

"Good." Tabitha took another sip of wine and frowned intently. "First lesson is never bite the hand that feeds you."

"W-wouldn't dream of it," Ron assured her.

"Second lesson…" Tabitha paused, trying to concentrate. Then she brightened. "Is never to play games."

"No games." Ron draped his arm around her shoulders and raised his glass in salute to the second lesson.

"No playing make-believe," Tabitha emphasized just in case he hadn't got the message. "I have discovered that men who are older and more set in their ways have a nasty habit of playing make-believe. My first husband did, you know."

"The bastard!" Ron exclaimed with great feeling.

"He pretended he was in love with me," Tabitha explained gravely. "But he wasn't."

Ron shook his head, baffled at such duplicity.

"The last man I met also played make-believe. All kinds of games. He wasn't at all the sort of man he pretended to be."

"A rat."

"No, a dragon," she corrected automatically.

"Dragons are worse than rats."

"Yes."

Tabitha was about to go on with the lessons when the

door behind them opened to reveal Sandra on the arm of the fisherman. "Oh, there you are, Tab. Jim and I were just leaving. Had a fantastic time. Happy birthday!"

"Thank you," Tabitha responded very politely.

"Think you can get home all right, Ron?" Sandra peered at her younger brother before the fisherman got her down the steps.

"Don't worry. I won't be driving. I'll walk," Ron said happily. "Then again maybe I won't go home at all."

"I see." Sandra tipped her head to one side and smiled at Tabitha. "You, uh, want me to see he gets home?"

"Heavens no! We're having a wonderful time," Tabitha assured her happily. "I'm giving him lessons."

Sandra slid a doubtful glance from Tabitha to her brother. "Interesting." Before she could say anything else the man named Jim tugged on her arm.

"Let's go, honey. It's late."

Sandra smiled. "Okay. Well, good night, you two. Be careful."

"Of what?" Tabitha asked very curiously.

"Never mind," Sandra groaned and let herself be hauled away by her new escort.

"Where were we?" Tabitha asked interestedly as Sandra and Jim climbed into a truck parked at the curb.

Ron's brows drew together in a thick line of forced effort. "Not sure. Next lesson was going to be number three, I think."

"Oh. Well, let's see. Ron, did I ever tell you about the mating habits of bestiary animals?" Tabitha began industriously. She'd had good luck with that technique once before, hadn't she?

"Nope." Ron swallowed the last of his wine. "How do they do it?"

"All sorts of fascinating ways," she told him gravely.

Once again the door to the house opened, however, interrupting Tabitha's words. This time a number of people were taking their departure, albeit reluctantly. By the time she got back to the conversation with Ron Adams the younger man had helped himself to still another glass of wine. He appeared to be having a great deal of difficulty in focusing. She managed to get him seated on one of the black couches before he toppled over, however.

After that accomplishment, Tabitha had to take another break to send off the last of her guests. Many of them had walked, and now they ambled happily back down the street towards their assorted homes. A few sang en route and there was a great deal of riotous laughter. Tabitha stood in her doorway and watched them go with a distinct sense of satisfaction.

It had been a very successful thirtieth birthday party. No doubt about it. And now it was time to get back to the business of seduction. There was a nice young man sitting on her couch just waiting for the techniques of an older, sophisticated woman. Tabitha smiled smugly as she turned back into the room.

"Animals!" Ron cried, hoisting his glass. "Tell me about the animals!" He leaned back into the corner, his feet propped on the cushions. Then he leered at Tabitha. "Always like to learn new things about animals. Almost became a zoologist instead of a sales rep, you know."

Tabitha blinked, studying her quarry craftily. Then she advanced farther into the room and sat down on the black couch across from him. Through the clear glass of the coffee table she could see the head of the dragon in the carpet.

"Such lovely silver eyes," she sighed, feeling a sudden wave of moroseness.

"Whose eyes?" Ron demanded aggressively.

"The dragon's."

"Umm. So how do dragons make love?" he asked with groggy interest.

Tabitha considered the question darkly, frowning down at the creature in the carpet.

"Magnificently. Once they're properly seduced, that is," she heard herself whisper in a blurry voice. Why did the dragon in the carpet have to stare up at her like that? He had no right to look so accusing. *He* was the one who should feel guilty! "But you can't trust them."

"Never trust dragons," Ron repeated dutifully. "Lesson number three." He waited expectantly.

"He has no right to make me feel guilty about this!" Tabitha hissed down at the carpet. "No right to interfere!"

"No right!" Ron agreed helpfully. Then he paused. "Who is 'he'?"

"The dragon."

"Damn right. No dragon's going to interfere."

"Nasty, vicious creature," Tabitha muttered, still staring down at the carpet.

"Probably an older dragon," Ron opined seriously.

"Nearly forty," Tabitha agreed with a nod.

"Much too old to be properly trained."

"You can't teach an old dragon new tricks," Tabitha sighed again. "They're born sneaky, though, so you probably couldn't teach a young one much, either."

"How about me?" Ron pressed with an inviting, if bleary, smile.

She glanced up, half-surprised to see him still there. She had been concentrating so hard on the damn dragon in the carpet that Ron had faded into insignificance. For a long moment she just looked at her last guest, trying to remember that she had planned to seduce him. Then Tabitha closed her eyes with a forlorn little groan. "It's no use, Ron. I can't go through with it. You'd better leave now."

"Leave?" He sounded vastly dismayed.

Tabitha opened her eyes, aware of a very sleepy sensation. "I can't seduce you tonight. I'm very sorry, Ron. I just don't feel like talking about the beasts anymore this evening."

"Not even a little bit?" he begged sorrowfully.

She shook her head. "I can't do it. Not with this stupid dragon staring up at me."

"Maybe we could get rid of the dragon," Ron suggested helpfully.

"Wouldn't work. He'd still be around somewhere. Oh, hell. I wonder how long he's going to hang around like this, ruining my new life. Nasty, vicious creature."

"It's not just your life he's ruining," Ron exploded ruefully. "I think he's going to ruin my evening, too."

Together with Tabitha he sat staring down at the silent laughing dragon and then, very slowly, Ron keeled over and fell asleep on the sofa he had been occupying.

Tabitha glanced up and then leaned back into the corner of her sofa and curled her feet under her. She was so sleepy. Since the dumb dragon in the carpet wasn't going to let her do anything else tonight, she might as well get some rest. In the morning she would figure out how she was going to get rid of the haunting presence in her home. Something had to be done. She was making such terrific progress on other fronts, she refused to let the dragon stand in her way when it came to organizing a whole new love life!

But even as she slid quickly off to sleep, Tabitha had the depressing feeling that it was going to be very difficult denying the dragon's claim. And her dreams were filled with images of a man with silver eyes and an ebony cane who kept fading in and out of the body of a dragon.

IT WAS A LONG WHILE BEFORE TABITHA separated the pounding in her head from the sound of pounding on her door. For long moments she lay very still, violently aware that daylight was streaming in through the curtains and that someone was at her front door.

Neither event was a welcome one.

"Oh, my God!" She shuddered, her hand going to her aching head. "Go away." But her voice was only a whisper, and it never carried as far as the door.

The knocking came more aggressively than ever.

"Oh, hell." Tabitha made a valiant effort and succeeded in rolling to the edge of the couch. Just as she did so a loud masculine snore came from the opposite sofa. Tabitha got her eyes open with an effort. The sight of Ron Adams sleeping across from her was a little too thought-provoking for eight o'clock in the morning. Even as she watched, he snored again and twisted a bit on the cushions.

Slowly Tabitha sat up, her hand still on her aching

head. Memory returned in a cold rush as her eyes swept the littered room. Everything was in chaos. Empty glasses were stacked on all the tables and scattered on the floor. Overflowing ashtrays reeked with a stale, morning-after aroma. A chair had been overturned at some point and still lay on its side. The flowers were wilting in their bowls. Someone had spilled the water, apparently. It lay in a pool on the hardwood floor.

She hadn't thought to put any of the leftover food away, Tabitha realized as she got shakily to her feet. Partially consumed appetizers lay on paper plates scattered around the room. Half-drunk bottles of wine were still sitting on the serving table. The once cozy living room was a mess.

And then there was the man sleeping on her sofa.

Tabitha winced as she walked past Ron Adams' recumbent form. She might not be on cordial terms with dragons these days but she did owe the one on the floor a favor. He had kept her from making an idiot of herself with Ron Adams. At least her memory on that score was perfectly clear. Ron had passed out just before she had! The discussion on the mating habits of bestiary animals had not progressed as far as it had the last time she had brought up the subject with a man.

The knocking on the front door came once again.

"Okay, okay, I'm coming." It was a weak response and probably went unheard. Tabitha couldn't help it. She had to concentrate all her strength just to get across the room; there wasn't much energy left for shouting.

Desperately she attempted to plan a course of action as she crossed the room. The first thing was to get rid of whoever was pounding on her door. Then she would have to wake Ron Adams and get him out of the house.

Then she would have a nice, long shower, followed by a huge cup of coffee. Following that, she would start cleaning house. Lord, what a day it was going to be.

"Will you kindly stop that damn pounding!" Tabitha commanded resentfully as she wrenched open the front door. "I'm opening the door as fast as I can!" Then her eyes went painfully wide as they took in the presence of the man on her doorstep. "Oh, my God," she breathed, stunned. "The dragon."

Dev Colter lowered the handle of the ebony cane, which he had been using to pound on the door. Bracing himself with it, he stared down at the rumpled, disheveled, bleary-eyed figure in front of him. The familiar silver eyes narrowed in mingled astonishment and gathering disapproval.

"What the hell happened to you?" he bit out.

Tabitha realized she was staring. Frantically she attempted to collect her scattered wits. "Dev," she managed weakly. "What are you doing here?"

"Isn't it rather obvious? I came to see you. Tabby, what on earth is going on here? You look awful." He scowled down at her, searching her face and the wrinkled black dress.

"Got run over by a herd of basilisks, I think," she got out in a thin voice. Maybe she was still dreaming. Perhaps she was still safely asleep on the couch and this was all some sort of crazy nightmare. Very cautiously she extended one hand and touched the unyielding surface of the blue, oxford cloth shirt he was wearing. "You're real, aren't you?" she groaned.

His scowl deepened and then he apparently decided he was getting nowhere trying to conduct a rational conversation on the doorstep. Stepping forward, he edged Tabitha aside and crossed the threshold into the chaotic room.

"Damn it to hell, Tabby. What went on here last night?" he snarled softly, scanning the disaster.

"Party," she explained succinctly.

"A party!" he snapped, eyes slitting ferociously.

"I turned thirty yesterday," she said. "And would you please stop shouting? My head is killing me."

Whatever Dev was going to say in response was cut off by another snore from the couch. He turned his head, clearly astounded.

In dreadful silence Tabitha listened as Ron Adams came awake with a muffled groan. Then, even as she watched, he sat up very slowly on the black couch, his dark eyes blinking balefully at the stranger with the ebony cane.

Dev, Tabitha realized, was absolutely thunderstruck. Even as that analysis was filtering through her confused mind, however, another realization dawned. As the shock in his rigid expression faded, it was being replaced by sheer rage.

Tabitha watched in morbid fascination as his steel gaze pinned her. Never had she seen this particular expression in a man's face. And she would happily live the rest of her life without ever witnessing it again. When he finally spoke, Dev's voice was as deadly as the secret sword in his cane.

"For the sake of formality let's run through a couple of quick explanations before I beat the living daylights out of you. *Who the hell is he?*"

CHAPTER EIGHT

HE HAD NEVER KNOWN THIS KIND of sheer, masculine outrage in his life, Dev realized vaguely through the haze of his fury. This emotion wasn't the cold, lethal anger he had felt toward the men who had threatened Tabitha. It wasn't the fatalistic, brooding feeling he had known for a while after the realization that his marriage was faltering. It wasn't the wary animosity he had been experiencing toward Delaney lately.

It was the primitive male rage that engulfed a man when he found his woman in a compromising situation with another male. Dev had never truly experienced the sensation before, but his instincts told him exactly what it was when the emotion washed over him.

Damn it to hell! He hadn't meant the reunion with Tabby to go like this at all! During the entire trip to Port Townsend, he had tantalized himself with daydreams which all revolved around the image of having Tabby in his arms. He had wanted only to hear her purr again.

Now he wanted to see real fear in her eyes.

He wanted her quivering beneath the force of his rage.

He wanted her throwing herself at his feet and pleading for his understanding.

He wanted her so terrified of him that she would

never again even think of waking up in the same room with another man; never even *look* at another man.

Especially not another man who only looked to be about twenty-five years old, by God!

But Tabitha wasn't shivering in terror or rushing to beg his forgiveness. She was holding her tousled head with both hands and glaring up at him in grim disgust. Dev had never seen her look at anyone in quite that way.

"If you don't stop shouting," she said with gentle dignity, "I'm going to have to ask you to leave."

"The hell you are! Who is he, Tabitha?"

"My name's Ron. Ron Adams." With grim determination Ron managed to get up off the couch. Cautiously he circled toward the door, leaving plenty of space between himself and the older man. "I, uh, was just on my way home. Honest. Bye, Tab. Great party. Happy birthday…"

Dev watched Ron's progress through evilly slitted eyes. At least this puppy was showing a bit of healthy fear. There was some satisfaction in that. "Don't rush off, Ron Adams. We have a few details to straighten out here."

"You leave him alone, Devlin Colter!' Tabitha hissed behind him.

Dev ignored her. He was having more success terrorizing Ron Adams, so he decided to pursue the task. "Just what the hell do you think you're doing spending the night with my woman?" He lowered his voice to that deceptively soft level that had been known to send chills down the spines of more resolute men than Ron Adams. When you are pushing forty and find yourself in a face-off with a twenty-five-year-old, you have a right to use a few tricks, Dev told himself.

"Look, Mr. Colter or whoever you are, I didn't know she was yours! That's the truth. Tell him, Tab!" Ron swung a pleading glance at Tabitha, urging her to defend him.

"I don't belong to anyone!" she stormed and then groaned as the sound of her own voice vibrated painfully through her head. "I wish you both would leave."

"What happened here last night?" Dev growled, paying no attention to her request. He concentrated on Ron Adams.

Ron put up a placating hand and shook his head. "Nothing," he declared earnestly. "I swear it. I came to Tab's birthday party with my sister and some friends. Had a few drinks. Then Tab and I started talking…" His voice trailed off weakly.

"Talking about what?" Dev prompted coldly.

"It's a bit fuzzy," Ron admitted morosely.

"The state of your memory might very well determine your physical condition when you leave this house." Dev waited with all the arrogant intimidation he could summon. It was a considerable amount and it had its effect.

"Animals," Ron remembered almost immediately. "That's all we talked about, wasn't it, Tab? Animals."

"Animals!" Dev thundered. He sent a ferocious glance at Tabitha. "*Animals!* You told *him* about the mating habits of medieval animals? How did you dare? You're only supposed to use that line on me! You have no right to go around discussing that sort of thing with every other male you come across! Tabby Graham, I really am going to beat you. I'm going to make certain you don't sit down for a week. Animals. I can't believe you actually went that far!"

"Why not?" she retorted spiritedly. "It worked so well on you I decided to try it out on another man. Field testing, so to speak."

"Field testing!" Dev realized he was nearly speechless with shock and outrage. He swung back to Ron Adams, who was almost safely out the door. "Listen to me, you young twerp. I'm going to let you go without breaking both of your legs only because I can see for myself that you didn't wind up in bed with Tabby. But if you ever come near her again, I won't be responsible for my actions, is that clear?"

"Very." Ron dashed gratefully for the door.

"And just forget everything you heard here about the mating habits of medieval animals. Understand?"

"Yes, sir," Ron assured him quickly, his hand on the doorknob. "Actually, I don't think we got past dragons. That's the truth. Scout's honor."

"You discussed dragons?" Dev asked ominously. Tabitha had called *him* a dragon. "What did she tell you about dragons?"

"I...I'm not sure. It's all a bit vague," Ron explained hastily.

"Think hard," Dev advised grimly.

"Oh, Dev, will you cut it out? I'm sick and tired of all this male nonsense," Tabitha complained.

"Not until I hear what you told him about dragons." He saw Ron trying to gauge his chances of escaping through the front door and swung his cane up to bar his way. Intimidatingly he leaned toward the younger man. "Try very hard to remember, kid."

Ron swallowed awkwardly. "I, uh, think I asked her how dragons made love or something."

"And what did she tell you?"

Ron frowned in desperate concentration. "She, er, said something about them doing it magnificently, I think."

"Did she?" Dev smiled his best highwayman's smile and slowly lowered the cane. "She ought to know. She's had personal experience of the matter. I'm the dragon in question, you see."

Ron gulped. "I was beginning to get that impression. If you'll excuse me, I'll be on my way." He didn't wait for permission, moving down the steps with unsteady haste.

Dev watched his fleeing foe with savage satisfaction; then he turned back to confront Tabitha, who was sinking slowly down into a nearby chair, still clutching her head.

"What the hell did you want with a kid like that?" he muttered. "He must be a good five or six years younger than you!"

"It's the latest trend," she gritted, massaging her temples. "Younger men start looking very good when a woman hits thirty, you know."

"No, I didn't know! Damn it, Tabby, I'm about at the end of my patience. What kind of game are you playing, anyway?" He stalked closer, wanting to see a little terror in her. But she had closed her eyes in obvious suffering.

"The theory is that you can train them properly if you get them young," she explained. "Older men are rather set in their ways, you know. They're sneakier, less trustworthy."

"Tabby!"

"Yes sir, give me a younger man every time," she said, leaning her head back against the chair cushion. "They're cute. Eager to please, too."

"I'll bet!" Dev stalked forward another step, his knuckles whitening as he gripped the handle of the cane. "My God, Tabby, you're really walking the edge this morning, do you know that? The only thing saving your neck right now is the fact that I know you didn't actually go to bed with him!"

"How do you know?" she taunted.

Where was she getting the courage to defy him? Dev wondered furiously. Why wasn't she cowering and apologizing and generally pleading for mercy? Belatedly it occurred to him that no one had ever said tabby cats lacked guts. "Well, for starters, you're both still fully dressed," he mocked brutally. "You've even got your pantyhose on. Most women who've spent the night in wild abandon with a young stud lose their pantyhose somewhere along the way."

"Oh." Tabitha opened her eyes and glared balefully down at her stocking-shod feet. "I always said you were very observant," she sighed.

"Furthermore, it's obvious he slept on that small sofa. There really isn't room for two on it. And it looks like you slept on the other one. One of your shoes is still on the cushion," he added derisively, flicking a scathing glance at the article of furniture in question.

"What good eyes you have, grandpa."

"Don't call me grandpa!" Dev roared. It was the last straw. He dropped the cane and closed his hands around Tabitha's shoulders, hauling her unceremoniously to her feet. "I may not be twenty-five any longer, but I'm willing to bet I can get further than that young puppy did last night! Shall we find out, Tabby? Let's see if a few years of experience make any difference! If you'd spent the night with me, you wouldn't have awakened this morning still wearing your pantyhose!"

"Maybe I'm not interested in your kind of experience," she shot back bravely. "Maybe I don't want a man who lies to me. Who makes me think he's someone he's not. A man who deliberately leads me to believe he's gentle and vulnerable and shy. A man who makes me think he's a lot like me! Who *deceives* me!'

"Tabby, I didn't deceive you!" Oh, God, he'd been afraid of this. How was he going to fight the accusations? How could he explain why he'd been another man when he was with her?

"Yes, you did. You go around cutting throats for a living with that…that sword you carry. You're not a travel agent!" she exclaimed furiously.

"Yes, I am a travel agent, damn it!'

"You see? Lying is second nature to you now that you're nearly forty! You've probably been doing it so long you don't know how to tell the truth! Are you going to try to pretend you're the emotionally sensitive and vulnerable man I thought I met on that ship?"

"Damn right, I am!" he blazed.

"Hah! It's too late, Dev. I've seen you in action. I know you were only using me. I made a nice cover for you, didn't I? Who would expect a real, live secret agent to hang around with a woman like me?"

"What makes you think you know what I do for a living?"

"Steve Waverly told me all about it during that pleasant little wait I had while you figured out I was never coming back from the rest room!" she fumed, remembering.

Dev sucked in his breath. "Did he?"

Tabitha frowned even more severely. "Why are you turning pale?"

"Probably because I'm realizing that he meant to kill you. He would never have told you anything if he'd intended to let you go free. I should have cut the bastard's throat."

"You see? That's exactly what I mean! An emotionally sensitive, gentle, vulnerable man doesn't go around threatening to cut other men's throats!"

"Tabby, you're going to listen to me if I have to beat the facts into you!" He gave her a small shake and saw her eyes widen abruptly. But it wasn't with fear. "Tabby?" he prodded with sudden anxiety. "What's wrong?"

"I think I'm going to be sick," she announced gravely.

"Oh, hell."

Her hand flew to her mouth. "Go away, Dev. Just go *away!*" She tried to twist free of his grip but Dev only gathered her closer.

"Which way is the bathroom?" he demanded. When she gestured mutely, he started purposefully forward. It was a little awkward holding onto her and balancing himself without the cane but they made it in time. Barely. He held her gently as she leaned over the porcelain bowl, and wiped her face with a damp cloth afterward. "Feel better?" he asked softly when it was all over. She was shivering now, not with fear but from reaction to being so ill.

Tabitha nodded but for the first time that morning her eyes slid away from his and Dev realized she was embarrassed. "Thank you," she said very formally.

"Come on, you need a good hot shower and a decent

breakfast." Holding her against his side, he industriously began getting her out of the black dress she was wearing.

"No, Dev, please!"

But she was really too weak to resist him, although she slapped futilely at his hands. When he simply ignored her small struggles, she appeared to give up and submitted meekly to being undressed and put into a hot shower.

"You didn't wear a bra last night!" he accused as he folded the clothing she had been wearing.

"Haven't worn one for several days," she retorted from inside the shower, where she was leaning precariously against the tile wall. "It's part of the new me."

"You're only supposed to go without one when you're trying to seduce me," he flung back in annoyance. "Damn it, forget it. We'll discuss this later. How's your head?"

"Hurts."

"Here, I found this in your medicine cupboard." He opened the shower door and pushed two tablets into her mouth. Then he handed her a glass of water and watched while she obediently swallowed them. "Ever had a hangover before?" he demanded critically, surveying her gently rounded body with a kind of professional interest. She was so soft and inviting. He'd been dreaming about her for days. It was hard to believe he had her back within reach finally.

When she became aware of his scrutiny her hands went up to cover her full breasts and she deliberately turned her back to him. "No," she mumbled. "I've never had a hangover."

"What the hell got into you, Tabby?" he groaned, his

eyes on the curve of her backside. Unable to resist, he put out a hand and shaped the wet, tantalizing globe of her buttock. She flinched and stepped nervously out of reach but continued to keep her back to him.

"I told you, it was my birthday party. I decided to make a new start. I was going to be a phoenix rising from the ashes."

Dev set his teeth and shut the shower door. He really didn't have the heart to grill her when she looked so washed out and weak. Later, he vowed, as he selected a huge towel from the closet. Later he would finish reading her the riot act. He glanced down at the towel and saw that it was embroidered with the head of a unicorn.

Inside the shower Tabitha turned her face up to the pounding water and tried to think. She really was feeling much better but it seemed safer somehow to go on pretending to be quite weak. Ever since she had warned him she was going to be sick, Dev had been treating her with great gentleness. His touch had been reassuring and kind; she had to admire a man who could deal with a sick woman. Most men were far too squeamish to handle that kind of scene.

Of course, a man who went around slicing people with his sword cane probably didn't have a squeamish attitude toward much of anything, she told herself violently. On the other hand, you wouldn't expect such a man to be quite so gentle with someone who was genuinely ill, either.

Well, she couldn't stay in the shower forever. Sooner or later she was going to have to emerge and find out exactly what Devlin Colter was doing in Port Townsend. With a groan she turned off the taps and opened the door a couple of inches. "Would you please hand me a towel?" she asked very politely.

"Come on out, honey. I'll dry you off."

"No, Dev, really, I'd rather…" But he was already pushing open the door and hauling her carefully out. There was nothing else she could do except stand quietly while he began to rub her down. He stood with his legs braced a couple of feet apart, and she realized that was the way he balanced himself when he didn't have his cane.

His hands on her body were intimate but they made no demands. It was the touch of a lover who wasn't intent on making love just at the moment but who still felt possessive. Tabitha shivered.

"Relax," he growled. "I'm not going to hurt you."

"You were threatening to beat me," she reminded him.

"I still might, but not until you're feeling more normal," he grunted. "There." He folded the towel around her breasts, his hands lingering on the full curves for a few seconds. "You go get dressed while I see about something for breakfast."

Tabitha nodded, turning gratefully away to make her escape.

"And this time put on a bra!'

She emerged cautiously from the bedroom after delaying the inevitable as long as possible. Feeling more normal in a pair of jeans and a loose turquoise and yellow striped long-sleeved top, she peered around the corner into the kitchen before entering. Dev had collected his cane again, hooking it over a kitchen chair while he worked industriously on an omelette.

"Come on in, I'm not going to bite you. Not yet, at any rate."

"I'm not afraid of you," she muttered. Deliberately she sauntered into the room and sat down with what she hoped was a careless sprawl.

"Maybe you should be," he advised laconically. "Finding you standing amid the aftermath of an orgy has not put me into a good frame of mind."

"It wasn't an orgy! I keep telling you, it was my birthday party."

"What did you do? Invite every young male in town so you could pick and choose among them?"

"I invited everyone I knew. Period. Some of that crowd included young men, yes." She lifted her chin defiantly. "I decided to take a few lessons from my recent cruise."

"Decided to try your hand at seducing everything in trousers?"

"Why not? I had so much luck with you!" she tossed back lightly.

"Really? If you were getting so good at that sort of thing, what went wrong last night?"

Tabitha winced. "That's none of your business."

Dev glanced up, one brow rising curiously. He didn't seem so angry now, Tabitha decided. Why not? Or perhaps a better question would be, why had he been so angry in the first place? Why was he even here, come to that?

"Did you really tell that kid that I made love magnificently?" he drawled, sliding the omelette out of the pan and onto a plate.

"We were discussing dragons at the time, not you!"

"The hell you were," he contradicted gently, setting the food in front of her. "I'm the only dragon whose mating habits you're familiar with. You told me yourself the bestiaries don't have much information on the topic."

"Dev, why are you here?" she demanded roughly, eyeing the omelette with caution. Was her stomach really steady enough for food now?

"I'm here to collect you, tabby cat." He poured himself a cup of coffee, shoved aside a tray of leftover cheese sticks which was sitting on his side of the table and sat down.

Tabitha heard the resolute note in his voice and bit nervously into a forkful of omelette. She would not let him put her off stride again. "Why?"

"Because I want you," he said simply and then leaned back to sip his coffee just as if he were discussing the weather. He watched her intently over the rim of the cup. "And I need you, Tabby."

"Need me! Men who carry swords in their canes don't need people like me!'

"Yes, we do. I do, at any rate," he countered softly. "You were falling in love with me on that ship, weren't you, Tabby?"

She flinched. "What if I was? I got over it in a hurry just as soon as I found out you had lied to me and used me."

"I didn't use you! What exactly did Waverly tell you?"

Her eyes narrowed. "That you were a government agent and that you had made a routine pickup for your department on St. Regis. He had decided to relieve you of the film you collected in that alley. What did happen in that alley, Dev? Who was it you left stuffed into the trash container?"

Dev hesitated and then lifted one shoulder indifferently. "Someone who tried to intercept the film."

"That's why you were all beaten up?"

Dev nodded once, watching her warily. "I very nearly lost, Tabby. With a little less luck it would have been me who got stuffed into that trash bin. I'm getting too old for that kind of work. I'd been telling Delaney that for two years."

"Who's Delaney?"

"Washington, D.C. type. You know, I told you how they were. Hard and cold. I used to work for him until my accident."

"Oh, yes, the famous accident. Did you lie to me about that, too? Were you really in a car wreck?" she demanded scathingly.

"Tabby…"

"Answer me!"

"Not exactly," he grated harshly. "On my last assignment for Delaney I had a little trouble with a couple of terrorists I'd been told to stop. They nearly stopped me, instead."

Tabitha winced in spite of her resolution to remain implacable. "Oh, Dev! What happened?" Her eyes betrayed the flash of concern she was trying to stifle.

"Against my better judgment, against my *instincts,* I agreed to meet with an informer. The guy was supposed to be supplying us with reliable information. The night I turned up for the rendezvous he turned up with the two guys I'd been trailing. I wound up with a bullet in my left knee and a few other assorted bruises."

"What happened to them?" she asked quietly.

"One escaped. The informer. A friend of mine got him for me later."

"And the two terrorists?" she whispered.

"Tabby…" he began.

"What happened to them?"

Dev sighed. "I shot both of them. There, are you satisfied? It's what you wanted to hear, isn't it? That I'm a violent sort of man? Capable of shooting people or slicing their throats? Tabby, that rendezvous was miles from the nearest town. I nearly bled to death before I got help. As it was, the doctor wanted to amputate my leg. I didn't dare let him give me any anesthetic for fear he'd go ahead and cut it off while I was under! I had to fight to keep him from doing anything drastic until Delaney got me to a decent hospital!"

"My God, Dev," she breathed, horrified at the bleak, remembered pain she could see in his silver eyes. "I didn't realize…"

"Afterward I told Delaney I'd had enough. I wanted out. He said all I needed was a few months to recover and I'd be chomping at the bit to get back to work. Tabby, I really am a travel agent. I opened the business after I got back on my feet. I had done a lot of traveling in my work for Delaney's department, and I figured if there was one thing I knew about, it was globe-trotting. I've been working hard for months to establish the business." Dev broke off and sighed. "Then Delaney contacted me a few weeks ago and asked if I'd make the pickup for him on St. Regis. The film was important, he said. It's got something to do with laser technology. Delaney thought it would be simple for me to take the cruise under my legitimate cover as a travel agent. And I…"

"You what?" she prompted grimly.

"Hell, I don't know. Maybe I was curious to see if he was right. He claimed that once I got my feet wet again, I'd be ready to go back to work on a full-time basis. I don't know, Tabby. I only knew that something was missing in my life. I was putting the travel business together all right, but it wasn't enough. I wasn't satisfied. And Delaney had once been a good friend. I agreed to do the job for him. But I started regretting it as soon as I got on the boat. I knew I was no longer cut out for that kind of work. Then you came to my rescue in that alley, and I began to realize what it was that had been missing in my life. It wasn't the excitement of working for Delaney. It was having someone care for me and love me and shower me with attention. What I really wanted was a sweet, gentle tabby cat who would curl up in my lap and make love to me."

Tabitha felt the warm flush rise in her face as she steadfastly refused to meet his glance. "I'm not going to play tabby cat any longer, Dev. I felt like an absolute fool the last time. You used me. Oh, maybe not as a cover for your work, although I have a hunch it suited your purposes to have me hanging around for that reason, too. But you took advantage of my unquestioning assumption that you and I were two of a kind. You more or less lied to me, Dev. When I think of what an idiot I was…"

"You weren't an idiot!"

Her head came up swiftly. "Oh, yes, I was. Do you know how I feel every time I think back to that night when I supposedly seduced you? I actually thought you were too shy to make the first move, did you know that? I thought you were such a sensitive man you were terrified of forcing yourself on me!"

"I *was* terrified of doing exactly that," he cut in savagely. "I knew you'd run for cover if I came on too strong. It seemed safest to let you set the pace until you felt comfortable with me."

"You mean you decided to let me wander so far into the trap I wouldn't be able to escape when you shut the door! But I'm out now, Dev, and I'm a different woman from the one who wandered so blithely inside. I learned a lot on that cruise!"

"Don't ever forget that what you learned, you learned from me!" he snapped abruptly. "I know what the problem is here: you've discovered the passionate side of your nature and now you're determined to find out what you've been missing. You want to be free to explore the side of you that's been locked up all these years. But if you think I set that side of you free just so you could turn around and throw yourself at every young stud who comes along, you're out of your head! You belong to me now!" The coffee cup crashed down onto the table as Dev straightened and leaned forward in his chair. His hard face was set in fierce lines as he challenged her.

"I'm a changed woman and there's nothing you can do about it! I'll live my life exactly the way I want to live it, and if I happen to feel like running around with nice young men like Ron Adams, I will, by God!"

With an obvious effort of will Dev brought his voice back under control. "Tabby, Tabby, I didn't come here to yell at you."

"No? You're doing a pretty good job of it."

He groaned in exasperation. "Honey, my instincts all tell me there's no way you could have changed fundamentally in the few days that have passed since you left the cruise. That's the real reason I let you and your young friend off so lightly this morning. I know damn well that whatever happened here last night, you weren't really very likely to have gotten yourself involved in a genuine one-night stand!"

"Why not? I did with you!"

"I'm different," he told her evenly.

She blinked owlishly, not trusting his expression of utter conviction. "What makes you so sure of that?"

"Instinct."

"Oh, shut up!" She reached for her coffee cup, glowering down at the dark brew.

"It's true. Tabby, I survived for years on my instincts. Let me show you that they can be trusted. Let me show you that you really do belong to me."

Tabitha eyed him uneasily. "You might trust your instincts, Dev, but I don't trust you."

A flicker of pain flashed briefly in his eyes, but his voice was steady as he said quietly, "Okay, so you don't trust me. Are you going to admit you're afraid of me?"

"I'm not afraid of you," she informed him aloofly.

He gazed at her consideringly. "What if I told you I came here to return the favor you did me on board ship?"

"You mean repay me for getting you out of that alley?"

He smiled slightly, a small, wicked twist of his mouth that stirred the delicate hair at the nape of her neck. "I meant the favor you did when you seduced me.

One good turn deserves another, Tabby. It strikes me that you've never really been properly seduced. Your ex-husband obviously didn't know how, and lately you've been making all the moves yourself. It's time you learned one of the fundamental pleasures of life, honey, and who better to learn it from than the man who's going to marry you?"

CHAPTER NINE

IT WASN'T THE WICKED SMILE OR THE blunt masculine aggression. It wasn't the fact that Dev had actually spoken of marriage. It wasn't even because she had been feeling uncomfortably hung over and was therefore in a weakened condition.

None of those had anything to do with the decision she had made, Tabitha thought resentfully as she whipped a feather duster over a shelf of books at The Manticore. No, she had accepted the date with Dev because of the flash of grim desperation she had seen in his silver eyes. It was that strange urgency coupled with a mental image of him nearly bleeding to death on some lonely road two years previously that had done her in, Tabitha knew.

Damn! What was the matter with her? Why hadn't she simply kicked him out of the house? Morosely she dusted a shelf of science fiction books and then abandoned the task altogether in favor of sitting on her stool behind the counter. The shop was empty at the moment; there was no distraction to stop her from dwelling on her own stupidity. The conversation at the breakfast table that morning kept replaying through her mind.

"Marry you! Not a chance!" she'd choked.

"You're afraid of me."

"I am not afraid of you," she'd gritted, meaning every word.

"Then prove it by having dinner with me, tonight."

"Dev, this is ridiculous. First you were talking about marriage and now you're discussing dinner!'

"One step at a time. Tabby, at least come out to dinner with me," he'd ordered softly. It was then that she'd seen the flash of urgent need in his eyes and her resolve had faltered. In the end she'd grumblingly agreed to have dinner with him, and now she could only sit, chin in hand, and berate herself.

Because she was in love with him.

She'd known that the moment she'd opened the door this morning and found him on the step. No, Tabitha corrected herself dismally, she'd known it last night when she'd looked down at the dragon in the carpet and realized through the haze of alcohol that she had no business telling Ron Adams about the medieval version of the birds and the bees. The only man she wanted to seduce was Dev Colter.

Travel agent! Likely story. But what the devil was he doing here in Port Townsend if he wasn't telling her the essential truth? If he'd only been using her on board the ship would he have bothered tracking her down now? And what was the meaning of that desperate determination she had sensed in him?

What if Dev Colter were now telling her the truth? He was the man she had rescued from that alley on St. Regis, after all, even if she hadn't known the real reason for his being there. One thing hadn't altered: when she had come across him in that brick alley he had needed her badly and she had taken care of him. She would have done the same even had she known he'd left his assailant behind stuffed in a trash bin. There was no way she could have turned from him in that moment.

Now here he was in Port Townsend telling her that he needed her again. He wasn't bruised and bleeding this time, but she had seen pain in his eyes and she wasn't at all sure she would be able to turn from him this go round, either. He was an annoying, demanding, somewhat deceptive sort of beast, but he was *her* beast, her very own dragon.

Tabitha sighed and reflected on that thought for a moment. Something about having rescued a man and then seducing him gave a woman a very possessive sort of feeling toward him. And the feeling must be somewhat mutual because she'd seen the aggressive fury in those silver eyes this morning when Dev had found Ron Adams amid the shambles of her birthday party.

She shuddered as the shop door opened. It occurred to Tabitha that she was very glad Dev's "instincts" had told him nothing serious had happened between herself and Ron. She didn't like to think of what he might have done if he'd felt the younger man had poached on his territory.

"Good morning, Tab," Sandra Adams called as she came through the door. "Just wanted to stop by and tell you what a fantastic party that was last night! Had a great time. Jim is absolutely the most interesting fisherman I've ever encountered. The strong, silent type, you know. At one with the sea and the storms," she continued melodramatically, "a part of the primeval forces of nature, etcetera, etcetera. Love those primeval forces.

And what the heck did you do to my little brother, by the way?"

Tabitha grimaced as her friend lounged against the counter and regarded her with amused eyes. "He fell asleep on my couch."

"And awakened to the roar of a dragon, according to him." Sandra grinned. "Naturally I hastened over to hear more about the beast." The shop door chimed just as she spoke and automatically Sandra glanced over her shoulder to see who was entering. "Don't tell me. The dragon, right?"

Dev arched a dark brow as he walked in, carrying two Styrofoam cups of coffee carefully cradled in one large hand. He used the ebony cane to shove the door shut behind him. "My reputation seems to have preceded me," he mocked dryly.

"No wonder my little brother was overwhelmed. You must have a good fifteen years on the lad."

"Don't remind me," Dev growled feelingly. "You're the kid's sister?"

"Sandra, this is Devlin Colter." Tabitha hastily made introductions, aware of a strange feeling of wariness as she saw the speculative gleam in Sandra's eyes. The hint of jealousy vanished almost at once, however, because Dev totally ignored the other woman's incipient interest. Just as on the ship, he seemed oblivious to the curiosity or the speculation in the eyes of any woman but Tabitha. Tabitha knew a measure of happy satisfaction which she instantly tried to squelch. "Dev and I met on the cruise," she explained weakly.

"It must have been some cruise," Sandra observed cheerfully to Dev. "Tab came back a changed woman."

"Not really," Dev murmured, handing a cup of coffee to Tabitha. He smiled gently as she avoided his gaze by hurriedly snapping open the plastic lid. "She just learned a little more about herself, that's all."

"Sandy's quite right," Tabitha announced defiantly as she swallowed a large sip of steaming coffee. "I'm changed."

Dev just smiled again and peeled off his own lid.

"Well, if the two of you will excuse me, I've got some grocery shopping to do," Sandra declared brightly, heading for the door. "I see that little dress shop next to you has closed, Tab. Going to lease the space and expand The Manticore?"

"I haven't decided yet," Tabitha said honestly, her mind not really on the subject. "I'm thinking about it. Goodbye, Sandy. Thanks for coming to the party last night."

"My pleasure, believe me!" Sandra shut the door behind her with a chuckle.

"Resigned yourself to having dinner with me tonight?" Dev asked mildly as he glanced curiously around the shop.

"Dev, I want you to understand that this is only a dinner date, nothing more," she told him severely. "Is that very clear?"

"Meaning I'm not supposed to seduce you?"

"Meaning we can have a pleasant evening if you behave yourself! I won't be pushed, Dev. I have a lot of serious thinking to do about us, and I don't want you trying to maneuver me."

"Yes, ma'am," he agreed humbly. "Let's just say we're getting together for the sake of old times. How's that?"

Tabitha glared at him suspiciously, declining to answer that one.

She was still eyeing Dev suspiciously that night as she sat across from him in the charming harbor-front restaurant he had chosen. But she felt reasonably able to hold her own that evening. Dev had been the model of gentlemanly behavior since the moment he had arrived at her door in a subdued, dark, linen jacket and trousers. She herself was wearing a white knit dress trimmed in black.

His refined manners had reestablished her own sense of equilibrium but she knew him much better now than she had on the ship, and Tabitha's innate caution was still in effect as they ordered lobster soufflés and celery, radish and olive salads.

"Stop worrying," Dev drawled softly. "I'll warn you when the seduction is about to start. Just as you warned me."

Her brows drew together in a fierce line. "What do you mean by that?"

"Well, first there was that charming kiss on deck in the moonlight," he mused. "I got my hopes up, but nothing came of it that night. The morning you met me at your cabin door wearing that loose, little cotton thing without any bra on underneath, I told myself that there was still a chance."

"You were laughing at me," she accused tightly. "All the time. God, I feel like such a fool."

"Tabby, I wasn't laughing at you," he said evenly. "I wanted you to make love to me so badly, and I was so afraid you'd lose your nerve."

"Too bad I didn't."

"Don't say that. The night you seduced me was the most memorable evening of my life," he said wistfully. "I wouldn't trade that memory for anything on earth."

She regarded him skeptically, desperately wanting to believe their night together had meant that much to him. "I'm sure you've enjoyed many similar evenings."

"I've never spent another evening like that one," he said simply.

"Hah!"

"It's true," he said. "I've never had another woman really make love to me. And you were making love that night, weren't you? Not just having a fling with me?"

"You've been married!" she protested. "Or was that a lie, too?"

A flare of anger at the accusation lit his eyes and then was firmly repressed. "I was married," he confirmed. "But she was in love with the image of my job, not with me. That's why she left me, Tabby, after I nearly lost my leg. She wanted a James Bond, and I was only willing to give her a mundane businessman."

Tabitha bit her lip as a pang of sympathy welled up inside. She knew what it was to be married for all the wrong reasons. "Is that the truth?"

"Tabby, I've always told you the truth except about the reason I was in that alley on St. Regis. Frankly, I wasn't free to tell you those facts. Not until you found them out the hard way by having a gun held to your head. I felt so damn guilty about getting you into that mess, honey. It was all my fault. Afterward I couldn't think of anything else but finding you and straightening everything out between us. But you were gone when I got back to the ship."

"I couldn't stand the thought of facing you after that. I was so angry. And I felt like an idiot for having mistaken a tough, hard-bitten secret agent type for a mild-mannered, gentlemanly travel agent who was…"

"…vulnerable, sensitive and shy. I know," he finished wryly. "But, honey, that's exactly what I am. Well, maybe I'm not particularly *shy*," he conceded honestly, "but I am vulnerable and sensitive and…"

"Dev, I think we'd better go on to another topic before I pour this excellent Chardonnay over your head," Tabitha threatened violently.

His mouth hardened and for an instant she thought he might override her demand. But he didn't. Instead he obediently changed the subject, asking her about Port Townsend and how long she'd had The Manticore. In a surprisingly short time Tabitha found herself chatting freely once again, just as she had on the ship. Slowly Tabitha began to relax. In spite of all the uncertainty, this was where she wanted to be and this was the man she wanted to be with tonight. She loved Dev Colter.

Dev watched her gradual relaxation with a sense of gratification. It was working. She was rapidly turning back into the charming, soft, feminine creature she had been on board ship. He was managing to undo some of the damage. She was seeing him now less and less as the ruthless agent she had watched in action on the island and more as the ordinary, non-threatening businessman he truly was. Dev began to relax a little himself. He hadn't realized just how tense he had been for the past few days.

It had taken careful planning and thought to decide

just when to pursue her to Port Townsend. His instincts had warned him to give her a little time to get over her hurt and resentment. But his instincts had very nearly kept him away too long, he thought in annoyance. Walking in on that little morning-after scene today had told him that much. How did the tabby cat dare play around with her newfound self-confidence?

Grimly Dev tamped down the rising irritation. He had arrived in time. There would be no repeat performance. Tabitha would not be practicing her unique seduction techniques on anyone except him from now on! Belatedly he realized that something of his determination must be showing in his face, because she was eyeing him a little warily from the other side of the table. Dev smiled blandly.

"Have some more wine, Tabby. It's very good. I had no idea your northwestern wines were becoming so competitive with California's."

The caution in her eyes eased once again and she went on to tell him about the thriving wine industries in Washington and Oregon. Dev listened attentively. He found her so soothing to listen to, he realized vaguely. Soothing and charming and sweetly exciting.

By the time he drove her home after dinner Dev was feeling quite certain of his progress. Tabitha, he decided happily, was very nearly back in his lap. The wariness in her had diminished to almost nothing and the warmth was back in her sherry-colored eyes. She hadn't resisted at all when he'd taken her hand to walk her back out to the car, and he felt quite sure she wouldn't resist when he took her in his arms later. Once he had her safely in his arms, he told himself, everything would be perfect.

He was right up to a point.

"Is this the beginning of the seduction?" she asked with grave interest as he closed the door of her cottage behind him, hooked his cane over the knob and started to pull her close.

He smiled sensually down at her, inhaling the tantalizing, female fragrance of her hair and skin. "I do believe it is," he murmured. Actually, the seduction had been going on all evening, but if she didn't realize it, who was he to tell her? His smile widened, lighting his eyes as he traced the line of her cheek with his finger. God, it was good to be touching her again. So very, very good. Dev sighed softly and bent his head to taste her lips.

"Well, in that case, this is where I say good night," Tabitha declared firmly and planted both of her small hands against his chest.

Dev blinked in surprise. "What?"

"You heard me. Good night, Dev. I had a lovely evening." She smiled a bit too brilliantly for his liking.

"Tabby…!"

"You have to go now, Dev, because I haven't made up my mind about us yet. I still have a lot of thinking to do," she explained very kindly.

He bit back the rather violent four-letter word which came to his lips. He wouldn't push her. She was almost back where she belonged, and he could afford to wait until she came the rest of the way of her own free will. He had the rest of his life to think about. Surely he could hold off for another night or so before securing his future? Where was all that much-vaunted patience he had learned through the years? With a supreme effort of will he summoned another smile and bent down to brush her lips.

"Thank you for trusting me enough to come out with me tonight, Tabby," he murmured, injecting as much humble gratitude into his voice as he could manage under the circumstances. "I'll call you in the morning."

For just an instant she hesitated, a worried expression coming to her eyes. "Have you got a place to stay?" she asked a little gruffly.

It took fortitude, but Dev succeeded in passing up the obvious opportunity. What would she do if he said he had nowhere to go tonight? Offer him a couch? He'd never know because he had already made up his mind to go on playing the gentleman. "I'm staying in one of those old Victorian monstrosities someone has converted into a bed and breakfast place. Don't worry about me, Tabby."

"I won't," she agreed with alacrity. "Good night, Dev."

"Good night, Tabby." He hesitated wistfully, but could think of no further excuse for staying. Without another word he grasped his cane and let himself out the door. Patience, he instructed himself grimly. You're supposed to be good at waiting. Just give her a little more time and she'll be yours. The woman's in love with you. She had to be in love with him, damn it!

Dev was still consoling himself with that promise four days later as he dressed for yet another evening out with Tabitha Graham. She had to be in love with him; he refused to consider any other possibility. But why the hell was she insisting on keeping him at arm's length?

With a savage twist, he finished knotting his tie and

reached for the jacket hanging on the chair. Automatically he checked for his keys and wallet and then headed for the door of the room. Was she playing some kind of game with him? Punishing him perhaps for not being the man she had wanted him to be on board ship? Or was she just uncertain of herself?

If it was uncertainty, he had to decide how long to let it go on before putting a stop to this nonsense. If she was playing games, he would damn well put a halt to them as fast as possible. And if she was trying to punish him… He winced at the thought. Perhaps he deserved it. Down in the tiny parking lot of the old Victorian Inn he slammed the rental car in gear and pulled out into the street, heading for Tabby's little cottage. One way or another he had to find out what she thought she was doing, and then he had to put a stop to it. His patience was nearly gone and all his instincts were coming uneasily alive in warning.

Warning of what? That Tabby might really have changed? That she might have become a harder, slightly vicious little cat? No, he didn't want to believe that. He couldn't believe it. He had seen the gentle compassion in her eyes too often during the past few days. She couldn't have changed so fundamentally.

So why was he feeling that sense of restless unease again tonight? God, he hated these prickly sensations of impending disaster, even if he did occasionally owe his life to their warning signals.

Tonight was the night, he decided grimly, his hands tightening on the steering wheel. Tonight he would settle matters once and for all. Tabitha belonged in his bed, and the sooner she rediscovered that fact, the better for both of them. This fencing game she was playing with him was going to drive him out of his mind. He had been so sure that she'd surrender right away. After all, she *loved* him.

God help him if she didn't.

With admirable self-mastery, he hid the growing sense of desperation he was feeling as he took Tabitha out on yet another dinner date. This time she had recommended an expensive French restaurant housed in yet another of the restored Victorian homes for which the town was famed.

"One of the best examples of Victorian architecture north of San Francisco," Tabitha had told him proudly as she had taken him through Port Townsend the day before. "We've been designated a National Historic District, you know."

"I didn't know," he'd murmured, wondering what she would do if he just dragged her down onto the grass of the nearest park and made love to her right then and there. But of course he hadn't. He was a gentleman.

But tonight urgent instincts were overriding the refined, sensitive gentleman in him. Dev knew he had to get things settled. His nerves, once thought by many to be made of steel, weren't going to survive this torture much longer.

"A new piece of jewelry?" he asked politely halfway through the shrimp in cognac cream sauce that they had both ordered. He peered at the necklace more closely.

"Do you like it?" she asked excitedly. "A friend of mine made it. It's a centaur. Half man, half horse. Supposed to be a very lusty animal."

As soon as the words were out of her mouth Dev

knew she regretted having dragged the topic of sex into the conversation. He saw the pink tinge in her cheeks and smiled to himself. At least the concept of sex was also on her mind!

"Lustier than dragons?" he asked innocently.

She coughed and reached for her wineglass. "Well, as I told you, no one seems to know much about the sex habits of dragons…"

"Except you," he reminded her bluntly.

"If you don't mind, I would prefer to change the subject," she replied loftily.

"Whatever you say, honey."

She could change the subject, but damned if he was going to let her get away with forgetting about sex altogether! Tonight he was going to make love to her and still these nagging, restless prickles of warning which had been haunting him all afternoon. He needed the reassurance now of having her back in his arms.

"Will you come in for a nightcap?" she asked easily at the door later on that evening. She'd invited him in for the preceding two nights and had found him simple enough to get rid of afterward, Dev thought wryly. He hadn't yet given her a reason to think tonight would be different.

"Thank you, Tabby. I'd like that."

He watched her disappear into the kitchen and then he carefully lowered himself to one knee in front of the fireplace and began building a blaze on the hearth. He was getting to his feet, using the cane as a lever, when she returned a short time later with two brandies in snifters. Dev winced and then smiled bravely.

"What's the matter?" she demanded in immediate

concern. "Is your leg bothering you tonight?" Hastily she set down the brandies and came forward to help him to the couch.

"A little. It'll be fine in a moment. All that walking around town yesterday afternoon might have been a bit much."

"I shouldn't have run you all over the place looking at Victorian houses," she chastised herself, assisting him onto the couch. "Here, have some brandy."

Gratefully he accepted the snifter. She sat down beside him and frowned intently until he took a sip and then assured her his leg was better in its present position. "I'll just have to stay off of it for a few minutes. It'll be fine by the time I leave."

Since he didn't intend to leave until morning that would probably not be a lie, he told himself. A night in Tabby's bed would be more than enough medicine to soothe the slight, aching twinge he had experienced when he'd used the cane to get to his feet a moment ago. Then he noticed she was still frowning.

"That's something I want to talk to you about, Dev," she began very precisely.

"Leaving?" He tensed but hid the reaction with a faint whimsical smile. "Already? I haven't even finished my brandy."

"I don't mean tonight," she countered carefully. "I mean for good. What exactly are your plans, Dev? How long will you be staying here in Port Townsend?" She raised her eyes determinedly to meet his quizzical gaze.

He took a long breath and let it out slowly. "For good, I think."

"For good!" The brandy sloshed precariously in her snifter as she stared at him. "What are you talking about?"

"About opening a travel agency in that shop next to yours, the one that's going to be for lease soon," he told her flatly, holding her eyes with his own. "About moving permanently from Houston to Port Townsend. About marrying you."

He watched the expressions chase each other across her sensitive features. She hadn't been prepared for anything quite so blatant tonight and it showed. Well, the waiting was over as far as he was concerned. There was no reason not to be blunt.

"But, Dev, surely you aren't prepared to make a major decision like moving to Port Townsend on the spur of the moment! I mean, there are so many things to consider...."

"I can't really see you in Houston," he remarked blandly. "So I think I will have to be the one to do the moving. You're not a Houston type, you see, just as you aren't a Washington, D.C. type."

The snifter in her hand trembled slightly. "And what type are you?" she asked anxiously.

"The type who was born to run a travel agency in Port Townsend. Tabby, why have you been keeping me at a distance for the past few days?" he asked with a hint of the aggression he had been repressing all evening.

She licked her lips cautiously. He could read the sudden wariness in her eyes. She knew he had just taken over the direction of the evening, and she wasn't at all sure how to stop him. "I've told you, Dev, I don't intend to allow you to rush me into anything. I don't want to make another mistake the way I did on the ship. I want to be sure of what I'm doing this time."

He stared broodingly down into the swirling brandy in his glass. "Time just ran out on you, Tabby. I'm staying the night."

"No."

Dev glanced up because the small word had been only a breath of sound on her lips. She was staring at him as if he really were a dragon and herself an unfortunate princess trapped in his lair. There was nothing to be gained by trying to reassure her. He was determined to be honest. He didn't want any more accusations of deception aimed at him.

"Yes." He set down his snifter and reached for her.

The paralysis which seemed to have her in its grip broke just as he wrapped his hand around the nape of her neck. The brandy in her snifter sloshed as she tried to evade him and her eyes opened wide with outrage and something else. Something Dev hoped very much was excitement.

"Damn it, Dev, you're not going to push me around!"

He held her at the back of her neck and carefully removed the brandy glass from her fingers. "I told you I'd give you fair warning of when the actual seduction started. Well, this is it, tabby cat. I'm going to hold you in my arms here in front of the fire and stroke you until you purr for me. I'm going to make love to you, Tabby Graham; seduce you until you can't think of anything else except making love back to me."

Dev knew that although the words were meant to sound sensual there was an underlying hardness he couldn't filter out. He was too desperate, too set on possessing her once more to infuse a mellow, seductive quality into his voice. Perhaps if he'd managed that feat he wouldn't have suddenly found himself tangling with a hellcat.

Tabby seemed to explode in his grasp, wrenching furiously away from his restraining fingers.

"Let me go, Dev, or so help me, I'll…" She didn't finish the sentence, wriggling fiercely out from under his hand and leaping to her feet.

If he didn't catch her quickly she would have an advantage over him, Dev acknowledged. His weak leg made running next to impossible and without the cane as an aid he would have a hell of a job catching her before she fled out into the street. The ebony stick lay a couple of feet away, just out of reach.

"Tabby, come here," he rasped harshly as she began to back toward the fire. There was a flame in her brown eyes which was as golden as that on the hearth; she shook her head violently. "Tabby," he repeated softly, "you know you don't want to run from me. I'm the man who helped you find out just how passionate you really are. Come here, sweetheart, it's time you repeated the experience."

Hell. He was handling this very badly, Dev realized grimly as he slid slowly along the couch toward her. She was set to run as soon as he got up off the black cushions. Then he was going to have a real job on his hands catching her again.

"Stay away from me, Dev Colter. I haven't made up my mind yet about you!"

"I know. I'm going to help you come to your senses. This game you're playing has gone on long enough, honey. Tonight it ends." He moved a bit closer. The cane, at least, was within reach now. She edged to the side of the hearth, her eyes never leaving him.

"This isn't a game, Dev. Can't you understand? You fooled me once before, and I'm not going to be tricked again."

"I did not trick you!"

"You're not the man I thought you were on that ship!"

"Well, we're even then, because you're not exactly the woman I thought you were, either," he gritted. A couple more inches he told himself. Just a couple more inches.

"What's that supposed to mean?" she blazed, clearly incensed at the accusation.

"It means I'm learning you've got claws, tabby cat. But that's all right, I'll teach you to keep them sheathed around me." Would she break to the right or the left? He eyed her with all his years of experience and decided that this little opponent would dodge to the right. She seemed to put just a shade more weight on that foot when she edged away from the fire. Yes, it would be to the right. He curled his fingers around the handle of the cane and tensed. "Tabby, don't fight me. You know you want this as much as I do."

"I'm still thinking about what you've been saying these past few days, Dev," she informed him aloofly. "And I'm going to take all the time I want deciding what to do."

"You're going to have your mind made up for you tonight," he growled.

"Why?" she demanded aggressively. "Why aren't you willing to give me a little time?"

"Because I have this funny feeling," he returned honestly enough. "A hunch, an *instinct* that something's going to go very wrong if I don't act tonight."

"You're going to rape me because of a hunch?" she exploded.

"You know damn well it's not going to be rape!" The accusation infuriated him. He was going to make love to her, not assault her, and she ought to know that. He wouldn't hurt a hair on her head. Although he might seriously consider taking his belt to her for what she was putting him through tonight, he amended. "Come here, Tabby!"

"It's time you left, Dev."

He feinted, using the cane to lever himself up off the couch. She misinterpreted the direction of his movement and did as Dev had expected, darting to her right. Bracing himself against the curving arm of the black sofa, Dev leaned forward and blocked her path of flight with the ebony cane.

"Damn you!" Tabby swore violently as she ran full tilt into the unexpected barrier of the cane which stretched across her path at the level of her waist. Before she could recover herself Dev swept her back against his chest with the ebony stick. Then he released it as he caught her in his hands.

She pummeled him, throwing herself against his chest in an attempt to force him off balance. Dev didn't try to fight the effort and as a result they both sprawled into a heap in front of the fire. The thick, white sheepskin rug cushioned their fall, although Dev made an effort to absorb most of the impact.

Tabitha landed on top of him, her breath hissing sharply between her teeth. He didn't give her a chance to catch it again. With a swift movement he rolled over, trapping her writhing body beneath his own. He saw the reflection of the firelight in her furious eyes, felt the thrust of her soft curves as she struggled, and his body leaped into vivid awareness.

"Tabby, I want you!" he muttered in husky wonder and then he bent his head to take her mouth. She parted her lips to protest and he took advantage of the opportunity to force himself intimately inside. There was a hint of brandy mingled with the natural warmth of her mouth, and Dev was exhilarated by the heady combination.

He held her easily, his strength and weight pinning her to the sheepskin rug almost effortlessly. With every twisting, struggling movement she only succeeded in arousing him further. His body was pulsating with the sheer pleasure of mastering her softness.

"Damn you, Dev!" she gasped, wrenching her mouth free of his for a moment. "Let me up!"

He lifted his head for an instant to stare down into her flaming eyes. "How can I let you go? I need you too damn much tonight." Then he very deliberately tangled his hand in her hair, holding her head still so that he could explore the line of her throat with his lips.

She raked his leg with her foot, trying to drive the heel of her shoe into his skin. "I'm going to trim your claws, cat," he vowed roughly. Then he used his knee to push her thighs apart. The soft emerald fabric of her dress rode high up on her legs, and Dev felt the warmth of her skin through the silky pantyhose. "The only thing I'm going to let you do with those nice legs is wrap them around me. Stop fighting, tabby cat. You know damn well you belong to me."

"The gentlemanly act sure fades in a hurry when you want something, doesn't it?" she charged between clenched teeth. Tabby got one hand temporarily free and dug her nails into the back of his neck.

"Hell!" he muttered, grabbing at the small, clawing fingers and yanking them to a safe distance. Snagging both of her wrists in one of his fists, he moved his free hand to her breast. "You know you've been asking me to touch you like this. You aren't even wearing a bra. You wanted me to see just enough of your softness to drive me out of my mind."

"No!"

"Yes, Tabby. And I like what I've seen. Now I'm going to take you. It was only a matter of time before I had you back in my arms. You knew that." Beneath the green fabric of her dress he could feel the taut peak of her nipple and he gloried in the response. He moved his hardening body against hers and groaned aloud as he felt the waiting softness. So feminine and inviting. His blood was pounding through his veins as the anticipation coursed along his nerves.

Eagerly his palm slid down over the curve of her breast to the contour of her waist and beyond. When he found the hem of her dress he fastened his mouth on hers to stifle the protest he knew would be forthcoming, and then he slipped his fingers boldly up the inside of her thigh.

"When you wake up in the morning you're not going to be wearing these," he growled, gliding his fingertips over the nylon of her pantyhose. He found the apex of her thighs and stroked tantalizingly, teasing her through the slick fabric. "How can you lie beneath me like this and say you don't want me when I can feel the heat in you? Tell me you want me, Tabby. Tell me the truth!"

He wanted to hear the words, Dev realized belatedly.

He wanted the reassurance of hearing her call his name. He wanted her to beg him to take her. When there was no response he stilled for a moment, raising his head once more to look down into her face. She gazed up at him through her lashes, her eyes unreadable and unbelievably mysterious. Her soft mouth was full and sensually parted as the breath came quickly through her lips. What the hell was she thinking?

For the first time that evening doubt assailed him. Panic suddenly overrode his body's urgent demands. Oh, God, what if she didn't love him? What if she no longer even wanted him? He hadn't counted on this. He had been so sure that her blossoming love could not be turned off at will.

"Tabby! Tabby, say my name," he ordered desperately, his whole body suddenly tense and unmoving. "Say my name," he pleaded harshly. What good would that do? he asked himself in surging panic. But he had to hear her say something, anything. Surely she couldn't have changed completely. God help him if he'd been totally wrong. She *had* to love him.

He knew she was searching his face but he had no knowledge of what she sought in his eyes. The tense stillness gripped them both now. In an agony of suspense Dev waited for some sign that his instincts had not failed him completely where this woman was concerned. He needed her so badly.

"Dev," she whispered, her voice suddenly throaty and deeply inviting. "Love me, Dev. I want you so, darling. Please, Dev…"

With a groan of heady relief and savage ecstasy Dev sank back down, gathering her into his arms. He knew

he was talking, saying things he didn't fully comprehend. The words were dark and intimate and exciting.
He was promising her everything he could think of, in
the manner of impassioned males from the dawn of
time. And she twined her arms around his neck and
drank the promises from his mouth.

She wanted him; loved him. Everything was all right.
Everything was perfect. His fingers shook a little as they
found the zipper of the emerald dress and lowered it.
Then he was pushing the material up her body and over
her head. The fullness of her breasts taunted him as the
firelight bathed her skin in gold.

"So lovely," he said in wonder. With a muttered exclamation of need he lowered his mouth to taste the
rigid berries which capped her curves. The scent of her
skin shot through his senses, sending his head into a
spin. Dev could feel her nails on his shoulders and
suddenly he was impatient with his own clothing.
Heaving himself slightly away, he yanked at the knot
of his tie and then, as she watched from beneath slum-
berous lids, he pulled at the buttons of his shirt.

In another moment he was pushing off the remainder of his clothing, his fully aroused body feeling magnificently free and primitively aggressive. Tabby raised
her fingertips to snarl them lovingly in the curling hair
on his chest and he sucked in his breath as she let her
hand follow the line of hair down below his waist.

"You're driving me wild, honey," he managed
shakily. The waistband of her pantyhose gave easily
beneath the assault of his fingers. Too easily, he realized
ruefully an instant later as the delicate nylon abruptly
tore. Almost immediately he forgot the small disaster,

losing patience altogether with the tight-fitting fabric. Swiftly he yanked the garment off, leaving it in tatters on the floor. Along with the pantyhose came her scrap of silky panties. At last she was lying naked and open, waiting for him.

"Love me, Tabby," he begged hoarsely as he stretched out along the length of her in slow delight. "Take me inside of you and warm me with your fire. Let me have all of you tonight. I need you, sweetheart. God, how I need you!"

In answer she wrapped him close, her arms circling his neck and her legs parting to allow him between her thighs. He heard his name on her lips as she kissed his throat and the crooning, inviting sound exploded the last of his restraint.

Gripping her shoulders, he surged against her, about to bury himself in her softness, when suddenly he remembered the way she had hesitated, the first time they made love, before accepting the full force of his masculinity. Above all he did not want to hurt her.

"Tabby?" he rasped.

"Yes, Dev, oh, yes, please!" She sank her nails into his shoulders, urging him to complete the union. Her eyes slitted almost shut.

Dev tried to go slowly, to ease himself into her, but the passion in him was too strong to allow for any further restraint. The need to possess her completely was overwhelming him and he succumbed to it with a fierce, driving energy.

She gasped as he forged deeply into her satiny warmth, but she made no move to resist or draw back. Instead she gripped him more violently than ever and lifted herself to meet the passionate, rhythmic power of his body.

Dev lost himself in the reckless, spinning emotions which enveloped them both. On some level he wanted to master her completely and on another he desired only to give himself up to the loving sensuality she offered. On and on he surged, ricocheting back and forth between the two equally powerful, equally sensual demands, and then he felt her responsive body tighten in that special, magical way.

"That's it, honey," he encouraged savagely, "give yourself to me completely. Let go and come to me. I'll hold you. I'll keep you safe."

"Dev!"

Her body shuddered delicately beneath his, gripping him more tightly than ever and pulling him into the vortex with her. Together they fought the last battle and won and then they were cascading down, down through the night, collapsing onto the sheepskin rug in a damp tangle. Dev kept her tightly against him, knowing he would never, ever let her go. She was his.

It was a long time before she stirred slightly beneath him, her lashes flickering open to reveal the drowsy, re-membered sensuality in her eyes. He braced himself on his elbows, a faint smile edging his mouth as he returned the knowing, intimate gaze.

"You're magnificent, Tabby. Utterly magnificent."

"So are you, dragon. Arrogant and demanding but quite magnificent." Her voice was soft and slurred, and Dev's smile widened affectionately.

"Sleepy?"

"Umm. You exhaust me. First you wrestle me to

the floor and then you ravish me. It's very exhausting, you know."

"I'm a little tired myself," he confessed dryly.

"Amazing."

"I think it's time we went to bed."

"Yes."

The firelight faded into flickering embers as the two people on the sheepskin rug got slowly to their feet, clinging tightly to each other. Together they walked, arms entwined, down the hall to the bedroom.

"I guess I should sweep you off your feet and carry you to bed," Dev sighed, "but the truth is, if I tried it, I'd probably lose my balance and we'd both wind up on the floor. This damn leg of mine…"

"I didn't notice that leg of yours slowing you down any tonight," Tabby drawled. "I never stood a chance, did I?"

"A chance of escaping me? No," he admitted flatly as they reached the bedroom. "I could never let you go, Tabby." he turned to her as she started to pull down the satin comforter that covered the bed. "Tabby?"

"What is it, Dev?"

"Promise me you'll never let me go, either," he rasped with a renewed sense of urgency.

"I don't seem to have much choice in the matter, do I?" she mused. "Come to bed, Dev."

He hesitated, watching her slide naked between the snowy sheets, and then he followed, reaching out to fold her close. What was wrong with him? he wondered restlessly as he lay in the darkness, absently stroking her shoulder. Why was he still getting those uneasy, prickling sensations? He had Tabby in his arms. He had been so sure that taking her would quiet his anxiety.

But now that his body was no longer clamoring with desire, the old, uneasy feeling was back in full force. What the hell was wrong? He gripped Tabby more tightly, seeking comfort. She moved against him in her sleep, offering that which he needed, and he sighed and fell asleep beside her.

CHAPTER TEN

FOR THE SECOND TIME THAT WEEK Tabitha found herself
waking up to the sound of an imperious knock on her
front door. At least this time she wasn't waking up with
a pounding headache to go with it, she thought wryly,
floundering to a sitting position beside the still-sleeping
man in her bed.

God, he was magnificent, she thought, drinking in
the sight of him as he lay there amid the white sheets.
Hard and lean and sleek. If he had a dragon's scales,
they would be gleaming in the morning sunlight. As it
was, his bronzed skin was dark and tantalizing against
the bedclothes. And she loved him. Once he had decided
to claim her last night there could have been no other
possible outcome to the evening other than the one he
had planned. How could she have gone on resisting the
man she loved?

The knock came again and with a muttered groan
Tabitha pushed aside the sheets and padded to the closet
to find her Chinese silk dressing gown, the one with the
dragon embroidered down the back and around the
hem. Strange that Dev hadn't awakened. His senses
were normally so much more acute than her own.
Perhaps he hadn't gone to sleep immediately last night.

She had awakened once or twice and found him rather restless beside her. When she had put her arm around him he had drifted back into a deeper slumber. Tabitha had taken a subtle pleasure in offering the small comfort. He seemed to need her as well as desire her.

Surely from such roots love could grow?

Hurrying out into the living room, she wrenched open the front door just as a thin, gray-haired man in a dark three-piece suit raised his hand to knock again. His thin, patrician features were set in remote lines.

For an instant they simply stared at each other without any trace of recognition. Then the older man smiled politely, his hazel eyes cool and aloof.

"Good morning. You must be Tabitha. I'm John Delaney."

"Delaney." Tabitha narrowed her eyes, sweeping the line of his conservative suit and the hard, chillingly polite expression on his face. "From Washington, D.C."

He arched one heavy, gray brow. "I see you know of me."

Tabitha abruptly started to close the door in his face. "Go away, John Delaney. You're in the wrong place. This is Washington, state of. Go back to D.C."

He shoved one polished, black shoe over the threshold, blocking the door. "I gather you know why I'm here."

She lifted her chin with fierce determination, her hand clenching into a small fist. "He's not going back with you, Mr. Delaney. He belongs here now. He belongs to me."

"Come now, Tabitha," Delaney murmured. "If you know Dev Colter at all well, you know he doesn't belong to anyone."

"He does now!" She pushed at the door again but the black shoe didn't move.

"What the hell?" Dev's question cracked across the room and Tabitha whirled to see him standing in the hall doorway. He was wearing only his slacks, which he must have just grabbed off the floor. He was still fastening the belt and yanking up the zipper. "Delaney," he muttered, coming forward far enough to see who stood on the threshold. "I should have known. No wonder I couldn't get that damn uneasy feeling out of my system last night. My instincts were right. As usual."

Delaney smiled, a speculative gleam in his hazel eyes. "Your instincts have always bordered on the precognitive. That's one of the things which makes you so valuable."

Tabitha gasped. "You're clairvoyant?" she demanded in astonishment, staring at Dev as if she hadn't quite seen him clearly before.

He frowned in annoyance. "No, of course not. I just get these hunches occasionally. Usually when something is about to go wrong. I had a feeling something was about to go wrong last night, but I thought…" He broke off. "Well, why are you here, Delaney? Just happen to be on the West Coast?"

"Why, yes, as a matter of fact," John Delaney began soothingly, inching his way through the door.

"Don't believe him," Tabitha ordered Dev. "He's here to get you back to Washington, D.C." She glared at Delaney, who took no notice.

"The little jaunt to the Caribbean should have reassured you that you've still got what it takes, Dev," Delaney murmured smoothly, focusing all his attention on the other man. "You not only got the film for us, you took care of Waverly, too. We knew there was a new in-dependent working the Caribbean region, but we had been unable to smoke him out. Handing him over to us was a nice bonus from you, Dev. We appreciate it."

"Your gratitude overwhelms me."

Tabitha switched her glare from Delaney to Dev. What was the matter with him? Why wasn't he telling the other man to get lost? Dev had made his decision.

Hadn't he?

All of a sudden fear lurched within her stomach. Had Dev only been playing with her? Had he been using her as a pleasant interlude before returning to a job with John Delaney? *Why wasn't he kicking Delaney out of the house?*

"Come now, Dev, you know it's time you stopped fooling around with that travel agency bit and with attractive, young women like Miss Graham. It's time you came back to work, back to what you do best."

Dev looked at him, his face totally unreadable. Tabitha waited in an agony of suspense. Was he really considering going back to Delaney's horrible depart-ment?

"No!" she burst out furiously. Dev swung his un-readable gaze to her tense face. "You're not going with him, Dev."

"I'm not?"

"You're a *travel* agent now, not a…a *secret* agent, remember?"

"Actually," Delaney interrupted easily, "his travel agency work makes an excellent cover…"

"It's not a cover!" Tabitha stormed, advancing on the older man with her hands curled violently at her sides.

"It's his job! His career! Furthermore, he's going to be a married man, soon. He can't be running around doing your dirty work for you. Not anymore!"

Delaney eyed her as if she was finally beginning to pose a mild threat. "Married?"

"That's right. I'm marrying him, Mr. Delaney, and I will not allow him to go on risking his life in dark alleys and mazes..."

"Mazes?" Delaney looked a little blank.

"Or anywhere else, for that matter! He's going to open a nice little shop next to my bookstore and he's going to sell airline tickets and cruise ship tours and that's all! He will be home every night, sitting right here in front of my hearth wearing slippers and sipping sherry. He's most definitely not going to be running your stupid errands or risking his neck. Do I make myself very clear, Mr. Delaney?"

Delaney stared at her now as if she were some strange, new animal. Then he glanced at Dev. "Where the hell did you find her?"

"I didn't find her. She found me. She rescued me from an alley on St. Regis."

"I found him and I'm going to keep him!" Tabitha blazed.

"Are you?" Delaney flicked another speculative glance at her, and then he pinned Dev with a cool, probing glance. "She seems quite determined to rescue you again. This time from me." There was a significant pause and then the older man asked almost gently, "Do you really want to be rescued from me, Dev?"

Tabitha, stricken, stared at Dev, too. There was not much she could do if Dev Colter didn't want to be rescued this time. Her heart raced anxiously as she held her breath. Her whole future hung in the balance. What would she do if Dev walked out with his old boss this morning? The heart which was pounding so nervously would break this time. She could not bear to lose him now.

"Dev," she whispered starkly. "I love you."

He looked at her. "Do you, Tabby?"

"With all my heart."

The sudden flare of warmth in his silver eyes seemed to light the whole room. "I won't be going anywhere, tabby cat. I think I've been in love with you since you dragged me out of that damn St. Regis alley. All I want is a home here with you."

"Oh, Dev!" Tabitha managed to unstick her feet from the floor and hurl herself into Dev's arms. He caught her, staggering a bit under the impact, but his braced feet supported them both while she buried her face against his chest and wrapped her arms around his bare waist.

Over the top of her head Dev smiled crookedly at his former boss. "You need a new, young dragon, Delaney. I'm afraid I've lost my taste for your kind of work. I wasn't altogether sure of that when I agreed to take the Caribbean job for you, but now I'm quite positive."

"I see," Delaney said with unexpected softness in his voice. "You do seem to have made up your mind. Strange, I never saw you as the home-and-hearth type."

"Home and hearth complete with my own tabby cat," Dev said, chuckling, his hand lightly stroking Tabitha's hair as she continued to cling to him. "You ought to try it sometime, Delaney. You don't know what you've missed."

Delaney watched the way Tabitha was holding his former agent. "How much of your past is she aware of?"

Tabitha turned her head to glare at Delaney. "It's not his past I'm concerned with, it's his present and his future."

"Dev?" Delaney made one last appeal.

"My present and my future are here in Washington, state of, Delaney," Dev said with quiet conviction.

"You're sure, aren't you?"

"Very."

Delaney sighed. "I was afraid of that. But it was worth a try. I don't suppose," he went on matter-of-factly, "that anyone would like to fix me a cup of coffee before you throw me out of the house?"

Tabitha slowly freed herself from Dev's grasp, eyeing her foe with deep suspicion. But John Delaney merely smiled pleasantly.

"It's okay, Tabitha. I know when I've lost. He's all yours. Wouldn't do me much good, anyway, if he kept thinking of you every time I sent him into the field. Being in love blunts a man's instincts."

"Not all of them," Dev retorted dryly, but he was suddenly grinning. "Come on, Delaney, I'll fix you a cup of coffee."

"Thank you. I need something warm. It certainly rains a lot here in Washington, state of, doesn't it?"

"Yeah," Dev agreed easily, "but somehow it never seems as cold here as it does in Washington, D.C."

THAT EVENING TABITHA CURLED HAPPILY against Dev as they sat on one of the black sofas in front of the fire. She hadn't really relaxed until John Delaney was on a plane heading back to Washington, D.C., but now her world seemed warm and right. Dreamily she ran her fingers through Dev's dark hair. His arm tightened around her in response.

"Thank you for rescuing me again, tabby cat," he drawled, nuzzling her earlobe with lazy anticipation. "That's twice now. I'm going to be in your debt for the rest of my life."

"Exactly where I want you," she teased, her eyes alive with love.

"I love you," he murmured simply.

"When did you first realize it?" she demanded.

"When I walked out of the bedroom this morning and found you trying to kick Delaney out of the house. I suppose I'd been in love all along, but the sight of you tangling with John Delaney for my sake made me put a name to it. Up until then I'd been thinking in terms of wanting and needing. But it all came together for me this morning. What about you, honey?"

"I knew I loved you that night I seduced you on the boat," she admitted with a ready smile.

"I kept telling myself you must love me, but when you skipped the island after that scene with Waverly I was afraid I was going to have a hell of a time getting you to admit you felt something for me. Then when I arrived here and found that young cub asleep on your living room couch and discovered you were bent on trying to forget me, I wanted to tear Port Townsend apart. Tabby, I may not have understood right away that what I felt for you was love, but I did know right away that I needed you desperately. Your love was what had been missing from my life. I could never let you go, sweetheart."

"I'll never want to leave you, dragon. You are my

very own, very fabulous beast." She raised her face invitingly, winding her arms around his neck.

"Are you about to seduce me again?" he demanded, silver eyes turning smoky with stirring desire.

"I'm engaged in a bit of research."

"Research on what?"

"On the mating habits of dragons."

"I can tell you one thing for sure about this particular dragon," Dev vowed as he lowered his mouth to hers. "This beast has just mated for life."

* * * * *

NIGHT OF THE MAGICIAN

CHAPTER ONE

"HISTORICALLY IT HAS NOT BEEN CONSIDERED wise to insult a magician," Lucian Hawk warned in a dark velvet drawl.

"Are you threatening to saw me in half?" Ariana Warfield demanded with great interest. "Or make me disappear into thin air?" She smiled up at him, smoky blue eyes wide and guileless behind the lenses of her oversized designer glasses.

It was her brother Drake who rushed to smooth over the incipient hostilities which had flared up a few minutes earlier when he had introduced Ariana to the magician. He did so with his usual forthright acknowledgment of what he considered his sister's failings. "Pay no attention to her, Lucian. She's always like this around men of, er, lower financial status." He grinned cheerfully. "She doesn't generally associate with men who earn less than she does, you see!"

"I see." Lucian nodded at the revelation, not appearing to be overly surprised. He studied the woman in front of him with a critical, speculative glance, topaz eyes examining her from behind the lenses of his own glasses. Lucian Hawk's frames were not as aggressively stylish as Ariana's. He hadn't opted for the chic aviator

look or even the academic style. His glasses were busi-
nesslike and very traditional. Strong black lines framed
the strange honey-gold of his eyes and matched in color
the intense velvet black of his hair.

Ariana, to her horror, was aware of a rush of embarrassed warmth as she endured the gleaming topaz of his
glance. Had she insulted the man? In self-defense she
turned on her brother, who was two years younger than
her own thirty years of age, and therefore fair game as
a scapegoat.

"I was not being insulting, Drake. I merely commented upon the rather hand-to-mouth existence which
must be the fate of the usual magician!"

"Asking a man why he doesn't settle down and get
a decent, regular job is often considered something of
an insult," Drake shot back dryly.

"Especially when the man is my age,' Lucian pointed
out. "I'm nearly forty, you know. It should be obvious
that I'm probably not going to amount to anything more
than I already am." There was a taunting challenge in
his gaze now, and Ariana was vividly aware of it.

"Be reasonable, Ariana," Drake went on, his Warfield
blue eyes laughing at his sister. "You didn't come to my
party tonight to meet a prospective husband. You came
to hire a magician."

"Voil;aga!" Lucian murmured, sipping from his glass
of whiskey and soda. "You see before you one magician
for hire. Maybe."

"Maybe!" Ariana swung her narrowed gaze back to
meet his. "What do you mean, 'maybe'? Are you interested in the job or not?"

"I'm interested in talking about it," Lucian temporized. "Why don't we let Drake get back to his other guests while we find a quiet spot and discuss the matter?" He took Ariana's arm and nodded at his host. "It's all right, Drake. I'll send for you if the insults start flying too thick and fast for me to stop them on my own."

"Now just a minute," Ariana began waspishly.

But her good-looking younger brother was already trading an easy man-to-man look with Lucian. "Okay, I'll see you both later. Try the den at the back of the apartment, it should be relatively quiet there. Be nice to him, Ari," he advised his sister. "You need him for what you've got in mind. And he's right, you know. It's not generally considered smart to insult magicians!"

Before Ariana could give her brother her views on the subject, he was making his way back into the throng of colorful people that filled his oversized living room. Drake's parties were always full of odd, eccentric, interesting and occasionally fascinating people. He collected them without regard to social or financial status. The only requirement for being invited to one of Drake Warfield's parties was being interesting. Drake was an inventor, and he claimed that he needed these parties to inspire his thinking processes.

He'd tried telling that to the IRS one year, Ariana recalled as Lucian led her firmly through the crowd. But the IRS hadn't agreed to his proposal for writing off the monthly parties as a business expense. As usual, it was Ariana who had been called upon to straighten out the resulting financial misunderstanding.

The masculine hand on her arm was beginning to become annoying, she decided as Lucian guided her toward the doorway. It was a large hand with a supple strength in the fingers, and her arm felt quite powerless in its grip.

"I think I can manage to make it all the way back to the den on my own,' she said dryly, attempting unsuccessfully to release herself. "Would you mind letting go of my arm? You're leaving imprints in the skin!"

Lucian arched one black brow as he glanced down at his captive. "Sorry. Didn't want to take a chance on losing you in this crowd."

"I'm not likely to disappear in the short distance between the living room and the den!"

"A good magician could make you disappear in about two seconds," he pointed out. "But as long as I've got a grip on you, you're safe."

"Thanks!" she muttered caustically. "Are there any other magicians here tonight of which I must be wary?"

"One never knows," Lucian said smoothly.

He whisked her through the doorway, out of the white-on-white living room which had been decorated for Drake by Aunt Philomena. Aunt Philomena redecorated both Drake's and Ariana's living rooms twice a year; not because they liked having their apartments redecorated so frequently but because Philomena loved to do it and Ariana and Drake loved her. It had been Philomena Warfield who had taken them in upon the death of their parents.

For the past six months Ariana's living room had been done in shades of French vanilla and papaya. One of the first clues to the fact that something unusual and disturbing had occurred in Aunt Philomena's life was Ariana's realization two weeks earlier that there had been no discussion of how to redecorate her apartment for the coming six months. But it was the new rash of checks being written on her aunt's money market account which had really alerted Ariana.

If there was one thing Ariana understood, it was money.

Surreptitiously she studied the man who was leading her down the carpeted hall. A magician. Did she really have to get herself involved with this sort of man in order to carry out her plan?

Lucian Hawk stood an inch or two under six feet, she estimated. And he looked the age he had hinted at a few minutes earlier. He was definitely nearly forty.

But it was a hard, tough, streetwise forty, not the slightly paunchy, fading, comfortable forty that seemed to visit softer men. Ariana had a hunch that there had never been much that was soft about Lucian Hawk or his life.

His midnight dark hair was cut relatively short in a casual, controlled style, and there was a lacing of silver in it. The depths of his topaz eyes held a cool, savvy intelligence. Whatever handsomeness the harshly carved face had once held had been transcended over the years by an almost fierce strength reflected in the aggressive line of nose and jaw.

At least he hadn't dressed with the kind of outlandish showmanship one might expect in a magician, Ariana decided thankfully. So many of Drake's eccentric friends advertised their highly individual lifestyles with their clothes. Lucian was wearing a pair of dark-toned cotton twill trousers that rode low on a lean waist, and a buttery-soft suede pullover shirt with an open collar. There was something very right about the suede on him, Ariana thought absently. It went with the quality of rough, virile aggression that she sensed lay close to the surface of the man. A pair of casual leather handsewns on his feet and a rather worn belt completed his outfit.

"Ah, here we are." Lucian threw open a door at the end of the hall. "It looks like whoever did Drake's living room didn't get her hands on his den!" He glanced appreciatively around at the warm, richly comfortable room with its leather and heavy wood furnishings. Then he shot a speculative glance at Ariana.

"Don't look at me," she told him wryly as he released her arm. "I don't do Drake's decorating. I have no artistic talent. Aunt Philomena's the one with that particular ability." She sank down into one of the oversized leather chairs. "Actually, she did do this room, but she did it to Drake's specifications, and when it was finished he made her promise never to touch it again. This is where he does most of his serious thinking."

"I can see why a professional inventor might need a room for that." Lucian smiled slightly as he took the opposite chair. There was something annoyingly casual about the way he settled so easily into his host's chair, as if it didn't bother him at all to make use of someone else's possessions. He looked quite at home on the expensive leather, his legs stretched out in front of him, his arms resting comfortably along the padded sides. There was a lithe, indolent grace about him that irritated Ariana. Where did Drake find his friends, for heaven's sake?

"My brother works hard, Mr. Hawk, even if his hours are a bit irregular," she told Lucian repressively.

He inclined his dark head with an unexpected, almost courtly gesture. "Implying, of course, that I don't work particularly hard?" The topaz eyes gleamed.

Ariana closed her eyes briefly, striving for patience. "I'm sure a professional magician must do something that resembles work occasionally."

"You mean when I'm not sponging off my more financially successful friends like your brother?"

"I didn't mean to imply that you were sponging off Drake!" she shot back coolly. "I know you aren't, as a matter of fact, at least not in any large way. If you were, believe me, I'd be the first to know about it!"

He watched her speculatively. "You keep close tabs on your brother's finances, Ariana?" he finally inquired very gently.

"It's none of your concern, Mr. Hawk, but yes, I do keep an eye on his financial situation."

"Money, I take it, is a primary interest of yours," he drawled.

She shrugged. It was the truth and she saw no point in denying it. "Perhaps we should get on with our business, Mr. Hawk."

"Call me Lucian."

"Fine. Lucian." Ariana nodded crisply and sat forward a little, her fingers laced together in front of her, elbows resting on the arms of the chair. "Has Drake explained any of this to you?"

"He merely mentioned that you're worried about your aunt. And he told me a bit about you," he added thoughtfully, as if he were trying to recall whatever it was Drake had mentioned about her and how accurate the comments had been.

Ariana didn't waste much time wondering what Lucian Hawk's assessment of her was. She had an honest, straightforward impression of herself and knew how she must appear to the magician. Along with her brother she'd inherited the rich cinnamon brown hair of their mother. She wore it shoulder length in a blunt cut, the sides pulled back behind her ears and held, tonight, with two small clips of gold. The look was controlled and chic, and it served to emphasize the wide, aware, faintly wary expression of her smoky blue eyes. The stylish eyeglasses enhanced those eyes, but they also provided a subtle barrier of defense. From behind the lightly tinted lenses Ariana could view the world from some indefinable point of safety.

Ariana had no illusions about her looks. She knew the slightly upturned nose and the gentle line of her cheekbones and jaw needed a lot more purity of shape to be considered beautiful. And the too-vulnerable mouth was another source of dissatisfaction. Ariana did what she could to hide the hints of softness in her appearance by dressing with a sophisticated polish.

Tonight she was wearing a narrow little black wool dress which held the drama of slashed white satin sleeves and a high-standing white satin collar. Delicate black patent leather pumps and dark stockings added to the cool impact of the dress. The sleek line emphasized the slenderness of her figure.

"To put it bluntly, I believe my aunt has somehow come under the influence of a man who claims to be a psychic," Ariana began, her voice laced with the disgust she felt. "Philomena is not a stupid woman—far from it—but she does have an exceedingly active imagination and she's fascinated with the notion of flying saucers and alien visitations. This character she's involved with is feeding on her interest in the subject, claiming to have had 'encounters.'"

"It's the modern explanation for psychic phenomena," Lucian observed. "In the old days spiritual mediums claimed to be in touch with the 'other side,' the world of the spirits. Now they often claim to get their powers from alien visitors."

"I do not like fraud or deception of any type," Ariana stated grimly, not caring for Lucian's calm acceptance of the existence of psychics.

"It can be entertaining and there's often some very excellent magic involved. If your aunt is enjoying the experience, why not let her do so? Perhaps she doesn't like to view the world from your more, uh, pragmatic perspective."

"If she wants a magic show, she can buy a ticket and go see one! This isn't the same thing at all. I believe this man is taking advantage of her and I want to put a stop to it. I want you to help me expose him."

"You're working on the principle that it takes one magician to catch another?" Lucian's mouth curved wryly.

"Something like that. Can you do it?"

He considered the question. "Possibly. I know you don't have a high opinion of my humble craft, but I am reasonably good at it. How, exactly, is this man taking advantage of your aunt?"

Ariana frowned intently. "Lately there have been some unusual withdrawals from her money market fund. When I mentioned them to her she avoided the question, claiming they were for some unexpected purchases. She's an artist, you see, and she's always involved with new projects."

Lucian regarded her with a mocking expression of wonder. "You certainly do keep track of your relatives' finances, don't you? I hate to mention the obvious, but doesn't it occur to you that your aunt has a right to spend her money any way she sees fit?"

"You clearly have no conception of the sense of responsibility needed to manage money, Lucian," she retorted quellingly. "And, frankly, I don't have the time or the inclination to try explaining it to you. Right now all I'm concerned with is this charlatan who seems to be fascinating Philomena!"

"Are you sure the money she's withdrawing from her account is going to the psychic?"

"I have a strong feeling that it is, yes."

"But you don't know for certain?" Lucian pressed.

"I haven't wanted to pin Aunt Philomena down," Ariana explained, shifting a little uncomfortably. "I don't want her to suspect I'm on to the situation."

"Why not?"

"Because if she thinks I'm suspicious of her new mentor, she won't let me get anywhere near him. We will have to get near him, won't we? In order to expose him?"

"In order to expose him in a suitably impressive fashion, yes," Lucian agreed. "I hope you realize, though, that true believers often go on believing in their chosen psychics even after most people have been convinced it's all a case of stage magic. I could bring about an elaborate expos;aae in the middle of one of this guy's performances and still not manage to convince your aunt that the man's not a psychic who's been endowed with special powers from alien spacemen. If she truly wants to go on believing in him..." He let the sentence end with a shrug.

"I understand, but my aunt is an intelligent woman

who, I think, will have the sense to see the man for the fraud he is once he's been exposed. Philomena isn't the only one who's been captivated by him, Lucian. Several of her friends are also making weekend trips to his place in the mountains for his so-called seminars."

"Perhaps they're really enjoying themselves," he suggested wryly. "Do you have a right to interfere? After all, it is your aunt's money and time and you claim she's intelligent. What, exactly, is your interest in getting involved?"

Ariana's eyes narrowed as she sat back in her chair. The toe of her black patent leather pump tapped impatiently on the Oriental carpet. "Are you implying I have ulterior motives? That I'm not simply interested in protecting my aunt?" she challenged softly.

"I think your rather overpowering interest in money may account for some of your concern," Lucian admitted blandly. "Presumably your aunt's money will someday constitute your inheritance?"

Ariana almost went white under the implied accusation. For an instant she sat perfectly still and then she was on her feet with a crisp, furious surge of motion, striding for the door.

He was on her before she could wrench it open, catching hold of her wrist in an unshakable grip. How had he moved so quickly? Ariana didn't pause to consider the question. Instead she let the momentum of his grasp spin her around and as she turned she brought her opposite hand up in a quick, short arc that connected effectively with the side of his face.

"How dare you?" she hissed tightly. "You know nothing about my relationship with my aunt and yet you virtually accuse me of worrying about her solely because I'm trying to protect my inheritance! Let go of my wrist, you bastard!"

He didn't release her, but his other hand lifted to touch the reddening mark she had left on his face. The topaz eyes glittered with an anger he was obviously making an effort to control. "Calm down," he ordered in an icy tone. "Calm down and give me a chance to do the same."

"I don't give a damn if you calm down or not!"

"You should," he growled. "I'm furious. It's unwise to insult magicians, but it's downright reckless to make them lose their tempers! Try to remember that, Ariana."

"I'm not going to worry about remembering it because I don't ever intend to see you again. Let go of me before I scream for Drake!"

"He'd never hear you over the noise of that stereo system he's got going in the living room. Come on back and sit down, Ariana," Lucian instructed with a sigh of resignation. "I suggest we start over. I shouldn't have implied that you were only concerned about your aunt because of the money, and you shouldn't have slapped my face. But I'll concede I may have deserved the latter," he added as he pushed her almost gently back down into the leather chair.

"You most certainly did! Are you apologizing, by any chance?" Ariana lifted her chin with royal disdain.

"It was not gentlemanly of me to ask about your motives regarding your aunt," Lucian said quietly, taking his own seat once more. Something approaching a sign of wry amusement edged his mouth briefly. "But, then, what can you expect from a lowly magician? A man who makes his living with techniques of illusion and deception can hardly be considered a gentleman, can he?"

Ariana stared at him, a little uncertain about his mood. A few seconds ago he had been furious. She'd seen it in the tight lines around his mouth and in the glittering gold of his eyes. Now that the immediate crisis was over she could even admit to herself that perhaps she ought to have been a little frightened for a moment or two. The only reason she hadn't experienced fear was because she, herself, had been so overwhelmingly angry.

"Are you going to accept my apology?" Lucian asked politely.

Ariana drew a deep breath and told him the truth. "Frankly, I doubt if I have much choice. I don't know where or how I'd find another magician at this late date."

"Don't go overboard with the gracious lady routine," he advised dryly.

"Rest assured I'm not tempted to do so. Not with you."

"Ouch." He winced. "I don't suppose you view yourself as owing me an apology?"

"For slapping you? You said yourself, you deserved it," she reminded him spiritedly.

"Just the same, I suggest you don't make a habit of slapping my face every time you lose your temper with me."

"More warnings about angering magicians?" she murmured with apparent interest. Inwardly she was beginning to ask herself if she had, indeed, gotten off lightly this time. The man, as he admitted, made no claim to being a gentleman and there was an aura of rough, steel-edged temper about him that should have cautioned her.

"I can see you don't take my profession very seriously," he retorted.

"Only when a member of it gets in my way or the way of someone in my family," Ariana said pointedly. "Believe me, I take my aunt's new acquaintance very seriously!"

"Don't classify me with that psychic your aunt's involved with!"

Ariana bit back a comment to the effect that all magicians, illusionists and deceivers were pretty much the same to her. But nothing would be served by further insulting the man, and right now, like it or not, she needed his cooperation. He must have seen the flicker of thought in her eyes, because Lucian smiled with a certain grimness.

"Very wise," he applauded in a low, velvety growl.

"Are you going to claim you can read my mind?" she scoffed irritably. "That you knew what I was thinking just then?"

"Any man sitting where I am right now would have known exactly what you were thinking about him. But, then, you're really not making much of an effort to conceal your opinion of me, are you?"

This was getting them nowhere. "Lucian," Ariana began in a determined, steady voice, "I think you were right a few minutes ago. We'd better start over. Let's accept the basic fact that you think I'm mercenary and that I have a few reservations about your chosen profession. All I want with you is a business relationship and I'm willing to pay well for your particular expertise. Will you help me expose the psychic with whom my aunt is involved?"

Lucian propped one elbow on the arm of his chair and rested his chin on his palm, his pose pensive. "Strangely enough, I'm tempted."

Ariana arched one cinnamon red brow behind the frames of her glasses. "I can't tell you how grateful I am," she said with exaggerated politeness.

"Don't get me wrong, what's tempting me isn't your kind offer of honest employment."

"No?"

"No. It's just that I'm intrigued by the thought of watching another magician in action and seeing if I can figure out how he's operating. I suppose you could call my interest in your offer a form of professional curiosity. I can make no guarantees, however, you do understand that? There is always the possibility that the man's so much better at his craft than I am that I won't be able to expose him. There is also the possibility that when I actually see him in action I'll decide that he's not really doing anything wrong, in which case I will *choose* not to expose him. A matter of professional ethics."

"You don't think it's wrong for a magician to use his skills to fleece my aunt and several of her friends?" Ariana demanded.

"If that is, indeed, what's happening, I'll do my best to put a halt to it."

For a moment Ariana regarded the man she was coming to think of as an adversary. "And how much do you consider fair payment for a job of this nature?" she finally asked coolly.

"You're in luck. The food stamps came in yesterday and I'm feeling generous. I won't charge you a cent," he drawled.

"That's quite unnecessary," she snapped. "I'm prepared to pay for your services."

"I, however, am not prepared to receive money from you," he snapped back, getting to his feet with a sudden lithe movement. She watched as he paced across to the bay window and stood staring out at the San Francisco skyline. What was he thinking now?

"Lucian, I see no reason for this particular argument. It was understood from the first that I wanted to hire 'a magician."

"Think of the bargain you're getting," he said a little too pleasantly.

"I'm not interested in a bargain magician," she responded behind him, and for the first time her sense of humor rose to the occasion. "They say you get what you pay for and I want the best."

He swung around and was in time to catch the trace of genuine amusement that touched her soft mouth. For an instant he seemed fascinated by the sight. "I guarantee I'll give you my best work. You don't have to worry about that. But I have this strange feeling that any man who gets involved with you had better make it clear from the start that he is putting the relationship on an equal footing. I think, Ariana Warfield, that if I actually accepted your money and went to work for you, you'd make my life hell. Therefore, our arrangement will be a partnership or you can forget the whole idea."

Ariana caught her breath at the absolute finality of his tone. He meant it, she realized. He had no intention of taking money from her and thereby putting himself at her command. Magicians, it seemed, had their share of pride. "All right," she agreed hesitantly, "if you're sure that's the way you want it."

"It is."

She got to her feet. "Very well, then, it's a deal." She glanced at the thin gold watch on her wrist. "We'll have to discuss the details later this week. Right now I'm late for an engagement and I had better be on my way. When would you like to get together to go over what information I have?"

Lucian flicked a hand uncaringly. "Tomorrow evening, perhaps? I'm afraid I'm going to be busy during the day," he said carefully, watching her intently.

"Tomorrow evening will be fine." Ariana nodded once in relief and satisfaction that at last matters were beginning to progress more smoothly. "Why don't you come by my apartment around seven o'clock?"

"Before or after dinner?" he inquired blandly.

"During," she told him crisply, moving toward the door. "And you can leave the food stamps at home. I'll feed you for free. It's the least I can do if you're going to donate your services to the cause!"

"Thank you," he said, moving silently behind her so that it was his hand which went to the doorknob first, not hers. "Where are you headed this evening?"

"I'm going to catch a cab to Chinatown. I'm meeting someone there for a late dinner," Ariana explained as he opened the door for her. She thought of Richard waiting for her and stepped briskly out into the hallway. It was getting late.

"Have you called the cab?" Lucian paced beside her down the hall toward the noisy living room.

"Yes, I phoned earlier and arranged for it to meet

me out in front in a few minutes. I'll get my coat and be on my way."

"I'll come with you," Lucian said flatly, drawing to a halt at the closet in the tiled foyer. "Which coat is yours?" He was already reaching for a rugged-looking black jacket with a corduroy collar and metal clasps.

"The white cashmere," she told him, nodding at the elegantly simple coat hanging to one side. "Listen, there's absolutely no need to escort me to Chinatown," she went on quickly as he helped her into the coat. "I'll be perfectly all right. Richard will be waiting for me at the restaurant."

"I know you don't think much of magicians' manners, but we do lay claim to a few," Lucian informed her as she finished tying the sash of the coat. "Besides, I was about ready to leave, anyway. I'll simply go on home after letting you off in Chinatown. Convenient."

"Oh," she paused, seeing the logic of the situation. It would be easier for him if he didn't have to call a second cab. "Very well, if you're sure you're ready to leave."

Lucian looked up as a particularly raucous laugh filtered into the foyer. His mouth crooked wryly. "Believe me, I'm ready. In a few more minutes someone is sure to start yelling for me to perform a little magic, and since my powers don't extend to making the whole crowd disappear, I think I'll take the easy way out and just make myself disappear."

"Hey, you two, going somewhere?" Drake materialized in the doorway, a glass of champagne in one hand, his other arm around an interesting woman with blue and green hair.

"I'm going to escort your sister to her next appointment and then go on home myself. I'll see you soon, Drake."

"Did you and Ariana come to some arrangement?"

"Oh, yes. We traded a few insults, she slapped my face, I apologized and we agreed we have the perfect basis for a working partnership," Lucian said smoothly as he finished fastening the clasps of his jacket and reached for Ariana's arm.

Drake nodded happily as he watched the other two move out into the chill, foggy night. "Sounds like a solid beginning. Good night, Ari. I'll give you a call tomorrow, okay?"

"Fine. Good night, Drake." Ariana eyed the blue-and-green-haired woman, who smiled back cheerfully. Then the door closed as Lucian firmly pulled it shut behind him. The cab was already waiting at the curb.

"Does this Richard person who's supposedly waiting for you so patiently know about your plans to expose the psychic?" Lucian asked as he bundled Ariana into the back of the cab and shut the door.

"No, I haven't told anyone except you and Drake about the situation." Ariana wondered why she found herself so aware of the way Lucian seemed to dominate the close confines of the cab. With the dark, masculine jacket, that silvered black hair and those topaz eyes, Lucian Hawk definitely constituted a somewhat overpowering presence in the small space. She moved a little uneasily, seeking her own corner of the seat. When she realized what she was doing, Ariana scolded herself silently. She certainly wasn't going to let this man intimidate her!

"Is Drake as worried as you are about your aunt?"

"No, but he agrees it would probably be wise to check out this psychic," she told him vaguely, turning to gaze out the window at the city streets. The fog was close tonight, wreathing the street lamps in an eerie golden glow. In the distance a foghorn sounded, and all at once Ariana shivered for no apparent reason. She turned back abruptly and found Lucian's cat eyes studying her intently. A perfect night for a magician to be abroad, she thought fleetingly and then firmly dismissed the fanciful image.

Nevertheless, it was something of a relief to see Richard Dearborn waiting patiently outside the expensive Chinese restaurant he had chosen for the evening. His pale blond hair glistened in the garish lighting of the busy Chinatown streets, and his stylish trenchcoat was belted with a rakish air. A handsome, well-mannered man, Ariana told herself. Not a rough, potentially dangerous magician. The cab drew to a halt and Ariana put her hand on the door handle.

"Goodnight, Lucian, I'll see you tomorrow evening."

"I don't have your address," he noted calmly, his gaze on the man approaching from the sidewalk to meet Ariana.

"Oh, yes, of course." Quickly Ariana dug a business card out of her small black handbag. On the front in engraved lettering it read Warfield & Co., Financial Planners. Hastily she used a delicate gold pen to jot down her address. "There you go." She handed it to him.

"Thank you," Lucian said gently, taking the card. He was still watching the blond-haired man who was leaning down to open the cab door. The driver was getting mildly impatient. "It's nice of you to invite me to dinner, Ariana. I mean, considering your opinion of me and all," he murmured.

She bit down on her lower lip and said quickly, "Yes, well, I'm afraid we're going to have to get accustomed to the idea of getting along with each other. You see, there are a couple of details about this situation I haven't had a chance to explain yet."

"Such as?"

She sucked in her breath and said very hurriedly as she opened the door, "Such as the fact that the only way I'm going to be able to convince Aunt Philomena to let us attend one of her psychic's sessions is to make her think you're a new, uh, close friend of mine."

That caught his full attention. At once the topaz eyes went from the waiting man on the sidewalk to her suddenly tense features. "I'm going to pose as your lover?" Lucian asked harshly.

"I'll explain everything tomorrow night!" Hastily Ariana extricated herself from the cab and almost stumbled with relief into Richard's arms.

The cab door slammed shut, and the driver shot away from the curb without a second's pause.

Lucian found himself staring out the back window, one arm along the seat, watching as Ariana disappeared into the restaurant on the arm of her escort.

Was that man with the pale hair and the three-hundred-dollar trenchcoat her real lover? More to the point, why the hell was the notion so strangely disturbing? Face it, the real reason he'd insisted on sharing her cab this evening was because he had been very curious to see the man she was rushing off to meet. Ariana was both an infuriating and an intriguing woman.

Lucian settled back against the seat as the cab left Chinatown behind and headed for the next address the driver had been given. His passenger glanced down at the engraved business card in his hand and thought about what it would be like to be Ariana Warfield's lover.

CHAPTER TWO

RICHARD DEARBORN WAS NOT ARIANA'S lover. He'd made it clear that he would have liked the role, but Ariana wasn't particularly interested in casting him in it. After the "disaster" of her twenty-sixth year she never again intended to be swept off her feet by something as dangerous and unreliable as a man's passion.

The price was far too high, and if there was one thing that Ariana had a talent for, it was analyzing costs.

On the other hand, she was more than prepared to consider marriage—much to the chagrin of her small family. Philomena and Drake made no secret of the fact that they thought her overly cautious and far too practical where men were concerned. What she needed, they insisted, was a wild, blazing affair to wipe out the memory of what had happened when she was twenty-six. They very much feared that life was passing her by.

A wild, blazing affair, however, was definitely not in the picture as far as Ariana was concerned. A stable, comfortable marriage was what she needed now.

Ariana reflected on the situation the following evening as she went about the task of preparing dinner for her newly acquired magician. Richard Dearborn had everything she needed and wanted in a man. He not only made as much money as she did, he made considerably more. He had a sterling reputation as a gentleman and a businessman. He came from a family that had been quietly successful for three generations in San Francisco, and he had proven his own native ability when he had assumed the reins of the family banking business three years earlier. At thirty-four he had shown himself a worthy successor to his father.

And being a solid businessman as well as a logical person in every respect, Richard would understand Ariana's unshakable insistence on a prenuptial agreement if she were to marry him. After all, given their respective financial situations and the practicality of planning for the uncertainties of a modern marriage, a contract made perfect sense. It would protect him as well as her.

Ariana's expressive mouth curved wryly as she popped the walnut torte she had just finished making into the oven. Yes, if and when the time came, she would present the idea of such an agreement to Richard in the context of how it would protect *him*. That approach should work well on a banker.

Heaven knew she didn't want to have to explain that she was the one who needed to have the psychological security of a marriage contract. With a small sigh of self-disgust she slipped off her apron and headed for the bedroom in order to dress for dinner. Explaining her own deep-seated need for an iron-clad agreement would only resurrect the humiliation and financial disaster which she had gone through at the age of twenty-six. That had been the year when she'd thought she had it all: Success and the man of her dreams.

The man of her dreams, however, had turned out to be a fraud, a charlatan who had destroyed her love and her fledgling financial empire in one fell swoop.

Never again.

It was ironic, she thought as she stood in front of the closet, that tonight she would be entertaining a professional deceiver, a man who had made deception and illusion into a fine art.

Ah, well, she needed such skills if she was to deal with the dangerous situation in which she suspected her aunt had become involved. What were the old sayings on the subject? One fought fire with fire. And there was something to the effect that it took a thief to catch a thief. She needed a magician to expose another magician.

At least Lucian Hawk was honest about his chosen vocation, she acknowledged as she selected a pair of narrow black velvet trousers. She didn't particularly admire his choice, but she was in no jeopardy from his magic. Almost absently she pulled out a full-sleeved silk blouse done in a rich amalgam of jewel tones. The ruby, sapphire and gold colors were vibrant against the dark velvet. A pair of black ballet-style slippers finished the outfit.

She brushed her cinnamon-colored hair back behind one ear, catching it with a clip, and allowed the opposite side to swing free. The chic frames of her glasses were a strongly accented accessory in and of themselves, and she decided not to wear anything else in the way of jewelry.

How, exactly, should she handle Lucian Hawk tonight? Ariana frowned consideringly in the mirror as she checked her appearance one last time. She'd startled him last night with that parting comment about having him pose as her "close friend." He'd understood the euphemism at once. Of course, magicians were reputed to be clever people, she reminded herself with an amused smile.

The flicker of humor faded, however, as she walked back into the kitchen to finish dinner preparations. Just how clever was Lucian Hawk? Smart enough, apparently, to refuse to take money from her. She reluctantly gave him credit for that piece of insight.

He was quite right. It would have been easier to control him if he were directly in her employ. Something about the exchange of money for services rendered gave the employer a strong element of advantage over the employee. There was a subtle form of power involved in that sort of relationship, and Ariana would have felt more comfortable and in control if she had been allowed to exercise it.

As matters now stood between herself and Lucian she would be dependent on persuasion and cooperation.

The first thing she had to persuade him to do was act out the role of a man with whom she was having a "meaningful relationship." Philomena was bound to be suspicious of almost any other explanation for a man accompanying her niece to the psychic's next session. For that matter, the so-called psychic was probably going to be damn suspicious, also.

A magician. She'd have to think of some other profession for Lucian when she introduced him to Philomena. Something respectable.

Her doorbell chimed right on time half an hour later. Ariana walked through the warmly decorated living room to answer it. It was a charming room. There was no doubt about Philomena Warfield's being an extremely talented woman. When it came to mixing colors and textures, few could match her. The papaya-shaded carpet made a dramatic backdrop for the vanilla-colored furniture. Each item in the room had been selected for both comfort and style, and there was an overall sophistication about the blend of Queen Anne and French designs. The resulting atmosphere perfectly suited Ariana's lifestlye just as the sleek, ultramodern look of Drake's apartment suited his rather unusual way of living.

"Good evening, Lucian," Ariana began with cool formality as she opened the door. "You're very prompt."

"I generally am for a home-cooked meal," he said as he stepped inside. Dressed in dark slacks and a deep green pullover sweater, Lucian looked casual and at ease. He slipped off the metal-clasped jacket, the same one he had worn the night before, and handed it to her to hang in the hall closet.

Ariana took advantage of the small distraction to adjust to his dark presence in her warm pastel living room. The fog had left a trace of dampness on his black hair, and he seemed as large and faintly intimidating as he had seemed the night before in the cab. It wasn't that he was an unusually big man, but there was definitely something about him that made her uneasily aware of his presence. By the time she had completed the job of hanging up his heavy coat, however, Ariana had herself firmly under control.

"Thank you for coming, Lucian. Please have a seat. What would you like to drink?"

Instead of obeying her casual wave toward the Queen

Anne sofa, Lucian fell into step behind her as Ariana walked into the open kitchen. He slid onto a stool on the opposite side of the breakfast counter as she opened a cupboard full of glasses.

"Whatever you're having will be fine."

"A glass of Johannesburg Riesling?" she inquired, opening the refrigerator to remove the Napa Valley white wine she had been chilling.

"Fine." He watched her.

"I don't suppose you'd like to help me economize by doing some nifty trick like turning my tap water into good Riesling instead of making me use up this expensive stuff?" Ariana asked pleasantly as she set the bottle on the counter and searched for a corkscrew.

"You don't look as if you have to worry about economizing to that extent," Lucian remarked with a significant glance at the expensively furnished apartment. "But I will offer to get that cork out of the bottle for you."

She handed him the wine bottle. "With magic, or do you need the corkscrew?" she inquired interestedly.

"I thought I'd just use my teeth," he growled. Then he held out his hand demandingly. "Of course I need a corkscrew. What is this? A test?"

Ariana smiled very brilliantly, handing him the implement. "It's just that I haven't met many magicians and I wasn't sure what to expect."

"We're even then. I'm not quite sure what to expect from you, either." Expertly he began uncorking the bottle. "So suppose we start satisfying each other's curiosity. Why will I be posing as your lover?"

Ariana winced at the blunt question. "Not my lover,

Lucian," she qualified. "Just a man I'm currently dating. Someone with whom I have a relationship. Enough of a relationship that my aunt will accept you without suspicion when I ask to bring you along to the s;aaeance or whatever her psychic calls his little get-togethers."

Lucian made a noncommittal sound as he removed the cork from the bottle.

"I can't very well tell her who you really are or expect her to welcome you with open arms, now can I?" Ariana went on determinedly. "Furthermore, that damn psychic will undoubtedly forbid you to attend the session if he knows who or what you are. He's not likely to want another conjuror watching him at work, is he?"

Lucian poured the wine, a thoughtful expression on his hard face. "Okay, so you need a reasonable excuse for bringing me along. Who else besides us knows what you're planning?"

"Just Drake."

"How about the man you met outside the restaurant last night?" Lucian asked quietly, handing her a glass and sipping at his own.

"Richard?" Ariana frowned. "No, I don't think I'll tell him what's going on. It would be a little embarrassing to explain."

"You mean about having me as a lover?" he drawled, topaz eyes narrowing assessingly.

"About Philomena having fallen for a psychic," she corrected smoothly. "I'd rather keep this within the family as far as possible."

"I gather from something Drake said last night that he and Philomena and you comprise the total Warfield family, right?"

"That's right," Ariana agreed evenly, leading the way back to the living room. Enroute she scooped up a silver dish laden with eggs which had been stuffed and decorated with caviar. "Our parents were killed when Drake and I were small. They were botanists. Very brilliant botanists, as a matter of fact. They died on a field trip up the Amazon." Her tone made it clear that she did not want to discuss the matter further.

Lucian ignored the tone. "Scientists, hmmm?" He helped himself to several of the stuffed eggs as he sprawled casually on the sofa. "Let's see. Drake is a highly ingenious and successful inventor, your parents were scientists and Philomena is an interior designer and artist of some renown. Your family seems to have more than the normal share of talent."

Ariana shrugged and munched a canap;aae. She had taken a seat across from him with the wide coffee table between them.

"What talent were you blessed with, Ariana?" Lucian asked almost silkily.

"Nothing very exciting or interesting like Drake and Philomena, I'm afraid," she tossed back coldly. "The only thing I do with any competence is make and manage money."

· "Which explains your rather extensive interest in the subject." He held up a hand as a spark flashed in her smoky blue eyes. "Relax. I'm not going to start another insult-slinging match. I learned my lesson last night," he added with a wry smile. "Warfield & Company, Financial Planners, I take it, is just what it sounds like? A comprehensive money management and counseling firm?"

"That's correct," she replied stiffly, sensing the underlying disapproval in his voice. "We sell a variety of financial services to individuals and businesses. The services are designed to help them make money and control what they do make so that it doesn't all wind up going to the IRS. What about you, Lucian?" she demanded firmly, seeking to change the direction of the conversation. "Has magic always been your chief interest?"

"I've loved magic since I was ten years old," he said simply.

Ariana couldn't help the question which immediately came to her lips. "For heaven's sake, *why?*" Her perplexed expression was totally honest. How could anyone truly love deliberate deception?

Lucian stared at her for a moment as if trying to ascertain her reasons for asking. "There's a real beauty in it, Ariana," he finally said quietly. "People respond to it in such a unique fashion. They're charmed by it. It creates a sense of wonder that's unlike anything else. I enjoy mastering the art that is capable of creating that wonder."

Ariana thought about that and then smiled reluctantly. "You sound like Philomena when she discusses a perfect room or Drake when he's working on something especially clever."

"But I don't sound like you when you're making money in an especially clever fashion?" he concluded perceptively.

She shook her head. "No. I've never thought of managing money as an art form. It's just an ability I have. I don't go around instilling wonder and appreciation in people, although I do instill a little gratitude when things go right or someone gets his financial world straightened out."

"Perhaps you manage to dazzle people in other areas of your life," Lucian pursued softly. "In your relationship with the man who was waiting for you at the restaurant last night, for instance?"

Ariana lifted her chin and gave her guest a quelling glance. "You seem rather fascinated with Richard."

"I'll admit I'm a little curious about him," Lucian said honestly.

"Why? He has nothing to do with this."

"That's one of the reasons I'm curious. What would he say if he knew you were feeding me dinner tonight and that you're planning to have me pose as your lover?"

"Not my lover," she repeated automatically. "And you don't have to worry about Richard. Please forget about him!"

"Does that mean you're not going to worry about him?"

"Of course I'm not going to worry about him. Why on earth should I?" she snapped. Somehow she had to get control of this ridiculous conversation.

"Then he's not your real lover?"

"Lucian, I don't know what makes you think you have the right to pry into my personal life like this, but..."

"I just want to be aware of all the potential risks," he told her flatly.

"Risks!" She stared at him, dumbfounded. "You're worried about the risk of Richard finding out you're pretending to be my—my *friend*, and taking offense?" She refused to use the word lover.

"There might not be time to explain that I'm only

pretending. A man in his position could be forgiven for losing his temper rather quickly if he were to discover that you're entertaining strange males in the evenings. All I'm asking is whether or not he has the right to lose his temper over such an event. Is he your real lover? Because if so, I think you'd better tell him exactly what's going on." There was a steel-edged note in his words that enraged Ariana.

She set her glass down on the table with a crystal clatter and glared furiously across the short expanse of space separating her from the magician. "Let me try and make a few things very clear, Lucian Hawk. First, you have no need to concern yourself with any aspect of my private life. You may rest assured that Richard Dearborn will not descend on you and beat you to a pulp, even if he were to misunderstand the situation. He's a gentleman. Second, I do not need or want your advice on what I should or should not tell him. I'll handle my relationship with him as I see fit!"

"Are you sleeping with him? That's all I'm asking," Lucian growled.

"That's none of your damn business!"

"It is my business! My God, woman, if you're having an affair with him and he finds out about me, you're asking for all kinds of trouble. What's the matter with you? Are you so naive that you think he won't care? A man who feels he has a claim on a woman isn't going to take kindly to the notion of said female pretending to be in love with another man, regardless of the situation or reason. And he's going to be even angrier about it if he finds out in a less than straightforward fashion!"

"You speak knowledgeably on the subject!" she flung back.

"I speak from a man's point of view. I know damn well how I'd react if I found out my woman was involving herself in a situation like this without consulting me first!"

For an instant Ariana could hardly speak, she was so enraged. It took the sum total of her willpower to ask far too sweetly, "And what, exactly, would you do, Mr. Hawk? Use your magic to turn the other man into a frog?"

He looked at her with a disconcerting directness that made her catch her breath. She had the impression that he was actually trying to put himself in Richard's place. "I would," he ground out at last, "be furious that you hadn't taken me into your confidence. To put it bluntly, there would be hell to pay."

Ariana took a savage grip on her temper. "Then it's fortunate you're not in Richard's position, isn't it? For the record, Lucian, Richard Dearborn is the man I may marry. That decision, however, lies in the future. He has no 'claim' on me, as you so chauvinistically phrase it. I assure you, you are perfectly safe."

Lucian looked down into his wine as if he'd discovered something fascinating floating on the surface of the Riesling. "If you're thinking of marrying him, you must be sleeping with him. If you're sleeping with him, you're asking for trouble by pulling off this little stunt behind his back. I, as the person most likely to be clobbered in the process, am afraid I must object."

"I am not sleeping with him!" Ariana yelped, losing the tenuous grip on her temper. "There! Are you satisfied? I'm not having an affair with anyone. You're safe, magician. Do you hear me? *Safe!*"

Lucian raised his head once more, and for the life of her Ariana couldn't read the expression in those topaz eyes, but that didn't lessen the impact of his glittering glance. Behind the lenses of his glasses, the honeyed depths of his eyes seemed to burn for a moment and then the fire was gone to be replaced by something much cooler and more controlled.

"I apologize for pushing you so hard about it," he said quietly. "I had to know exactly what I was getting into." His voice sounded strained.

Ariana shifted restlessly as she got her emotions back under control. "Forget it. I just didn't realize how upset a man in your position would be about the prospect of Richard misunderstanding the situation."

"No," he agreed. "You didn't."

"Believe me, Richard would not be a threat, even if things between him and me were as you thought."

"I see," Lucian said very neutrally.

Ariana sighed in exasperation. "I don't think you do see but it really doesn't matter as long as you'll still agree to help me in this project."

"Oh, yes. I'll help you. I made up my mind about that last night."

Her eyes widened. "Then why the hell did you just put me through that inquisition?" She got to her feet abruptly. "Oh, never mind. I don't think I want to hear any more of your convoluted masculine reasoning. I'll serve dinner." With a regal, impatient stride she headed for the kitchen and once more he followed. This time he leaned in the kitchen doorway, watching as she prepared to serve.

"I take it that if and when you do decide to marry

Richard, you envision a very modern sort of arrange-ment?" he finally queried in a very conversational tone. He sniffed appreciatively as she withdrew the baked salmon from the oven.

"If you're talking about a so-called open marriage when you say 'modern,' most definitely not. I am a firm believer in fidelity. But if, on the other hand, you're talking about a financially and legally modern marriage, then, yes, I do want a modern relationship," she agreed almost absently, concentrating on arranging the fish on a warmed platter. She could feel his eyes on her as she worked, and wondered at the intensity of his gaze.

"What's that mean?" he asked.

"It means that I would never enter into marriage without such things as a clear and binding prenuptial agreement, for example," she told him, swinging around to thrust the platter into his hands. "Here, make yourself useful and take this over to the table."

"A marriage contract?" He accepted the platter, but his attention was on her as she turned back to the oven for the tray of Duchesse Potatoes. She heard the startled tone in his voice.

"Exactly. A contract protects both parties. It's the only sensible way to go about something as uncertain as marriage."

There was a silence behind her, and when she moved to carry the potatoes to the table she found that Lucian had already placed his platter on the round dining room table. "I take it you don't agree, Lucian?" she smiled, faintly amused. She put down the potatoes and went back to the kitchen for the spinach salad.

"My feelings on the subject are immaterial," he said

slowly, holding her chair for her. There was a curious remoteness in his words. "I was married once and I plan never again to repeat the error. Therefore, such modern issues as prenuptial contracts don't arise for me."

He sat down across from her and met her steady gaze. For an instant a strange tension hovered in the air between them and then Ariana broke it with a supremely condescending smile. "So, magician, it would appear we are fated to be on opposite sides of yet another fence. You and I have, apparently, drawn different lessons from our past mistakes."

He poured out more of the wine and then lifted his glass. "To the lesson I learned," he murmured sardonically. "Never trust a woman who says she's in love and wants to marry. She can damn well prove her love by taking the risk of having an affair with me."

Ariana's chin lifted imperiously, and her smoky eyes gleamed as she raised her own glass. "And to the lesson I learned. Never trust a man who says he's in love. He can damn well prove his love by taking the risk of marriage with a prenuptial contract that's been cast in iron."

Wordlessly they each downed a symbolic swallow, and when they had finished, Ariana felt as if somehow they had arrived at a fragile understanding. It was time to go to work.

"My aunt is due to attend another of her psychic's sessions this coming weekend," she began in a business-like fashion. "I've already told her I was curious, myself, and wanted to attend. She didn't object when I said I'd be coming up with you; not when I explained that you were someone I've been dating who is also curious. She's quite confident her new guru can with-stand a little scrutiny, I guess."

"Where does this guru live?"

"He has a sort of retreat up in the mountains about a hundred miles from here. Sounds very gothic. Lots of atmosphere, I gather," Ariana said dryly as she tasted the salmon. "Anyhow, a small group of people is allowed to attend the s;aaeances each weekend. Philomena doesn't seem concerned about getting per-mission to bring a couple of guests."

"There's a charge for attending?"

"Naturally. A stiff one, too. Actually, I wouldn't be so concerned about the situation if that was all it appeared to be costing my aunt. One expects to pay for any sort of performance, after all. I would assume she'd grow bored with this latest fad after a while and go on to something else."

"But the withdrawals from her account have added up to considerably more than just entrance fees for the sessions?" Lucian hazarded.

"Considerably more," she emphasized.

"What's the name of your aunt's psychic?"

"Fletcher Galen. Mean anything to you?"

Lucian shook his head. "No, I'm afraid not. That doesn't mean much. Probably a, er, stage name."

"You mean an alias!" she scoffed, passing him the salad bowl which he took with alacrity. She suddenly noticed the way he was enjoying the meal she had cooked. Didn't the man ever get home cooking?

"Okay, an alias," he agreed. "Could I have some more salmon, please?" He looked hopefully at the platter.

The discussion continued, but it became increasingly clear that it was the meal which was commanding Lucian Hawk's attention. By the time the walnut torte had been produced he was clearly satisfied with the progress of the evening.

"I warn you I may drag out our working relationship indefinitely if you'll guarantee to keep feeding me," he chuckled as he polished off the torte. "Sure beats eating off of the food stamps!"

"Thank you," she said dryly.

"Don't worry, I know how to pay for my dinner," he told her easily as he helped her carry dishes back into the kitchen.

"You do parlor tricks?"

"How did you guess?"

Ariana set the last of the dishes in the sink and turned to him, wiping her fingers on a hand towel. "All right," she challenged. "Let's see what you can do."

"Are you serious?" he half smiled, eyeing her curiously.

"Why not? I'm hiring a magician, aren't I? I might as well see how good a magician I've got!"

Lucian hesitated. "You're not hiring me, Ariana, remember? This is a partnership."

"Sorry, I'll try to remember," she murmured and reached into a cupboard for two brandy snifters. "Show me your stuff, magician," she commanded, leading the way back to the living room with a bottle of brandy and the glasses.

"Something simple, I think, to start," he said with a trace of amusement as he sat down in the center of the papaya-colored rug. "Got a dollar bill?"

She might as well get into the spirit of the thing, Ariana told herself, locating the required dollar bill in her purse. Then she sat cross-legged in front of him and poured brandy into the two glasses. She assumed he would need a few minutes to arrange whatever little trick he intended to perform, so she occupied herself with pouring out the brandy.

The sound of the dollar bill being torn into shreds brought her head up sharply. "My dollar!" she gasped with the natural chagrin of someone who has a very healthy respect for money. The last of the shredded dollar was just going into Lucian's left hand. "You've just destroyed my money!"

"I thought that would get your attention," Lucian said pleasantly. He showed her the ball of once perfectly good money which was now in the palm of his hand. Then he closed his fingers back into a fist, made a pass or two with his other hand and proceeded to unroll the wad which had been the torn bill.

The dollar bill was again in one piece.

Ariana frowned, her suddenly intent gaze going from the dollar bill to Lucian's topaz eyes. "How did you do that?" she demanded.

"Magic," he reminded her blandly.

"Don't give me that," she ordered impatiently. "How does that trick work?"

"I just told you. Magic."

"Do it again."

Obediently Lucian repeated the trick, tearing the dollar bill into several pieces and then unrolling the ball of fragments to reveal a complete and whole dollar.

Her brows drawn together in a line of unswervable

concentration, Ariana inched a little closer and took a sip of her brandy. "Do it one more time. Slowly."

Lucian smiled and obligingly repeated the sleight-of-hand. Once more Ariana was forced to admit that it looked very much as if her dollar bill had been torn to shreds and then magically made whole. She shifted a little closer on the papaya carpet. Her curiosity was thoroughly aroused now.

"Given your interest in money," Lucian said in low, luring tones, "you might like this little piece of magic, too." He reached into his back pocket and removed a handkerchief and a coin. Then he picked up an empty glass he'd carried in from the kitchen and carelessly rolled up the handkerchief into a small ball which he dropped into the glass. He set the glass with the wadded-up handkerchief onto the carpet between himself and Ariana and then casually made the coin, which had been sitting beside the glass, disappear.

"You palmed the coin!" she accused at once.

"Did I? Look inside the handkerchief," Lucian advised, mouth crooked upward in amusement.

Suspiciously Ariana reached into the glass and pulled out the handkerchief. Out fell the missing coin. She shook her head in annoyance. "Do it again."

"What's the matter, Ariana, don't you believe the evidence of your own eyes?" he mocked, obediently making the coin disappear and then reappear inside the handkerchief.

"Tell me how it's done!" she insisted, moving a couple of inches closer.

Lucian took a sip of his brandy and regarded her speculatively over the edge of the glass. "No," he said finally. "I don't think I will. But I'll give you another chance with another bit of magic. Hold out your hand."

At once Ariana did as instructed. Her frustration was growing by leaps and bounds. With her decidedly practical and intellectual approach to most matters she found it infinitely disturbing not to be able to detect the secrets involved in Lucian's magic. She was determined to catch him in the middle of a piece of sleight-of-hand and find out exactly how he did his tricks.

Carefully Lucian counted out five coins into her palm. Ariana watched with total concentration. "Now count them back into my hand," he instructed in that gentle, come-hither voice. He held out his hand.

Carefully, never so much as blinking, Ariana counted back the five coins.

"We agree there are five coins?" Lucian questioned, watching her avidly alert face with a veiled expression that Ariana ignored. She only wanted to discover how the trick was going to work.

"Agreed."

"Good. Hold out your hand again," he told her and promptly dumped the coins back into her palm, closing her fingers tightly around them. His own hand was clearly empty. "Now watch," he smiled, "while I make one of the coins you're holding so tightly leave your hand and come to mine."

Almost at once he produced a coin from between the fingers of his right hand. Hastily Ariana opened her own closed fist and discovered that she was now holding only four coins. Her patience snapped.

"Damn it, Lucian! Tell me how it's done!"

He smiled tantalizingly, topaz eyes clearly mocking. "I'll give you one more chance to see if you can figure it out."

Once again he began counting coins into her palm. Ariana followed each movement carefully. She couldn't explain, even to herself, why his magic was annoying her so thoroughly. Somehow it had become a matter of paramount importance to expose his secrets. It was as if she wanted to prove to both of them that he was no faster or cleverer than she was.

Deliberately she counted the five coins back into his hand. Whatever he did had to be done at the point where he dropped the coins into her palm and then closed her hand into a fist around them. That must be the moment when the sleight-of-hand took place. She waited, poised to strike.

Lucian saw the tension in her slender body as she sat waiting to pounce. The cool determination in her appealed to him, prompting a sense of amusement and challenge. She was so grimly set on finding out how the magic worked.

But he had been deliberately luring her closer and closer on the plush papaya carpet, because ever since last night he had been wondering what made Ariana Warfield work.

The woman was a mystery to him, and Lucian knew an overwhelming urge to discover what lay behind her cool exterior. What were the secrets hinted at by that unexpectedly soft and vulnerable mouth?

So she wasn't sleeping with Dearborn, the man in the three-hundred-dollar trenchcoat....

He held his hand above hers, ready to back-palm one of the coins so that only four of them would fall into her hand. Ariana waited expectantly, her eyes focused on his palm full of coins. She was going to grab for his hand just as he was concealing one of the coins, Lucian realized with a flash of humor. She was very, very close and when she moved to trap his hand she would be off balance. Which was just the way he wanted her.

Deliberately he started to drop the coins back into her hand.

"Oh, no you don't!" Ariana cried, reaching for his hand with her free fingers.

Lucian didn't argue. He simply encircled her wrist and yanked her gently off balance and onto her back. An instant later she was lying partially trapped under him. He felt her go unnaturally still as she stared up at him wide-eyed.

Very calmly he removed her eyeglasses and then his own. For a timeless moment topaz eyes burned into unreadable smoky blue depths and then Lucian said huskily, "It's dangerous to interrupt a magician at work."

Slowly, savoring the heightened awareness of all his senses as his body responded to the woman beneath him, Lucian lowered his mouth to Ariana's.

CHAPTER THREE

ARIANA'S IMMEDIATE RESPONSE TO THE position in which she found herself was astonishment; not that Lucian had decided to kiss her but that she had been concentrating so intently on his magic that she hadn't even been aware of his real goal. The whole magic act, it seemed, had merely been an elaborate diversion, a piece of misdirection. She had been neatly lured into a very old trap.

The knowledge that he had handled her so adroitly was what held Ariana still as Lucian's mouth came down on hers. She simply wasn't accustomed to being so easily maneuvered by a man.

Lucian took full advantage of the moment of astonishment. Holding her wrists firmly but gently pinned to the carpet on either side of her head, he moved his lips with warm deliberation. Ariana felt as if she were being carefully tasted; as if her mouth were being explored to the fullest possible extent. There was a hungry sensuality behind the kiss, and it occurred to her vaguely that she was the subject of his curiosity as well as his desire. Was Lucian Hawk really curious about her?

The realization that he might be searching for some answers about her was disturbing. When his tongue emerged to lightly trace the outline of her lower lip in a coaxing manner, Ariana stirred beneath him.

It was at that point that she had to acknowledge that more than astonishment and surprise was holding her flat on her back on the carpet. Ariana tried to move again and realized that she was physically trapped, as well. Lucian was using the weight of his body and the casual strength in his hands to hold her where he wanted her.

Ariana felt a returning surge of irritation as well as the beginnings of something suspiciously akin to a physical response, and she parted her lips to protest both.

"Lucian, that's enough!..." she whispered more un-steadily than she might have wanted.

But he simply took the opportunity to drive his tongue between her lips, filling the warm interior with such shocking completeness that her protest was cut off before it had really begun.

She felt the accompanying surge of his body as he intimately invaded her mouth, and a small answering tremor went through her slender frame. The effect of her own response was like a tiny dose of electricity passing over the surface of her skin. Every nerve ending seemed to come alive; she was exquisitely aware of a tighten-ing at the nape of her neck and across her midriff, and inside the black ballet slippers her toes curled. Ariana moaned, a small, primitive sound that was half locked in the back of her throat.

Lucian's response was a husky stifled groan that emanated from deep in his chest, and the weight of him seemed to increase. His tongue moved inside her mouth now with a rising urgency, its motion deliberately imitating the far more intimate union to which it was only a prelude. The primitive rhythm seemed to thrill Ariana's senses, freeing them from the bonds of her normal, cool thought processes. Slowly, with ever more complex patterns, they began to whirl.

Magic, she tried to tell herself as her lashes fluttered tightly shut and her hips arched of their own accord into his. He must be using magic on her.

As if the instinctive movement of her thighs were a signal of some sort, Lucian growled her name deeply into her mouth.

"Ariana!" And then his leg moved boldly across hers, sliding aggressively between her knees. He guided one of her hands to the back of his neck, where her garnet-colored nails slid into the black and silver of his hair with trembling expectancy.

The sense of expectancy was as much a shock to her as anything else that had yet happened. Ariana found herself striving to forget about the significance of what was happening. For a few minutes, she told herself, she would sample a bit of what was being offered. The promise of magic had never seemed so tantalizing.

"My God! You feel good lying here under me," he breathed, reluctantly breaking the hot contact with her mouth to trace a silky pattern of kisses along the line of her jaw. "I knew you were going to feel good!"

"Lucian?"

The uncertain, questioning note in her voice ended in a sharp little intake of breath as he nipped gently at her earlobe. Simultaneously his hand came down on her breast. Her body's response was immediate. There was a sudden, aching tautness, and she knew the nipple beneath his palm was hardening. The silk of her jewel-colored blouse and the scrap of lace which was her bra offered little protection. She knew he must be aware of the budding nipple.

His deep growl of anticipation and pleasure was ample evidence that he was satisfied with her reactions. A part of Ariana wanted to retreat; to deny this man the knowledge that he was having such a strong effect on her senses. It was dangerous for a woman to let a man know the extent of his power over her, she reminded herself.

But those words of wisdom were making no impact on her brain tonight. It was easier to listen to the urgings of her senses. Her fingers threaded luxuriously through the darkness of his hair, and she was rewarded with the shudder that coursed through him. His leg moved purposefully along the inside of hers.

His lips were on her throat now, and he arched her head back over his arm, exposing the vulnerable, sensitive curve. When he began to unbutton her blouse Ariana moved restlessly. The danger in his magic was coming closer, and she knew she ought to resist it.

"Oh, Lucian!" The tiny cry came as he unclasped the front fastening of her bra and found the swelling outline of her breast. Instinctively she turned her face into his shoulder, inhaling the warm, male scent of his body.

"So soft," he whispered hoarsely against the skin just above the nipple he was delicately exciting with his thumb. "Soft and gentle and passionate. I was sure there would be something special behind that cool exterior. I had to find out." The words came brokenly, punctuated by small, stinging little kisses that moved closer and closer to their goal until suddenly he had taken the tip of her breast into his warm mouth.

Ariana gasped and clung heedlessly to him, her hands finding pleasure in the thrusting contours of his strong shoulders. "Lucian, Lucian, please! I don't know...I don't think..."

"Hush," he murmured, his voice lulling and deliciously hypnotic. "Hush, Magic Lady. I want to discover all your secrets." He slid his palm down across her stomach, searching out the fastening of the velvet trousers. "By morning I'm going to know exactly how you work."

Morning? Good lord, did he think he was going to stay the night with her? Awareness jolted through her, sending the magic fleeing. What did she think she was doing letting this near-stranger make love to her! Was she out of her head?

"No. No, Lucian! That's enough. Stop it!" Tremulously and then with gathering conviction Ariana shifted beneath his weight and began pushing at his shoulders.

"Relax, honey," he crooned, voice still hypnotic and full of promise. "Just relax and let me take you where we both want to go."

Ariana sucked in her breath, her head moving in a fierce negative. "Lucian, stop it. I mean it. Let me up!"

He must have heard the underlying element of panic that was seeping into her voice because he stopped his sensual assault and raised his head to gaze down at her intently. She saw the embers of passion that still flickered in the depths of his topaz eyes and held her breath for a tension-filled moment.

What would she do if he didn't release her?

"What's the matter, Magic Lady?" he murmured, gentling her with his fingertips. His mouth curved reassuringly. "Don't you want me? I could feel you responding, honey. Why the panic now?"

"I am not panicking," she retorted angrily. "I'm simply calling a halt to an after-dinner kiss that has gone much too far. I don't know where you got the idea you might be staying until morning, magician, but you're wrong. You're going to pull a quick disappearing act with the assistance of my front door. Let me up, Lucian."

He didn't move. "And if I don't?"

"You will." She returned his gaze unflinchingly, her voice very steady.

He waited a moment longer and then rolled onto his side, propping himself up on one elbow to watch as she hastily sat up and began arranging her clothing. "You're right. I will leave. This time." The last words came very meaningfully.

"Don't make it sound as if there's going to be a next time!" Ariana scrabbled on the carpet for her glasses and pushed them onto her nose in a small act of defense.

"You're one heck of a quick-change artist," he observed almost casually, reaching for his own glasses and sitting up. "A minute ago..."

"A minute ago things were getting out of hand!"

"No," he countered softly. "I had everything under control." The look in his eyes sent a wave of warmth through her from head to toe.

"You mean you were going to call a halt of your own accord?" she mocked skeptically as she got to her feet and scooped up the brandy snifters.

"I didn't say that, I merely said I had everything under control." He picked up the bottle of brandy and followed her back to the kitchen where he set it on the counter.

"Well, magician, your idea of things being under control varies somewhat from mine, so I think it's time we ended this evening."

"You're scared of me, aren't you?" he asked wonderingly. "What's the matter? Doesn't Dearborn make you react like that?"

Ariana swung around to face him, cold fury in her eyes. "Let's get something straight, Lucian. I am not in the market for an affair with a magician or anyone else. You and I have a working relationship together and that's all. Stay out of my private life and I'll stay out of yours. Agreed?"

He smiled abruptly, a devastating, wholly masculine smile that was guaranteed to raise the hackles on any woman's neck. Ariana was no exception. "You're quite welcome to invade my private life," he drawled provocatively. "And as long as we're setting the record straight, I'd just like to point out that you were enjoying at least part of that little session on the carpet a few minutes ago!"

Ariana's chin lifted proudly. "I can enjoy an after-dinner kiss as much as anyone!"

"You make it sound like an after-dinner mint!"

"I put it in exactly the same category. A couple are very pleasant. A whole package would be far too much. Good night, Lucian Hawk. I will phone you later this week and let you know the final arrangements for the trip to Fletcher Galen's retreat."

"Would you let me stay if I offered to tell you how to make the coin disappear from the floor and reappear inside the handkerchief?" he tried.

She saw the dawning laughter in his eyes and almost succumbed to it. With firm resolve she managed to keep her face set in unyielding determination. "You can't bribe me, Lucian. Not by promising to teach me the tricks of your craft."

"What would it take to bribe you?" he asked with a deep curiosity.

"Nothing you have to offer! Good night, Lucian!" Imperiously she went to the front hall closet and hauled out his black jacket.

He took it almost meekly and absently shrugged into it. His eyes never left her face.

"Do you need to call a cab?" she inquired belatedly, feeling unaccountably guilty at the way she was pushing him out the door.

"No. I drove tonight."

"Oh. Well, in that case..."

"In that case there's no excuse for not being on my way, is there?" he finished for her amiably.

The guilt rose a little higher. "Lucian, I'm sorry if I gave you the wrong impression tonight," Ariana said in a contrite little rush. "You're not really angry?"

One black brow climbed above the frames of his glasses, and his mouth curved cryptically as he eyed her. "What's the matter, Ariana? Finally beginning to worry about the consequences of angering a magician?"

That restored her sense of balance very neatly. Ariana flung open her door and wordlessly ushered him out into the foggy night.

"Thank you for dinner, Ariana," he murmured politely and then he was gone.

There was an unnatural trembling in the tips of Ariana's fingers as she closed the door solidly behind him. Now why in the world should that be? she asked herself uneasily. What was the matter with her? This wasn't the first time a man had tried to take more than she was willing to offer.

But it was the first time in a long while that she had been so tempted to forget all the fine decisions she had made when things had gone so wrong four years ago.

Well, she'd come to her senses and regained control of the situation in time, she reassured herself as she trailed through the living room. She could handle Lucian Hawk.

It was an impulse which made her reach for the phone beside the Queen Anne sofa. Her brother kept very odd hours, and it was a good bet that he was still awake. When he answered cheerfully on the other end of the line Ariana plunged in with the question that was at the top of her list.

"What, exactly, do you know about Lucian Hawk, Drake?"

"What's wrong? Isn't he going to work out?" Drake yawned extravagantly in her ear. "He's a hell of a good magician. A real artist."

"Okay, I'll buy that, but what do you know about him, personally? How did you meet him?"

"Through a friend, a guy who's trying to write a book on Houdini. He knows a lot of magicians. It's all right, Ari. My friend has known him quite a while. He vouched for Hawk. And after I met Lucian I liked him, too. Don't you?" Drake added innocently.

Ariana ignored the question. "Is that all you know about him?"

"Well..."

"Well, what, Drake?" she prodded coolly.

"Lucian and I had a few drinks one night last week and talked a bit." Drake sounded more vague than he usually was when he had his mind on a new project.

"And?"

"And nothing really. I gather he's done a lot of varied things. Only to be expected I suppose. I mean, he didn't have a smart sister like you to manage money for him and help him get rich, did he?"

"Drake, if there's something I ought to know before I leave with Lucian Hawk Saturday morning, I'd certainly appreciate it if you would tell me!" Ariana got out acidly.

"Look, the best I can do is to tell you that the friend who introduced me to Lucian swears he'd trust the man with his life. Furthermore, I, myself, like Hawk. I'd trust him, too. What's the matter with you? Has something happened to make you nervous about the man? I can get some more details from my friend if you want to know them, but I had the impression that Hawk's a relatively quiet person who can be trusted and who knows magic. What more do you want?"

Arian sighed. "Nothing, Drake. He'll have to do. There really isn't time to find anyone else. I've already told Aunt Phil I would be attending the session with her this weekend and that I was bringing someone with me."

"I still think you're worrying over nothing, Ari. This is just another of Aunt Phil's passing fancies. You know how wild she was about all those films and books claiming that Earth had been visited by alien spacemen thousands of years ago. She always gets excited about the possibility of visitors from outer space. But she'll realize this guy Galen's a phony soon enough."

"I'm not so sure, Drake. This time there's money involved," Ariana stated decisively.

There was a chuckle on the other end of the line. "And when there's money involved Ariana Warfield sits up and takes notice, doesn't she? Good luck, Ari. I'll be anxious to hear the results of this weekend's big expos;aae. Good night, I've got to get back to this nifty little gadget I'm working on. It's the solution to a single woman's fears in the big city. It looks like a normal lipstick case, but..."

"Good night, Drake," Ariana interrupted. She wasn't going to get any more out of him tonight, she told herself wryly. "I'll phone you when I get back from the mountains."

LUCIAN HAWK REAPPEARED AT ARIANA'S door precisely on time the following Saturday morning. He got out of the cab carrying a small leather overnight bag and the familiar black jacket. Ariana watched him through the curtains, wondering disgustedly why her pulse had quickened at the sight of the dark-haired magician. She had convinced herself that her body had forgotten the sensuous attack it had undergone on her living room carpet earlier that week.

Now, as Lucian paid off the driver and loped easily up the steps to her front door she was forced to acknowledge that some forms of illogic died harder than others. The sight of him had an uncanny effect on her, and she wasn't sure how to fight it. Remember that you know very little about him, she told herself as she went to answer the door. As if she needed that added bit of caution. Wasn't the fact that he was a professional deceiver enough to make her keep her distance?

"Hello, Lucian, come on in. I'll be ready in just a minute," she said politely, opening the door and stepping aside. He was wearing a pair of faded jeans, a maize-colored oxford cloth shirt and a pair of canvas shoes. Her eyes went over him, assessing his appearance.

"What's the matter? Don't I look acceptable enough to introduce to Aunt Philomena?" he inquired easily, setting down his leather bag.

"I think we can fake it," Ariana said quickly, aware of a red stain on her cheeks. "It's not that you look bad or anything," she tried to explain.

"It's just that I don't look rich?" he hazarded perceptively. He smiled blandly.

"Never mind. You'll do just fine. Everyone dresses casually these days. Aunt Phil won't notice the jeans and shoes, I'm sure!" Hurrying off to the bedroom, Ariana made her escape. What a way to begin the trip! She picked up the shoulder purse lying on the bed and double-checked her own appearance in the mirror.

She was wearing a sassy loden green wrap jacket over a pair of pleated taupe trousers. A crisp yellow tuxedo-style shirt and a pair of elegant glove-leather casual shoes added to the overall effect of easy sophistication. How was she going to look to Philomena when she stood next to Lucian in his jeans? Ariana grimaced to herself and promptly decided to put the issue out of her mind.

She could put the matter of clothing aside but not the underlying problem it had pointed out. "I think we should discuss your background," she announced firmly to Lucian as she emerged from the bedroom.

"I beg your pardon?" He watched her with sudden wariness.

"Not your real background," Ariana assured him hastily. She felt herself flushing again and covered the moment of uneasiness by making a production of collecting her chic yellow cotton duck carryall. "The background we'll have to give Aunt Phil in order to make you sound like a plausible romance possibility. She's going to want to know something about you. Only natural, I suppose. When I told her I was bringing a friend she immediately got excited."

"Has visions of marrying you off, I take it?" he said pleasantly enough, following her outside and waiting while she locked the door.

Ariana glanced at him in surprise and then grinned wryly as she realized that he had no real knowledge of her unusual relative. "Not at all. You need have no fears on that score! Aunt Phil doesn't really believe in marriage. She thinks a good love affair is far superior to a bad marriage any day. She'd love to see me embroiled in an affair, but I don't think she has any particular wish to see me married. She's never been married herself." Which hadn't stopped Aunt Phil from enjoying more than one discreetly glorious affair of the heart, Ariana thought privately. She headed toward the sleek black Porsche parked at the curb. It was a cloudy, zesty San Francisco day, and the chill of fall hung in the air. "She does know the kind of man I generally date, however."

"And I may have trouble measuring up to the image," he observed dryly. "Your aunt sounds like an interesting woman." He stowed the luggage. "Here, toss me the keys. I'll drive."

"That's all right, I'm used to doing my own driving."

"So am I," he said, pointedly extending his hand.

An imp of mischief came to sit on Ariana's shoulder and she grinned, folding her fingers tightly around the keys. "Why don't you just magically make these keys disappear from my hand and reappear in yours the way you did the coins last night?"

"Okay, watch this," he ordered, grasping her wrist before she realized his intention. An instant later he had pried open her fingers and stolen the keys. "Voil;aga! Magic! I now have possession of the keys." He held them up with a flourish.

"Some trick!"

"It worked, didn't it? That's all a magician asks of a piece of magic."

Surrendering to the inevitable, Ariana went around to the opposite side and slid into the bucket seat. "About your fictional background," she began repressively as he started the engine and expertly put the thoroughbred car in gear.

"Don't worry, I've got that covered, too," he said easily, his eyes on traffic as he headed for the Golden Gate Bridge. "It occurred to me that your aunt might ask a few questions sometime during the visit."

Ariana shot him a sharp glance. "All right, let's hear it. What sort of background have you decided to give yourself?"

"How about my posing as a reclusive but eminently successful real estate speculator?" he suggested.

"Hmmm. The word 'speculator' is a little sleazy sounding. Let's make it real estate developer and financier," Ariana said thoughtfully, considering the matter closely. "It carries connotations of quiet wealth. I like that."

His mouth crooked wryly. "Because the words 'developer' and 'financier' have a more established ring to them, Ariana?"

"I think so," she said slowly. "'Speculator' has a somewhat here-today-gone-tomorrow sound, don't you think? It smacks of slick dealing and fast maneuvering. Yes, I definitely prefer developer and financier."

"Whatever you say," he agreed neutrally. "As long as it sounds wealthy enough for you."

She heard the mockery in his voice and decided to ignore it. He couldn't possibly understand her fears, and she had no intention of trying to explain them to him.

But what if, Ariana found herself thinking wistfully as they crossed the elegant span of the Golden Gate Bridge, what if Lucian Hawk really did meet her specifications for a husband? Instantly she put a brake on her flight of fancy. That was ridiculous. Even if by some miracle he had money and a spotless reputation, even if he were to fall in love with her, there was still the overriding fact that he had no interest in marriage. He had made that very clear the other night.

She was a fool to even be thinking such wild thoughts, Ariana scolded herself. With a touch of aggression which caused Lucian to slide her a sideways glance, she changed the subject.

The picturesque inn at the edge of the tiny mountain

town was charming; quaintly Victorian in architecture. Nestled cozily in the towering pines and fir trees which surrounded it, the place looked as if it had been at home there in the mountains for a hundred years. Aunt Philomena had happily told Ariana that in reality the place had only been built five years previously and that the plumbing, thank God, could be relied upon.

Lucian guided the black Porsche into the small parking lot and glanced around curiously as he switched off the engine. "This is where Fletcher Galen conducts his magic act?"

"The actual retreat is located a few miles from here according to Aunt Phil. People aren't allowed to stay overnight on the grounds. Most of them stay here at this inn. If you do succeed in exposing Galen, the owners of this place probably won't thank you. They're undoubtedly doing quite well on the tourism he inspires!" She opened her door, not waiting for him to perform the small task. "Oh, good. We should be just in time for afternoon tea. Phil will be pleased."

"Tea?" Lucian occupied himself collecting the baggage.

"Umm. Aunt Phil says it's one of the attractions of the inn. That and the late evening sherry hour!" She smiled as they walked into the lobby.

Ariana recognized immediately the apparition standing at the front desk engaged in what could only be politely described as a forceful discussion with the middle-aged clerk on the other side.

Only Philomena Warfield could have pulled off the fashion coup of combining a flowing, flowered caftan, hand-tooled cowboy boots and a brilliantly patterned headscarf wrapped gypsy style around her long silvery hair. And only Aunt Phil would have the audacity to be conducting such an outrageous argument. Ariana felt the heated rush of embarrassment as a blush rose up her throat and stained her cheeks. By now she ought to be accustomed to Philomena's eccentric ways, but there were still times when she could be caught flat-footed and totally embarrassed by them.

"I don't care what you thought I ordered two days ago. I no longer want two rooms for my niece and her friend. I want *one* room. What's the matter with you, man? Are you living in the Dark Ages? This is a modern world we live in and my niece is a very modern woman. Men and women do spend weekends together at places like this, you know! All the time these days! Ariana is thirty years old, and she's entitled to share a room with her male friend!"

"Madam," the clerk began grimly, "the question of your niece's love life is not at issue here. I don't care who your niece sleeps with or where she chooses to spend her nights. What is at issue is the little matter of two guaranteed room reservations. These rooms were held at your request. They could easily have been booked for the evening by other people whom we had to turn away. Now if your niece wants to share a room with her *friend,* that's clearly her business. But someone is going to have to pay for the extra room!"

"That's ridiculous," Philomena declared grandly. "Why should I pay for two rooms when I only require one for her? However, if you're going to be chintzy about the matter, I will pay for both rooms on one condition! You're to tell my niece and her escort when they arrive that there is only the one room available, do you understand?"

Ariana managed to find her tongue. "Aunt Phil!" Caught between the embarrassment of her aunt deliberately trying to arrange a compromising situation and the tall, dark figure of Lucian looming behind her in the lobby with a wickedly amused smile on his face, Ariana could only wish for a genuine act of magic. Something along the lines of having the floor open up to allow her to disappear without a trace. Instead there was only one alternative and that was to get the situation in hand immediately.

"Aunt Phil, you can forget it. It won't work," she grated with what she hoped was cool amusement. There was no hiding her flaming cheeks.

"Ariana, darling!" In a floaty little rush of caftan and perfume Philomena's dainty figure flew across the room to greet her niece. At sixty-two, Philomena Warfield was still a striking woman. Full of energy and talent she lit up any room in which she found herself. "You finally got here! I've been dying to meet your new friend. Drake has been telling me all about him just this morning on the phone. Please don't waste another second. Introduce us, dear!"

Ariana sighed. "Philomena, this is Lucian Hawk. Lucian, my aunt."

Lucian dropped one of the bags he was holding and stepped pointedly around Ariana in order to accept Philomena's delicately held fingers. He inclined his head with a gracious manner which Ariana presumed he had developed in the course of performing before an audience. "I'm very pleased to meet you, Miss

Warfield." The words were gravely polite, but the topaz eyes gleamed as he continued, "And I appreciate your efforts on my behalf with the desk clerk."

Philomena glowed. "Well, I wouldn't have bothered," she confided as they both ignored Ariana, "if you'd been that Richard Dearborn person Ariana's been seeing so much of lately. But I had a lovely chat with Drake this morning, and he told me all about you. I came to the conclusion that you may be just what Ari needs. In the past four years she's become terribly, terribly cautious about interesting men."

"I understand," Lucian said, nodding.

"Aunt Phil that is enough!" Ariana interrupted vengefully, wondering what in the world Drake had told her. "Lucian, stop encouraging my aunt, do you hear me? Both of you are causing me untold humiliation. Just look at all these other people watching us! Aunt Phil, that was a perfectly ridiculous little plot you were concocting with the desk clerk. It wouldn't have worked at all and you should have known it! If Lucian and I had arrived to find only one room, I would have shared yours!"

"Oh, dear." Philomena appealed to Lucian. "She's so unimaginative, isn't she? Well, I did my best. It was worth a try. Come along, both of you, they're just starting to serve tea and I'm sure you could use a cup after that long drive."

Ariana turned a helpless look on her escort, but Lucian merely smiled kindly and took her arm to guide her in the wake of Philomena.

One thing which could be said about Philomena, Ariana consoled herself despairingly as her aunt commandeered a table and ordered a sumptuous tea, there was never any lack of conversation in the older woman's vicinity. Philomena kept up a lively monologue while she arranged tea and scones. Most of the discussion was aimed at Lucian, who listened attentively. Ariana could only set her teeth and endure. For his part, Lucian appeared entranced.

"Has Ariana always been so interested in financial matters?" he inquired blandly, oblivious of the seething glance bestowed on him by the lady in question. He lathered butter on a scone and took a satisfyingly large bite as Philomena responded with an indulgent chuckle.

"Oh, my, yes. Since she was in high school. Always seemed to have a talent for handling money, didn't you, Ari?" Before Ariana could answer, Philomena plunged on. "Naturally Drake and I are both extremely grateful, you understand, Lucian."

"You are?" He looked across at Ariana who sat in tense silence.

"Definitely. Drake and I, I'm sorry to admit, would undoubtedly be flat broke today if it weren't for Ari. My nephew and I are both quite talented in our own fields, but we have absolutely no feel for money at all. We simply enjoy spending it. It's Ariana who has invested our earnings over the years for us and built them into comfortable amounts. Drake and I both recognized what an asset she was early on and started turning everything over to her as soon as possible. I don't mind saying she's made us a nice little mint, bless her heart. I do so like having money to spend, don't you?"

"It can be...very convenient," Lucian admitted, still watching Ariana, who was, in turn, focusing totally on the contents of her teacup.

"Everyone likes money." Philomena nodded complacently. "And Ariana is so good to Drake and me. Why, she doesn't even charge us a cent in commission! But she can be awfully proud, too. After that messy business four years ago when she lost everything of her own and was forced to borrow from Drake and me she insisted on paying back every last dollar with interest. We tried to tell her there was absolutely no need but she..."

Ariana turned on her aunt, smoky eyes full of desperate appeal. "No more, Phil," she begged quietly. "Not on that subject. Please."

Philomena was instantly contrite. "I'm sorry, darling, I didn't realize you probably hadn't told Lucian the full story. I should never have reminded you of that awful year."

"Never mind. Just find something else to discuss." Over the rim of her cup Ariana met Lucian's glittering, inquiring eyes. She held that gaze with a steadiness which was belied by the faint trembling in her fingers. She held his gaze, but she didn't like the deep, probing expression she saw there. A wave of uneasy premonition swept over her. But before she could think of anything more to say, Philomena was rushing forward once more.

"No sense rehashing ancient history is there?" the older woman declared cheerfully as she poured more tea. "The present and the future are the only things that matter, don't you agree, Lucian?"

"Definitely," he stated firmly.

"Well, then, tell me something about yourself, Lucian," she invited brightly. "Drake says you live in San Francisco and that he introduced you to Ari at one of his parties."

"Lucian is in real estate," Ariana said distinctly, wondering why she was bothering to give her escort a re-spectable cover now. Philomena clearly seemed quite taken with him as it was! "He's a developer. He finances large projects in and around the city."

"Oh, a speculator! How exciting!" Philomena clapped her hands once in appreciation. "I'll bet you're very slick, aren't you, Lucian? Fast and sharp."

Lucian began to laugh. A deep, rich, velvety chuckle that held all the male amusement in the world. Ariana glared at him, but nothing could have quelled that laughter. Philomena stared in puzzled delight, clearly wondering what was so funny, but Lucian was laughing too hard to explain.

Ariana lifted her eyes beseechingly toward heaven, recalling with forceful clarity the conversation she'd had with Lucian in the Porsche about the difference between a speculator and a financier and developer. His sense of humor, it appeared, was as unpredictable and unreliable as that of her aunt's.

"Tell me something," Philomena went on irre-pressibly as Lucian managed to control his laughter. "Has Ari told you about her plan to insist on a prenup-tial contract in the event that she ever marries?"

"Phil!" Ariana turned once more on her aunt, but Lucian was already answering the question.

"As a matter of fact," he said smoothly, still grinning, "I believe she did mention the subject."

"And what did you think of the idea?" Philomena pressed interestedly.

"I hope I made it very clear that I didn't plan on signing such an agreement," Lucian said flatly, the last of the humor fading from his eyes.

"Excellent," Philomena approved at once. "I've been saying for four years that a man who could convince Ariana to take another chance on love and passion was exactly what she needed. Someone has got to rescue her from this obsession she's developed about protecting herself with contracts and marriage and money! A wild, wonderful affair would do her so much good, don't you think?"

Ariana ran out of fortitude. "I think," she stated grimly, rising to her feet with the royal grace of a queen, "that I'll go to my room and unpack."

She fled the tearoom, leaving it to the magician and the mischievous imp who inhabited it.

CHAPTER FOUR

SEVERAL HOURS LATER THAT EVENING Ariana sat in a pitch black room, a room so dark that she couldn't even make out the features of the people next to her, and learned that there are situations in this world that are far more unnerving than that of holding one's own with a magician and a wickedly good-natured aunt.

Ariana had never been so uneasy, so primitively alarmed in her life, and the intellectual knowledge that everything she was witnessing was nothing but sophisticated stage magic did nothing to quell the incipient dread.

The lightless room held about twenty other people, including her aunt and Lucian. Philomena knew most of the other attendees at the psychic demonstration and had introduced many of them to Ariana and her escort before the group had been conducted through the high gates of Fletcher Galen's "retreat" and into the massive stone mansion in the center of the grounds.

Galen's assistants had all been sober-faced people dressed in dark, concealing robes that resembled those of a medieval monk. They had said little as they collected the so-called donations at the gate and led people into the darkened chamber where Galen was to make his appearance.

At first Ariana had tried to tell herself that the whole thing was like going to the haunted house at Disneyland, but somehow the seriousness with which everyone took the events made it difficult to keep thinking in those terms. There were, she was learning, some very interesting factors of group psychology involved. When the people around you clearly believed that they were about to witness something wondrous and inexplicable, you found yourself in danger of suspending your own rational thought processes, too.

What Ariana couldn't fully comprehend was why she found herself the most thoroughly frightened person in the room. No one else seemed unduly terrified, merely fascinated and enthralled. Why was she, one of the two people in the room who had come to expose the trickery, so alarmed? Ariana shivered as a faint glow appeared on the small platform in front of the audience. She was suddenly very glad of Lucian's presence beside her.

The glow at the front of the room increased steadily until it revealed a table and a single chair. Ariana didn't care for the eerie, phosphorescent green of the light, but a ripple of anticipation went through the rest of the audience as if it were some sort of signal.

"Relax, will you?" Lucian leaned over to whisper in her ear. "You're the big-time exposer of charlatans and frauds, remember? You're not supposed to lose your nerve at your first s;aaeance!"

She could hear the smile in his voice, although she couldn't see his face. With an effort of will she took a grip on herself. Damned if she was going to provide him with another source of amusement tonight. He'd laughed enough at her expense this afternoon.

Before she could think of a snappy response to his bantering, however, a deep, vibrant voice seemed to effortlessly fill the room, and a figure appeared on the stage behind the table and chair. A figure dressed in a shapeless robe of yellow, the front of which was worked with a strange design. There was a hood to the robe, but it was thrown back to reveal the starkly handsome features of a man in his mid-forties. It was a lean, ascetic face, dominated by dark eyes and a strong nose—the face of a man who might have conducted inquisitions in his spare time. The face of a man with a cause. The face of a man who carried a heavy, demanding burden with great dignity.

Fletcher Galen had what was casually referred to as "presence." It was the special gift that made for the finest actors, the most persuasive politicians and the most charismatic public figures. From the moment he entered the room, Galen was the center of attention.

"Good evening, friends," he said. There was a murmur of respectful response. Galen went on in slow, measured tones. "I thank you for coming once more to witness along with me the gentle power of our good friend Krayton." Galen took the chair behind the table.

Ariana shivered and moved restlessly in her seat. On one side Philomena sat expectantly, and on the other side Lucian sat in thoughtful silence, his eyes on the figure in front of them.

"Krayton's abilities to work through me increase daily," Galen announced in a pleasant yet humble tone. "As our mind-to-mind link solidifies and grows strong, so does his ability to channel his other-worldly talent through that link. But as I have explained in the past, your assistance is also a powerful component of these experiments. Through me Krayton can tap your energy and goodwill and use it to conduct the various tests. As with everything else in the universe, all power feeds on energy and energy feeds on power. The two are intertwined and inseparable. Only the nature of the energy changes. Here on earth we have tapped very primitive forms of energy such as fossil fuels and the atom. But Krayton's people have gone far beyond such sources. Tonight you will see just how far they have gone."

Ariana jumped a little as she realized that another person had materialized at the corner of the stage as Galen had been talking. The assistant had his hood up over his face and nothing could be seen of his features as he carried forward a tray of small objects.

"Concentrate with me," Galen intoned as he passed his hand over the tray of objects. "Let Krayton tap into the power of your minds and demonstrate to you the rich resources of the human brain that wait to be set free, just as the resources of his own mind have been set free by the psychic science of his planet. You are the Keepers of the Energy here on Earth."

There followed a demonstration of psychokinesis, the movement of objects by the power of the mind. The assortment of items on the tray alternately floated in midair, snapped in half or disappeared entirely from the room.

It was all accompanied by eerie lighting, the sincere, heavy-toned voice of Galen and the indefinable power of an audience that was only too happy to believe in psychic powers. This was the same crowd who also believed in the Bermuda Triangle and ancient spacemen, Ariana reminded herself periodically. But no matter how frequently she told herself that it was all stage magic, she couldn't control the uneasy reaction of her body and her mind.

The demonstrations grew in complexity until Galen himself floated in midair at one point. Then a member of the audience was put into a trance and declared he could actually see an image of the mysterious Krayton as if he were viewing him through a camera. Philomena leaned over to whisper to Ariana and Lucian that she knew the person in the trance and couldn't wait to talk to him about the experience later.

Gradually the tension and the sense of other-worldliness built in the dark room until almost anything that could have happened would have been blamed on Krayton's psychic intervention. Ariana knew it was all a razzle-dazzle operation, but for the life of her she couldn't fully convince her senses. She sat quietly crouched in her chair, every fiber of her being taut and alarmed. She began to pray that the session would come to a quick close.

And then a soft rush of wind seemed to fill the chamber. Instantly a thrilled silence swept over the crowd, and Fletcher Galen, himself, went absolutely still, as if he, too, was stunned. His dark eyes peered into the space above the heads of the audience, and everyone else's eyes followed.

There was another glowing light, apparently emanating from midair, and in the center of it was the faint outline of an unhuman face.

"Krayton!" The shocked gasp was from Galen. "Krayton, is it possible? Have you actually found the strength to project yourself so far?"

The image in the darkness seemed to turn its head slowly with great effort, and then, as if from across the vast reaches of interstellar space, came a distant voice.

"Not enough. Not yet. Not yet..." The image and the voice began to fade.

Ariana shuddered and felt the last of her rational thoughts desert her. She gasped aloud and groped blindly for Lucian's hand. It closed around her own with instant reassurance, and she turned her head into his shoulder, burying her face in the fabric of his jacket. Immediately his arm came around her in a protective motion that was also somehow very possessive.

But Ariana wasn't concerned with such fine nuances just then. She wanted only to hide from the magic that was fraying her nerves to an extent she would never have believed possible. She was horrified not only by what she had seen but by her own reaction to it!

"Let's get out of here," Lucian ordered abruptly. He leaned over to catch Philomena's attention. "Come on, Phil, I want to take Ariana back to the inn. She's had enough."

"Of course," Phil whispered back, rising immediately to her feet. "But I can't see a foot in front of me!"

"Here, take my hand." Lucian extended his free arm to catch hold of Philomena's wrist. His other arm was still wrapped around Ariana, who was shivering uncontrollably as she crowded close to his warmth.

As she lifted her head from the security of his shoulder another light appeared on the floor at her feet, allowing her to see the carpeted aisle. The addition of yet another inexplicable light made her suck in her breath.

"Flashlight," Lucian whispered dryly. He was holding

the pencil-slim object in the hand that was wrapped around Ariana's shoulders, and he used the light to guide his two charges to the curtain through which they had entered earlier. On the other side an assistant in the usual flowing robes hastened to open the door.

"Is the lady all right?" the man asked in solicitous tones.

"She's fine. Just a little nervous," Lucian said blandly, shepherding Ariana and Philomena out of the room and into the wide hall beyond. Without pausing, he led them outside to the lot where Philomena's Mercedes was parked. The keys to the car, which he had driven earlier, appeared in his hand, and in a matter of seconds he had Philomena and Ariana safely inside.

"Ari, dear, are you all right?" Philomena leaned over the seat as Lucian drove back toward the inn. "What's wrong? There was absolutely no danger, you know. Krayton would never harm a soul!"

Ariana shuddered and stared fixedly out the window. It was Lucian who succinctly explained what had happened. "She'll be okay, Phil. Ariana just forgot to make allowances for the power of suggestion on the human mind. Some people are more susceptible than others. It can be a shock to find out you don't have all the control you think you have over your own senses."

Ariana found her voice. "It was magic, wasn't it? All of it. Stage magic." She knew then that she was asking for reassurance. Her voice was a harsh whisper.

"Yes, it was magic," Lucian said quietly. "The man's good and he has a hell of an ability to handle an audience. But it was all stage magic. With a little practice and a skilled lighting technician anyone could have done what he did tonight."

"What!" Philomena swung around to stare at Lucian. "Are you saying it was all trickery?"

"I'm afraid so, Phil. A lot of sleight-of-hand, invisible wires and lighting effects. Nothing unduly complicated." He smiled gently.

"I don't believe you! The man's a direct conduit for Krayton! Everything we saw was an example of Krayton operating through Fletcher Galen!" Philomena exclaimed.

"Phil," he said patiently, glancing at her in the rearview mirror. "I could duplicate any one of the effects you saw tonight and have you believing that you were seeing Krayton in action."

"I'm not saying a good magician couldn't find ways to imitate Krayton's powers, but that doesn't mean that what we saw tonight wasn't real! I've seen it done before, don't forget! I've seen people in the audience go into trances and actually have visions of Krayton's home world!"

"People in a hypnotic trance can be persuaded to have all sorts of interesting visions," Lucian explained quietly. "Look, Phil, let's talk about this in the morning, okay? Ariana's upset enough as it is."

Instantly Philomena was concerned again for her niece. "Ari, dear, listen to me. Krayton is quite harmless. You have no need to fear him or Fletcher Galen. They mean only the best. Don't be alarmed, dear. Goodness, I had no idea this was going to upset you so much!"

"I'm all right, Aunt Phil," Ariana managed huskily, her attention still on the darkened scenery outside the car's window. "Really I am. I just wasn't expecting quite what, uh, happened."

"I know you didn't expect to see such an amazing display of Krayton's abilities," Philomena soothed chattily. "And knowing your practical approach toward life, you probably thought it was all some silly old-fashioned spiritualist s;aaeance when I told you about it, didn't you?"

"I just wasn't expecting what happened," Ariana repeated bleakly as Lucian pulled into the inn's parking lot.

"What Ariana needs is a good dose of that sherry I saw sitting on the mantel in the lobby," Lucian announced as he assisted the two women from the car. "I take it it's there for the guests?"

"Oh, yes, help yourself." Philomena nodded quickly. "I think that's an excellent idea. I believe I'll have a little nip, myself."

Lucian seated both women in the cozy Victorian parlor and went to fetch the sherry. They had the place to themselves, since most of the inn's guests were attending Fletcher Galen's s;aaeance.

"They'll all be back fairly soon," Philomena explained as Lucian handed her a glass of sherry. "We have the most intensely interesting group discussions afterward."

"I think I'd rather give the discussion a miss if you don't mind," Ariana said as she downed a large swallow of the sherry. "I'm exhausted. I think I'd like to go to bed."

"Of course, I quite understand," Philomena murmured sympathetically.

"I'll take her on upstairs." Lucian poured more sherry into Ariana's glass and helped her to her feet. "If you'll excuse us, Phil?"

Philomena smiled benignly. "Certainly. But don't think this is the end of our little argument, Lucian. Fletcher Galen is not a fake!"

He nodded. "We can discuss it in the morning."

"You don't have to lead me off to bed as if I were a child," Ariana muttered resentfully as he steered her in the direction of the staircase.

"Be careful that you don't spill the sherry," he countered mildly, quite as if she were, indeed, a child.

At the top of the landing she whispered warningly, "If you dare laugh at me over what happened tonight, I swear, I'll steal your magic wand!"

"I'm not laughing at you," he said gently, guiding her to her door.

Ariana took a deep breath as he thrust the key into the lock. Then she took a large swallow of the sherry. "Thank you for getting me out of there, Lucian. I've never been so unnerved in my whole life!" she told him honestly.

"I understand and you're welcome." He closed the door behind them, standing with his back to it as he watched her pace restlessly across the room.

"Well, I don't understand! I knew it was all trickery! Who could possibly believe such drivel?"

"Someone who wants to believe it," he said simply. "And there are a hell of a lot of people who get a charge out of the idea of being visited by alien beings."

"And yet I was the only truly frightened one in the whole room," Ariana whispered, shaking her head dejectedly.

"Some people have a stronger reaction to the power of suggestion than others. You're the kind of person who should never volunteer for a hypnosis experiment,

Ariana. I'll bet you were a lot of fun to take on a roller coaster ride or through a haunted mansion at an amusement park," he added with a crooked grin.

She shuddered. "I used to hate both of those forms of entertainment!"

"I can see why. Your head is telling you one thing and your senses another, and the resulting conflict is definitely hard on your nerves. But you were perfectly right, you know. Galen is a first-class fake." He left the door and paced thoughtfully across the room to stand in front of the window. Beyond the glass stretched a darkened vista of pine and fir.

"I thought you were going to stand up and do something dramatic like turn on all the lights and show the invisible wires and the lighting arrangements," Ariana grumbled, flinging herself down on the foot of the bed and kicking off her high-heeled shoes. "What happened to the grand expos;aae? Houdini made a real name for himself doing that sort of thing, didn't he? Exposing charlatans and frauds who claimed to have connections to the spirit world?"

"Yes." Lucian continued to gaze thoughtfully out the window, his hands shoved into the back pockets of the jeans. "He did."

"I thought you'd see this as your big chance or something," Ariana sighed, taking another sip of the fortifying sherry.

"It wouldn't have been quite that simple, Ariana. I'm sure Galen's smart enough to take protective measures against the possibility of someone in the audience declaring him a fraud and trying to prove it."

"Protective measures?"

"You don't think all those strong young men in the robes and cowls were there purely for atmosphere, do you?" he asked dryly.

Ariana blinked in astonishment. "My goodness, I never thought of that. Do you suppose he hires them to keep the audience in line?"

"I'd say that's probably one of their functions. Anyone who tried to cause real trouble would undoubtedly be escorted rapidly out of the room and thrown off the grounds."

Ariana winced. "How are we ever going to prove anything to Aunt Phil?"

"Your aunt's an intelligent woman, as you have already observed to me. I think she'll see reason." Lucian swung around to face her. "After all, she's smart enough to know that you and I could be very good together," he added deliberately.

Ariana's head came up sharply in response to the new tone in his voice. In a flash the uneasiness she had been experiencing since the s;aaeance was given another source. It wasn't Galen's magic she needed to fear tonight, it was Lucian's.

"My aunt is an incurable romantic," she said firmly. "Don't get the idea that just because you have her approval you can therefore have me."

A distant roll of thunder drummed across the night sky.

"There's a storm coming in," Lucian said as if she hadn't just issued a challenge.

Ariana smiled a little grimly. "Thunderstorms are not on the list of things of which I am afraid. I won't be needing any comfort to get through a storm, if that's what you're about to suggest, Lucian."

"Are you sure?" he drawled gently. He was watching her the way she imagined a sorcerer watched a magic pentagram, waiting to see what would appear in the center. The fateful sense of premonition that she had experienced briefly during tea swept over her again.

Irritably Ariana got to her feet, shrugging off the prickle of awareness and the strange, intoxicating fear that accompanied it. She could feel those topaz eyes on her, sensed the waiting quality in him and she wanted to hide, just as she had wanted to hide from the other kind of magic earlier in the evening.

But somehow Lucian's brand of magic was far more threatening. "I think it's time you left," she ordered huskily, meeting his gaze in the mirror over the dressing table. "Good night, Lucian."

He said nothing but moved slowly to stand directly behind her, watching her in the mirror. She could feel the desire in him and with a shock felt the answering flicker of sensual tension that sprang to life in her veins. His jeweled eyes held hers with invisible bonds as he stood behind her.

"Do you really want me to go, Ariana?"

She swallowed and unconsciously steadied herself by holding onto the edge of the dressing table. "Yes." She didn't think she could move. What would she do if he reached out and took hold of her?

"I want you," he whispered and then his hand moved to stroke the line of her shoulder. "Badly."

Wordlessly Ariana shook her head, trying to stifle the shiver that coursed through her at his touch. What was it about this man that tantalized her so? Why did it have to be Lucian Hawk of all people who could have this effect on her?

"Just tell me that you know how much I want you," he murmured persuasively. "Tell me you are aware of the attraction between us."

"Lucian, there's no point..." she began urgently.

"Tell me and I'll leave," he interrupted coaxingly. "I want to hear you say the words."

"Why?" she got out starkly.

"Because there's magic in the words." He half smiled, dropping the most delicate of kisses into her cinnamon hair. "Didn't you know that? And the magic is strongest when you say the words aloud. Tell me you know how I'm feeling." The tips of his fingers moved again on the curve of her shoulder and Ariana quivered.

"I...I know that you want me," she said and instantly regretted having spoken. He was right. Saying the words aloud gave them some kind of power. It was as if by having voiced them herself, she had in some fashion acknowledged his *right* to want her. "But *I* don't want you, Lucian," she grated fiercely, turning to face him. "I do not want an affair with you! How many times do I have to say it?"

"Until you've convinced yourself, I suppose," he said politely. "Good night, Ariana. I'll be right next door if you decide after all that you're scared of thunderstorms." He bent and kissed her lightly, lingeringly, as if casting a tiny spell on her mouth, and then he turned and left.

There was a crackle of electricity in the night time sky as the door closed behind him, and Ariana was left wondering why there was power in his words but none in her own.

With an effort she shook off the effects of his presence and doggedly went about the process of getting ready for bed. Too much had happened this afternoon and this evening, she consoled herself as she undressed and slipped into a lacy peach-colored nightgown. It was no wonder she was feeling overwrought.

Overwrought. Now there was a fine old Victorian expression suitable for use in an inn such as this! She glanced wryly around at the hotel room, which had been done as an excellent reproduction of a romantic, old-fashioned lady's bedroom. The wide bed came complete with four carved posts and a thick lace-trimmed quilt. The furniture was heavy and solid, and there was a charming flower print on the wallpaper.

As she climbed up onto the high bed, Ariana decided that she understood now why ladies of the past century occasionally gave way to a fit of the vapors. There were times when no other reaction would quite do! Leaning across the quilt, she turned out the bedside lamp and idly watched the gathering storm outside her window. It was going to be a violent one from the looks of things.

It seemed perfectly suited to the events of the evening, she thought with a sigh. Memories of the s;aaeance drifted back into her head, and she knew a surge of anger at Fletcher Galen for having shown her the weakness in herself. The man deserved to be exposed!

The rain began then, pounding fiercely against the sliding glass doors that opened onto her balcony and had been patterned to resemble French windows. She lay on her side, watching the light and crackle of the thunderstorm, and thought about Lucian Hawk.

What right did he have to want her? What right did

he have to force her to acknowledge that wanting? And why had she been so weak as to admit it at his command?

There were a lot of "whys" and "ifs" going through Ariana's head, but the most treacherous question of all was why did it have to be Lucian Hawk who left her mind and body tantalized and aware?

He was wrong for her. All wrong.

Slowly her lashes closed as sleep came to claim her and quiet her churning thoughts. There was a lot to talk over in the morning, not the least of which was how they were to go about convincing Aunt Philomena that she was involved with a fraud.

In the morning she would be stronger, Ariana told herself just before she drifted off to sleep. Her normal will and common sense would reassert themselves after the shock they had undergone at the s;aaeance. Stupid, being so easily frightened like that. Very stupid. Thank goodness Lucian had realized how upset she was and had taken steps to get her out of that damn chamber.

And in her dreams it was that sense of Lucian's reassuring presence that seemed to hold sway that night. The element of magic seemed irrevocably bound up with the reassurance and protection. It didn't make any sense, really, because what Lucian offered was unstable, unreassuring and dangerous.

Outside, the storm continued gathering its forces, streaking the sky with lightning and rumbling through the air with thunder. Curled in the middle of the four-poster bed, Ariana dreamed of a dark-haired magician who wanted to claim power over her.

And because he was so interwoven in the fabric of her dreams, Ariana knew only a sense of inevitability when her lashes fluttered open two hours later in response to a particularly loud crash of thunder. There on the balcony, silhouetted by a burst of lightning, stood her magician.

Ariana stared at the night-shrouded shape of him, unable to move as Lucian calmly opened her sliding glass door and stepped into the bedroom. He was a man of midnight and shadow as he crossed slowly to her bed.

And when he stood at last looking down at her tense, still figure, Ariana knew that the magic he wielded tonight was strong enough to suspend the future and all her logic.

CHAPTER FIVE

IT WAS A NIGHT FOR MAGICIANS TO BE abroad.

Behind Lucian the wind howled and light flashed in the black sky. It was a night that belonged to the elements and to the man who could wield their power.

Ariana watched the magician by her bed and knew that for her this man commanded that power. The attraction between them was unlike anything she had ever known before, and even though her logic dictated the safe path of avoidance, this was not a night for logic.

Above her the topaz eyes were pools of ancient mystery and unshielded masculine desire. Lucian towered over the bed for a long, lingering moment, drinking in the sight of her, and then his voice came, soft and deeply intent.

"Ariana, I want you tonight."

He reached down to touch her tangled hair and then he was shrugging out of the black jacket, letting it slip unheeded to the floor. Underneath he wore only his jeans.

It seemed to take all the energy in the world just to say his name in gentle question. "Lucian?"

"Come and take a chance with me, Magic Lady," he whispered, sitting down heavily on the edge of the bed and leaning over her. He trapped her body with his hands and stared down into her heavy-lidded eyes. The dark-framed eyeglasses had been left behind in his room, and without the shield of the lenses his gaze seemed to gleam with honey-colored fire. Ariana stirred and knew her pulse was quickening rapidly.

"I'm afraid of you, Lucian."

"You aren't afraid of me," he countered. "You're wary of me and cautious, perhaps, but you're not afraid of me. By morning you'll know all you need to know about me." He lowered his head slowly. "And I'll know all I need to know about you."

His mouth closed over her parted lips, allowing the combined warmth of their bodies to intermingle at that one point. Otherwise he didn't touch her, although she sensed the weight of him poised just above her breasts. The kiss was a slow, hungry, luxurious caress meant to be a prelude to the banquet from which Lucian wanted to feast. His lips slipped damply across hers, persuasive and full of promise.

How could anyone be afraid of this kind of magic? Ariana asked herself as she moaned beneath the touch of his lips. This was the kind of sorcery a woman could search for and never find during the whole course of her life. A thrilling quiver of desire raced through her, tightening an invisible coil in her lower body.

"Yes, Lucian. *Yes,*" she breathed on a sigh of passionate surrender.

He groaned huskily against her mouth. "You won't regret it, Magic Lady. I swear I'll take care of everything."

She didn't understand his words, but there was no chance to ask for an explanation. In a swift, wrenching movement that spoke volumes about the level of his own urgent desire, Lucian pulled himself away from her and unfastened his jeans. In a moment he stood perfectly nude, perfectly male beside the bed.

She thought that he would come to her then, but instead he seemed to be waiting. Ariana looked up at him and tried to read the taut, harsh lines of his face. Then she took hold of the edge of the covers and tugged them aside, her eyes never leaving his.

The invitation was as eloquent as it was ancient, and Lucian accepted it with a rasping exclamation. "Ariana!" He slipped into bed beside her, gathering her in his arms and pressing her onto her back.

Ariana's hands came up to first touch and then cling to the curves of his smoothly muscled shoulders. The strength in him was a source of excitement, conveying both a physical and a mental power that appealed on several levels. She tested his skin with the tips of her nails as he began to explore her mouth with his tongue.

The violence of the storm was a fitting backdrop for the storm of passion that Lucian began to unleash. His tongue surged again and again between her lips, demanding a response from the sensitive interior of her mouth that she could not have withheld even had she wanted to do so. Her own tongue emerged hungrily to involve itself in a passionate little duel that ended on the inside of his mouth. Once there, Ariana's desire seemed to escalate more and more rapidly as she tasted the essence of him.

He let her revel in the experience, parting his lips willingly and encouraging her with husky little groans and little nips with the edges of his teeth.

And while she lost herself in the thrilling discovery

of her own power, Lucian slid his hands along the line of her throat to her shoulders, seeking the lacy straps of the peach-colored nightgown. The garment was lowered to her waist before she realized what had happened, and by then it no longer mattered.

"Oh, Lucian!" Ariana's mouth broke free from his long enough to gasp his name as his palm cupped her breast with a possessiveness that should have startled her but didn't in that moment. *"Lucian!"*

"Can you feel the tightness here?" he growled hoarsely as his thumb grazed one aching nipple. "Can you feel the way it's becoming tight and hard for me? And the softness here," he breathed, caressing the underside of her breast. "My God, Ariana, you are going to make me lose my head tonight, do you know that?"

He touched each nipple again, circling them with thumb and forefinger and tugging slowly so that Ariana cried out softly in passion and nipped at his shoulder. With lingering, teasing movements of his hands and lips Lucian built the tension between them until Ariana began to writhe beneath him. When he took her fingers and placed them against his thigh she responded willingly, touching him with intimate gentleness. "Ariana, Ariana," he whispered again and again as she slipped her fingertips along the thrusting hardness of him. "Touch me all over, sweetheart. All over!"

Quivering under the force of her own desire, Ariana sought to obey, longing now to please as much as she was being pleased. Her hands moved with soft wonder, learning the flatness of his stomach, the feel of the muscular, male buttocks and the driving power of his manhood.

In turn Lucian was lost in a tantalizing exploration of her soft, exquisitely feminine body. His lips closed over one nipple as his hand passed over her hip and around to the inside of her thigh. Ariana trembled and he soothed her with his low, hypnotic, deeply sensual voice. "Tonight you're going to take a chance with me, sweetheart. There's no other way. Tonight we'll both take a leap in the dark. Open yourself for me, darling. Let me touch you the way I need to touch you."

Over and over the husky words were crooned in her ear until the magic of his voice was as much a caress as the feel of his hands. Ariana's nails dug passionately into his thigh as she obeyed the lulling, encouraging commands and parted her legs.

"Ah, sweetheart!" He sought the silk of her, threading his fingers through the tangled thatch of dark, cinnamon brown hair. Ariana sucked in her breath as he inevitably found the ultrasensitive heart of her passion. She turned her face into his shoulder, clinging to him as she had clung earlier that evening when fear had been the impetus.

And as it had on the first occasion, Lucian's arm closed around her with fierce possessiveness as he held her close and teased the center of feminine sensation. It flowered for him, revealing mysteries and a need that was as strong as his own. The flowing warmth was a heady, exhilarating call to his senses.

Ariana's lashes closed tightly against her cheeks as she gave herself up to the moment and the man. "Please, Lucian. Please come to me. I need you so," she whispered in a throaty tone filled with unchecked wonder. Never had she known a need so strong that it caused her to plead for a man's fulfillment. But never had she been under the spell of magic before, either.

"I want you so badly, Magic Lady." He loomed over her, broad shoulders blocking out the shimmer of lightning in the sky behind him. For an instant the golden brown jewels of his eyes burned over her face, and then Ariana shut her eyes once more, unable to endure the intensity of his gaze.

Slowly, with infinite masculine power he brought his body to hers, his rough legs sliding aggressively between her soft thighs, the crisp, curling hair of his chest enveloping the berry-hard peaks of her nipples, his mouth taking hers in absolute possession.

Ariana felt him ready himself for the final union. It was as if he were gathering her completely to him. Then his hips surged strongly against her, and he filled her slowly and totally.

Lucian's breath caught in his throat as the impact of the physical bonding washed over him. He felt its reverberations going through the soft frame of the woman under him and knew he was not alone in sharing the sensation. She was right for him, so very *right!*

Burying his head in the curve of her shoulder, he held her with near-violence and began to build the magic rhythm that would bring them both the secrets of the universe. He knew an utterly primitive, utterly glorious satisfaction at the evidence of her response. It was essential that she find pleasure in his arms. He had to begin staking a claim somewhere, and this was the most basic method of all for doing so. The need to satisfy her thoroughly, to wipe out the memories of any other man she had ever known was a powerful goad to all his senses.

The biting pain of her nails in his shoulders, the tightening pressure of her soft legs around his hips and the little gasps which came from her lips were sources of infinite gratification. Lucian's body and mind were both thoroughly caught up in the turmoil of passion and need. The words he whispered against her throat were dark and heavy with an elemental excitement. He reveled in her response to them. He reveled in *all* her responses.

At last he felt the fragile tightening of her body beneath his and knew that she was on the brink of the ultimate physical sensation. His own body reacted fiercely to the knowledge and threatened to overwhelm what little was left of his self-control. With ferocious willpower he kept his senses in check. It was essential that she be satisfied first. He had to know that she had given herself completely at least on this level.

"Lucian! *Lucian?*"

He caught his name as it left her lips and heard the uncertainty in it, the hint of panic. "Take the chance, Magic Lady. You have no choice. Take the chance!"

He slid his hand below her tenderly rounded derriere and arched her tightly against his hips, his fingers clenching deeply. It was enough to send her into the final, delicate convulsion.

"Oh, my God, my God!" The low moan was half-stifled in her throat as every fiber of her body tightened and then went into shimmering release.

Lucian felt the roaring exultation in his veins and surrendered to the mindless climax at last. He had made her his, irrevocably his.

Ariana came languidly out of the pleasant haze of the

aftermath, aware first of the weight of Lucian's body which still sprawled across hers in magnificent abandon. No, in magnificent possession.

The second realization came quickly on the heels of the first, and Ariana stirred with a faint unease. There was a sense of complete and total possession in the way the magician lay along her body, his head on her breast, his hands somehow having caught hold of her wrists. The heaviness of his thighs trapped her legs.

Ariana felt a return of the incipient panic that had blossomed just before she had surrendered completely to Lucian's lovemaking. Firmly she squelched it. There was no cause for panic. She was a mature adult, a woman with needs that had been too long held in check.

But even four years ago when she had thought herself so wildly, blindly in love, the need and the desire hadn't been like this.

Nothing had ever been like this.

And that thought brought back the hint of panic. After so many years of being so very, very careful how did she come to find herself in this situation? In bed with a magician, a man who was totally at odds with every one of the requirements she had set down for a husband. *A man who didn't even have any intention of becoming a husband!*

"What is it, Ariana?" Lucian lifted his head, and she knew that he must have felt the tremor that had gone through her. His eyes smiled down at her, warm and tender but with an underlying expression of lazy victory that couldn't be masked. His mouth crooked with indulgence and remembered pleasure, and he lifted a hand to stroke back a strand of hair that lay along her cheek. "Are you starting to worry already?"

Her lashes shifted as she looked up at him with clear honesty. "I always worry when I take chances."

"You won't have cause to regret taking this one, honey," he drawled reassuringly.

"Won't I?"

"No. I can give you what you want. But I had to know that you would surrender first without demanding financial statements from the banks and an iron-clad contract. I was a little afraid to take a chance, myself," he added with a wicked little smile. "But now we've started off on the right foot. Everything's going to be okay."

She stared up at him in confusion. "What are you talking about, Lucian?"

"Forget it. I'll explain everything in the morning. Right now all I want to do is enjoy what's left of the night. Magicians always do their best work at night, you know."

He leaned down to kiss her, and the toe of his foot moved excitingly along the calf of her leg. Ariana felt the faint stirrings of renewed passion and wondered at it.

Magic. It was the only explanation. She let her arms circle his neck once more and pushed aside the confusion and doubts that had begun to assail her....

In the morning both the storm and the magician were gone.

Ariana stirred and woke, instinctively feeling for the warmth of the man who had lain beside her during the night. When she found only the empty bed next to her she sat up groggily, blinking away the last traces of sleep.

There was still an indentation on the pillow where

Lucian's head had rested, and when she buried her nose in the down-filled thickness of it she thought that she could detect a hint of the unique and satisfying scent that was his alone.

What was the matter with her, sitting there amid the sheets and inhaling Lucian's fragrance from a pillow? Tossing it aside, Ariana tried to bounce lightly off the high Victorian-style bed and nearly stumbled as her body proved unexpectedly sore in various places.

She drew in her breath in surprise. Her body was rather forcibly reminding her of the solid strength of the man who had spent the night with her. Holding onto the bedpost, Ariana stretched, working out the voluptuous aches in her muscles. Lucian had been a demanding lover, but he had repaid her for the response he had taken with a seemingly inexhaustible masculine passion.

When had he left? Continuing on her way to the bathroom, Ariana frowned as she tried to figure out what would happen next between them. Obviously he had gone back to his own room sometime near dawn. There had been no further chance to talk. What did a woman say to a man over breakfast the next morning after a night such as the one that had just passed?

Ariana felt restless and confused as the shower water cascaded down around her. Last night Lucian had refused to deal with the crisis he had created, using sensual magic to take her mind off the subject of their future whenever she would have tried to return to it.

She didn't have the impression he was ignoring that future, only that as far as he was concerned, it was settled and there was no real need to discuss it. He had promised to explain everything in the morning.

What did that mean? What was there to explain? The restlessness and confusion grew as her thoughts became more chaotic. She could hardly believe that she had been so cautious for so long only to wind up giving herself in a blaze of desire to a man who wasn't at all what he should be. That thought kept clanging around in her brain, occasionally colliding with a memory of that same man's tenderness or a recollection of his concern for her during the s;aaeance. Images of the startling, overpowering figure he had made silhouetted against the storm as he walked into her bedroom also intruded, sending little frissons along her nerves.

The night had belonged to the storm and the magician who was a part of it. What of the day?

Deciding that her only defense against the unknown lay in such familiar feminine tactics as choosing clothes that would enhance her self-confidence, Ariana walked back out of the bathroom and carefully dressed for the trauma of breakfast.

She belted a shawl-collared long-sleeved blouse in a foulard print over a slim yoked skirt that fell to her calves. Then she added a pair of soft suede high-heeled boots. The overall effect was sophisticated and dashing. Just the impression she wanted. Sophistication and dash could cover up a multitude of uncertainties and vulnerabilities, she told herself as she picked up her hotel room key and started for the door.

The realization that she had been safely locked in her room last night swept over her just as she put her hand on the doorknob. Hesitantly she turned to glance at the sliding glass door through which Lucian had entered. She could have sworn that door had been locked before they had left for the s;aaeance. Which meant that he must have deliberately unlocked it before he had left her room the first time last night. She remembered how he had been standing near the window with his back to her, and she remembered how good he was at sleight-of-hand. Lucian had known full well that he would be returning when he had said good night to her that first time.

A little dazed at the sheer audacity of the man, Ariana continued downstairs. Aunt Phil would be waiting to have breakfast with her in the inn's dining room.

As soon as she walked through the double doors of the charmingly decorated room she saw that her aunt was not alone. Seated at the table across from her was Lucian, his dark hair, jeans and black pullover sweater making him a strong note against the white linen of the breakfast room. He looked up almost at once, as if sensing her arrival, and then he was on his feet, coming toward her with a satisfied smile and a look of anticipation in his eyes.

"Good morning, Ariana," he murmured huskily, bending down to brush the lightest of husbandly kisses against her mouth before taking her arm and leading her back to the table.

Husbandly? No, that was definitely the wrong word, Ariana reminded herself firmly as she greeted her aunt. Philomena looked rather like a large bright-eyed tropical bird this morning, dressed as she was in the colors of exotic plumage, which somehow flowed together quite perfectly.

"Good morning, dear. Feeling recovered from your bit of shock last night?"

Ariana reached for her coffee cup, and her eyes collided with the topaz ones across the table. She firmly resisted the urge to inquire which shock her aunt meant. The shock of the s;aaeance had, after all, only been the prelude to the evening!

"I'm fine, Aunt Phil. Sorry I made you leave early last night. I hope you didn't miss anything important," she muttered, diligently searching the bread basket beside her and discovering a warm scone.

"No, no, not a thing. The session ended soon after we left, according to my friends. Poor Krayton.was unable to get through, but we are all vastly encouraged by how much was accomplished this time," Philomena said cheerily.

Ariana bit her lip. "Aunt Phil," she began sternly, striving to find the right words to squelch her aunt's cheerful belief in the quackery of Fletcher Galen.

"Never mind, Ariana," Lucian interrupted quietly. "Your aunt and I have come to an agreement."

Ariana looked up in surprise, frowning. "What sort of agreement?"

"I'm going to check into Galen's background a bit further, and if I find out anything Phil ought to know, I'll tell her. Fair enough."

Ariana opened her mouth to say something about the money involved, but the warning expression in Lucian's eyes made her close it again. She subsided in annoyance and buttered her scone.

"I'm quite sure Lucian won't find out anything bad about Mr. Galen," Philomena assured her chattily. "But I've agreed to keep an open mind."

"Well, that's something, at least," Ariana sighed.

"Lucian also tells me you'll be leaving early today for the drive back to the city," Phil continued. "Lovely day for a drive, isn't it? That storm certainly caused a fuss last night, but it made everything so bright and fresh this morning, didn't it? Did the storm bother you on top of the session with Krayton, Ari, dear?"

"I managed to get through it all right," Ariana said dryly, not looking at Lucian.

"Good." Phil smiled and nodded. "I was afraid it might have added a bit too much *atmosphere* to the evening for you!"

It was Lucian who injected the last comment. "I, for one, found it contributed to a very memorable evening." White teeth gleamed in a laughing masculine grin that made Ariana seriously consider inserting the tines of her fork into his hand. With an effort of will, she resisted.

An hour later, Lucian had packed their bags back into the Porsche and said his good-byes to Philomena Warfield. "Take care, Phil. I enjoyed meeting you and I look forward to seeing you again soon."

"Enjoy the rest of your stay here at the inn," Ariana said a little hesitantly as she kissed her aunt good-bye. "You'll be here for a week?"

"Yes, Fletcher Galen has passed the word that we came very close to a major breakthrough with Krayton last night. As long as the energy level is running so high he feels we should all take advantage of it. There are going to be several intense attempts to make direct contact this week. So exciting!"

"Yes, well, uh, good luck," Ariana said weakly as Lucian wrapped an arm around her shoulders and began steering her toward the Porsche. "Call me as soon as you get back to the city!"

"Oh, I will!" Philomena watched Lucian bundle her niece into the front of the Porsche and smiled grandly. The older woman looked quite pleased with herself, Ariana decided uncomfortably. Or pleased with Lucian.

"Why are we rushing off so quickly?" Ariana demanded as Lucian slammed the car door and started the engine.

"Because we have things to do back in the city and we've done all we can do for the moment here," he explained as if she weren't too bright.

"You mean you're going to start checking out Galen today? On Sunday? Won't all the agencies you'd have to contact be closed?"

"Galen can wait until tomorrow." He glanced at her with a small smile edging his mouth as he guided the Porsche out onto the main road. "You and I have other things to accomplish today."

"Such as?" she asked, hearing quite clearly the slightly waspish tone in her own voice. Ariana's sense of unease and her innate wariness had not been dispelled. She felt uncertain and far too vulnerable beside this man.

"Such as clearing up one or two matters between ourselves."

"Oh. I see." She looked at him blankly, not knowing what else to say.

Lucian grinned and put a hand on her knee in casual affection. "I doubt it, but you soon will."

"I wish you wouldn't try to be mysterious this

morning," she complained, massaging her temples. "I'm really not up to it."

He squeezed her knee. "You did look somewhat beleaguered when you appeared in the dining room doorway this morning. I'm sorry, sweetheart, I've been a little rough on you, but that's because I'm not accustomed to taking chances, either. At least, not the kind we were taking last night."

"What are you talking about, Lucian?"

"I'm talking about the way we were both trying to circle the other at a wary distance until we knew for sure what we wanted. It could have gone on indefinitely, you know, and my nerves weren't up to that! That's why I forced the issue last night."

"Are you trying to tell me the logic behind your decision to...to come to my room last night?" she asked carefully, gazing directly ahead of her through the windshield.

"I suppose so. I couldn't figure you out, Ariana. On the one hand you seemed like such a mercenary little witch," he chuckled wryly. "I wanted to take you across my knee and paddle you the first night I met you. Even your relatives freely admitted you wouldn't look at a man who didn't meet your financial specifications. It was infuriating!"

"A woman has a right to limit the risks she takes," Ariana said woodenly.

"Maybe," he agreed surprisingly, "but I didn't want you to apply those standards to me and find me lacking. I wanted you to want me the same way I wanted you. And I kept telling myself that there was a lot more to you than met the eye. Your brother and Philomena both seem to adore you. I sensed a softness and a vulnerability in you just below the surface and I wanted to tear away the facade and find it."

"Lucian," she began anxiously, not at all sure where this was leading.

"I'm not very fond of mercenary women, and you're not very fond of men who don't have bank accounts that match your own. We were at an impasse, honey, and I decided one of us was going to have to take a chance." He shot her an apologetic sideways glance. "Last night seemed like a good time to get the initial clash of arms over with."

"You mean you decided I could be the one to take the chance," she clarified dryly.

"I'm afraid so," he agreed regretfully. "I wanted to know you'd come to me willingly even though I didn't meet your financial requirements. And you did," he concluded with deep satisfaction. "You surrendered so beautifully, sweetheart. I'm going to remember last night as long as I live, do you realize that?"

The panic began to swim like a shark in her stomach. "And what am I supposed to remember?" she managed bleakly. "That I let myself be pushed into taking a chance on a man who doesn't believe in commitments?"

He swung his head around in a quick movement, astonishment plain in his expression. "I know how to make commitments, Ariana. And I know what I expect in return."

"An affair?"

"Most definitely an affair," he growled, downshifting for one of the many curves in the mountain road. "We still have a lot to learn about each other, Ariana, but we know enough already to realize that what we feel for each other is special; full of potential. I'm not one for wasting that kind of potential, are you?"

Ariana felt the shark of panic swim a little closer to reality. "I...I need time to think, Lucian."

His hands tightened fractionally on the wheel. "Now that the basic decision has been made we'll take it easy," he promised quietly. "I want you to get to know me better and I want to get to know you. But like it or not, the affair began last night, sweetheart, and there's no going back for either of us."

The feeling of inevitability which she had known when she'd opened her eyes the night before and had seen him waiting at her window returned. It was true that all Lucian wanted was an affair and she had promised herself never to take that kind of chance again. Yet a part of her was urging her to do exactly that: To take a chance on an affair with this man.

They would take it easy, he said, get to know each other. Perhaps, just perhaps, there really was something special here, something she should take the risk of discovering. Last night had been unlike anything she had ever known. Did she really want to walk away from such warmth and passion?

It was true that Lucian was a far cry from what she had promised herself she would look for in a man, but Drake and Philomena both liked him. She no longer fully trusted her own emotional reactions, but she'd never had any cause to doubt theirs. They were good judges of character.

My God, she thought, sitting deeply into her seat as she watched the mountain scenery. What was she doing? Trying to rationalize her own desires? Probably. She was on the brink of throwing away all her long-held requirements for a man, even the requirement of a marriage with a contract. For it was unlikely that there'd be any kind of marriage at all with Lucian Hawk.

The churning of her inner thoughts kept her silent for most of the return trip to San Francisco. Lucian didn't try to push her into conversation, apparently lost in his own considerations. It wasn't until after they'd crossed the bridge and had begun heading for an affluent section of the city that was some distance from her own neighborhood that Ariana finally realized that something was wrong.

"Lucian, where are we going?"

"Home."

"Your home?" She didn't want that, she realized. It was too soon.

"Ummm. I want to show you something." He smiled, looking quietly pleased with himself.

"Show me what? Lucian, what are you up to now?" she demanded suspiciously.

"I only want to prove that there are rewards for women like you who take chances on men like me," he drawled as they climbed one of the city's most quietly elegant hills.

"Rewards!" Genuine alarm filtered through now.

"Ariana, last night I asked you to give yourself to me without any strings attached. I know that put you in a vulnerable position. Today I'm going to make it up to you."

He turned the Porsche into the underground garage of a handsome condominium building which overlooked the Bay. Without a word he parked the car and helped her out, ignoring her taut, questioning glance. In silence they rode the plushly carpeted elevator to one of the top floors, and in silence Lucian led Ariana down the hall to a heavy oak door.

Then he inserted a key in the lock and pushed the door open to reveal a brilliant vista of San Francisco Bay as seen from the living room of an expensive, beautifully decorated condominium. Ariana simply stood on the threshold of the elegant room, staring at the expanse of windows ahead of her.

"Welcome home, Magic lady," Lucian said quietly from behind her.

She whirled around to face him. "This is your home?"

He nodded, watching her expectantly. "When it comes to money, sweetheart, I could buy and sell you a couple of times over. Does that reassure you about the chance you took last night? You've made it clear that you want a man whose income level at least matches your own. Well, I'm more than able to do that."

"Why didn't you tell me?" she managed tightly, a cold fury beginning to build inside her as she stared up at him.

"Because I wanted you to take the chance of giving yourself to me first," he admitted calmly as if it were the most natural thing in the world that she should be the one to take the risks.

"You deceived me," Ariana whispered. "You created an illusion and let me believe in it."

"You jumped to conclusions and chose to believe in that illusion," he countered a little roughly, topaz eyes narrowing.

"You could have straightened me out at any time!"

"I could have, but I wanted to make you mine first," he said deliberately.

Her rage soared higher as she confronted him with sudden fierceness. "My God, magician, did you think this would miraculously make everything all right?" she grated, waving a hand to encompass the richness around her. "Did you think you could play the rich king in the fairytale who dresses as a pauper and then sets out to win the princess?"

"Ariana," he began firmly, clearly beginning to perceive that something had gone awry with his plans. "Listen to me."

"Listen to you! That's what I did last night! That's what I've been doing all along. I've been listening to you spin a web of illusion and deception, and now you expect me to tell you it's all right? Did you think that like the princess in the fairytale, I was willing to take you for what you pretended to be, but I'd be thrilled to find out you're actually rich and that we're all going to live happily ever after? Well, you'd better think again, magician," Ariana declared furiously. "I might have been willing to accept the fact that you didn't meet my financial requirements, but *there's no way in hell that I will ever accept the fact that you deceived me!*"

"Damn it, Ariana!" He moved, intending to block her path, but Ariana was too quick. She snatched the Porsche keys from his hand before he realized her intention.

And then she fled down the hall to the waiting elevator as if all the magicians in the universe were after her.

CHAPTER SIX

Ariana made the phone call to her brother as soon as she walked into her apartment. Flinging down her carry-all, she crossed the papaya-colored carpet to pick up the white phone beside the sofa. Drake Warfield sounded rather vague on the other end of the line, and she knew that she'd caught him in the middle of some serious bout of thinking. Ruthlessly Ariana fought to get his full attention.

"You heard me, Drake, I said what exactly do you know about Lucian Hawk?"

"Ari, you asked me that question a few days ago, and I told you that I liked the guy and had heard he could be trusted. What more do you want to know? What the hell happened up there in the mountains, anyway? You sound a little upset."

"Upset is an extremely mild word for what I'm feeling! And don't you dare tell me you don't know much about Lucian! I think you knew a lot more than you told me a few days ago!"

There was a thoughtful pause on the other end, and Ariana could practically hear her very intelligent brother putting two and two together. "I take it you found out he's more than just a magician?" Drake finally asked carefully.

"Oh, yes, Drake," she bit out furiously, "I found out. This morning. But you and Aunt Philomena knew all along, didn't you?"

"Well, I knew he wasn't exactly a pauper, Ari, and I did mention to Aunt Phil when I talked to her Saturday morning that he seemed perfect for you..."

"Perfect for me! *Perfect for me?*" In the face of such brotherly audacity she couldn't find a suitable response. Ariana felt stunned. "Why the hell didn't you tell me he was rich?"

"Now, Ari, he's not super rich, just wealthier than you are," Drake temporized. "But what's the matter with that? I thought you'd be pleased!"

"So did he!" she grated. "But you didn't answer my question, Drake. Why didn't you tell me? Why did you allow me to believe he was just a magician?"

"He is a magician. A damn good one."

"Drake!"

"Okay, okay, Ari. I didn't tell you because he asked me not to," Drake said simply.

Ariana went momentarily silent in the face of that response. "I see," she finally managed icily.

"Ari, it's not as bad as it sounds," Drake said, trying to placate her. "After we were introduced by our mutual friend, I told Lucian why you wanted a magician and he sounded very interested. He was curious about you. We, uh, had a few drinks and I told him how cautious you are about men. How you wouldn't consider dating someone without money...."

"For God's sake!"

"Now, Ari, it's true," Drake pointed out gently with brotherly forthrightness. "You've been vetting your dates on the basis of their financial statements for the past four years and you know it."

"That's my business, Drake!"

"At any rate, we kept talking about you, and I told him you were really very nice except for this hangup you seem to have developed about men who don't have as much money as you do."

"Did you tell him what happened four years ago, Drake?" Ariana demanded.

Drake sounded shocked. "Of course not, Ari! I would never tell anyone about that! But you're letting it ruin your whole life and I think it's time you started being realistic. Anyone can get conned, and while I'll admit it's not very pleasant, you shouldn't judge everyone else you meet on the basis of what a con artist did to you!"

"Forget it, Drake. You just don't understand," Ariana interrupted bleakly, lowering her forehead into her hand and massaging it. "Just finish telling me what happened between you and Lucian."

"Nothing much beyond that. As I said, over a couple of drinks I told him why you needed a magician and that you tended to be a little prejudiced about men, but that basically you were okay. Hell, I can't remember everything I said, Ari. You know how it is when a couple of men start sharing a few drinks!"

"No, I don't know how it is, but I'm beginning to get an idea!"

"Now, calm down. That's really all there was to it. He said he was interested in meeting you and discussing the job you had in mind, but he asked me not to say anything about his main line of work. I think he's in real estate or something," Drake added as if struggling to remember the conversation. "I like him, Ari. On Saturday morning I phoned Aunt Phil and told her you were going to arrive with someone who was a nice change of pace from Dearborn. She asked a lot of questions that I more or less had to answer. After all, I didn't want to talk about the fact that he was also a magician and that his main reason for going with you was to check out her psychic. It seemed safer to talk about Lucian's background, or what I knew of it."

"And what, precisely, do you know about his background, Drake?" Ariana snapped. "What else did you learn about him while the two of you were having that lovely man-to-man chat and getting drunk?"

Drake sighed. "Just that he's made his money in real estate and that he seems to have come up the hard way. I think maybe he was in and out of trouble a lot as a kid. Not much of a family life from what I could gather. Parents split up or something and more or less let him fend for himself. I don't think there was much money. Anyhow, he ran away from a foster home where he'd been stashed one year when he'd gotten too wild for his mother to deal with. I think he told me he lied about his age and got a job with a traveling carnival. I guess that's when his hobby of magic began to come in handy."

"My God," Ariana groaned weakly. "A carnival magician. A natural con man."

"Now, Ari, that's not fair," Drake told her grimly. "How do we know what we would have been doing if we found ourselves in his shoes? You and I were just damn lucky there was someone like Aunt Phil to look after us!"

"Never mind. Anything else, Drake? Any other little tidbits you might want to tell your trusting sister?" she whispered scathingly.

"No, that's about it, except that I like and trust him. I honestly thought he might be good for you. When he asked me not to say anything about his financial status I agreed. Now it's your turn, Ari. What happened up there in the mountains?"

Ariana closed her eyes and thought of the storm that had taken place outside her window and inside her bedroom. Then she said very steadily. "Galen's a fraud, of course. Lucian says he could duplicate any of the stunts that were used in the s;aaeance. Aunt Phil is having too much fun thinking she's helping to make contact with someone from another planet, though. She doesn't want to hear about Galen being a charlatan."

"So what happens next?" Drake persisted.

"Aunt Phil apparently agreed to listen to Lucian if he could supply her with some proof that Fletcher Galen's a con man. Ironic, isn't it? I wanted a magician to catch a magician and I got something even better. I got a con artist to catch another con artist. Except that my *partnership* with my con man/magician more or less terminated this morning, so I may have to find another con man. No, that's not necessary, is it? I already know Fletcher Galen is a crook, so maybe my next working relationship should be with a private detective! I'm meeting such an interesting crowd of men lately, Drake!"

"Ari, you sound bitter," Drake began worriedly. "You've told me what happened as far as Galen's concerned, but what happened between you and Hawk?"

"Exactly what you and Hawk planned to have

happen," she flung back fiercely. "I was deceived, conned, misled and generally made a fool of. Rather like I was four years ago."

"Ari! What the hell are you talking about? Lucian wasn't after your money!"

"No," she agreed. "I'll grant you that much."

"Then why do you say he made a fool of you? Just because he didn't bother to present you with a financial statement?" Drake demanded. Then he seemed to finish putting the pieces of the puzzle together in his mind. "Wait a minute, I get it. You started falling for him, didn't you? That's why you're so furious this afternoon. You're mad because he misled you for a while about his true status and you're piqued."

"You don't understand, Drake. You never did understand," Ariana repeated, suddenly very tired. "But never mind. It doesn't matter. I'll talk to you tomorrow." She hung up the phone and leaned her head back against the French vanilla sofa cushion.

It wasn't really Drake's fault for not understanding. Ariana admitted as much to herself. She had never told either her aunt or her brother the full extent of her involvement with Marsh Sutcliff four years ago. Oh, they knew about the financial aspects of the situation and they knew that she had been dating Sutcliff, but they never realized that it wasn't a simple swindle he had conducted. Ariana had trusted him with all her money because she had loved him to distraction. She would have done almost anything for Marsh Sutcliff.

Almost, but not quite. Somehow she had managed to draw the line at turning over Drake's and Philomena's money to him along with her own.

The phone beside her rang imperiously, and Ariana automatically reached out to pick up the receiver. "Yes?" It would be Drake calling back.

But it wasn't Drake. "Ariana, I want to talk to you," Lucian said bluntly.

"That's going to be tough, because I don't want to talk to you," she whispered.

"Have lunch with me tomorrow. You'll have calmed down a little by then and we can sort this out."

"No." She hung up the phone again and unplugged it from the wall.

That night before she went to bed Ariana double-checked all the locks on her doors and windows. There was no trusting a magician.

The next day she sought refuge in the pleasant, busi-nesslike hum of activity at the downtown offices of Warfield & Co., Financial Planners. It was not a large business in terms of employees, but it was a highly suc-cessful one, and the offices of its president had been decorated by Philomena Warfield to reflect that success.

Ariana sat in a padded leather chair behind an ultra-modern glass-topped desk and deliberately lost herself in her work. There was a soothing quality about the paneled walls, which had been hung with works of abstract art that Philomena had produced. The paintings had already appreciated three times since she had signed them and hung them in Ariana's offices. A Japanese kimono stand displayed a brilliantly designed ceremonial robe on one wall, and the white carpet, which ran from wall to wall, set off the black leather fur-niture and glass fixtures.

With a diligence that had built her success twice

from scratch, Ariana applied herself to the reports in front of her. The coffee cup at her elbow was never empty, and she had lost track of the number of cups she'd had since arriving at the office at seven-thirty that morning. Too many, she was sure. She was beginning to notice a fine trembling in the tips of her fingers. Well, at lunchtime she would eat something solid. Perhaps that would mitigate some of the effects of the caffeine. On the other hand, she needed the caffeine to offset the effects of a restless night. It was a vicious circle.

It was twelve o'clock when her secretary buzzed her from the outer office. Ariana had just been staring morosely at the coffee cup, wondering whether or not to refill it one more time before lunch when the discreet interruption came.

"Yes, Beth?"

"There's a Mr. Lucian Hawk to see you, Miss Warfield," Beth Dexter's voice said briskly. Beth only called her Miss Warfield when she was conveying strong disapproval of the visitor in question. Lucian must have created a stir in the outer office, Ariana decided grimly.

"Tell him I'm busy, Beth." Lucian would be able to overhear that on the speaker that sat on Beth's desk. She made no effort to soften the crisp executive sound of her voice. Ariana used, in fact, the same tone of voice she used when she was trying to avoid a salesman. There was instant silence as Beth cut off the connection. Ariana realized that she was holding her breath and watching the closed door of her office as if there were several dozen cobras on the other side. Hadn't she read somewhere that one of Houdini's greatest tricks had been the art of walking through walls?

She didn't have to wait long. Lucian didn't literally walk through the door. He simply flung it open and strode across the white carpet to stand before her desk. Then he leaned over, planting his palms on the glass surface, and pinned her to the chair with a glittering gaze.

"I came to take you to lunch."

Ariana's fingers clenched into the padded arms of her chair as she glared back at him. "I'm not interested in going to lunch with you. I thought I made that clear last night. Please leave my office at once."

Even as she spoke a part of her was noticing the transformation in his appearance. Until now she had only seen him in casual clothing that could have been worn by almost anyone at any point on the economic scale. Today Lucian Hawk had effected another piece of magic. He had transformed himself into the essence of the powerful corporate executive. His black and silver hair was brushed to perfect obedience. His vested chalk-stripe wool suit was tailored with an assertive, conservative hand to define his lean waist and broad shoulders. His button-down shirt was subtly striped to complement the suit, and his tie was silk, Ariana decided, or she'd eat the silk blouse she, herself, was wearing under her own white suit.

"We're having lunch together, Ariana," Lucian announced evenly, every line in his harsh face etched with masculine assertiveness.

Ariana swallowed uncomfortably and refused to back down. "No."

"You won't leave the office with me?"

"Absolutely not!"

Lucian didn't move except to lift one hand off the glass and snap his fingers in the direction of the doorway behind him. His eyes never left Ariana's as a figure pushing a wheeled table appeared on the threshold.

"What in the world?..." Ariana broke the glaring contest to stare at the scene taking place in her office. The man pushing the cart was dressed in a black and white waiter's outfit, and the cart was set with white linen, silver and china. A display of food could be seen under the glass dome cover. Without glancing at Ariana, the waiter began setting up the meal.

"Magic, Ariana," Lucian explained dryly. "You won't come out to lunch, so I have no choice but to make lunch appear here in your office."

"Lucian, you can't do this!" she stormed. "Tell that man to take that cart away this instant!"

"Do you really think I'm going to do that after going to all the trouble of arranging the trick?" he growled sardonically.

Helplessly Ariana watched as the waiter finished arranging the repast to his own satisfaction and then, with a formal bow in her direction, left the office, shutting the door behind him.

"First we'll have a little of this very excellent Monterey County Pinot Blanc," Lucian decreed, stepping to the cart and hauling a bottle of wine out of the silver chiller. "And then we'll get down to business." He poured out two glasses and handed one to Ariana with a flourish. "To the future," he intoned, downing a healthy swallow.

Ariana reached for the wineglass, not because she

intended to drink to his toast but because just then she needed something to settle her jangled nerves. Silently she sipped the wine as Lucian surveyed the linen-draped cart.

"Shrimp and scallops in pastry shells, mushroom and celery salad and a ham mousse with peach chutney. Shortcake for dessert or fruit and cheese. Which will you have to start, Ariana?"

The sensation of utter helplessness in the face of unpredictable behavior kept Ariana in her seat. "The salad and the seafood, I think," she heard herself say very distantly. He served her with a style worthy of the tuxedo-clad waiter.

"I've waited a few tables in my time," he explained easily as she watched him.

"Was that before or after you did the carny circuit?" she shot back coolly.

One black brow arched behind his glasses. "I see you've been talking to your brother." He drew up a chair across from her and sat down to enjoy his meal. "What else did he tell you about me?"

"That you were in and out of trouble a lot as a kid, that you ran away to join a carnival and that you are currently in real estate. You really are a speculator, I take it?"

"Financier and developer," he corrected smoothly, biting into a sourdough roll. "Remember?"

"Speculator," she asserted cuttingly and focused on her shrimp and scallop dish.

"Words," he said. "It amounts to the same thing in terms of success. I don't need your money, Ariana. Have you settled down enough today to at least admit that I'm not a financial threat to you?"

"How do I know what kind of a threat you might be? You've deceived me once, why not again?"

His face hardened. "Ariana, you have a way with insults that is going to land you in trouble one of these days."

"More threats about the dangers of angering a magician?" she tossed back in icy tones. "Don't bother. I'm not interested in hearing them."

He eyed her, the fingers of one hand drumming lightly on the surface of the table. "Just remember that you've been warned."

"Thanks. I'll keep it in mind!"

He clearly made a grab for his patience. "Ariana, are you really so angry just because I didn't tell you the truth about my financial status?"

Her head came up abruptly. "Funny you should ask that. My brother asked me very much the same thing. What's the matter with you men? Can't you understand?"

"I could understand your being a little annoyed," he said calmly. "But in the end what does it matter, honey? You were willing to accept me in your bed, to take a chance on me, when you thought I was merely an itinerant magician. I can't believe you have lost all interest just because I turned out to fit your financial requirements!"

"You don't understand!" she exploded furiously. "You just don't understand!"

"So tell me," he growled. "What is it I don't understand? Ariana, I'm not after your precious money. I've got enough of my own. Furthermore, you and I are more than compatible in several areas," he added meaningfully. "It's true I'm not interested in signing a marriage contract with you, but since I'm not a threat to your financial empire, what the hell does that matter? You don't have to protect yourself from me, so there's no need for the prenuptial agreement."

"Is that an offer of marriage *without* an agreement?" she inquired far too sweetly and had the satisfaction of seeing his eyes narrow.

"I've told you from the beginning that I'm not interested in marriage," Lucian said quietly.

"Oh, yes, that's right, I almost forgot. You want a woman to take a *chance* on you, don't you? You want her to take all the risks."

"What risks?" he grated. "You don't need my money any more than I need yours. You're not taking any financial risks by having an affair with me, and the only other risk I asked you to take was Saturday night when I came to your bed. That particular risk is behind us now. You took a chance then, I'll admit, giving yourself to a man who apparently didn't meet your monetary requirements. But you were willing to overlook that little matter Saturday night. Why the hell are you so upset, now that you've found out it never was a genuine risk in the first place?"

Ariana lost her temper. The strain on her nerves had become too great to ignore the provocation of his words. She flung herself out of the leather chair and stood facing him with the air of a small cornered animal that no longer has any option but to lash out in self-defense.

"I'll tell you why I'm so angry, Lucian Hawk," she breathed in a ragged tone. "I'm angry because while it's true you managed to meet one of my requirements in a man, you failed miserably to satisfy the other one, which I have always considered even more important. You lied to me, Lucian. Not only that, but your whole background suggests that you've made deceit an integral part of your lifestyle. Just what sort of trouble were you in when you were a kid?"

He hesitated. "That was a long time ago, Ariana."

"Tell me!"

He leaned back in his chair, watching her warily. "I ran with a gang of boys for a while. It was a little rough, but where I grew up it was the logical social organization. Just ask any social worker," he murmured blandly. "I seem to recall talking to a number of them up until I was sixteen."

"And after that?" she persisted, her mouth dry as she pictured him wearing leather and carrying chains and knives. A gang member. Probably its leader, she thought savagely.

He shrugged, his eyes never leaving hers. "After that I joined a carnival. I was the chief magician." Lucian's mouth turned down wryly. "I was also the guy who repaired the equipment, settled squabbles between townies and carnies when they arose, rigged the arcades so that the paying customers didn't win too often, you name it. After that came the army and Southeast Asia. After that came a decision that it was better to be rich than poor."

"And how did you carry out that decision, Lucian?" she questioned starkly.

"The same way you did. With a lot of hard work."

"Hard work and a little slick maneuvering?" she persisted.

"Slick maneuvering, as you call it, is the name of the

game in real estate, honey," he informed her bluntly. "That's why I laughed so hard the other morning when you were trying to draw lines between speculators and financiers. There aren't any lines."

"And how about the lines between legal and illegal?"

"Those are a little vague at times, too, Ariana," he told her stonily.

"Are you telling me you've crossed them on occasion?"

His fingers tightened around the stem of the wineglass as he raised it to his lips. Something dangerous showed in the depths of his eyes. An angered magician, Ariana thought fleetingly. "I don't think I'm going to tell you anything else until I find out what this is all about," Lucian stated coldly. "Why the inquisition?"

"Because you've lied to me once, and I just wanted some idea of how long a history you have of deceiving people," she flung back. "Apparently you've been walking pretty close to the edge for a long, long time." She leaned forward, planting her own palms on the glass top of her desk very much the way he had done earlier. She spaced each word out very carefully. "Not only do I make it a point to avoid men whose financial backgrounds don't match my own, Lucian Hawk. I also avoid men whose reputations won't stand the light of day. I am looking for a man of honor, something you'll probably never understand. I might have been willing to bend the first requirement, but I will never again bend the second!"

She saw the cold fury in him, but she also saw that he had it under control. The knowledge wasn't particularly reassuring. Somehow the control he was exerting over his anger seemed to make him all the more dangerous. "Meaning you bent that rule once before?" he rasped softly.

"I made that rule along with the one about finances four years ago, Lucian," she gritted.

He was suddenly on his feet across from her. "Tell me about it!" he commanded even more softly.

Ariana couldn't stop herself. She had gone too far now. "His name, or rather, one of his names, was Marsh Sutcliff. He was handsome, charming and sophisticated. I fell in love with him. I trusted him. I gave him a tremendous amount of money to invest. *And after that I never saw him again.*"

He waited, as if knowing there would be more.

Ariana drew in her breath. "After he disappeared, leaving me financially devastated, I learned that Marsh Sutcliff was a professional con artist. Under a variety of names he'd run scams all over the country. The one he'd run on me had been one of the easiest of his career, apparently. I was in love with him, or thought I was. It was like taking candy from a baby for him, I'm sure," she concluded in disgust. "If I'd done a little serious checking on him, I would have learned that his past was murky, to say the least. But I didn't. The law finally caught up to him somewhere in Florida where he was running a land fraud scheme. But I was a fool and it cost me."

"How much did it cost you?" he asked brutally.

"My money, my heart and all of my pride!" she tossed back savagely.

He glanced around the office. "You've rebuilt the financial end, and I learned Saturday night that you're not breaking your heart over some other man. You couldn't have given yourself to me the way you did if there was another man who held the key to your love. So that leaves us with your pride, doesn't it? That's the one point that is still vulnerable, isn't it, Ariana? You've recovered from everything else but not the humiliation of knowing you'd fallen for a con man. That's why you made those rules of yours. To protect yourself from ever making the same mistake again. To protect yourself from that kind of humiliation!"

"I congratulate you on your powers of perception, magician!"

"So now you think that I'm another Sutcliff?" he asked in a voice of steel.

Ariana flinched at the direct question. That was what she'd implied, wasn't it? "I took the risk of bending one rule for you, Lucian, and look where it got me. In bed with a man who doesn't worry overmuch about a little deception when it's in his own interests. You deceived me. You have to admit that your actions don't speak very well for your sense of honor. At least I was never anything but honest with you, Lucian!"

His hard mouth tightened. "No," he agreed roughly. "You were always honest. You were also bigoted, prejudiced and snobbish. There was also the very real possibility that you were exceedingly mercenary. Hell, woman, can't you see that I was as nervous about you as you say you are about me?"

"I won't take any more risks for you, Lucian!"

He swore, a short, graphic oath that made Ariana step back a pace. "Oh, yes, you will, Ariana Warfield. You bent one rule for me on Saturday night. I can promise you that sooner or later you're going to bend the second rule for me, too! You're going to accept me, murky past and all! You're going to take me as I am, ex-gang leader, ex-carny-showman, ex-G.I. and full-time sleazy real-estate speculator and magician. And you're going to admit that I have a sense of honor, after all!"

"Why the hell should I do that?" she yelped furiously. "Damn it, magician, why should I take one more risk for you?"

"You haven't got any choice," he gritted. "You belong to me. You've belonged to me since Saturday night and probably before that if I wanted to start dissecting the relationship."

"That's not true!"

"It is true," he countered quietly. "But if it makes you feel any better, you have the satisfaction of knowing this relationship works both ways. I belong to you just as surely as you belong to me."

He moved then, his hand making a slight, graceful motion in midair, and then he extended his palm, uncurling his fingers to display a single yellow rosebud on a stem.

Ariana stared at it in consternation as he laid it gently on the glass in front of her. "Good-bye, Ariana. Thank you for lunch. And, honey, try to remember all those warnings about the dangers of getting a magician angry. Don't do anything you'll regret."

She tore her gaze away from the small rose and lifted it back to his face, her own features a study in mingled astonishment, chagrin and anger.

But Lucian was already at the door and through it before she could summon the words to tell him that he had no place in her life and never would. Slowly, the wind leaving the sails of her temper, Ariana sat down at her desk. Unable to stop herself she reached out and touched the rosebud with the tips of her fingers. Trust Lucian to have the last word and the last trick up his sleeve.

Dear God, what was she going to do now? Lucian Hawk would have no qualms about using whatever means necessary to achieve his goals. Any man who had run with a teenage gang, worked the carny circuit and scraped together a successful real estate empire probably knew a hell of a lot more about getting what he wanted than she did.

Ariana shivered and stared at the rose.

He wanted her.

What really made matters difficult was the frightening knowledge that she wanted him. With a shaky sigh, Ariana forced herself to admit the truth. What she felt for Lucian Hawk was more than desire. Simple physical attraction she could have dealt with, Ariana was certain. This strange emotion that had begun plaguing her was far more insidious; far more potentially dangerous.

Her hand folded shut around the rose and, holding it in her lap, she swiveled around in the leather chair to stare out the sixth story window of her office.

Why couldn't Lucian have been perfect? Why couldn't he have fit her image of an honorable man the way Richard Dearborn did? Why couldn't Lucian have arrived in her life complete with a spotless reputation and a sense of personal integrity that couldn't be doubted? Why couldn't Lucian Hawk have been safe?

Ariana blinked as she recognized the paradox of her own thoughts. The truth was, she *didn't* doubt Lucian's personal integrity. A man or a woman was the product of his or her experiences. To wish that Lucian's background was different was to wish that he was a different man altogether.

And she could not imagine herself with a different man now. It was Lucian Hawk, the product of a checkered past and a business career that probably used as much sleight-of-hand as did his hobby of deception, with whom she was in danger of falling in love.

CHAPTER SEVEN

THE FLOURISH WITH THE ROSE HAD COME out all wrong. He'd meant to give it to her with a kiss, not a threat.

Lucian's mouth turned down in self-disgust, and the hand that had produced the rose twenty minutes earlier balled into a large fist. He was standing at his office window gazing with unseeing eyes at the sailboats on the Bay.

It wasn't only the bit with the rose that had gone awry. Everything was going wrong! Damn it to hell! He ought to have realized that it wasn't just her concern with money that stood in the way. She was far more vulnerable than he'd guessed. After what had happened to her, it was no wonder she insisted on complete honesty in a man.

With classic masculine arrogance he'd thought the discovery of his true financial status would remove any doubts that she might still have been harboring. After all, she'd already taken the risk of giving herself to him. Finding out that there was no need to worry about his being impoverished ought to have been the grand finale to the sleight-of-hand act he'd been carrying out since meeting her. But instead of amazing and delighting his intended audience, the magic revelation at the end had precipitated disaster. Lucian groaned feelingly and turned away from the window. He threw himself into the chair behind his desk and stared broodingly at the final subdivision report for the condominium development he was supposed to be considering.

He couldn't focus on business today. All he could think about was the magic lady who was trying to disappear from his life. He couldn't let her go. Lucian knew that with chilling clarity. The well-developed instincts that had brought him so far from the streets of Los Angeles were screaming at him to reach out and grasp this woman. He didn't try to put a label on his emotions. Lucian only knew that he wanted Ariana Warfield.

Why in hell hadn't he realized that with a woman like her things were going to be a lot more complicated than just resolving the financial problem? He'd thought he could simply pull that particular rabbit out of the hat and she would move in with him! What a fool he'd been.

The money had only been part of it. Rule number one, as she'd called it, and he'd managed to make her break it. But rule number two left him with no defense. He'd have had to be one hell of a magician to pull off the impossible feat of making his actions over the past few days disappear! Why hadn't he seen the potential trap he'd been setting for himself when, out of a curiosity he couldn't even explain at the time, he'd decided to keep silent about his personal background the night he'd met Ariana?

Face it. He'd out-finessed himself. A fine magician! But if there was one thing he'd learned in the past thirty-nine years, it was that a man couldn't afford to look back. The only route out of a dilemma was to keep plowing forward, using whatever tools came to hand.

Deliberately Lucian forced himself to cool down and think logically. Ariana was angry now; hurt. But that was something to which he could cling, wasn't it? Better by far to have her feeling some intense emotion toward him than nothing at all. Everything would have been hopeless if she'd simply dismissed him from her life with casual, disgusted indifference.

The drawback to having a passionate woman like Ariana in this particular mood was that it might impel her to do something rash; to lash out recklessly at him. She was woman enough to sense instinctively that her greatest weapon would be another man. Lucian's stomach knotted as he thought of Richard in the three-hundred-dollar trenchcoat. And that image, of course, was what had prompted him to throw out the warning along with the rose.

It should have been a kiss. He knew that he could make her respond to his kisses. Why the hell had he succumbed to his territorial instincts and delivered a threat, instead?

With a wrench he dragged his raging thoughts away from that fruitless path. Logic was what was needed now. Coolly he examined the alternatives available to him. Then he leaned forward and stabbed the button on the intercom.

"Mrs. Kingsley, get hold of that private investigator we used last summer on the Morrison project. Tell him I want to see him this afternoon."

"Yes, Mr. Hawk. Shall I tell him what the conference will be in reference to?"

"A con artist named Fletcher Galen."

Lucian released the button and sat back in his chair, steepling his fingers. He eyed the glass paperweight on his desk as if it were a crystal ball. The strongest tie he had to his magic lady right now was the tenuous partnership they had originally agreed upon. She was probably already thinking of it as dissolved, but Lucian told himself that he would use every trick he had up his sleeve, and helping her prove Galen a fraud was the single most elaborate one he had available. He had to let her know that he still considered the business partnership active. Once again he leaned forward and stabbed the intercom button.

"Yes, Mr. Hawk?"

"Mrs. Kingsley, after you've contacted the investigative service, I want you to call a florist and put in an order for six yellow roses to be delivered here this afternoon."

Mrs. Kingsley had been working for the man who was part magician, part real estate entrepreneur for over five years. She'd learned to expect the unexpected. Her proper secretarial tone didn't alter by so much as a nuance as she acknowledged the unusual request.

But safely out of sight in the outer office Elvira Kingsley allowed a small satisfied smile to brighten her pleasant middle-aged features. It was about time Lucian Hawk found someone for whom he cared enough to order yellow roses on company time. Mrs. Kingsley realized that Hawk had a social life but never had it been permitted to encroach on business hours. Now, in the course of one day she had been obliged to order a catered lunch for two, and a half-dozen yellow roses. Hawk had arrived back from the luncheon with the most deliciously forbidding expression on his hard face. And now the roses. Things were becoming interesting, she thought as she reached for the phone.

THE FIRST OF THE YELLOW ROSES GREETED Ariana when she opened her apartment door the following morning. She had been running late after a restless night and was feeling irritated with herself and with life in general when she threw open the door and nearly ran into the rose.

It wasn't lying on the mat, it was floating in midair at eye level.

After her initial start of surprise, she realized that only one person would have arranged to deliver flowers in such a fashion. Cautiously she extended a hand to clasp the levitated rose and found it attached to an almost invisible nylon string that was, in turn, suspended from the top of the doorway. There was a tiny card dangling from the rose stem.

Knowing that Lucian had been so close gave Ariana an unexpected sense of excitement which lightened momentarily the depression that had been plaguing her. He had been there sometime during the night, standing right outside her door! What would she have done if he'd knocked?

Hastily she tore down the rose and opened the small note. The inside read merely: *I'll get Galen for you.* It was signed with a handsomely scrawled "L."

Ariana's fingers trembled ever so slightly as she stared at the note. She was aware of both a sense of disappointment over the fact that the note was almost busi-nesslike and a conflicting sense of relief that Hawk intended to carry out his end of the partnership.

The business between them would make it necessary for her to see him again.

The ambivalent feelings she experienced at that thought were chasing each other about in her head as she walked to the black Porsche parked at the curb and turned the key in the lock. The yellow rose waiting inside the car on the dash made her draw in her breath.

There was no note attached this time, but Ariana acknowledged to herself that the placement of this flower was a little trickier than the first. Her car had been locked all night, and there was no sign that it had been tampered with.

But it was the rose waiting for her in her office chair that elicited an unwilling admiration for the sheer audacity of the man who had placed it there. The highrise office building that housed Warfield & Co. along with several other businesses was well patrolled at night. Lucian would have had to get past the guard and at least two locked doors. Unless, of course, Ariana reminded herself with a strange little smile, the man really could make roses materialize behind locked doors.

The fourth rose was waiting for her on a stack of letters that Beth brought in for her to sign that morning.

"Don't ask me how it got there," the secretary said, grinning. "I went to pick them up and bring them in to you and there it was!"

The fifth rose was waiting for Ariana on the seat of the Porsche when she left work that evening.

But it was the sixth rose that sent an atavistic chill

down her spine. She found it on her pillow that night as she turned back the covers of the bed.

Lucian Hawk had been there, standing beside her bed, sometime during the day.

It was a long time before Ariana went to sleep that night, and it seemed as though she had just barely managed the feat of getting her eyes closed when she was awakened at four in the morning with an irrational thought. If Lucian Hawk were to fall in love, would he know how to go about asking for love in return? Or would he try to force a response by utilizing his magician's bag of tricks? She went back to sleep again before she could ponder the significance of the question.

The call from Richard Dearborn came at ten the next morning, and even as she accepted it, Ariana was forced to realize that a part of her had hoped it would be a call from Lucian.

"Ariana," Richard began in his pleasant, well-cultivated voice, "I'm going to have to leave for New York on a business trip in the morning. Any chance you could have dinner with me tonight?"

The first thing that popped into her mind as she listened to the invitation was Lucian's warning about the dangers of angering a magician. The second thing that came into her head was a grim, reckless desire to reestablish her independence from the man who had deceived her this weekend. Damn it! She most certainly did not belong to Lucian Hawk, whatever he might think!

"I'd love to, Richard," she heard herself saying smoothly. "What time?"

"I'll pick you up at seven, darling. We'll go down to

the Wharf. Mario is promising to hold some fresh swordfish for us and an excellent Chardonnay. How does that sound?"

"It sounds wonderful, Richard. I'll look forward to it."

And she honestly did try to look forward to their date, but even as she dressed carefully in a violet blue pleated column of a dress that fell narrowly over her slender figure, Ariana kept wondering what Lucian Hawk was doing and what he would say if he knew that she was seeing Richard.

Richard Dearborn was at his most urbane and charming that evening, clearly looking forward with anticipation to a successful business trip the following day. Ariana did her best to make conversation, trying to keep her mind off the realization that with this man she would never find the spark that had ignited so easily between herself and Lucian. Something just wasn't right.

There was no magic with Richard Dearborn, she finally told herself wryly as the evening drew to a close. And after having had a sample of the real thing, she no longer wanted to content herself with a pleasant facade. Ariana wanted the magic.

What had Lucian done to her? How could she have allowed such a man to disrupt her life to such an extent? Why couldn't she put him out of her mind and out of her life?

"I hate to have to take you home so early, Ari," Richard sighed as he assisted her into a cab, "but I've got to leave at six tomorrow morning. Don't hold it against me, darling. I promise I'll make it up to you when I return."

"Don't worry about it, Richard. As a matter of fact I've had rather a difficult day and need some sleep. Have a good trip to New York," she responded as the cab drew up in front of her door.

"I'll see you inside," Richard said gallantly, signaling to the driver to wait. He climbed out of the cab and escorted Ariana to her door. As she turned the key in the lock and pushed it slightly ajar, he took her into his arms.

Ariana felt his lips on hers in a sophisticated, polished embrace, and all she could think about was the magic she had known when Lucian had held her.

"Good night, Richard," she whispered almost sadly as he took his leave. She felt as if she were really saying good-bye. Whatever happened, she would not tie herself in marriage to Richard Dearborn. She knew that now with stoic resignation. In fact, she had known it earlier that evening when she had dressed for him. Lucian's impact on her senses had left no room for another man.

That realization was occupying her thoughts as she reached out to flip on the foyer light switch.

"Have a nice evening, Ariana?"

For an instant she thought her mind had conjured him up out of thin air. Ariana froze in the doorway, her hand still on the switch as dappled light from the faceted globe overhead illuminated Lucian's dark figure lounging in the arched entrance to the living room.

"Lucian!"

He regarded her with a raking gaze. Even though he was leaning almost casually against the wall, his arms folded across his chest, one foot crossed over the other, all Ariana could think about was the peril of offending a magician.

Lucian Hawk was coldly, dangerously furious.

"At least you had the good sense not to bring him inside," he drawled.

From out of nowhere it seemed, Ariana managed to recover her nearly stifled voice. Behind the lenses of her designer glasses her smoky eyes were wide and wary. The door was still open behind her and some sixth sense urged her to leave it that way.

"What are you doing here, Lucian?"

"Waiting for you, naturally." He straightened and took a step forward. Instantly Ariana moved backward a pace until she was standing on the threshold outside her own door. Lucian halted, topaz eyes glittering angrily. "Come inside and close the door, Ariana."

"Not unless you'll give me your word you're not going to harm me!"

He appeared to consider that. "I ought to beat you."

"Lucian!" She stared at him, appalled. There was enough tension in the way he stood before her to make her believe him capable of it.

"But I won't," he went on heavily. "I will remind myself that beating you would only serve to reenforce your already low opinion of my background and morals."

Something about the way he said that made Ariana long to tell him that she really didn't have a low opinion of him. Before she could stop to think, she had stepped back into the foyer and was closing the door behind her. "Lucian, I don't know what you hope to accomplish by materializing inside my apartment in this way," she tried to say with a coolness she was far from feeling, "but I can guarantee you that I'm not going to applaud the act!" She tossed her evening bag down on a nearby table and faced him.

"What did you hope to accomplish by going out with Dearborn?" he grated. Dressed in charcoal slacks and a black chamois shirt, he was a dark, intimidating figure standing amid the French vanilla and papaya shades of her apartment.

"I went out with Richard because I wanted to go out with him! I've been dating him frequently for over a month!" Ariana stormed.

"You went out with him because you knew it would infuriate me! He was the strongest weapon you could find to use against me, wasn't he?"

"I don't need a weapon against you!"

"No, you don't *need* one, but you wanted one, didn't you?" Lucian came a step closer. "Did it work, Ariana? Can Dearborn make you forget Saturday night?"

Ariana flinched. Nothing on earth would ever make her forget that night, and she knew from the gleaming gold of Lucian's eyes that he was aware of it. Because he would never forget it, either? Somehow, Ariana desperately wanted that to be the case.

"This is a pointless discussion, Lucian," she managed to say very steadily. "What are you doing here?"

He arched one black brow. "My original reason for stopping by was to give you some information on Fletcher Galen. We're still partners in that little enterprise, remember?"

"I remember," she whispered shakily.

"But that can wait," he went on grimly. "When I got here and realized you were gone for the evening I had a hunch you were out somewhere trying to show me that you can do as you please with other men. So I decided

I'd hang around until you got back. I think we need to get a couple of things clear between us."

"Such as?" she dared, her head lifting haughtily.

"Such as the fact that whatever else happens between you and me, neither of us is going to use someone else as a shield." He took another step forward and quite suddenly he had his strong fingers curved around her shoulders. Ariana was trapped. "Damn it, you know you don't want him," he rasped harshly. "If he'd been important, you would have been sleeping with him long before I came on the scene."

"That's a typical male conclusion!" she flung back. "I'm building a relationship with Richard. One that might end in marriage. I have no wish to rush such an important event. Just because you find it necessary to take a woman to bed after knowing her only a couple of days, that doesn't mean all men work the same way!"

"Only those of us who crawled up out of the gutter the hard way? You could be right," he went on as she tried to freeze him with a glance. "I expect I do work a little differently from Dearborn. But that's because I've learned that moving quickly is the only sure way to get what you want in life. And I want you, Ariana Warfield. I want you so badly I'm not going to take a chance on losing you by playing the game your way."

"I'm not playing a game, Lucian! Damn you! Let me go. Say what you have to say about Fletcher Galen and then leave. It's late and I want to go to bed."

Too late she realized that goading him verbally was probably not the best way of handling an irate magician. She saw the flicker in his golden eyes a scant second before he moved, and then there was no time to escape.

His hands slipped down her body and under her thighs. In an instant she was swept off her feet and high in his arms.

"Going to bed is exactly what I had on the agenda for this evening," Lucian assured her in an intense and velvet dark voice that ruffled all her nerve endings. "It seems to be the most efficient method of communicating with you!"

"Put me down." Ariana's arm rested on the black chamois cloth that covered his shoulder as she glared defiantly up into his set features. "I mean it, Lucian. Let me go this instant. I won't allow you to manhandle me this way!"

He turned with her in his arms and started across the living room to the hall that led to her bedroom. "I'm not going to hurt you, Ariana, and you know it. I'm going to make you feel what you felt on Saturday night. And afterward, when you're all soft and glowing in my arms, we'll talk."

"Why, you arrogant bastard," she breathed as her pulse began to race. "If you think I'm going to melt in your arms after the way you've behaved this evening, you're out of your mind."

"Probably. You've had me half out of my mind for almost a week." He strode down the hall and turned into her bedroom with an assurance that made Ariana recall he'd been there once before when he'd left the rose. And that thought brought with it another. But it was too late and in any event there was little she could have done to hide the evidence.

Reaching out to turn on the wall switch with the hand that extended from under Ariana's back, Lucian saw the half-dozen roses in the crystal vase beside her bed as soon as the lamp flared into brightness. Ariana had a moment in which to regret the impulsive way in which she had preserved the six roses he had materialized for her and then she felt the tightening of his arms.

Desperately trying to think of some scathing dismissal of the obvious fact that the roses had meant something far too important to her, Ariana said tightly, "It seemed a shame to just throw them out."

"Ariana," he got out hoarsely, ignoring her faint defense. "I really should beat you for putting me through so much hell!" Then his mouth came down on hers in a fiercely possessive kiss.

Ariana tried to think as he took control of her mouth. She tried to think about her ambivalent feelings toward this man. She tried to think of what a perfect escort Richard Dearborn had been that evening. She tried to think of how angry she should have been with Lucian Hawk. But all she succeeded in thinking about was the undeniable fact that she was back once again in the presence of magic. Real magic.

Her fingers, which rested at the nape of his neck, found themselves entwined in the black and silver of his hair, the gold and crimson nails providing a sensuous contrast. Her lips parted beneath the onslaught of his mouth, allowing him into the warmth he sought.

She was barely aware of being carried the rest of the way to the bed. There was the sensation of softness under her as her back touched the plush papaya-colored spread, and then there was only the hardness of Lucian's body as he followed her down onto the bed.

"My God, woman, you don't have a prayer of escaping me tonight, not after I've seen those roses!"

He grated the words against the curve of her throat. "Tell me why you saved them. *Tell me!*"

But she couldn't tell him. She didn't want to take the step of admitting aloud that she was so far under Lucian's spell. Instead she moaned something unintelligible into his shoulder and encircled his neck with her arms.

He seemed willing to take the response as sufficient answer. His teeth nipped with teasing passion, and then his tongue came out to soothe as he found the fastening of her violet blue gown. The solid feel of him beat at her senses, making her totally aware of his mounting desire. One heavy thigh lay across her own, anchoring her on the bedspread so that he could touch her at his pleasure.

Ariana was held in sensual captivity as the pleated dress was lowered to her waist. She heard his muffled groan as he followed the retreating line of the soft fabric with his lips. Her unconfined breasts seemed to swell to fill his hand as he touched her.

"Ariana, my Magic Lady, I could never give you up. Didn't you realize that? I've waited too long to find you!"

"Oh, Lucian," she breathed brokenly. Already the swirling tension of passion was staring to tangle her in its coils. She knew a tightening in her lower body that brought warmth and dampness in its wake. Ariana's nails began to test the resilient muscles of her lover's back, following the contours down to where the chamois shirt disappeared into his slacks.

When Lucian pulled away a few inches to finish removing the pleated dress, Ariana closed her eyes and slid her fingers into the waistband of his black slacks.

She felt him remove her glasses and toss them along with his own onto the nightstand, and then he was back beside her, whispering heated encouragement.

"Undress me, Magic Lady. Let me feel your fingers in all the right places. I haven't been able to get the memory of your touch out of my head!"

As if to punish her gently for having haunted his mind, Lucian caught one nipple between his teeth and tugged carefully. The resulting sensation sent tremor after tremor through Ariana's body.

"Your body knows what it wants," he growled in satisfaction as the nipple grew hard and tight under his caress. "Listen to your body, Ariana."

She moaned his name again and fumbled with the buckle of his belt. As if he were suddenly too impatient to wait for her awkward movements, Lucian lifted himself away and pulled off the clothing he wore. She lay looking up at him through her lashes as he stood for a moment beside the bed. Inwardly Ariana acknowledged that the insistent need of her body to know the totality of him was a heady drug. No other man had ever succeeded in drugging her senses like this. Drugging them or casting a spell over them?

He lay alongside her, pressing himself into her hip so that she knew the fullness of his arousal. Gathering her against him with one arm, Lucian flattened his palm at the base of her throat and slowly drew his hand downward. It grazed each breast in turn and then glided over her stomach to the upper edge of the small silken garment that was all she still wore.

Lucian raised his head from her throat to look down into her face as he deliberately moved his palm across the triangle of satiny nylon to the warmth between her legs.

"Oh!" Her gasp was involuntary as he began to draw delicate circles on the surface of the thin material. The exquisite sensation was conducted through the fabric the way electricity was conducted through water. And it had almost the same effect. Ariana writhed beneath the touch.

"I can feel the heat in you, Magic lady," he rasped. "Already you're hot and warm and sweetly damp. I couldn't leave you now if I tried."

He rolled on top of her, thrusting provocatively against the nylon that still barred the path. Ariana cried out softly as she felt her body respond to the knowledge that he waited at the gate. Instinctively she arched her hips, only to know a pulsating frustration as the nylon of her underwear continued to prohibit his entrance.

For some reason the teasing sensation made her go wild in his arms. It was as if, having realized that she couldn't have him within her immediately, she suddenly *had* to have him. Her senses clamored for the release only he could provide.

"Lucian, oh, Lucian, *please*," she begged, arching passionately once more against him.

He caught her wrists gently when she would have lowered her hands to remove the garment that still remained between them. Pinning her hands to the bed on either side of her head, Lucian kissed her deeply, moving his tongue in and out of her mouth in a rhythm which he repeated with his hips.

Ariana shivered and lifted herself against him in a helpless turmoil of desire.

"A little longer, Magic Lady," Lucian muttered thickly in a voice that betrayed his own frayed control. "I want you to know what it feels like to need someone the way I need you." He released her wrists and began to explore further.

The sweet torment continued until Ariana was a restless, raging wild thing in his arms. Her senses spun and her passions rioted as he steadfastly provoked her. Her legs wrapped around him, urging him as close as possible and her hands danced a primitive pattern across his back. Ariana thought that she would go mad, and her only consolation was the knowledge that Lucian was very close to losing his iron control. She would push him over the edge and make him finish what he had started if it took all the strength in her body!

"My God, woman! I knew I wouldn't be able to resist you very long in bed, but I thought I could hold out longer than this!"

Sliding one hand down her spine to her hips, Lucian lifted her and slipped off the panties that had barred the way to her softness. Instantly Ariana sucked in her breath and clung, pulling him close. Lucian needed no further urging.

With a deep, husky groan he surged against her body, sheathing himself in her hot, damp warmth. "Yes, Magic Lady, oh, *yes!*"

Then he was riding the storm he had unleashed, inciting it to new heights even as he quickly became its victim. Ariana shut her eyes tightly and abandoned herself to the power that was driving her body. The shimmering magic blossomed around her until she could no longer think at all.

Her body reacted to every touch, every new sensation being visited upon it. Her palms flattened against the curves of his back and her mouth flowered to receive him.

Gradually the intensity built to the bursting point. Ariana sensed the precipice and knew once more that curious instant of panic. As if he felt it approaching and refused to let her succumb to the strange fear of the unknown, Lucian sank his teeth lightly into her lower lip and simultaneously slid his fingers to the rounded cushion of her buttocks. There he clenched with calculated pressure.

Ariana went hurtling over the edge, losing herself entirely in the glittering magic. She heard Lucian's hoarse cry of satisfaction, and then there were only the shifting colors of the dissipating spell as it slowly broke apart and released the two it had held captive.

It was a long time before Ariana felt Lucian's body shift slowly and roll to one side. She opened her eyes to find him watching her with a gaze that revealed undeniable masculine gratification.

"Promise me," he ordered softly with the arrogance of a man who is certain that he is in control of his woman, "that there won't be any more nights in which I'll have to pace the floor waiting for you to come home from a date with Dearborn or anyone else!" Lucian drew a fingertip up along her throat to the corner of her vulnerable mouth as she lay watching him.

Ariana didn't have the energy to attempt a lie, so she told him the stark truth. "I won't be going out with Richard again." She had known that much when she'd stood on her doorstep and watched the other man drive off in the cab. There didn't seem much point in trying to pretend otherwise to Lucian.

He let out a long sigh of satisfaction that might have been tinged with relief. "So that much is settled, at least." He leaned over and brushed a surprisingly tender kiss against her lips. "Ariana, there's something I want to explain to you," he went on slowly as he lifted his head again.

"Yes, Lucian?"

Lucian's mouth was edged with the smile of a man who is about to indulge his lover and is already anticipating her delight. His eyes were soft and full of his own pleasure. "You told me once that marriage was on your list of demands. You said you wouldn't consider an affair. I told you I wasn't interested either in marriage or in signing your damn prenuptial agreement. You've explained why you were trying to insist on a safe marriage. Well, now I'd like to explain why I told you I wasn't about to marry again. And why I'm having some second thoughts."

"Second thoughts?" she queried uncertainly.

"Oh, not about that business with the contract. I'm not about to sign anything like that," he assured her gruffly, "but with you I think I would take another chance on marriage." His smile widened as he waited for her reaction.

But Ariana merely smiled in return and closed his mouth with the tips of her fingers as she sat up beside him. "That's all right, Lucian. You don't have to explain anything to me."

"I want to, Ariana," he insisted, the first hint of a frown pulling his dark brows together as she turned away to sit up on the edge of the bed.

"It's not necessary, Lucian," she said, glancing back over her bare shoulder with the expression of a woman who is surrendering totally to the idea of an affair and is demanding nothing in return. "I've dropped my demand for marriage along with all my other demands. You don't have to worry about it anymore. I'm not going to go on fighting you. I can't. I won't ask for marriage."

She got to her feet and reached for the robe that hung inside her closet door. As she belted it around her narrow waist she hurried to the bathroom and shut herself inside. With fingers that fumbled violently she switched on the taps in the shower and stuffed her hair up under her cap. Her whole body was trembling with the tension of anticipation.

The bang of the bathroom door being thrown open behind her came just as she was about to step behind the striped shower curtain. Ariana turned to face a chillingly furious Lucian. For an instant they stared at each other across the short distance separating them, and Ariana felt her heart pound as she acknowledged the enormity of what she was doing and the violence of his reaction to her words.

"Are you telling me," Lucian grated in a deadly soft voice, "that I'm not good enough to marry?"

CHAPTER EIGHT

"I DIDN'T SAY YOU WEREN'T GOOD enough to marry, Lucian, and I certainly wasn't implying any such thing!" Feeling terribly vulnerable as she stood nude on the threshold of the shower, Ariana took the only escape possible and stepped behind the plastic curtain. The bold, lean maleness of him seemed to dominate the pastel bathroom.

Good lord! She ought to have foreseen that potential reaction! What was the matter with her? Couldn't she have guessed he'd take her lack of interest in marriage as an insult? It was just that in the soft aftermath of his lovemaking she had finally convinced herself that he cared for her. There was an elemental quality about Lucian Hawk that told her he wasn't playing tricks, not on the fundamental level of their strange relationship.

When he had gone so far as to mention marriage she had decided to take the biggest risk of her life and gently fling the offer back in his face.

She wanted marriage, Ariana admitted freely to herself, but she didn't want it presented to her indulgently as a reward for her surrender the way news of Lucian's financial status had been presented. Ariana had no intention of marrying Lucian Hawk unless he wanted the binding tie as much as she did.

Lucian had to learn how to ask for love.

The conviction was firm in her mind, but Ariana was honest enough, even in those first moments of arriving at the decision, to acknowledge that she was gambling for very high stakes. What if she were wrong about her magician? What if he didn't feel anything more than mere desire? What if passion was all he required from her?

The only way she would ever learn the truth of his feelings for her was to let him discover for himself that an affair was not enough. The realization of what she was doing sent a small shiver through Ariana. There had been warnings aplenty about the dangers of angering a magician. What kind of penalties existed for a woman who tried to use the contents of her own bag of tricks against him?

The shower curtain was rudely swept aside as Lucian stepped inside the tiled stall. A quick sidelong glance revealed that he was far from convinced of the sincerity of her words a moment earlier. He reached to catch hold of Ariana's arms, his face set in uncompromising lines. She was vividly conscious of his raw masculinity.

"If you think for one minute that you can have an affair with me while you wait for a proposal from a more suitable candidate," he ground out roughly, "you're in for one hell of a shock!"

"There's no need to play the heavy-handed male," Ariana managed in a soothing tone. Daring to lift her hand to his cheek, she stroked it with a featherlight touch. Her eyes were soft and luminous. "I have no intention of trying to find another man. I told you I believe in fidelity. I'm simply attempting to tell you that you've won. You and my aunt and my brother are all right and I was wrong. There is no reason to insist on a marriage license. We're two adult people who should be able to give our word to each other and keep it. I was only seeking marriage and a wedding contract as a way of protecting myself. I suppose it was a way of asking a man to prove himself. But there's no need to do that with you, is there? You're certainly no threat financially, and I think I can trust you in other ways. You'll be honest and straightforward with me when the time comes that you decide you no longer want me?"

He frowned ferociously. "Sweetheart, you're the only woman I want. For God's sake, of course you can trust me!"

"Then there's no reason for this argument, is there?" she whispered and stood on tiptoe to kiss the taut line of his mouth.

Instantly he wrapped his arms around her and swept her close against his wet, muscled frame, his mouth putting her butterfly kiss through a passionate metamorphosis. It emerged as a breathless, clinging embrace that left Ariana feeling thoroughly branded.

"God knows the last thing I want to do with you tonight is argue!" The statement came with great depth of feeling as Lucian reluctantly broke the sensual contact. His palms slipped down her shoulders to cover her breasts as his eyes met hers. "But I want to explain why I've been so cautious about marriage."

"You said you were married once?"

He nodded. "A long time ago. She was very beautiful, and I was just beginning to make something of

myself. She seemed perfect to me, like a lovely doll.
Just the right woman to have beside me as I made my
fortune. When she insisted on marriage I didn't argue.
Unfortunately I discovered too late that a perfect little
doll was just exactly what she was. Beautiful but inca-
pable of caring about anyone other than herself. When
she met me I was the most successful man she knew. A
year of marriage to me, however, put her into contact
with several men who were far more successful than I
was at the time. I came home from work one day to find
she'd filed for divorce in order to marry one of them.
Frankly I was glad to see her go. The whole experience
left a sour taste in my mouth for the noble institution
of marriage, however."

"And so you became very wary of women who
seemed somewhat mercenary, hmmm?" Ariana smiled
serenely, her fingers splayed against his chest. "I understand, Lucian." Deliberately she brushed the topic aside.
"There's something you should know about tonight,
though. I didn't date Richard with the intention of punishing you."

"No?" He looked skeptical.

She shook her head firmly. "I think I just wanted to
make one last comparison before I accepted the inevitable."

"And what was the result of your 'comparison'?" he
demanded with a returning touch of aggression.

"Just that there is no magic for me with Richard.
There's never been any real magic for me with anyone
except you," she told him simply.

"Ariana!" He pulled her close again, burying his
face against the wet skin of her neck. She felt him

shudder. "You won't regret this, sweetheart. I'll make it all right, I swear!"

The subject of marriage was dropped, and Ariana didn't know whether to be pleased or depressed.

With the contented humor of a large, satiated jungle cat Lucian turned what remained of the shower into a teasing frolic that finally drove Ariana to seek a laughing escape. She stepped out of the shower, grabbing for one of the thick towels on the rack, and left him to finish by himself.

"When you come out I want to hear what you discovered about Fletcher Galen," she called as she slipped back into her robe and went to the door.

"Oh, yeah. I almost forgot. I guess I got sidetracked," he called back.

"Uh huh." Ariana's mouth crooked wryly as she opened the bathroom door and stepped out into the hall.

By the time he had emerged from her bedroom wearing only his charcoal slacks, Ariana was waiting in the kitchen. She'd made a pot of hot chocolate and had put out a plate of cookies.

Lucian accepted the offering with alacrity, reaching for three of the little cookies as he sat down. "I put a good private investigative service on Galen two days ago."

"Is that his real name? Fletcher Galen?" Ariana asked curiously as she sat down across from him.

"Yeah, surprisingly enough. He's got a couple of other names apparently, but Galen is the one he uses when he's running the 'Contact-an-Extraterrestrial' scam." Lucian reached for his cup of hot chocolate.

"He's gotten away with this before?" Ariana was disgusted.

"Apparently he tried something similar down in Arizona a year ago. Bilked a lot of retirees of several thousand dollars over the course of a few weeks."

"Why doesn't someone stop him?"

"A lot of people won't file a complaint or testify. They're too embarrassed at having been taken in so easily. Also, Galen keeps on the move. By the time the Arizona authorities became aware of him, he'd skipped. This kind of con game is amazingly common, honey. The first-class con artists often operate with impunity for years. Even when they are caught they rarely go to jail. They just jump bail and head for South America or somewhere until things cool down."

"How does Galen's scam work? Is he making his money off those horrendously high fees he charges?" Ariana asked, frowning.

"No, the fees are just established to keep out the riffraff," Lucian told her dryly. "When the pitch is made for money, Galen wants to be sure he's hitting the right crowd, people who can afford it."

"Those large checks my aunt has been drawing on her account?" Ariana pressed.

"If this scam is like the one he pulled in Arizona, your aunt and the others have been donating toward a 'research' facility which will be used to set up continuing contact with Krayton after the initial breakthrough has been made."

"Oh, my God! And Aunt Philomena fell for this?"

"According to the investigator I hired, a lot of people have. And when Galen skips town with their money most won't complain."

"They'll be too humiliated over having been duped." Ariana sighed. "I know the feeling. How are we going to explain all this to Aunt Phil?"

"The investigator is compiling a lot of documentary evidence like the articles which ran in the Arizona papers after the last operation and reports the authorities made, that sort of thing. He's going to collect what he can and then we'll show it to Phil. That's about all we can do, unless..."

Ariana narrowed her eyes as he let the sentence trail off thoughtfully. "Unless what?"

Lucian shrugged. "Well, it might be interesting to see what the audience's reaction would be if Galen's performance failed to come off as scheduled one night during a session," he said slowly.

"What are you suggesting?" Ariana waited breathlessly, her eyes lighting up with anticipation.

"You have to understand that people are very odd in their reactions to the kind of evidence the investigator is going to come up with," he began carefully. "A lot of them will tend to dismiss it as yellow journalism or deliberate slander. If they want to go on believing, they will. But the one thing a magician can't survive is the embarrassment of tricks that go awry."

"If things go wrong during a performance, couldn't he just claim that proper contact hadn't been made?"

"Not if things go wrong in an embarrassing fashion," Lucian drawled, his eyes concentrating on some point in the middle distance as he ran several things through his mind.

"You said that if you were to leap up during the middle of a performance, you'd probably be subdued by those characters in the monk suits," she reminded him worriedly.

"I'm not suggesting I pull anything quite that grand. The essence of a good piece of magic is adequate preparation. I'm suggesting that I help Galen prepare for one of his performances."

Ariana went very still as she sensed the direction of his thoughts. "You're going to tamper with his bag of tricks?"

"Ummm. It could produce some interesting results."

"But to do that you'd have to get inside that compound, and once inside the gates you'd have to get into the room where he conducts those s;aaeances."

"Exactly." He brought his attention back to her face and smiled wryly at her expression of dismay. "It shouldn't be any more complicated than getting that rose onto your office chair."

"Lucian! Are you serious?" she whispered, her mouth suddenly very dry as she remembered the forbidding gates and the hooded men who walked inside the compound.

"I think it's worth a look. What do you say we drive back to the inn tomorrow afternoon, arranging to arrive around nightfall?"

"I don't want you taking any chances!" she declared.

He grinned, a wicked magician's grin, and the topaz eyes gleamed. "The only dangerous chances I've taken lately are with a reckless little red-haired witch who has nearly driven me out of my mind. Compared with those hazards, getting into Galen's setup and rearranging his performance should be child's play!"

Ariana gasped as he lunged to his feet, reached around the table, caught her wrist and dragged her into a tumble on his lap. With one arm cradling her, Lucian continued to munch cookies. "Tell me what made you save the roses, Ariana," he challenged.

She lifted a hand with deliberate vagueness. "I told you. They were too pretty to throw away."

"I don't believe you," he announced complacently. "Tell me the truth."

That she was wildly, heedlessly in love with him? Not a chance, Ariana decided resolutely. She had done all the surrendering she intended to do. Sooner or later Lucian Hawk was going to have to learn that love was a two-way street and that each party took some risks.

"There's nothing to tell, Lucian, except that I suppose I knew as I collected each rose that you were becoming more and more inevitable." That much was true, she reflected. Ariana ran her fingers through his tousled dark hair and smiled up at him. "How does a woman defend herself against a magician?" she asked whimsically.

"I couldn't leave you any defense," he said quietly, his eyes turning very serious. "I wanted you too much to take a chance on your escaping me."

"Did you, Lucian?"

He swallowed the last of the cookie, and then he nudged her chin with the edge of his hand and lifted her mouth for his kiss. "Damn right," he muttered. Then he was surging to his feet with her in his arms.

"Lucian?"

"I'm going to take you back to bed and show you some nifty sleight-of-hand," he explained as he strode down the hall.

Ariana nestled her head against his bare shoulder and

gave herself up to what remained of the night. In the morning she would deal once more with the future. The night belonged to the magician.

LUCIAN PICKED ARIANA UP LATE THE NEXT afternoon in a dark green Jaguar. He was dressed in faded jeans and a chocolate brown corduroy shirt. Suitable clothing for sneaking around the camps of enemy magicians, Ariana thought nervously. The closer the trip had approached, the more anxious she had become. Even a quick visit to talk things over with her brother had not allayed her fears. As she went down the front steps to meet Lucian, her brows were drawn together in a severe line.

"Nothing like having your woman greet you with a radiant smile the day after," he drawled, his eyes roving appreciatively over her designer jeans and royal blue sweater. He leaned down to kiss her firmly. "Cheer up, honey, nothing's going to go wrong!"

"Famous last words! Listen, Lucian. I've been thinking about this..."

"Heaven help us," he teased.

"I'm serious! If you're determined to go through with this, then I'm going to wait in the car while you sneak inside the compound. We'll synchronize our watches, and if you don't return at the agreed-upon time, I'm going to go for help!"

"There's no need to synchronize our watches," he pointed out amiably as he started the engine of the Jaguar. "We're both wearing quartz watches. They keep time almost perfectly."

"Don't tease me, Lucian!"

"Okay. If you want to wait in the car and stand prepared to go for the cavalry, you can. I don't see any problem with that. Just promise me you won't jump the gun!"

"Tell me how much time you think you'll need, and I'll wait exactly that long."

"An hour and a half should do it. Probably won't take that much time." He shifted smoothly for a stoplight and turned to flick her a laughing-eyed glance. "You're really worried, aren't you?"

Ariana, who had been worried all day, glowered at him. "And you're really enjoying this, aren't you?" she tossed back.

"Makes a pleasant change of pace from real estate."

"Lucian?"

"Hmmm?

"How did you get inside my office that night to leave the rose?"

"I'll tell you on our first anniversary," he promised.

"Since we're not going to be getting married, I think that's too long to have to wait," she retorted firmly, repressing a spark of hope.

"Ariana, you were the one who wanted to get married," he reminded her in a neutral tone.

"I've changed my mind," she declared with false breeziness. "Who needs it?" Then she hurried to shift the topic again. "Are we going to stop for a snack somewhere on the way or are you going to perform your walking through walls trick on an empty stomach?"

He frowned as if not particularly pleased at the direction of the conversation and then he asked politely, "I take it you're hungry?"

"You're a mind reader!"

"Actually, I never went in for that kind of magic," he said wryly. "It takes an assistant and I prefer to work alone."

"How do they do those mind-reading acts where one person goes down into the audience and the mind reader is blindfolded on stage?" she demanded.

"Codes," he explained easily. "That's why it takes two people. The person who goes down into the audience has to communicate with the mind reader by a variety of subtle codes. If she holds up a man's gold watch, for instance, she might say something like, 'Tell me quickly, quickly, what I'm holding in my hand.' The mind reader knows that 'quickly, quickly' is a code for gold watch. The codes can get extremely elaborate, depending on how well the two performers can memorize. Sometimes silent codes are used. Electronic gadgets and such. It can get very involved."

"And what about some of the other famous tricks? How about the one where a woman is sawed in half inside a box?" Ariana asked eagerly, sensing he was in a communicative mood.

"There are a variety of methods. Some revolve around having a table that is quite deep beneath the box. It doesn't look deep enough to hold a second woman, but that's because the edge of the table is beveled out to only a couple of inches. The center is actually thick enough to hold the second person, and there's a trap door in the bottom of the box."

"So the second woman can put her feet out the opposite end of the box?"

"Right. The first woman is curled up inside the first

half of the box. There are other methods, but that's one of the oldest."

"Okay," Ariana went on with relish, "how about all those escapes Houdini did?"

"Well, to begin with, he was an expert on locks. He was also an expert at concealing implements with which to pick locks. Also, the more elaborate a box or a bunch of rope ties or chains are, the more opportunities there are for having trick mechanisms for escape built into the apparatus."

"Why is it his name that everyone remembers when they're asked to name a famous magician? What was so special about his performances?"

"It's hard to say. He was a fabulous showman and he had a flair for dramatic, death-defying stunts. There have been whole books written on why his name lives on, but no one can really put it into words. He was a magician," Lucian concluded simply.

"He made a practice of exposing spiritualists and psychics, didn't he?"

"Yes, for all the good it did. The people who wanted to believe kept right on believing, Ariana. That's a blunt fact of human nature. We may succeed in persuading your aunt that Galen's a fraud, but you can bet that even if I manage to have him make a fool of himself in front of the audience, several members of it will still go on believing in him. Right up to the point where their money disappears and Galen skips town!"

They stopped for a quick supper, and half an hour before they reached their destination, night began to fall heavily around the mountains. Lucian briefly explained his plans. Ariana was aware of the increasing tension in him. It wasn't a nervous tension, rather the anticipatory heightening of awareness that a man might experience prior to going before an audience or into battle. She stirred restlessly on her side of the car as second and third thoughts assailed her.

"Lucian, maybe we should call this off."

"Would you rather I took you to the inn, first?" he offered dryly.

"No!"

"Okay, then stop suggesting we call it off. It's too late for that."

"Are you going to tell Aunt Phil you've rigged Galen's performance?"

"It's going to be pretty damn obvious someone's interfered with it." Lucian grinned. It was a feral sort of grin and Ariana didn't care for it. "I think we'll stop by the compound first. I'll make my little adjustments to Galen's bag of tricks, and then we'll drive on to the inn. Everyone there should be just about finished with dinner and preparing to go the s;aaeance. We'll attend along with the others. Yes, I think I will warn Phil, but no one else. If Galen got wind of my tampering in time, he might be able to salvage the act. Phil will keep quiet and let the chips fall where they may."

Ariana nodded. "Yes, she'll be willing to give him a fair test."

It was quite dark when Lucian pulled the Jaguar well off the road several hundred yards from the secluded retreat. He parked out of sight and turned in the seat to deliver last minute instructions to Ariana.

"Remember, no panicking. Everything's going to be fine, but it could be one hell of an embarrassment for me if you get nervous and go for help!" he lectured sternly.

"Then you'd better not be late getting back to the car," she retorted grimly. "I'd rather see you embarrassed than hurt!"

"It's nice to know you care," he drawled gently. "Ariana, when this is all over I really don't see any reason why we shouldn't go ahead and get married. What difference would it make? And I know you'd be more comfortable with a ring on your finger."

"Nonsense," she scoffed with credible nonchalance. "I'm not even going to get any family pressure to legalize things, remember? My aunt and my brother don't believe in the necessity of marriage, and I know how you feel about it. Relax, Lucian. I've come around to your way of thinking. Now off you go and take care of yourself," she urged.

He scowled at her for a long moment, and then with a violent little wrench he opened the Jaguar's door and stepped outside into the night. Leaning down, he said, "Sit in the driver's seat with the key in the ignition in case something comes up and we have to leave quickly. And keep the doors locked until you see me, understand?"

"I understand." She slid across into the driver's seat as Lucian straightened and slammed the car door. A moment later he was lost in the shadows of the surrounding forest.

Almost at once the darkness and quiet seemed to close around the Jaguar. Ariana glanced at her watch and knew that she would do so again and again as she waited for Lucian to reappear. She recalled Drake's words of advice to her that morning and smiled wanly. All she could do was sit and wait.

For lack of anything more productive she thought about the idea of marrying Lucian Hawk. Damn it, she wasn't going to let him do her any favors! If Lucian wanted marriage, it would have to be because he loved her so much he wanted all the trimmings. Not because he wanted to indulge and reward her for giving herself to him.

She knew that she was taking a terrible risk by pushing him this way. If he wasn't genuinely in love with her and was concerned only with possession, then he would grow bored with attempting to do her the favor of marriage. He would be content with an affair.

If that was the way things worked out, Ariana knew that she was going to be devastated. She wanted so much to believe that Lucian was in love with her as deeply as she was in love with him. She wanted him to comprehend his own feelings, and that, she knew, was asking a lot. She had the feeling that Lucian had made a habit of reaching out and taking what he wanted in life. He had probably rarely been called upon to analyze his own emotions very thoroughly. He knew he wanted her, but did he know that what he really wanted was her love, not just her passion and warmth?

For that matter, Ariana reminded herself sadly, did *she* know that he wanted more than just the physical side of their relationship? She was staking so much on an affirmative answer to that question.

Time was what they needed, she told herself as she sat staring into the shadows. Time to get to know each other well, to become accustomed to the feelings that had sprung up so quickly between them. An affair would give them that time, even though it might end in disaster for her if it turned out that Lucian didn't truly love her.

Ariana didn't see that she had much choice. She had already taken her chances. She had surrendered to him just as he had demanded. Now she could only pray that he would be willing to take the risk of admitting that what bound them together was love. Lucian Hawk had to take a few chances of his own.

Time dragged on as she sat impatiently in the front seat of the Jaguar. Philomena didn't know that they were due to arrive at the inn that evening. Lucian had called for reservations late in the afternoon just before they had left San Francisco, and unless the desk clerk thought to mention the fact to Philomena, she wouldn't be expecting her niece and Lucian.

How would she react when she realized that this time only one room had been requested?

Ariana's mouth curved ruefully at the thought. Two rooms last time had definitely been a waste of money. She was contemplating the memory of that fateful night when the magician, himself, materialized out of the darkness in front of the car.

As he loped toward her she unlocked the car door and slid into the passenger's seat. He looked grimly pleased with himself, she decided, aware of a vast relief that he was safe.

"What happened? How did it go? Did anyone see you? Could you get inside?"

He threw her a wide grin as he turned the key in the ignition. "One question at a time, I've had a hard night!"

"Waiting is much harder work, believe me!" she

assured him feelingly. He leaned over and kissed her soundly before putting the powerful car in gear.

"Here, I brought you a little reward for your patience." He dropped a yellow rose into her hand.

"What in the world? Lucian! Where did you get this?"

"Magic," he explained succinctly.

She looked up from the rose as he pulled the car out onto the winding road that led to the inn. "Did you accomplish what you set out to do? Could you find Galen's tricks?"

"I'm afraid our extraterrestrial visitor is going to be in for a shock tonight when he tries to traverse the spaceways," Lucian chuckled.

"You're really quite pleased with yourself, aren't you?"

"It's going to be an amusing evening, Ariana."

She glanced down again at the rose in her palm. Somehow he had smuggled it all the way from San Francisco, carried it with him when he made the foray to Galen's retreat and had had it ready to produce when he returned to the car.

Magic.

Ariana took a deep breath and told herself that she didn't want him to continue to reward her with this kind of magic. She wanted the real thing: Love.

CHAPTER NINE

ONCE AGAIN ARIANA FOUND HERSELF sitting between
Philomena and Lucian in pitch darkness. The evening
s;aaeance conducted by Fletcher Galen was about to
begin. Even though she knew that the whole thing was
fake and that Lucian had rigged the already-rigged performance, the sensation of uneasy dread was as strong
or stronger than it had been the first time. She didn't
understand it. Why should she be even more nervous
now that she knew how most of the tricks worked?

Philomena leaned over to whisper in her ear, "This
is going to be so interesting." The older woman was
delighted at the prospect of the drama which was
about to unfold. "I can't wait to see which magician
is the stronger!"

"It's not a question of which of them is stronger,"
Ariana muttered. "It's a question of whether or not
Galen discovered that his pranks had been tampered
with before the performance. I suppose you could say
it's a matter of which of them is more clever than the
other. Not stronger."

"Same difference," Lucian murmured laconically.
He reached out and took her hand in his own, and she
could hear the indulgent smile in his voice as he went

on softly, "What's the matter with you? You're trembling again. Don't you have any faith in the magician on your side?"

"I just wish it was all over!"

"It will be fairly soon now," he assured her gently.

Ariana also wished that she wasn't the only one in the room who seemed to sense some kind of impending danger. It was just a magic show, for heaven's sake, and it was about to go amusingly awry. So why did she feel as if there was a genuine threat hovering in the atmosphere? Only Philomena had been told that she was about to see Galen exposed. None of the other attendees at the s;aaeance had any reason to suspect a somewhat different show tonight.

For her part, Philomena had been more than willing to see the challenge carried out. With her bubbling enthusiasm for the extraordinary and the bizarre, she was just as intrigued by the prospect of Galen's being dramatically exposed as by the possibility that he was a genuine psychic with contacts in outer space.

On the other side of her, Lucian seemed calm, even faintly amused at the prospect of the show that was about to unfold.

Ariana shivered and wondered again why she was the only one who was so nervous.

Then there was no longer any time to reflect on her premonition of danger. The eerie green glow on the stage slowly bloomed into existence, and the audience hushed with expectation. After a suitably dramatic pause Fletcher Galen appeared with the timing of a real showman. His robes swirled around his feet as if disturbed by an invisible wind. The movement gave an appearance of crackling energy surrounding him.

"Offstage fan," Lucian whispered dryly as Ariana stared. "A new addition to the repertoire, apparently."

"My brothers and sisters who are the Keepers of the Energy," Galen intoned, "tonight there is raw power in the very air around us. Tonight great strides can be made. Tonight, perhaps, will be the breakthrough night. We must concentrate together, focus on the power within and without. We must form a channel for Krayton!"

Ariana stirred restlessly as Galen continued with the dramatic patter. When the tray of items scheduled to be broken or levitated was brought forth she felt Lucian's fingers tighten fractionally around hers.

"Now we'll see how good Krayton is when confronted by a little household glue," he growled in anticipation.

On stage Galen went through the ritual of building the "energy" that he'd told his audience was practically arcing through the room that night.

"We must not rush," the fraudulent psychic cautioned his audience as he prepared to bend and break silverware with the power of Krayton. "Great power must be controlled and channeled. We must guide it through the routes we have been establishing for the past few weeks."

Slowly, with grand emphasis, Galen moved his hand over the tray of objects. The audience held its breath, even though they'd seen variations on this particular trick several times previously.

When nothing happened, the reaction from the onlookers was one of stunned dismay. A gasp of disappointment seemed to emanate as if from one throat.

Philomena Warfield merely watched with fascination and then reached over to prod her niece in the ribs. "Interesting. First time this particular event has ever failed. Your magician may be the stronger."

"It's going to be interesting to see how he talks himself out of the problem," Lucian whispered blandly.

Fletcher Galen was more than equal to the occasion. He immediately launched into an explanation for the failure of the trick. "Too much power!" he exclaimed in tones of ringing wonder. "There is too much power in the room. Krayton does not dare to loose it on such small efforts. It might literally explode if channeled too tightly! We must move on. The energy has built up even more than I had dreamed!"

A low murmur rippled through the room, but the audience seemed willing to buy the explanation. At once Galen moved on to the next piece of magic in his act.

But the direction of the evening had been firmly established by Lucian's tampering. One after the other the magic tricks failed. Galen managed to hold his audience with explanations of energy and uncontrolled power, but it was obvious that he was getting harried.

"I just hope he doesn't quit before he gets to the good part," Lucian said dryly into Ariana's ear.

The hypnotic trance went well for Galen. Lucian had explained ahead of time that there wasn't much he could do about that one. People susceptible to hypnosis would see what Galen wanted them to see. But when the so-called psychic went into his own trance and prepared for levitation, Lucian's hand tightened once again around Ariana's.

Disaster struck. The concealed wires and bracing that were the apparatus behind the trick failed dramatically, sending Galen into an undignified heap on the stage floor.

Shock was the first reaction of the audience. There was nothing that could have stunned it more than to see its cherished psychic sitting unexpectedly on his rear on the stage floor amid a tangle of robes.

"Krayton!" Galen called, lifting his hands to the ceiling. "What do you want from us tonight? Why is your power being withheld?"

"I'll have to give him credit for being a real trooper right to the end," Lucian chuckled. "Of course, the thought of losing all the money he hopes to get from this audience is probably something of an inspiration."

"Krayton," Galen called again and motioned to the audience to join him in his plea.

At once a cry went up from the confused people watching the debacle of a performance.

"Krayton!"

"Krayton!"

The chant continued as Galen went through more rituals of gathering power.

"He's really damn good with an audience," Lucian said in admiration as the people around them went into a frenzy of desperate chanting. They didn't want to believe the evidence of their own eyes. They wanted an explanation for the failures, and only the mysterious Krayton could give it to them.

"This is the most amusing thing that's happened in a year," Philomena confided cheerfully to Ariana.

Ariana didn't respond. The sense of impending dread

was building in her even as the so-called energy around them was being built up in preparation for the dramatic arrival of Krayton.

"Try not to go through the roof," Lucian advised Ariana.

"Why? What's going to happen?" she pleaded urgently, not wanting any more surprises of any kind.

"You'll see."

Lightning crackled dramatically across the room.

"I left the voltage generator alone," Lucian explained as the current arced vividly over the heads of the spectators.

"Oh," Ariana said a little weakly.

Galen called upon Krayton to appear. The audience pleaded with Krayton to make the effort to project himself across the galaxy. Philomena waited with cheerful expectancy. Ariana wanted to cringe as her anxiety mounted, and Lucian lounged in his chair, just waiting for the inevitable.

Lights came on overhead, deeply mysterious lights designed to imitate the imagined colors of another world, and the inhuman face of Krayton began to revolve slowly into view.

The audience shrieked with excitement. Ariana dug her nails into Lucian's hand and felt him wince.

Then Krayton fell into the audience.

Pandemonium broke out and someone at the rear of the room found the light switch. In an instant all was revealed.

The plastic features of the extraterrestrial lay across several quickly vacated seats. Clearly the face of Krayton was a very human bit of creativity. As the lights came on the exotic creature was illuminated, revealing nothing more than cleverly painted plastic dangling from several broken wires.

The strangled gasp of outrage and pain that came from the audience as everyone turned to stare at poor Krayton went like a wave through the room. On its heels, Philomena Warfield rose majestically from her seat and announced to all and sundry, "Well, we certainly have been a pack of fools, haven't we? Thank heaven there are a few honest magicians in this world to help weed out the charlatans like Galen. If it hadn't been for the man who is soon to be my niece's husband, we'd all have been parted from a great deal more of our money, wouldn't we?"

As one, the heads of the audience turned toward the stage. It was quite empty. In the furor, Fletcher Galen had clearly opted to retire as Krayton's power source.

"Come on," Lucian said firmly, rising to his feet and pulling Ariana up beside him. "Let's go. That's the end of the show."

Philomena and Ariana were ushered up the aisle and through the curtain at the opposite end. In the glaring overhead light the mysterious, heretofore dark room was revealed to be only a small theater. Ariana glanced around worriedly. The performance was over, but her sense of disaster was heavier than ever.

"We'll see you to your car, Philomena, and then meet you back at the inn," Lucian instructed, guiding the two women before him.

"This is so exciting!" Philomena declared happily as they joined with the crowd that was milling around in the compound.

There was no sign of the men in monks' clothing who had been so evident earlier in the evening.

"Galen undoubtedly knows how to cut his losses and pull a genuine disappearing act when things go wrong," Lucian growled as he glanced around the courtyard. "We'll probably never see him again. God knows where he'll show up next."

"Well, I, for one, intend to file a complaint with the authorities just on general principles!" Philomena exclaimed firmly.

"Go ahead. The problem is that the authorities won't be able to find Galen," Lucian sighed as he reached Philomena's Mercedes and assisted her inside.

Philomena had insisted on taking her own car earlier in case Lucian was proved wrong and wanted to leave before she did. Now she smiled brightly up through the open window as he closed the door for her. "You put on quite a show tonight, Lucian. It's going to be interesting having you in the family."

"I wish you would stop saying things like that, Aunt Phil," Ariana hissed, her already taut nerves being tightened further at the references to marriage that Philomena had been making since Lucian's and Ariana's arrival at the inn that evening. The older woman had taken one look at the couple and beamed, apparently drawing her own conclusions. When she learned that they had ordered only one room this time she had been quite certain of the future.

"But, darling," Philomena began soothingly.

"Lucian and I are not getting married, Aunt Phil," Ariana tossed back deliberately. "We're having an affair. Just the kind of affair you've been suggesting I have.

How many times am I going to have to explain it to you? Now drive carefully back to the inn. We'll see you in a little while."

Philomena glanced sharply at Lucian's narrowed eyes and shrugged philosophically. "See you soon. And thanks for a most entertaining evening, Lucian."

He nodded once and stepped back as Philomena put the car in gear and joined the line of vehicles exiting rather hastily from the parking area.

"Well, that's about enough excitement for me for one evening," he drawled as he took Ariana's arm and led her across the almost empty lot to where the Jaguar was parked.

"You certainly achieved some dramatic results!" she admitted feelingly. "Did you have any trouble earlier this evening figuring out how to sabotage all that stuff?"

"No, I was pretty sure of how most of the apparatus worked. There was nothing particularly innovative or mysterious about any of it. The only problem was to locate the pulleys and wires and arrange to weaken them."

"How did you get inside the compound and then into that room, though?" she demanded as they neared the car.

"I picked the locks," he said casually, as if it were merely a commonplace skill. "Like Houdini, I've always had an interest in locks. The ones on the gates at the rear of the compound aren't nearly as imposing as those on the front gates. Once inside it was all fairly simple."

"So why don't I have a great feeling of relief that it's all over?" Ariana asked half aloud as Lucian reached to open the car door. Neither of them noticed the movement of several dark shadows beyond the car.

"Perhaps," drawled Fletcher Galen as he emerged from the other side of a hedge, "because it isn't over. Not quite." He was holding a gun in one hand.

Ariana froze, the sense of impending dread finally fulfilled as disaster at last materialized. Beside her Lucian went equally still.

"You'd better get moving, Galen. Some of your fellow Keepers of the Energy are feeling a bit annoyed with you this evening," Lucian said coolly.

"They're all intent on vacating the premises. You and the little lady here are about the only ones left. Except for a few of my staff," he added meaningfully as two of the men in monks' robes appeared on either side of him.

"What do you hope to accomplish?" Lucian asked quietly.

"Nothing much, just a little satisfaction," Galen murmured. "Come here, Miss Warfield."

Ariana didn't move. Galen lifted the gun a little higher and aimed it, not at her, but at Lucian. "Come here or your boyfriend is a dead man. Which would be a pity from your standpoint, because, unless you force me, I really have no intention of killing him. I only want to punish him for interfering in a perfectly good operation."

Ariana sucked in her breath and took a step forward even as Lucian snapped her name tightly between his teeth. She threw him a helpless glance, and then her attention was solely on the gun in Galen's hand.

Her fingers plunged into the pockets of her stylish suede jacket and her head lowered as she took another couple of paces toward Galen. What else could she do?

The threat to Lucian was sufficient to bring her into absolute obedience, and she had a hunch that an accomplished con artist like Fletcher Galen knew enough about human nature to recognize the weapon he held over her.

"Very wise, Miss Warfield," Galen growled as she came within reach. In a flash his free arm came out to wrap around her throat and draw her back against his chest.

"Ariana!" Lucian rasped, his face savage in the shadows. The topaz eyes burned as he looked at Galen. "Let her go, Galen. It's me you want."

"Exactly. But I think I have a better chance of keeping you under control as long as I have her. I should have been suspicious that first time you and the little lady attended one of my sessions. But I thought Philomena Warfield was sufficiently hooked and that I could trust her to bring only others who were equally interested in helping poor Krayton cross the universe. In any event, I didn't see much harm in allowing you to stay that first time, even though my staff knew nothing about you. Apparently I was wrong. Just out of curiosity, when did you tamper with my act?"

"Earlier this evening." Lucian had apparently decided that for the moment the only thing to do was to keep talking. "Getting inside the grounds was a snap, Galen. Next time you'll have to introduce better security measures."

Galen nodded almost pleasantly. Ariana swallowed awkwardly, the arm across her throat almost painful. Dear God. What were they going to do to Lucian? All of her fear now was for him. She dug her hands deeper into the pockets of her coat.

"You're quite right," Galen was agreeing easily. "Well, live and learn. The last time I tried this particular operation there weren't any glitches, so I suppose I made the mistake of thinking it was reasonably foolproof."

"There was nothing very brilliant or creative about your apparatus," Lucian growled scornfully. His eyes never left the other magician's face.

"No, but that was part of the beauty of the plan. I believe in the virtues of simplicity, Mr. Hawk." Galen's voice hardened. "I also believe in the virtue of teaching interfering people a lesson that won't soon be forgotten!" He waved the gun in a short arc and instantly the two monks grabbed for Lucian's arms.

He didn't struggle. Lucian stood quietly as they tied his wrists behind his back, his whole attention on Ariana as she watched in horror.

Fury was whipping through Ariana now, and she managed to speak for the first time since Galen's arm had gone around her throat. "What are you going to do?" Her voice was a raw whisper.

"I'm going to see to it that Mr. Hawk thinks twice before he goes around ruining other people's acts!" Galen declared grimly. "This way," he added as his men finished binding Lucian. "I think we want a little more privacy for this, just in case some busybody is still hanging around the parking lot."

Ariana's groping fingers clung to the small gold lipstick case that Drake had given her that morning. She held it tightly within the pocket of the suede jacket as she and Lucian were marched through the hedge to a clearing that was illuminated by a light on top of the fence which encircled the compound.

"Now!"

Without any warning Galen shouted the command. Lucian was hurled back against the wire fence, and Ariana realized what was about to happen. The two men in robes were going to beat him.

"Stop it!" she grated. "Stop it, Galen. You're free to go, for God's sake. What more do you want?"

"Don't panic, my dear. I really don't intend to have him killed. Just made to reconsider the wisdom of his actions!"

The first of the men drew back his fist and launched a solid body blow at Lucian's midsection. Ariana screamed and pulled the gold lipstick case from her pocket. It was now or never. If she waited much longer, Lucian would be bleeding and unconscious. If only Galen didn't have a gun! Grabbing the gun would be the hardest part.

Her scream was ignored by the men as the first blow sent Lucian sagging into the fence. The men who did this kind of work for a living probably expected women to do a lot of screaming. Even Galen didn't seem overly concerned, although he idly shifted his arm to cover her mouth.

But Ariana had the lipstick out of her pocket and was aiming it over her shoulder at her captor's face. Galen was so intent on punishing his other victim that he didn't even see the small object in her hand until it was far too late.

The blinding stream of acid spray flashed into his face.

Instinctively Fletcher Galen yelled and dropped the gun, clawing for his blinded eyes. Ariana had tensed, knowing that she would only have one chance at the weapon before the two toughs at the fence realized what was happening. She dived for it even as Galen stumbled backward, screaming in rage.

She caught the gun just as it struck the ground. Without hesitation she brought it up, leaping away from Galen but focusing the weapon on the two men in robes, who had turned to stare at her.

"Move and I'll shoot!" she said as she edged away from Galen, who had gone to his knees, his hands covering his streaming eyes.

But the two men seemed to know exactly what they were doing. They kept themselves in line with Lucian as they moved forward. "Shoot at us and you'll probably hit your lover," one sneered.

Terrified at that possibility, Ariana tried to edge further to one side. She needed a clear shot and they weren't going to allow her one.

Then the problem was taken out of her hands.

On silent feet Lucian came away from the fence in a menacing rush. Ariana had only time to realize that his hands were free and then he was on the other two men. His fists came down simultaneously at the base of their necks, sending them sprawling forward into the dirt.

"Ariana! The gun!"

She stepped toward him and he swept the wicked instrument out of her hand, turning in one fluid motion to cover the three on the ground. "Honey, why don't you get my glasses for me," he went on softly. "I'd hate to miss and hit someone's chest when I really meant to aim for his shoulder!"

The chilling possibility held the three men on the ground in near stillness, except for Galen who was whimpering softly. Ariana circled the trio warily and scooped up the glasses, which had come off during the rough treatment Lucian had received. She hurried back to him.

"Ah, thank you. That's much better," he drawled, sliding them into place. "Are you okay?"

"Yes! Yes, I'm fine," she managed tightly. "What about you? They hit you so hard, Lucian."

"I'm all right," he assured her, his eyes never wavering from his captives. "Just feeling a bit stupid for not having planned for this contingency."

"How did you get your hands free?" she remembered to ask in amazement.

He grinned. "Magic."

"Lucian! I'm in no mood for jokes!" she stormed furiously, reaction setting in as she realized what a close call they had both had.

"Okay, okay. I'm sorry. It's just that I've learned a lot about rope ties in the course of being a magician. All I needed was to allow a little leeway in the ropes when they tied me, and I accomplished that by tightening the muscles in my hands and wrists while they were busy practicing their Boy Scout techniques. Satisfied?"

"Yes," she groaned.

"So tell me how you managed to incapacitate Galen the way you did," he ordered with grave interest.

Ariana couldn't quite stifle the nervous little smile that sprang to her lips. "Magic."

"Uh huh," he chuckled in mocking admiration. "Some of your brother's magic, perhaps?"

"I'm afraid so. I visited him this morning to see if he could give me some form of protection. He invented that little lipstick for single women alone in the city," she explained.

"Come on, let's get these back to the main building and call the authorities. Your aunt will begin to wonder what's happened to us."

Ariana sighed at the thought of what almost had happened to them as she followed Lucian and his captives back to the now-deserted main building of what had been Fletcher Galen's retreat.

"My eyes," Galen wailed accusingly. "What about my eyes? I need medical help!"

"You'll get it. I'm sure the local police will be glad to take you to a doctor," Lucian shot back uncaringly.

"His eyes will be all right," Ariana whispered. "The effects are only temporary."

It was some time before Ariana and Lucian were free to return to the eagerly awaiting Philomena. The questioning of the local authorities was extensive, and there were papers to be signed. Galen and his men were taken away to the local jail, and Ariana could hear the defeated magician insisting on being allowed to contact his lawyer as the police car drove off.

"The sad part is, he'll probably be back actively pursuing his career within a year," Lucian noted wryly as he at last parked the Jaguar in the small parking lot of the inn.

"Well, at least it won't be at Philomena's expense," Ariana declared in relief. "Thank you, Lucian. I'm sorry my plan got you into danger, though. I've never been so terrified in my life as I was when Galen had his men start beating you!" She shivered at the memory.

Lucian smiled as he took her arm and walked her

toward the lobby. "You were brilliant, sweetheart. Remind me to congratulate your brother on that lipstick invention of his! If you hadn't used it when you did, I don't know when I would have gotten the opportunity I needed to deal with those two creeps!"

"Ariana! Lucian!" Philomena was waiting at the lobby entrance, a crowd of former Keepers of the Energy standing curiously behind her. "Thank heavens you're here! We were all so worried when you didn't show up back here, and then when the police called and explained what had happened, we were absolutely shocked! Who would have thought that nice man capable of such things?" She stepped aside and motioned them through the door. "Come inside, come inside. I've already phoned Drake and told him the news. He's on his way up here."

"Tonight?" Ariana asked, startled.

"Well, of course, dear. He wants to know exactly how the lipstick worked in action!"

Lucian was grinning as he followed Philomena into the lobby and threw himself down onto a sofa, pulling Ariana along with him. Galen's former audience gathered close, questions and demands for explanations filling the air.

Patiently Lucian explained everything. A bellhop was dispatched upstairs to bring down the briefcase he'd brought along. When it arrived he opened it up and dug out copies of the documentary evidence the private investigator had had time to find.

"I'm sure there's a lot more than this to be found, but I'm going to call the investigator off the case," Lucian concluded as the newspaper clippings and reports were passed around. "It's the job of the police now. Ariana and I have had enough of the business of exposing fraudulent magicians, haven't we, honey?"

"Definitely!" There was a great deal of feeling in the single word of agreement.

"You two must be exhausted," Philomena finally declared. "Don't feel obliged to stay up while the rest of us rehash our interesting little experience."

"Now that you mention it," Lucian began, getting to his feet, "you have a point, Phil. If you'll excuse us, Ariana and I are going to take your advice."

"What about Drake?" Ariana thought to ask as she was led out of the room.

"You can see him in the morning," Lucian told her bluntly.

Ariana yawned as they started up the staircase. "You know, Lucian, you have a strong, dictatorial tendency. I hope you're not going to try and make a habit out of telling me what to do."

"Oh, I'll probably *try*," he chuckled as he opened the door to their room. "But I doubt whether I'll always succeed. You have your own brand of magic, sweetheart, and it's pretty potent."

"My lipstick?" She smiled sleepily as he took her lightly into his arms.

"No, your magic is real, not mechanical," he murmured urgently. He shook his head, as if slightly dazed. "God, Ariana, when that man held a gun on you and put his arm across your throat..."

She felt his tension and lifted her fingers to stroke the sides of his face. "It's over, Lucian. Believe me, I felt just as sick when I realized what those two men were going to do to you!"

He hugged her close and for a long moment they simply stood together in the middle of the room, comforting themselves in each other's embrace. And then Lucian gently put her aside and turned to pull back the covers of the bed.

"Never again, honey," he promised fervently as they slowly undressed and made ready for bed. "I'll never let you get that close to danger again. I was so furious with myself for not having realized how dangerous Galen could be! I thought he was just another average con man and most of the professionals steer clear of violence. They make their living by their wits, not with guns."

Ariana looked up at him dreamily, vaguely realizing how exhausted she really was. He bent down and kissed her forehead as he tugged off his shirt. "No fair tempting me with that inviting look of female compliance!"

"Tempting you?" she repeated, yawning again. Her lids were beginning to feel irresistibly heavy, and it was a pleasure to lean against him while he finished the task of undressing her.

"Ummm. What you need tonight after your little adventure is sleep. I'll save my husbandly demands for some other evening."

"Not *husbandly* demands," Ariana remembered to correct sleepily as the last of her clothing fell to the floor and her nightgown was slipped over her head. "We're not married, Lucian."

"Not yet," he agreed, but there was a touch of grim determination in his voice as he lifted her and carried her over to the bed. "We'll discuss that issue in the morning."

"There's nothing to discuss," she tried to explain, but

he was already crawling in beside her, pulling her deeply into the curve of his body and cradling her against his chest.

"Go to sleep, Magic Lady."

She did as she was told, allowing sleep to calm the last of her body's tension. The warmth of Lucian's hard, lean frame was as comforting as a fireplace in winter and as protective as a sorceror's magic. Ariana sighed once and gave herself up to it completely.

THE MORNING LIGHT FILTERED THROUGH the swaying pines to awaken Ariana slowly and gently. She stretched luxuriously, her toe automatically extending expectantly to find Lucian's bare leg. When she encountered only an empty bed beside her she sat up in rueful annoyance. He seemed to be making a habit out of leaving her to awaken alone when they stayed at this inn!

Last time, she recalled, she had found him downstairs with her aunt. This morning she would probably find him in the same place perhaps along with Drake.

Ariana smiled as she considered how pleased her brother was going to be when she told him how well his "lipstick" had worked. And Aunt Phil would be eagerly awaiting her so that the events of the previous evening could be rehashed once more. And Lucian should be in a pretty good mood, too, Ariana concluded as she showered and dressed for the day. He had held her so tenderly and protectively during the night. Three cheerful, happy faces waiting for her in the sunny dining room. It was going to be a good day.

On that thought Ariana quickly slipped into a dolman-sleeved, diagonally buttoned tunic done in a soft white silky fabric. She paired it with gray pleated trousers. Hastily double-checking her hair in the mirror, she grabbed her room key and headed downstairs to meet her waiting relatives and the man she loved. Her feet, shod in black cuffed suede boots made fast work of the curving staircase.

Ariana came jauntily off the last step, using one hand on the banister to pirouette in the direction of the dining room. Smiling expectantly she sauntered through the open double doors.

But she was not met by the sight of cheerful relatives and an approving lover.

Ariana faltered in surprise at the expression of grim determination which met her on the face of each of the three people waiting for her at the table across the room. Not one of them looked bright or cheerful, she thought vaguely.

Even as she gathered her composure and started forward, Lucian was getting to his feet to meet her halfway. His face looked the grimmest and most determined of the lot, Ariana decided. What on earth had happened?

"Ariana," he greeted her almost formally, "I have been talking to your family and they and I are agreed. You're not really cut out for an affair. It's okay for some people, but not for you. We've decided you need marriage." He drew in his breath and then proclaimed flatly, "So, I'm going to marry you."

CHAPTER TEN

AS THE IMPACT OF LUCIAN'S UNCOMPROMISING statement hit her, Ariana pulled off a little magic of her own. She hid the tremor that went through her and successfully managed a gracious smile. Then, as if politely declining a small gift she said, "Thank you all for being so concerned about me, but there's really no need. I'm quite happy as things are." She took a seat at the breakfast table, ignored the expressions of the other three and reached for the bread basket. "Are there any scones left? I'm starving. Drake, did Lucian tell you how well the lipstick worked? I think you ought to go ahead and patent the chemical spray and the mechanism. It will sell like hotcakes in every big city in the country. A woman can't be too careful these days, you know."

"Which is exactly why I think you ought to consider Lucian's proposal, Ari," her brother shot back relentlessly. "You need a stable, established relationship. You're definitely the careful type!"

"No, I'm not," she contradicted lightly, holding out her cup as the waitress poured coffee. "Not anymore."

"Ariana," Lucian began urgently, "listen to your brother. You've been very cautious for four years. There's no reason to stop now. It's obviously part of your nature!"

"Ari, dear," Philomena interjected in a patiently reasonable tone, "I know Drake and I accused you of being overly careful..."

"And bigoted and prejudiced and several other things which escape me at the moment," Ariana concluded cheerfully. "But that's all changed now. You see before you a new woman. Could you please pass the cream?"

"Damn it, Ariana," Lucian ground out forcefully, "this is no time to go into your stubborn act."

"He's right, Ari," Drake said. "He wants to marry you and I think you should marry him! You're just being stubborn!"

"Am I?"

"Well, of course, you are. What other reason could you have for not accepting Lucian's proposal, dear?" Philomena demanded.

"How about for the simple reason that I haven't been asked?" Ariana bit hungrily into a scone as the other three at the table were stricken with stunned silence.

Lucian managed to break through the barriers of shock first. "Ariana, what the hell's the matter with you? What do you mean you haven't been asked? What do you think I'm doing this morning?"

"*Telling* me to marry you," she explained gently. Poor Lucian. So used to taking what he wanted in life that he hadn't ever learned how to ask for it politely. As his topaz eyes narrowed furiously she gulped another large swallow of coffee and announced to the table in general. "I'm surprised at the three of you. You're all such modern thinkers, but you don't seem to realize that in this modern age women are not told whom to marry. Some man must take the risk of rejection and *ask* the woman of his choice to marry him. Another scone, Philomena?"

"Ariana, listen to me," Drake began heatedly, only to be interrupted by his aunt.

"Ari, dear, you're being ridiculous. Lucian wants to marry you! Why in the world are you choosing this time and place to engage in a game of semantics?"

"You're being stubborn and outrageous and you know it, Ari," Drake charged hotly, glaring at his sister.

It was Lucian who halted the flow of accusations. His body tense and still, he sat staring at Ariana, who met his eyes over the rim of her coffee cup. "No, she's not being stubborn or outrageous or ridiculous," he said slowly, heavily, as if working it all through in his mind. "She just wants me to learn how to take a chance on something that's crucially important to me."

There was an unnatural silence around the table as Philomena and Drake turned to look at him in astonishment. Ariana broke it by saying very gently, "Is my answer crucially important to you, Lucian?"

He got slowly to his feet and reached down to take her hand. "So important that I haven't got the nerve to ask the question in front of anyone else. Will you please come out into the garden with me, Ariana, while I beg you to marry me?"

Her eyes glowing, Ariana followed him obediently through the lobby and out into the English-style gardens at the rear of the inn. For a long moment they walked in silence. She could feel the tension radiating from him, and part of her longed to soothe and comfort this man who wasn't used to asking for love. But some things had to be done the hard way.

He drew her to a halt beside the fountain, his hands resting lightly at her waist. Never had his eyes seemed so unreadable. Every line of his hard face was grim.

"Ariana, will you please marry me?"

She swallowed tightly. "Why, Lucian?"

He closed his eyes briefly in silent anxiety and then opened them to tell her in a steady, tightly controlled voice, "Because I am so much in love with you that if you don't marry me and come to live with me, I think I will go out of my mind. I need you, sweetheart, in a way I've never needed any other woman. I want you. I can't face the thought of living without you. I know you haven't had a chance yet to fall in love with me, but I can wait. The seeds of your love are there; you couldn't give yourself to me the way you do if they weren't. You wouldn't have put up with me this long if you didn't feel something for me. For God's sake, honey, put me out of my misery and tell me you'll marry me!"

Ariana lifted her hands to cup his tortured face, her own expression full of the love she had been masking all morning with flippancy. "Of course, I'll marry you, Lucian. I've loved you from that first night here at the inn."

He blinked, catlike, looking down at her with wonder and surprise. "You love me?" His fingers probed her waist in a small, urgent movement. *"You love me?"* he repeated, dazed.

She nodded, smiling gently. "Yes."

Lucian groaned and swept her tightly against him. "Sweetheart!" he growled hoarsely into her hair. "Sweetheart, you won't ever be sorry, I swear it. I didn't even understand what it meant to be in love, much less how to ask for it in return before I met you. Now I couldn't survive without it and I would be willing to beg for it! My God, Ariana. Oh, my God, how I love you!"

The two figures by the fountain were still entwined in each other's arms when Philomena and Drake eventually risked a peek from the window in the lobby. Drake grinned in satisfaction and his aunt smiled with blissful assurance.

"I can't quite figure out which of them has the other wrapped around his or her little finger," Drake chuckled.

"That's what makes it a perfect relationship," Philomena explained in satisfaction. "When things are that perfect, a couple might as well marry." She turned away from the window with a distant look in her sparkling eyes. "Now, let's see. They'll be needing a little interior decorating for their new home, don't you think? I wonder how Lucian feels about the color red."

* * * * *

REQUEST YOUR FREE BOOKS!

2 FREE NOVELS
FROM THE ROMANCE/SUSPENSE
COLLECTION PLUS 2 FREE GIFTS!

YES! Please send me 2 FREE novels from the Romance/Suspense Collection and my 2 FREE gifts. After receiving them, if I don't wish to receive any more books, I can return the shipping statement marked "cancel." If I don't cancel, I will receive 4 brand-new novels every month and be billed just $5.49 per book in the U.S., or $5.99 per book in Canada, plus 25¢ shipping and handling per book plus applicable taxes, if any*. That's a savings of at least 20% off the cover price! I understand that accepting the 2 free books and gifts places me under no obligation to buy anything. I can always return a shipment and cancel at any time. Even if I never buy another book from the Reader Service, the two free books and gifts are mine to keep forever.

185 MDN EF5Y 385 MDN EF6C

Name _____ (PLEASE PRINT) _____

Address _____ Apt. # _____

City _____ State/Prov. _____ Zip/Postal Code _____

Signature (if under 18, a parent or guardian must sign)

Mail to **The Reader Service:**
IN U.S.A.: P.O. Box 1867, Buffalo, NY 14240-1867
IN CANADA: P.O. Box 609, Fort Erie, Ontario L2A 5X3

Not valid to current subscribers to the Romance Collection,
the Suspense Collection or the Romance/Suspense Collection.

Want to try two free books from another line?
Call 1-800-873-8635 or visit www.morefreebooks.com.

* Terms and prices subject to change without notice. NY residents add applicable sales tax. Canadian residents will be charged applicable provincial taxes and GST. This offer is limited to one order per household. All orders subject to approval. Credit or debit balances in a customer's account(s) may be offset by any other outstanding balance owed by or to the customer. Please allow 4 to 6 weeks for delivery.

Your Privacy: Harlequin is committed to protecting your privacy. Our Privacy Policy is available online at www.eHarlequin.com or upon request from the Reader Service. From time to time we make our lists of customers available to reputable firms who may have a product or service of interest to you. If you would prefer we not share your name and address, please check here. ☐

BOB07

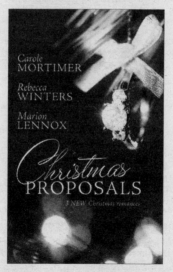

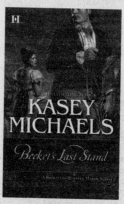

JAYNE ANN KRENTZ